WHITE AND RED CHERRIES

Tanja Tuma

Imprint

White and Red Cherries: A Slovenian Civil War Novel
Copyright ©Tanja Tuma, www.tanjatuma.com
US Coryright Office #TXu 1-959-930
Slovenian title: Češnje, bele in rdeče, roman o spravi
Edited by Jerneja Jezernik
English translation by Tanja Tuma
Copyedited by Arlene Ang

All rights reserved. No part of this publication may be reproduced, stored in a retrieval system, or transmitted in any form, or by any means, electronic, mechanical, photocopying, recording, or otherwise without either the prior written permission of the publisher or the copyright holder. This book may not be lent, hired out, resold or otherwise disposed of by way of trade in any form of binding or cover other than that in which it is published without the prior consent of the publisher.

Self-Published in March 2016
ISBN: 978-1530621637
CreateSpace Independent Publishing Platform
North Charleston, SC

Author's Note

Map of present-day Slovenia with neighboring countries.

Like many other countries in Europe, Slovenia suffered severe consequences during and after WWII. Many historians claim that WWII was the continuation of WWI, which had ravaged Slovenia and, in consequence, divided its territories and citizens.

Before WWI, Slovenia was part of the Austro-Hungarian Empire. In 1915, Italy attacked Austria and opened the Isonzo Front, one of the cruelest series of battles during WWI, ending in the defeat of the Italian army at Kobarid (Caporetto). Hemingway wrote about the battle in Farewell to Arms. Nevertheless, Italy was on the side of the winners, and consequently gained vast territories of Slovenia, Istria, and Dalmatia according to the Treaty of Rapallo. The people under the Italian rule were soon subjected to the genocidal policies of the Italian Fascists that came to power in the 1920s.

In April 1941, the Nazis defeated Yugoslavia and occupied northern Slovenia, leaving their Axis partners with the rest: the Hungarians took the east while the Italians annexed the south including the city of Ljubljana. Slovenian patriots organized a guerilla fight within the Liberation Front, consisting of various political groups together with the Communist Party. Within two years, the Communist Party completely took over the national resistance movement and played dirty with anyone who did not suit its interests, namely, the revolution to establish a socialist state in the manner of the Soviet Union. The novel begins in 1943 in the hinterland of Trieste that has been under Italian rule for more than two decades.

Slovenian anti-communist militia, who opposed such course, emerged. Yet, lacking of material support of the Allies, they all ended on the side of the Axis as collaborators. The two factions – the Home Guard (Axis) and Tito's Yugoslav resistance (Allies) – engaged in a bitter, fraternal fight that ended in 1945 resulting in massacres perpetrated by Yugoslav Partisans. In consequence, until today, Slovenians remain divided in their views on how to build a democratic state and society based on tolerance.

The names of locations are written in their original language to make it easier to find out more about them on the internet. Less common words and notions are printed in slanted letters and explained in the Glossary at the end of the book.

Non-English letters, i.e. consonants with a caron or acute, are pronounced in English as follows:

č, ć like ch in chair
š like sh in shut
ž like s in pleasure

My wish is to draw some sympathy for the characters who, in the course of the war, could never do the right thing, since war and violence had taken over their lives.

Tanja Tuma

Anna and Martin, Trubar Literature House, 2014

There is only one man
all the others around him are his different faces.

– Srečko Kosovel, For Mechanics!

I cast a furtive look at Martin's face. His cheeks trembled with the effort to subdue and hide the pain inside. Oh, the secrets we have kept in our souls for so long. The wrinkles around his eyes glittered. Were those tears? He must have tried to brush them away, buried them into the sleeve of his shirt so that nobody would notice. On a day like this who would have noticed anything anyway? At the roundtable on the consequences of WWII, the ravaging civil war in Slovenia, everyone was absorbed in their own thoughts and memories. Even now we remain children of war, young like spring and old like winter. Martin and I, we are older than most of them. We are pushing seventy.

Suddenly, my brother gasped for air. Fearing he would cry out or something, I put my right hand on his elbow, which rested like a motionless piece of wood on his knee. Without a word, he turned his palm upward, bony fingers squeezing mine gently. He didn't even dart me a glance. His eyes are fixed on what's happening on the stage. His chest shook and his eyelids quivered. A tear slid down his cheeks and remained hanging from his lips.

Then he turned and looked at me. I saw his eyes clearly. Gradually, the hatred and the pain in them faded away as the hell inside his brain dwindled, until only love and grace twinkled like millions of stars in the universe. He was my brother Martin again. Marty Smarty, my boy with diamonds in his round black eyes, was back. My Marty Smarty had been a Humpty Dumpty for a long time, far too long. Yet, the moment had come to put him together again. My hero with whom I played in the sand and swam in the sea until our lips turned blue. I felt the moment had come.

"Martin, shall we tell them now?"

His eyes bulged, and he looked into the distance, into the times past and places lost. Then he focused on me again. "What's the use? Look at how they're all tearing each other apart."

I'd made up my mind. This time I would not give in. "They must be told once and for all. This is no way to build a society. We're torn apart as if caught in a blood feud in the Middle Ages."

Martin nodded wisely. "True. The Slovenians are walking backward. Like cancers. This feud is the cancer of our society."

My body ached from standing up. The Rex chair was lower than I thought. My hands smoothed the blouse and straightened the skirt.

"Let's go!" I said.

Martin had even more trouble getting up. I wondered whether

it was the illness or age that caused his shortness of breath, or both. I could tell he was very upset.

"All right, Anna Banana, here I go." He offered his hand like the first time he had taken me across the road as a little girl. Now he was to take me across another road, more like a border than a road.

Our anonymity was over. We were about to step into the spotlight. From the obscurity of hatred and pain, we would pass into the brightness of love. We would show the world how useless it is to divide between traitors and murderers in war. People are good or evil, no matter which ideology they follow. Our sad long life is proof of that. Our confession would stamp a signature under the peace treaty of all Slovenians. If we could do it, they all could – and they should.

Slowly, the terrible weight lifted off my tired shoulders. I glowed with pure and all-inspiring love. It was beautiful to inhale the air of love at last.

Valerija Batič, 1943-1949

A bridge to be,
over which my mother's and
my daughter's hand
join in unity.

– Katja Špur, Ties, Murska Sobota 1970

"*Burja* in spring, damn it, what kind of weather is this?" murmured Valeria, keeping her wide brown skirt close to her knees as she descended the village path to the public well. She held an empty tin bucket in each hand, which made her skirt rescuing endeavors more difficult.

"Haven't you gone? Come on, girl, move it!" Mother nagged in a shrill voice.

Valeria Batič came from a big family – three daughters and four sons. Her eldest sister Maria was over thirty, Justina was two years younger, followed by twins Drago and Anthony, twenty-five. Mario was over twenty and escaped into the woods with the partisans. Valeria, seventeen, and her the youngest Franjo were the only two children, who lived at home. Three of her siblings were married with children and families of their own. Justina worked at a hotel in Rijeka and came home only for big holidays. Valeria thought lovingly of her sister Maria, who got married, and started a family in the neighboring village Vatovlje. She would often visit her and play with her nephew and nieces as well as run to exhaustion across the orchards with their funny little bitch Pika. It was a steep and long way back home to Kozjane where Mother and work waited for her. Valeria did not mind the hard job of working the land. However, she longed for education and knowledge. For many generations, the Batič family managed to set up a profitable farm despite the scarce soil. The village of Kozjane was at the heart of the *Brkini Hills*. It was a struggle to produce adequate food on the Karstic soil with its sinkholes, dolines, and caves (the most famous being the Škocjan Caves).

Yet, the villagers of Kozjane had a good life; there were orchards of cherries, apples, pears, and plums, and vineyards producing sweet wine. In these hills, winters were cold and dried by *burja* and summers were hot with enough rain. Since early 19th century, the authorities enforced growing fruits, which shaped the landscape into a little Tuscany. The law required each groom to plant fifty fruit trees if he wanted to bring his bride to the altar. The results were excellent. The farmers were innovative and industrious; they developed a network of dealers to reach good customers for their agricultural products in two major seaports of the region: Trieste and Rijeka or Fiume as Italians called it. Their major crops beside fruits were potatoes, wheat, and oats. They were also famous for their tasty prosciutto that only few could keep for their own tables. Usually, they sold the air-dried pork legs at the highest price to rich customers in the cities. With the money, farmers purchased textiles, shoes or technical gear for farming. Their cows were fat and the milk creamy. In front of each house, there were tall walnut trees where the Elders sat in the shadow. The sweet nuts made a thick filling for *potica* at all big festivities. Since Valeria could remember, there was running water in all houses of the village. Instead of wooden pipes, they laid new leaden ones in the years before WWI.

In the spring of 1943, the fields were glowing in red, waiting to receive the sun's warmth and the growing seeds. Soon they would start planting potatoes, cabbage, beans, beets, and other vegetables for delicious dishes in summer. Bright green strips of winter wheat spread among barren fields, their tender straws ascending to the bright sun in the blue sky. It was a magnificent view. White cherry trees in full bloom and tender pink buds of apple trees shaken by the harsh wind.

Precisely on a chilly *burja*-swept day like this, the major water pump for the whole village broke down, and Valeria's father, an able technician, rode his motorbike to Trieste to buy a spare part. It was Friday, so he wanted to get the pump working before the weekend when cooking, cleaning and personal hygiene increased the water demand. It would be hours before he came back and repaired the pump. In the kitchen, Mother needed water.

Valeria was also planning to take a bath. On Saturday night there would likely be a dance. She daydreamed about the boys she would wrap around her little finger. In men's eyes, Valeria was a real beauty. She was tall and her figure well-formed. Her curly chestnut hair surrounded a cute face with thin rose lips. Her step was light and energetic, her face always smiling. She was quick of mind and even quicker at repartee. When she turned down a young suitor, her green eyes sparkled with mischief; the right man was yet to come and conquer her heart. Although he came from a large family, her father never forced any of his girls to marry in haste and leave home. He often said, "When there is a mouth to feed, there is also a pair of hands for the work."

Ears reddened by the cold, she descended the narrow path lined by huge blackberry bushes on both sides, her hair blinding her view. Too late, she saw a group of Italian soldiers. They were sitting around the well, smoking, chatting, and drinking brandy. Before she could turn back, she heard whistles and cries.

"Che bella donna!"

"Bellissima!"

"What is your name, lady?"

Valeria froze. Italians, where did they come from? Nobody reported anything about them arriving today. Did they find out about their post at the barn behind the house where partisans rested before continuing their marches around the woods? A lump formed in her throat. She shivered in the strong wind. Her gaze turned to the blue sky and sank to the hills toward the vast, dark-green pinewoods in the north. Then she remembered: Mother had told her this morning that her older brother Mario and his partisans would come to their house, which was why the minestrone pot was full to the brim and fresh bread was baking in the oven. Mario could come any time now, around noon, and from another direction. The partisans frequently used the steep track from the neighboring village Vatovlje, which led deep into the valley, across the stream and sharply uphill. That tiny road was safe against the military patrols for no vehicles could climb the slippery rocks.

Raucous laughter made her focus on her immediate problem: a dozen of Italians. Valeria looked at them: lousy morons in black uniforms, laughing and joking like a bunch of spoilt boys who had managed to escape the stern supervision of their mothers. Yet these boys were playing with guns and bombs. Their merry smiles could turn to bullets in the whim of a moment.

Like every Slovenian, Istrian, and Dalmatian who lived, thanks to the Treaty of *Rapallo*, under Fascist rule ever since the end of WWI in 1922, Valeria hated Italians with all her heart. Slovenian was banned in every school, public office, and church. At school, Valeria learned only about Italian poets and writers, Italian art and history, and Garibaldi. She had to recite tedious heroic verses composed by their foolish war poet Gabrielle d'Annunzio alongside Dante and Machiavelli, who seemed to enflame the Fascist spirit. Every morning school started with their bombastic national anthem. The hair on her back stood up each time she had to repeat the pompous praises of sacrifice for the fatherland Italy. She well knew the other side of the coin, the side of the people under their muddy boot. Here, in the *Brkini Hills*, the Fascists showed their true nature: primitive, mean and stupid, completely blinded by the propaganda of their commander Benito Mussolini whom they called Duce – the supreme leader. These young boys with thin mustaches, aimlessly strolling around their villages might seem harmless, but they were killing and torturing the civilians, terrorizing the elders and raping women, stealing food from children as well as relics from churches. Worst of all was their systematic deportation of Slovenian folks under the pretext that they worked for the partisans. It could be anybody. They seized whole families and loaded them on countless of trains from Sežana somewhere to Dalmatia, nobody knew where. Then they settled some scoundrels from southern Italy in the empty houses and farms. Illiterate and lazy, these Italians were unable to tend to the orchards and the land.

Valeria was aware of all that, for everybody in Kozjane was working for the partisans. They had joined the *Liberation Front* more than a year ago in 1941. The village had given shelter to the resistance fighters ever since. The Italians must have suspected something. Many times, they strolled around the village like a pack of wolves smelling the blood of lambs. They must be undertaking a new offensive to cleanse the hills of the partisans, as they often did, luckily without success.

Valeria looked around the road and back to the village. She was alone, and the soldiers have noticed her; too late for an escape. It would only provoke them to enter the village. She swallowed her fear and thought of a way to distract them. Should they find her brother and his partisans in their house, they would kill them all, plunder their supplies, and burn down the village.

In the spit of a moment, Valeria had an idea. In the clear voice of a trained choir singer, she started singing the Fascist anthem:

> *Giovinezza*, giovinezza,
> primavera di bellezza,
> nel fascismo è la salvezza
> della nostra libertà.

It worked – even though Valeria was singing the old version without the name of Benito or, as she always thought of him, Bandito Mussolini. The soldiers jumped to their feet and took out their bayonets. With their right arm stretched into the air as a salute to their Fascist cause and their beloved Duce, they sang all ten stanzas in high-spirited voices. She also stretched out her right arm and sang, leading the tune with her girlish crystalline voice. It was pathetic; tears glistered in the eyes of the men as they filled their lungs with air. During the song, the soldiers formed a line. Valeria stood in front of them as though she were their war fairy. No smile, no twitch of the cheeks, no wrong movement betrayed the quantities of brandy they must have drunk. Only their shirts were undone, their gun belts swaying around their waists. Their war spirit was like their garments – a mess of dirty rags. Valeria thought how easily she could have shot them down with one machine gun. No such luck, she would have to think of something else.

Still stiff in their exalted salute, they sang the last line: "Del fascismo redentor." After a brief silence filled with awe, Valeria spoke in an authoritative voice.

"Dear brothers, Italians! I am one of you, an Italian. I am lucky to be still alive in these barbaric hills, but here I am, and I can help you save your lives."

Cheeky smiles returned to soldiers' faces. What was this wonderful girl with lovely long hair and vivid green eyes talking about? There was no threat here in this tiny village. They had sharp weapons. Besides, thousands were attacking the center of the resistance from every side. They had not heard a shot since they pulled out of the barracks in Trieste. Certainly, the partisans must be somewhere in these hills. However, there must be a lot of false propaganda, too. Their Fascist leaders probably wanted to impress the Germans who were experiencing strong resistance and subversive activities in northern Slovenia. The Italians felt that they knew these lands well. After all, they had done everything to make the people Italian. They had brought culture and education to these poor peasants – *Ščavis*. That's what they thought. Soon they planned to raid some rich peasant's pantry for a whole leg of prosciutto or a long chain of dried sausages to spice their meal of savory polenta. There were no partisans around here. The one wretched idiot they found at Barka was hung two days ago, which should teach these *Ščavis* how to behave. How amusing to hear this girl babbling about saving their lives.

"What do you mean, my beauty?"

Valeria played her card. She continued in her bookish Italian, "Honestly, you must believe me, soldiers. You're in the crosshairs of a partisan brigade, over one hundred bandits or more. I don't know where they've come from, but they are everywhere. They come out of the blue and disappear like ghosts into the fog."

The commander with the black beret felt compassion with the young pretty woman who sang "*Giovinezza*" so well. Wanting to console her, he came closer.

"But where are they, your partisans, bellezza, where? Tell me, and I will shoot them all."

"I am not sure where. I just heard they have surrounded the village and would not leave without your guns. I've come to warn you, boys. Maybe if they get the guns they will leave you alive."

The Italian commander gazed into Valeria's green eyes. She detected a tinge of fear and concern, but not for long. He knew the partisans could not have broken the thick lines of tanks and heavy machinery surrounding the *Brkini Hills*. It was simply impossible. The girl was frightened for no good reason. His lips broke into a wide smile. It was such a lark, this beautiful young peasant speaking in melodic grammar-school Italian.

"What do you want me to do, amore?"

Valeria held his look and spoke with drama and pathos. "Please, Comandante, listen to me! Maybe it isn't the last time we shall sing the beautiful *Giovinezza* together. Maybe they haven't noticed you yet. You should drop your guns and run for the woods as fast as you can. They will not pursue you and probably leave you alive. Well, they only want the guns."

The commander turned to his men with his arms stretched to the sky in the woeful gesture of a poor worshiper before his god. He grinned widely. What else could he do but continue playing this farce? Powerless men in the hands of a beautiful girl. The wet dream of every soldier.

"Men, let us listen to this beautiful girl with eyes as deep as the crystal waters of Adria! Let's drop our guns! I would do anything for her, wouldn't you?" He dropped his gun belt first and made a deep bow in front of Valeria.

The rest of the troop, a dozen stocky black-haired men did the same, finding it a good joke to surrender to the whim of a beautiful girl on a windy, early spring morning. This would make a wonderful story to tell their neighbors over a glass of red wine after the war.

As the last weapon fell on the ground, Valeria stepped between the guns and the soldiers. "You must go now! Run!"

She tried again to scare them away, but the men found it extremely funny. They were laughing heartily, exchanging gestures of fear, shock, and to her alarm obscenity. The brandy was finally doing its job.

One of them started to fuss with his belt. "I can drop the pants, too, amore! Would you like to see?"

An older man around her father's age was tearing his shirt open to expose the pale skin on his torso. "Do you want to see the scars from *Isonzo*? Here, cara mia, here! Feel it!"

Valeria's heart missed a beat, her eyes widening in horror. She had to do something quickly. In war, rape struck quicker than lightning. Although she heard more rumors than facts about the violence of Italians against women, she realized she was in a hopeless trap. Alone with a dozen of drunken soldiers who she inflamed with her song.

She felt cold sweat trickle down her spine. The black hair on the chest of the *Isonzo* hero quivered as he shook with lascivious laughter. She stared at the grinning mouths trickling with saliva. Her stomach turned at the thought of a drop falling on her face

'Oh, Mother! Where have you sent me?'

When Valeria was a little girl, her mother used to take her by the hand and lead her into the shadow of the old lime tree on the other side of the road. There, under the green crown, Mother would read her stories. Valeria would make long plaited garlands of bright yellow dandelions while listening. It was their time together; they were alone, away from the big family, away from the noises of the village. The bees hummed in the crown of the mighty tree where millions of sweet-smelling flowers were bursting with balmy nectar. When the sun moved lower on the horizon, they would pick lime flowers for tea that healed all ailments during gray winter evenings. When Valeria reached her teenage years, she would play hide and seek in the shadows of the ancient lime tree, away from the supervision of their parents. In the bush behind the big rock, a boy secretly kissed her lips once.

A short pudgy soldier stood at the trunk of the old lime tree, fiddling with the buckle of his gun belt, which got stuck in his belly fat. He wanted to play a part in this farce, too. Valeria shivered at the thought of his fat body squashing hers. She froze. Then, the sight of the machine gun at the top of the heap gave her an idea. She slowly bent down. Excited male voices commented about her behind.

"Oh, look at those buttocks, the picture of ripe watermelons."

Swiftly, Valeria picked up the machine gun and fired. A few shots blasted in front of the men's feet. They froze and turned pale before her, their faces showing bewilderment and anger, but no fear.

Valeria cried at the top of her voice, "Go away! Run or I'll shoot you, dirty, lousy macaroni bastards!"

Bewilderment left the soldiers' faces and panic came over them. The girl was not joking. The commander, still oblivious of the danger, tried to reason with her.

"We didn't mean you any harm, amore, honestly. We would not hurt a lovely girl like you. Look, bellezza, the party is over. Give us back our guns now!"

"You still don't understand, do you?" To show how serious she was, Valeria fired a few shots in front of the commander's feet, careful not to hurt anybody. It only would complicate the situation even more.

"Stop wasting bullets, girl! That gun is not a toy!"

The commander tried to grab the machine gun from Valeria. She leapt backwards and fired another burst. Some soldiers fell to the ground, covering their heads with their hands. Valeria did not hurt anybody. Fortunately, Mario had taught her how to shoot. And at school, she had eagerly come forward when the Fascists were recruiting volunteers and teaching them how to handle guns. When would they finally grasp the situation, the morons?

"Go and I will leave you alive. If you stay, I will have to kill you all, stupido!"

Finally, they picked up their military vests and ran. The hero of *Isonzo* fussed with his backpack for a while, wondering if he could cut her throat with a hidden bayonet before she could pull the trigger. Yet one look at her grim expression made him decide to keep his head on his shoulders. Valeria held the gun firmly, aiming at their waists. They knew it had a whole charge of bullets with their names on them.

Damn! They might be running now, but they would come back with reinforcements, hang the bitch, and burn down this crazy village with its mad Kozjane people. Nobody messed with brave Fascist heroes, certainly not a *Ščavi* cunt like her.

~~~

The harsh wind had stopped, and the sun began to warm Valeria's shoulders. She watched the soldiers' backs as they ran along the rows of white plum trees in bloom toward the oak bushes and dark pinewoods.

"You've got your amore and your bellezza now, shitty cowards!"

She felt all powerful, though at the back of her mind she knew the feeling could not last. She had made the Fascists run, but they would come back and take revenge for the humiliation. They were vicious and fanatic. Her fear of getting raped was not groundless. Yet, maybe this time, she had gone too far. Would they have raped her so close to the village? My God, when the old man started to undo his pants, darkness dimmed her senses. Dancing with death had become common these days. What would happen to Kozjane now? She looked at the empty buckets on the ground. She had no idea what to do next.

The buzz of an engine from the valley made her squint. She saw a man on a motorbike meandering on the winding road toward the village. It was her father. She dropped the machine gun and sagged against the concrete wall by the well, hiding her face in her palms. Only jolts of her back showed she was actually sobbing. What would her father say?

He found her slumped beside the empty buckets, amidst a heap of guns, hand grenades, and a couple of machine guns.

"What happened here, Valeria?" he asked in a stern voice.

"I, Father ... I couldn't help it ... I had to disarm a troop of lousy Italians."

Old Batič thought she was joking. "Valeria, what are you saying? What did you have to do? Whose are these guns, anyway?"

Valeria slowly lifted her head, and her father feared of the worse. Her eyes filled with tears of horror as she recounted what happened. His austere face remained unmoved.

"But, what – "

She finished his sentence, "What will happen to us now?"

Father dismounted his bike and started to collect the weapons. He was a tall man in his fifties, his face paler than gray stone and weathered by the tough lands he farmed. Like all the villagers in Kozjane, Father was a *Liberation Front* activist and knew how to make use of the guns. He put all twenty something pieces in his trunk, where the spare part for the water pump shone silvery. Finally, he turned to Valeria.

"Tell me again, Valeria. How did you manage to do it on your own?"

With the indifference that had come over her body and soul, Valeria retold the episode. Father smiled here and there, froze when she related the bawdy remarks of the soldiers and her fear of being raped. Afterward he took her in his wide arms and held her tight. Slowly, warmth flooded her veins again.

"My poor girl, this was terrible. Let's go home. We'll think of something."

Tears that she had been holding back for too long welled up again in Valeria's eyes. "Father, I will go to the woods with Mario and the partisans. You can burn all photographs of me and deny I ever existed. You can say you don't know a girl like me, that I am not from Kozjane. They did not check my identity, so they don't know my name. Nobody else has seen me."

"I could have guessed they were not interested in your passport, darling," he said, still holding her.

She brushed the tears from her eyes while her father filled the buckets with water and hung each at the side of the forks.

"Come, get on the bike. Let's go home."

Valeria climbed on the back seat, and they drove home.

From the yard, they heard Mother screaming angrily from the door. "Have you seen Valeria, Bruno?"

"I'm here, Mother!" Valeria cried, dismounting from the motorbike.

"What took you so long? Have you been waiting for the rain to fall? Mario and his men are here. They have a package for you to take to Vatovlje."

Father intervened. "Nadja, please, stop screaming! We're not all deaf. Let's have a bite to eat first."

Mother came out of the house and saw Valeria's face. Reading her distress, she asked anxiously, "Valeria, are you all right? You look like you've dined with death."

"A near brush, Nadja ...She disarmed a troop of Italians at the well. Our little Valeria is no less than a war hero. A very brave girl ..."

The talk about Italians brought Mario to the courtyard, too. Father showed him the weapons, and Valeria related what had happened in a more relaxed and even with some humor. The partisans gathered around her and cheered. They particularly liked the trick with the *Giovinezza* and, of course, the part where she set the Italians running. When she stopped, a question floated in the air: "What to do next?"

"Italians must have started a new offensive. We heard they are moving from Suhorje and Tatre, too. This time we will defend the village. We will set a trap for stinky Italians," Mario proudly said. "We're about thirty and we have weapons and ammunition to last for days. Reinforcements are on the way, too. We want to create a safe territory to be able to cure the wounded and organize the partisan propaganda, so there are a couple of battalions coming to join us. We will chase the dirty Fascists out of Kozjane once and for all."

The rest of the day was spent in frantic activities to raise the village's defenses. A couple of young men quickly built a rocky wall at the entrance of the village to shield the fighters from bullets.

'We have no artillery,' thought Mario. 'The Italians will bring guns and ammunition. This is not going to be easy.'

He had an idea and called his little brother Franjo.

"Franjo, get the kids together! I have an assignment for you. Collect as many old nails, pieces of broken glass and sharp metal. Then go to the road in the valley and spill the shards around the last corner just before the bridge. That should keep the bastards busy."

Franjo was twelve, tall and skinny like a stick. He gazed at his older brother with endless admiration. "So the macaroni will go swimming in the creek?"

Mario nodded with a smile and the boy ran off.

The Italians arrived the following morning. The partisan scouts reported that a couple of trucks slipped off the road as their tires blew up. The soldiers were swearing and sweating from the heavy repairs they had to make. The partisans waited for them on the hill to the village. They did not dare to start the fight in the open field. The enemies were too many. Some of the armored cars had light cannons in tow, approaching the village from the open field below. Immediately, they opened cannon fire on the houses, which burst into flames. The villagers snatched their valuables and evacuated the animals. Pigs and cows ran into the bushes in panic.

The partisans, however, had positioned their posts so well that the Italians could not break their lines for a week while heavy fights took place below the village. Two partisans were shot dead and one was wounded. The number of Italian soldiers wounded or dead was supposed to be much higher.

On Friday, March 12th, the partisans ran out of ammunition. Reinforcements were nowhere in sight. They had no choice but to retreat. In Bruno Batič's house, the family gathered for their last meal together. In spite of everything, the house miraculously remained undamaged.

Mother cooked a big pot of *jota*, a thick soup with potatoes, beans, and sauerkraut, and baked fresh bread. After the last bite, they heard loud explosions of heavy artillery that opened fire on the village and the surrounding hills. The Italians were gathering territory. Father looked at Valeria, who fell silent.

"Don't worry about us, Valeria. We'll be fine. I think you should escape from the Italians. You'll be safer with the partisans."

Mario moved in his chair uncomfortably. "Father, this is impossible. You see, Karlo, our commander, is not very keen on having women in our unit. Valeria will have to run to Ljubljana and get a new identity. I can't take her with me, I'm sorry."

Father looked at Mario with disappointment. "The city of Ljubljana is surrounded by barbed wire and practically impassable. Italian posts are checking everyone passing from one side to the other. How can Valeria get through and stay alive? Besides, where would she go in Ljubljana?"

"Father, I'm sorry."

"Don't sorry me, son. You let me down. We all work for the *Liberation Front*, including Valeria. We expect from you to protect us when we're in danger. We're talking about your sister here."

"I know." Mario nodded, sinking in his chair like a little boy taking Father's reprimands.

Nadja, a tiny peasant woman with an iron spirit, was weary of war and politics. In an attempt to find the best solution for her seven children, she spoke up.

"I think Valeria should go to live with Ada Skarpin, who is renting a flat in Ljubljana while she studies at the Teachers' College. Maybe you can go back to school and get an education, Valeria. You know Italian, my dear," she hinted at her daughter with a smile. "You could even get a job at an office working for the Fascists. It would be safe and far better than joining the partisans. Woods, guns, and rough men are not for a young girl."

Valeria's situation was hopeless in every way. Besides, in her mother's eyes she would always be a little girl. She looked at her with disappointment. "Mother, why do you think women cannot be as good fighters as men?"

Showing his support, her little brother Franjo said, "After all, our Valeria has single-handedly dealt with a whole troop of Italians, hasn't she? I don't know any man who did that."

Valeria threw him a grateful look; she loved him so much. She sighed with sorrow at the thought of leaving her family behind. Where would she go? How would she live without them? She loved them all so much.

"Nadja, you speak reason. Valeria should finish school. We can afford to support her, and she can do much more for the resistance in Ljubljana than here, if she got a new identity, a new passport," added Father slowly.

Mario jumped at the idea. "Of course, we'll take care of it, Valeria. Don't worry, you will be easily admitted to the Teachers' College. I can get you a new passport in a couple of days just to pass the barbed-wire border. In Ljubljana, we have a very good connection with a printing office. During the day, they print cellophane bags, during the night passports. The quality of their documents is excellent. You will get a new passport in a better quality than the one you have from Trieste. What do you say, Valeria? Will you go to Ljubljana and help the *Liberation Front* there?"

Valeria thought about it. Maybe Mother was right. She could live with Ada; they have been friends since their birth. Besides, war or no war, it was much more amusing in the city. The cinema, the theater, and the dancing hall were all there.

"Will Ada have space to accommodate me? Isn't Ada's sister Marjana living with her in the flat?"

"I heard Marjana is working in one of the Fascist hospitals in Italy or Croatia. She's not there as far as I know. I spoke about this with Ada's mother two days ago. I am sorry, Mario, but I don't see your troop having a chance to defeat the Italians," concluded Mother in a low voice.

Mario responded firmly, "Not yet, Mother. But there will come a day when the shitters will run quicker than rabbits to their stinky Italy, and as the poet says: *Close linked* be Slava's every child, // That again // We may reign // And honor, riches now regain!"

"That's the way to go, my son," said Father.

In the distance, gunshots drummed their morbid song.

"Where shall I get my passport for Ljubljana, Mario?"

"Do you know the mill in the valley of river Reka near village Ribnica?"

"Of course. How many times have we been fishing trout and crab there?"

"Right, there's a hiding post in the cave behind the mill. Go there and wait for one of our couriers to get in touch. Take good shoes and warm clothes. It may prove safer to walk to Ljubljana instead of riding the train from Pivka. There is always police on the train."

Shots were coming closer, and it was time for the Batič family to part. They kissed each other farewell, eyes gleaming with tears of concern and worry. There was little hope that peace would come soon, although news reached them that Hitler had lost a whole army in Russia, in the battle of Stalingrad. Maybe the Führer should reconsider and negotiate what's best for Germany out of the positions won, instead of continuing his devastating march around Europe. Still, the news that the Nazis were retreating from Russia bore hope. The partisans were eagerly awaiting ammunition and support from the Allies. However, it was not to be. The Allies were unsure of these ragged men, dwelling in the woods, relying on their people, and opposing three strong invading armies. One thing was sure: they fought not only for their lands but also for Communism, and their best friend was Stalin.

Old Batič was the last to leave the house. He locked the door and hid the key under the terracotta flowerpot where pale pink buds of roses were bursting to life. Would he live to see them in bloom? Would he ever again be able to sit lazily in the shade of the walnut tree and talk to Nadja on a Sunday afternoon? What would happen to his children and grandchildren? He would give anything for his people to live free under the sun of his hills.

~~~

Indeed, strong shoes and warm clothes proved to be the right choice. Valeria was waiting in the cave behind the mill for days before a courier brought her new passport and a little package to deliver at a city address. She memorized it and threw the scrap of paper away. She did not ask the boy what was in the package. Better not to know. She knew she was in danger as long as she stayed in *Brkini*. She must quickly move on.

She took the road toward the Pivka train station. In spite of her brother's warning, she was tempted to take the train to Ljubljana. The weather changed. It was spring and should be warm in the second half of March 1943. However, thick snowflakes fell from the black sky, melting into sticky, brown slush on the ground. The fruit trees that had already sprouted buds and their first light green leaves of the season were crushed under the masses of heavy white snow. No cherries and apples this year.

From the bush above the train station, Valeria could see hundreds of Italian soldiers hanging about the platforms. They seemed nothing like the brave Fascist army. The men were in despair, dragging their feet like lepers in the fog. The only light came from the burning butts of cigarettes hanging from their mouths. They were cold, drenched, and tired. Somewhere between this train station and the barracks of Trieste, they seemed to have lost their war spirit. Save for the moans of the wounded men lying on stretchers under the blankets, the falling snow wrapped them in silence. From afar, the platform looked like a row of white tombs in a graveyard.

Valeria swallowed hard and changed her mind. It was too dangerous to ride a train with hundreds of sullen soldiers, probably starving, yet high on brandy and looking for a fight. She followed the old road to the north, stopping at barns and abandoned houses to spend the night. She had been walking for days when she reached Brezovica, a tiny little village close to Ljubljana. She stopped at an old coachmen's post where she washed and changed before her final passage through the barbed-wire post.

Fresh and rested, she could charm the sentinels with her flawless Italian and a wide smile. Her papers declared her to be Gina Novella, born in Trieste, with license to work at the Ljubljana Bureau for Displaced People. Her main qualifications were in languages: Slovenian, some Croatian, and Italian. They let her pass, and finally she reached Ada's address at the corner of Wolfova Street. Her friend was already waiting for her. The two girls fell into each other's arms.

"Valeria, you look like a ghost. Your hands are as cold as ice. Come in, sit by the stove."

Valeria put down her heavy coat and removed her dripping shoes. "Thank you for taking me in, Ada."

"Think nothing of it. I had a letter from my mother a couple of days ago saying you would come. You must tell me what happened at Kozjane. Mother wrote that Italians attacked the village. Who is after you? The Fascist police?"

Valeria hesitated. Ada had been away from Kozjane for more

than a year. Much had changed since. Ada knew little about the risk the village was running by helping the resistance. Most of the villagers as well as the people of *Brkini Hills* supported the *Liberation Front*, yet rules of conspiracy and binding secrecy were the basic rules of survival. Valerie decided not to tell the truth as it happened. She embellished the story of *Giovinezza*, adding that young girls were in danger of rape, so she had to flee when the soldiers became annoying. The second reason for her move to Ljubljana was school; in order to change the topic of their conversation, she asked about the possibilities of enrolling at the Teachers' College.

"They are taking anybody who can speak Italian. Valeria, you can come with me tomorrow. I am certain you will be able to make up for the lost semester."

"That's wonderful. But I have to get my papers in order first and report to the *Commissariato civile*. I will go with you the day after tomorrow. You know I will have to use a different name, don't you, Ada?"

"I know. Is it really necessary?"

"It's better this way. I don't want anybody, least of all you, to get into trouble."

"I guess you know what you're doing. Here in Ljubljana, Italians are far less oppressive than they are in Trieste. We somehow manage to get along with them."

"Really? What about the resistance?"

"What about it?"

"Well, is there any?"

"There is, of course. But we don't hear much about it. I guess the barbed wire somehow obstructs the courier paths. The month after *Natlačen*'s assassination was terrible."

"Were there reprisals afterward?"

"Yes, it was horrible. Italians rounded up a dozen innocent people from the street and shot them that same day in the little alley where *Natlačen* was killed by the Communists."

"Of course. The Fascists want to exterminate us, Slovenians."

"If only the Communists would stop provoking them. It always gets worse after their actions."

Valeria nodded to her friend and yawned. It had been a tough week and she badly needed to rest. However, Ada wanted to know everything about home. About the boys, about the weather, about the fruit trees, and about the animals. They had a hearty dinner of polenta with pork cracklings, and when darkness finally fell, they went to bed. Valeria chased away her worries about home and slept like a rock.

~~~

In the next few days, Valeria found the secret print shop, her connection with the *Liberation Front*. It was indeed under the factory of *Brothers Tuma*, so well hidden that nobody could suspect anything illegal, particularly since the owners were respectable and successful business people. She also delivered the mysterious little package to the assigned address and enrolled into the Italian Teachers' College for Girls. As Ada had said, Valeria managed to sign in without any trouble. Her command of Italian and her charm opened all doors; her fake documents did the rest.

The weather changed. The sun was shining with its full force when the spring of 1943 came in full bloom to Ljubljana. Yet, Valeria felt that the hearts of its citizens remained cold. Everyone she met and spoke to quickly shut up in suspicion and walked away. Their melancholic Slavic souls and broken hearts lived in constant fear and terror. The citizens were not allowed to move freely and had to stay inside the barbed-wire fence. Armed sentinels at every fifty meters were danger points. Already on edge, young soldiers could put anyone in prison for nothing. Life in Ljubljana changed to worse. After WWI, the city flourished socially and culturally. The first Slovene university was founded, theaters and concert halls, the opera. Business and trade expanded, so life was generally much better than under the Austro-Hungarian Monarchy. Now, the white city around the *Castle Hill* became a trap, a huge cage in a Fascist zoo.

During meetings, the Liberation front activists explained the situation to Valeria. Generally faithful Catholics, Slovenians tended to follow the words of their priests, who preached about accepting a sustainable solution with Italians. It was the world turned upside down from Valeria's point of view. Their priest at Kozjane was breathing with the villagers, supporting their resistance against the Fascists, while here in Ljubljana, the rumors said that some priests even denounced their parishioners and Jews to the police. In spite of all this, the patriotic Catholic youth joined the *Liberation Front* and continued their support even after 1942 when the Communists took over. Everyone wanted to get the invaders out of their land.

Valeria was astonished to see resistance fighters coming from all walks of life: farmers, factory workers, intellectuals, business owners. They came from various political groups – social democrats, liberals, Christian democrats and so on. They were young and old, women and men. Valeria was glad to see women playing an equal role in the fight. Sometimes they were even better, for women were generally less suspicious. However, secrecy was top priority at all levels. Everybody was afraid of everybody.

In Valeria's mind all this was very confusing. Like a huge foggy swamp. Her judgment of the situation was black and white. The Slovenians were the good ones, the Fascists the villains. However, it was not so in Ljubljana. Here Slovenians fought against Italians, but did not want to do it side by side with the Communists. Then other Slovenians wanted to wipe out the Communists. And some Slovenian Communists wanted the other freedom fighters who were not in the Communist Party expelled from the *Liberation Front*. There were Slovenians who wanted to wait for the Allies to liberate their land and chase off the invaders; their loyalties went to the government in exile and the Yugoslav King. And last, most Slovenians considered the resistance pointless, that it would be better to lie low until the Axis forces were defeated. All they wanted was to stay alive. These groups had only one thing in common: they were all at each other's throats because of recent and long-standing animosities. The more Valeria tried to comprehend the politics of the big city, the less she understood. At Primorska, the people who felt betrayed by the British after WWI and had come under the Italian rule always thought that the other side of the *Rapallo* border, in Yugoslavia, was the land of milk and honey. There, the southern Slavs, Slovenians, Croats, and Serbs lived united in democracy and peace. However, the reality was different. Serbian King Alexander and his dictatorship threw the people praying to God in different languages and religions – Catholic, Orthodox and Muslim – into an abyss of mutual hate.

Her fellow activists kept reminding her to beware of Slovenian informers who would quickly find a reason to put her in jail. They merged with several paramilitary groups to fight against the Communism, eventually ending up with Italians who could procure military equipment. One of these was *Milizia Volontaria Anti Comunista*. Their headquarters at the little hill *St. Urh*, just outside the barbed wire, was a place everyone, particularly resistance activists, dreaded. A place of torture and murder. The saddest fact was that atrocities were committed within the walls of the church, a sacred place. Valeria was flabbergasted. How could a Slovenian betray, torture, or murder his fellow citizen? Didn't they all want to get rid of Italians?

She was even more surprised to find out that many non-Communist activists had to leave the *Liberation Front* as they did not conform to the Communist leadership within the organization. Why would they let anyone go during such difficult times? Couldn't they see that the resistance needed anybody who was willing to help? The worst were some vague suspicions when several non-Communist resistance fighters disappeared overnight. Some said they were betrayed and imprisoned by the Italians; others said they were killed by the secret police of the *Liberation Front*. In Valeria's judgment, this was wrong and insane. Yet she could not do anything but be quiet and leave such conflicts for the future once they were free. Freedom and justice were her focus, leading her thoughts and actions, the way the Polaris star brings ships to their course on a rough sea. Although Valeria came from a financially solid farmer's family, she embraced the ideas of socialism like common ownership, equal opportunities, and peaceful coexistence among people. She admired the Communist leaders who so bravely opposed the Fascists.

Ada, on the other hand, was more moderate as to her political views and refused to join the *Liberation Front*. One of her close friends, Valeria suspected it could have been a lover, was among the hostages killed during one of the Italian reprisal operations. Ada sincerely blamed extreme Communist actions for the suffering of the civilians. She was convinced that Italians would leave Slovenians in peace as long as they did not oppose them. Once the friends had openly aired their views, they avoided further political discussions. They could still love each other despite all the chaos around them.

One day in April, Ada received a telegram that her older sister Marjana was being released from the Ljubljana Mental Hospital Studenec. Since her sister was not able to work as a nurse for the Italian Army anymore, Ada was to come and take her home.

What a shock. Marjana Skarpin was one of Kozjane's toughest women. She was almost twenty years older than Ada, who was born after WWI when her father finally came home from the Russian POW camp in Galicia. It had taken him five years before he could return to his homeland, starved and ill, yet alive. In the early twenties, Marjana became a trained nurse, working at the *Custoza* Veteran Hospital near Verona. She was an amazing woman; her curly black hair and wide hazel eyes seduced men and women alike. Her full lips, light skin, and fine features seemed frail, but her determined expression showed a strong will and commitment to her work. She was full of humor, and her witty remarks made a handicapped life tolerable for many a soldier. At some point, Marjana made up her mind not to get married. Nobody knew why. Yet, after the suffering she witnessed at *Custoza* Veteran Hospital daily, it was no wonder. Valeria and Ada avidly listened to her stories about the patients when she came home to the village every summer for a month-long vacation. She spoke about her work in Italy while turning sweet-smelling hay on the racks. In 1941, her assignments moved her to other Italian facilities. First, she went to *Kampor* at the island of Rab, then to *Gonars* near Trieste. She had not come home for a holiday in two years, and her family hardly received any letters from her. Until now.

The news about her illness and the ambiguity surrounding it worried Ada a lot. With her heart full of dark premonitions, she hired a cab while Valeria cooked a meal of *gnocchi* with tinned tomatoes and Parmigiano cheese, all goods obtained at the black market. She even found a bottle of red wine to celebrate Marjana's return.

Hours went by. Ada and Marjana didn't come home. Valeria wondered what was taking them so long. It was already dark and the curfew was about to start. Finally, she heard the sound of an engine at the corner of the street. From the kitchen window on the fourth floor, she saw Ada walking next to a hunched old woman. It took her a while to realize that it was Marjana. What had they done to her, the bloody Fascists?

The doorbell rang, and Valeria hurried to open it. She met Marjana's empty look. It was as though she had never seen Valeria before.

"Valeria, please help Marjana with her coat. She's ill, you know..."

"Hello, Marjana. Don't you remember me?"

Marjana's head seemed tiny, wrapped in a huge woolen shawl. In spite of the hot weather, she was also wearing a nurse's winter cape. Her hazel eyes were blank, focused on some images in her head. Valeria could see Ada shaking her head at the back.

"Marjana must take her medicine and go to bed. She's tired."

"What about dinner? I made real *gnocchi*, Marjana. Potatoes, flour, salt, and butter…They're delicious."

Marjana's face grimaced with pain, and hot tears sprang to her eyes. She cried out as though a snake had bitten her. Shrill pain. Then she burst into uncontrollable sobs, convulsions shaking her frail body. Valeria froze.

"Dear God, Valeria, can't you do as you're told for once? Marjana needs a rest, not your *gnocchi* now!"

Ada's voice broke with emotion. Valeria shut up. She embraced Marjana and pulled her into the apartment. She took off her shawl, her cape, her bonnet, and her boots. Aghast, they saw that Marjana's head was almost bald; a few gray tufts of short wiry hair among deep scars and still bleeding scratch marks. Valeria noticed several cuts on her throat, cheeks and wrists. Did they torture her? Why? She patted Marjana's back, caressing her cheeks and holding her cold body in her embrace. She wanted to infuse life into her friend, whom she had always admired so much. Ada stood aside, rooted like a tree, unable to act.

At last, Marjana stopped wailing and was calmly waiting to be led somewhere. Valeria brought her to bed, freshly made with white linen smelling of lavender. She undressed her bony limbs, and finally tucked her in. Fighting a feeling of utmost despair, she planted a kiss on each of Marjana's wrinkled cheek and silently closed the door behind her.

Ada was sitting at the kitchen table with a tiny glass of grappa in her hand.

"They said she became like that after working in *Gonars*. I don't understand. She was assigned to care for children. She loves children. It should have been better looking after the little ones than tending to psychotic war veterans. If she hadn't had such a brilliant record from *Custoza*, they would have left her to die with the other internees at the *Gonars* hospital. But they sent her to Studenec where she was treated for several months. To think that all this time, she had been so near me."

"Why didn't they notify you earlier?"

"They thought she would get better and return to work. But she has lost her mind completely. They say there is little hope. For a month or so now, she has been refusing food. That's why she is so thin. And she keeps scratching her scalp. Did you see her head?"

"Yes, terrible...How did she survive without eating?"

Ada sighed and drained her grappa in one gulp. "I guess they force-fed her. She drinks some water though. She's lucky that one of the nurses at Studenec knew her from their training days in the twenties and took extra care of her. They used to be friends. I spoke to her."

Valeria poured herself a glass of wine. "What did that nurse say? Is there a diagnosis?"

"The nurse said that according to the Italian psychiatrist who examined Marjana regularly, she has catatonia or whatever that means...She has completely lost the touch with the world around her. They said she hasn't spoken a word in months."

"Were they treating her in any way?"

"They administered electroshocks. They said it usually helps, but Marjana showed no signs of improvement. Oh my God, Valeria, what has happened to my sister? If Mother and Father find out..." Ada burst into tears.

Valeria came to her side and embraced her tightly. "Ada, we're strong and healthy. We'll bring Marjana back from the dead. We will cure her with love. You'll see. She'll get better." After a few moments, she sighed. "God knows what they did to her. We'll have to be patient, Ada."

Between sobs, Ada spoke. "*Kampor* and *Gonars* are concentration camps. The sisters told me this today. We know nothing about it. Did you know they're detaining children? What could they have done? They're innocent...They can't be Communists, can they? They can't sabotage trains and assassinate soldiers. If only the *Liberation Front* would stop their pointless actions..."

Valeria looked over Ada's shoulder into the distance, anger building up in her. She could not help but speak in a low, menacing voice.

"Ada, the Fascists are targeting not only the Communists, they are seizing every Slovenian or Croatian – women, children, old people, everybody. They want to annihilate us. They're exterminating us from the face of the earth. After the Fascists have done their job, there will not be a Slovenian soul alive on this planet. They're bastards, the Italians, Fascist bastards!"

Ada shook her head at Valeria's harsh words. "It's not true, Valeria. No...Italians...They're a nation of poets and artists...Michelangelo...Dante...Virgil...They bear the Roman legacy. No..."

"And what did the Ancient Romans do in their occupied territories? They crucified Jesus."

Ada was still shaking her head in disbelief, denying the obvious. She needed to believe the world was better than it was. Valeria gave up. Tomorrow she would try to talk some sense into her again. Tonight all Ada needed was a hug. The girls held each other until complete darkness crept into the kitchen and engulfed the stove, the table with its four simple chairs, and the sofa where Valeria made her bed that night.

When they pulled apart, Ada stumbled into her bedroom while Valeria checked once again on Marjana. She was moaning in her sleep, shaking in agony, and turning around. Valeria took her cold, bony hands in hers, sat on the bed, and started to sing a soft lullaby. Marjana's face relaxed. She finally sank into a deep sleep. Unwilling to pull back her hand for fear that Marjana would start wailing again, Valeria lay beside her and fell asleep, too. For the rest of the night, she shared her dreams with the bony carcass entangled in a war that felt like the countless webs of a million evil spiders. Like a giant black widow, the war held millions in its cold lethal claws.

~~~

The next morning Marjana wasn't any better. For a moment, she seemed to recognize them and nodded as though in approval. Yet the light in her eyes faded as soon as it appeared and Marjana fell back into stupor.

Breakfast was a project. Ada prepared the table with white cloth, fresh bread, milk, and chicory coffee. Valeria tried to make Marjana eat, but she spat out every bite of bread and spoon of milk. Finally, Valeria managed to feed her a few spoons of warm chamomile tea.

Once Marjana had crawled to her room to rest, Ada went to the hospital. Marjana needed treatment, a proper head doctor, a professional. Ada went to Saint Joseph's Hospital where they told her to wait for Doctor Strainar. She sat on a cold bench in the lobby and waited.

"Are you Miss Ada Skarpin?"

"Yes."

"My name is Andrej Strainar. I am a psychiatrist. How can I help you?"

Wondering how such a nice young man could have become a head doctor, Ada described the symptoms of her sister's illness.

After asking some questions now and then, he said, "We're unable to admit your sister to Saint Joseph's Hospital. We are already at double capacity. But I can make a house call. Will you be able to take care of her at home?"

"Certainly, Dr. Strainar. A friend of mine, Valeria, is living with us. We all come from the same village."

"Where might that be? Forgive my curiosity, Miss Skarpin, but your accent is so melodious."

"Indeed?" Ada was surprised. "Well, we all come from the same village, Kozjane."

"Kozjane?" A dark cloud seemed to pass over Andrej's friendly face.

"Yes, it's a village in the *Brkini Hills*."

"Aren't they all s there?"

Ada looked firmly into his eyes. "I assure you I am no , Dr. Strainar. My sister was a military nurse for ten years. She worked in *Custoza* at the Veteran Hospital before they moved her to Rab and *Gonars*. My friend Valeria and I are studying to become teachers."

Andrej nodded. "I'm sorry, Miss Skarpin. It slipped out of my mouth. Politics has nothing to do with my profession. I will visit your sister today. But Kozjane, you know what happened there, don't you?"

"What do you mean?"

Why do doctors always have to be the bearers of bad news? Andrej's blue eyes were moist with compassion as he continued, "The partisans occupied it last March. The village came under their rule for a whole week, with the locals helping them. Then the Italians launched another offensive and regained control of the village. All the young men were sent to labor camps. Many of the houses were burnt down."

Ada stared at him, her brown eyes wide with terror. "What about the women and children? What happened to them?"

"I think they escaped to the woods. I don't know. The news is a couple of weeks old."

"Do you know the exact date?"

"No, I'm sorry. You haven't heard anything from your family?"

Ada stared at his blond curls and thin lips. How can such a nice man bring such horrible news? "No, my whole family is there: Mother and Father. I've written to them a few times, but didn't get any reply. Shall I go and see them?"

Andrej, taller than most men she knew, looked down at her. "I don't think that's a good idea. There's still fighting going on in the hills."

She burst into tears, and he put his arms around her, holding her against his warm chest. After a while, they pulled apart.

"How did you find out?" Ada asked. "Was it in the papers?"

"Yes, I read about it in the paper."

"I read *Slovenec* regularly, too. I must have missed it."

"It was in Corriere, not in *Slovenec*."

Ada looked at him with astonishment. "You read Italian newspapers?"

"I lived in Rome during my medical specialization. I try to read all the Slovenian and foreign publications I can find. I want to get a bigger picture of what's happening."

An awkward silence engulfed them. Ada rummaged in her handbag for a tissue, but Andrej was quicker. He took a piece of gauze from his coat pocket and wiped her wet cheeks. His strokes were tender and light. Ada felt her pulse quicken every time his skin touched hers. She flushed in confusion. So much going on in a few minutes ...What happened to Father and Mother? What has become of their house?

"Look, Miss Skarpin ..."

"Ada, please call me Ada. Andrej, isn't it?"

"Yes, Andrej."

"Will you come and see my sister, Andrej?"

"Of course, I will. I finish work in a couple of hours and I can visit her afterward."

"It is on Wolfova Street, on the corner of the Congress Square."

"All right."

"We have some leftovers from yesterday. My friend made *gnocchi*. You must dine with us."

"Wonderful! Thank you. The food at the hospital is terrible. Goodbye, Ada."

"Goodbye, Andrej."

Ada's first thought was to go the post office. She sent a telegram to Kozjane:

MARJANA ILL STOP SHE IS WITH ME AND VALERIA STOP HOW ARE YOU STOP REPLY STOP LOVE STOP.

~~~

Outside, a warm spring sun was shining, and birds were singing their irresistible chant of seduction. The walls of the mental hospital, however, were thick and cold, and life inside was gray and sad; so many patients, so many souls fragmented and broken like crushed glass never to be repaired and made whole again. The working hours dragged into eternity as Andrej talked to his patients. He was trained to see reason where there was hardly any left. Wars inflicted so much misery that his patient load continued to pile up. All were urgent. Human beings, who had once been treated like animals or, worse, stocked like objects, handled like spare parts in a goal-oriented, mechanized, and heartless society. In the whim of a gunshot, these men and women could be disposed of, once they stopped serving the hungry mouths of the greedy machine. Andrej Strainar had a big warm heart, which was why he had studied to become a doctor. He believed in all these disturbed men and women. He viewed them as part of one big picture: humanity. His idea of civilization was a society that did not leave anybody behind.

However, Andrej's mental patients in spring 1943 were very much different from those he had been treating before 1941. The war had been raging on for three years, causing ills a thousand times worse than the neuroses and depressions of the pre-war period. Of course, psychiatrists had also discovered so much more about man's psyche and the terrible consequences of the violent events since the end of WWI. Terms like "shellshock," "amnesia," and "trauma" acquired new meanings even since Freud issued his memorandum on the treatment of mentally ill soldiers during WWI, written at the request of the Austrian War Ministry in February 1920. Freud criticized the brutal electroshock treatments of traumatized soldiers and the violent therapies that had only one objective: to make them fit enough to get back on the front as quickly as possible and continue fighting. In his report, Freud was merciless toward his fellow physicians who sent soldiers with tremors back to the front lines, where they lost their lives, confused, unable to escape the shower of bullets and shells. Medicine had become a servant of war; rather than curing, it was killing people. Two decades went by, and gradually the war victims either died or sank into oblivion in the numerous veteran hospitals around the world.

Despite Freud's criticism of electricity in treating mentally ill patients, Andrej appreciated the positive results that moderate electrical shocks had with certain mental conditions; the emphasis was on moderate. He had followed the studies of *Ugo Cerletti* and *Lucio Bini* closely, even spending two years with their team to specialize in treatments using electrical current. Andrej introduced the therapy two years ago at the Ljubljana Mental Hospital Studenec, and at the Saint Joseph's Hospital, a subsidiary of Studenec, only a year ago.

He left his job at the Studenec Hospital, the center for mental illnesses at the outskirts of the city, for the one in the center of Ljubljana. The main reason was, his older sister had returned home from Russia sick and lonely. Sanja Strainar used to be a famous pianist, now she walked about like a shadow. Another broken soul. She needed him not only as a brother but also as a doctor. Her condition showed Andrej that medical science understood little when it came to a human being – just a modicum of knowledge about bodily function and far less about the soul and psyche. He researched the cause of her long illness, but no tests or analyses gave him insight. Sanja would stare at the falling snow for hours and hours without moving. There was only one reasonable explanation. Men could strive for the truth, but only God led the way to it. Although Andrej grew up in a family of atheists, he found God and truth in the soul's immortality beyond the borders of life, and faith in the justice of his heavenly Father. As a psychiatrist and a scientist, he felt he had failed for he could not cure Sanja.

The thought of his talented and beautiful sister Sanja Strainar saddened Andrej. He was her first fan and admirer. He would sit on the sofa behind her, a decade younger little boy, while her fingers glide across the keys of the piano. By the time she turned twenty, she was famous for her sensitive interpretations of Mozart's piano sonatas. Soon she spent most of her studies and life in Berlin, Paris and Vienna, where she filled the concert halls. In the early thirties, she received an invitation to play with the famous musicians of the Moscow Conservatory in Russia. Of course, Sanja, the daughter of a well-connected Social Democrat, was thrilled. That was twelve years ago. Sanja had loved her life in Russia where she seemed to fit in. In the photographs, she looked like a protagonist from a Tolstoy's novel: long blond hair and sky blue eyes, tall and thin. Her letters home were full of enthusiasm; the society and its egalitarian spirit, the socialist economy and its dashing energy, the arts and their spirit of fairness – everything in the Soviet Union had fascinated her. In her last letter from Moscow, Sanja wrote that she had fallen in love with Sergej Sukorov, a solo violinist in the orchestra. She planned to bring him to Ljubljana to meet the family. Sergej and Sanja were only waiting for were the papers to allow them to travel together.

Then, silence... All the letters from the family to Sanja remained either unanswered or returned. Almost a year had gone by without any news, and Father, old Strainar, started to worry. Using his international political network of Social Democrats, he tried to obtain more information by corresponding with people who had visited Russia or lived there. Everyone told him the same thing: the Soviet Union had become a tyranny, and Stalin a hangman instead of a political leader of the new world. Russians and foreigners alike were disappearing overnight under mysterious circumstances. They all feared that Sanja was among those dead souls, rotting away in one of the gulags. Mother Strainar became ill with worry. She found it impossible to cope with the loss of her beloved daughter. After a short illness, she died in 1938, and old Strainar followed her six months later. In 1939, Sanja suddenly returned from Russia. Only her younger brother Andrej was there to welcome her. In their vast city apartment on Miklošičeva Street, the siblings lived like shipwrecked survivors of the old times, when their parents still believed in the alluring social ideals of the Russian Revolution.

At first, Sanja did not want to talk about Russia. She seemed to blend in with the cultural life in Ljubljana. The *Slovenian Philharmonic Orchestra* soon invited her to perform with them. In 1941, in spite of the Italian occupation, she was giving concerts regularly. Two days before the Christmas of 1942, on a cold winter night, she was to play Tchaikovsky. After the opening notes, the conductor raised his baton in her direction. Her thin fingers were set to strike the first keys of Piano Concerto No. 1 when she collapsed on stage. Unconscious, they brought her to Andrej, who arranged immediate admission to the General State Hospital. Despite their efforts, the doctors could not find what caused her collapse. There was no real diagnosis. It seemed that Sanja fell ill with a mysterious fever. Days and months passed while she lay in bed delirious, crying, suffering. After a while, Andrej realized that her illness was more mental than physical. A memory, a past horror, something must have happened to her in Russia, and the wonderful music, the notes of angels on earth as surely Tchaikovsky was one, must have triggered it. He tried to pry the secret out of her, but she remained silent as a grave.

Then one spring day, six months after Sanja's illness and inability to play in the Orchestra, a letter came from Russia. Sanja burst into tears. She finally spoke up. Andrej would never forget what she told him. Such cruelty was beyond humanity. Since that day he profoundly hated the s. From his point of view, they were the root of all evil and far worse than any occupying Italian or German forces could ever be.

He closed his last patient file of the day and put on his trench coat. The willow trees along the banks of Ljubljanica River were shooting light green buds. Ducks were quarrelling over a piece of food – not bread, for the citizens of Ljubljana rarely had enough to fill their stomachs nowadays. The bread that the bakers were selling contained so much bran that even ducks would not care for it. With Ljubljana cut off from the rest of Slovenia, the supply chain had broken down. The prices of food had risen to almost sixty percent since before the war. After the New Year of 1941, in accord with the Italians, the local authorities introduced food coupons. Every citizen with no workable land received wheat flour – four kilos a month per person, but three kilos or even less for a child. White bread became a remote dream; most days they had corn bread that was so wet and heavy that people called it baked polenta. Everything was rationed – butter, coffee, sugar, and cooking fat.

Andrej usually had his meals in the hospital. This way the coupons could cover Sanja's needs comfortably, even though she wasn't eating much. Hence, Andrej was looking forward to a tasty Mediterranean supper tonight with his new acquaintance, Ada.

His heart leapt at the thought of the charming young woman to whom he delivered such devastating news about her home village. He could still see her oval face and tiny lips, her wide hazel eyes filling with tears before him. Her chestnut hair was straight, and she wore it short in a modern bob. Her body showed a strongly built young woman with heavy breasts and a small waistline. He loved what he had seen. Moreover, he loved what he anticipated with his sixth sense: a passionate woman who was able to love and receive love in return. Andrej had been single for too long. He needed a woman and a soul mate. It was time he started a family. Sanja's health had improved so much and she had even started to play the piano again. To make ends meet more easily, they agreed she would give private piano lessons.

He passed a flower stall, made a few steps toward it, but changed his mind. It was a professional visit. He was to examine Ada's sister, not Ada's lips. He burst into a cheerful laugh at the thought and quickened his step.

~~~

Several weeks had passed since Marjana opened up and told them about what had thrust her spirit into the darkest pit of human existence. She had only one thought on her mind: death. Andrej, Ada, and Valeria were still in shock. Having become close friends in the meantime, each of them deduced different conclusions from Marjana's account of atrocities in the two Italian concentration camps – *Kampor* on the island of Rab and *Gonars* near Trieste. The sad destinies of the babies and children infused their veins like black, sticky tar. The horror stuck to their hearts, freezing them in pain.

Andrej's analytical mind focused on the intensity of human compassion, which drove Marjana to experience the same agony and suffering as the children. Yet, it was more than that. In a way, Marjana felt responsible for the terrible murders. Guilt ravaged her good heart – guilt that she did not do enough to oppose the Italians. He despised men who were not brave enough to break the chain of vile commands and allowed children to die in front of their eyes. The eerie account of life in the camps made Andrej's hair stand up. It shattered not only Marjana's mental state, but also his beliefs. He had never looked at the Fascist occupation from this perspective.

Like every Slovenian patriot, he had supported the *Liberation Front* until the s monopolized the resistance not only in the name of all Slovenians, but also in the name of the proletarian revolution. He abhorred a political solution based on such tyranny. It was too similar to the Russian way. He broke all connection with the *Liberation Front*, for he did not want to have anything to do with the s. His criticism of their politics was a well-known fact among the citizens of Ljubljana. Consequently, Andrej Strainar was soon approached by the Anti-Communist police force – *Milizia Volontaria Anti Comunista* – which was connected to the Italian occupation forces. He used to think the Italians would do less harm than the Communists. But now this! Marjana's confession challenged his political views and confused him. His head was spinning with her recollections. The Fascists were criminals. He carefully distanced himself from his contacts at the Anti-Communist Volunteer Militia, which collaborated with the Italians. Andrej was a doctor; he did not want blood on his hands. Under no circumstances did he approve of concentration camps and such ungodly treatment of human beings. Besides, he was falling in love with Ada and wanted to cure her older sister. The image of himself as her savior flattered him. He stepped into the role of the knight on a white horse and jumped at each opportunity to console the young woman, who was often sad beyond saying, with a hug. She had grown melancholic and gloomy, shedding bitter tears every time she thought of the horrible images evoked by her catatonic sister.

Valeria's reaction to Marjana's disturbing confession, however, was outrage. All she could think of was she wanted to fight, fight, and fight. Valeria worked for the *Liberation Front* without caring who was in charge. They could be Communists, Christian Socialists, or aliens – as long as they were going to kick the Italians out of Slovenia forever, Valeria was with them. Her zealousness for the organization provoked and upset Andrej and Ada very much. On many occasions, they asked Valeria to be careful for she could put all of them in great danger. Gradually, Valeria began to invent little white lies to cover her dubious errands, and everyone pretended not to know what she did outside the house.

On that hot late August morning in 1943, Valeria was on her way home much earlier than usual, approaching the southern post of the Trieste Road in Ljubljana. There were no courses at the Teachers' College because of the summer break, or so they said. Valeria noticed that several Italian professors had left the city without setting any dates for the autumn term. She heard on the BBC Radio that the Allies had started an invasion of Italy via Sicily; they wanted to occupy and annihilate the crumbling Fascist state. The Slovenian *Liberation Front* increased the pressure on the Italian occupying forces by sabotaging the railways, blowing up ammunition warehouses, and attacking Italian troops where they could. Valeria took an active part in all these operations, traveling from Ljubljana to the *Brkini Hills*, to Notranjska, and as far as the Karst Plateau, carrying messages, light ammunition, spare parts for weapons as well as medicines. The cover story for her activity and absences from Ljubljana was a bogus practicum at a nursing school in Postojna. Marjana had provided her with the papers. As her health improved bit by bit, Marjana turned into a bitter opponent of Fascism. Occasionally, she would still fall back into a dark state of stupor, but Andrej's careful treatments that combined psychoanalysis, mild electrical shocks, and sedatives brought her back to normal within a week of her relapse. Still, she was unable to resume her work as a nurse, for which there was a great demand at the hospital.

Although Andrej was Marjana's doctor and main confidant, she related the scenes of horror first to Valeria, who could not forget that May morning. The situation was getting out of hand. Marjana had become so thin that Andrej considered admitting her to the hospital and feeding her by force. They were alone with Marjana in the small, cold apartment. It was raining for days, and cold winds shook the pale green leaves outside. Once again, Marjana refused to eat, staring at her nourishing breakfast of bread and milk as though it were a heap of vomit. Valeria lost her temper.

"Damn it, Marjana! I scavenged the black market behind the Opera House yesterday to get some milk and bread for you, and you're not having any! You're looking at it as though it were a heap of shit! But you know what, Marjana? It is you, you are shit! You're a shitty coward, that's what you are!"

Marjana howled with pain like a wounded wolf. She screeched back at Valeria: "You, you know nothing, young girl! Nothing, *pupa*, nothing ..."

"Instead of fighting me and Ada, who wants to cure you, you should fight the Fascists! You should help us kick them out of our lands! You should prevent more of our children to fall in their hands. Yet all you do is howl, wail, and moan. Tears won't save the world, you know!"

Marjana's her frail body was trembling all over. "You don't know anything! You have never held the hand of a dying child! You have never seen death, have you, Valeria?"

Valeria lowered her voice to a menacing hiss. "But I know well who is responsible for the deaths! And I fight them, dirty bloody Fascists! I fight them. And you, you're dying ...They don't even need to kill you! By dying, you're helping them!"

"Holding those tiny hands, a pair of lifeless tiny hands ..."

"Wake up, Marjana. Start living for God's sake! I am holding your bloody hands every night, aren't I?"

Valeria was out of her mind with anger. Marjana sat there, shaking her scratched, nearly bald and bleeding skull in despair. Tears streamed down her gray wrinkled cheeks as her words turned to harsh whisper: "There was nothing I could do. They sent me to

Kampor because I can speak Slovenian and Croatian. They asked me which age group I wanted to take care of, and I said children. You see, I love children. But I didn't know then...Oh, God! I didn't know then..."

Marjana hid her face in her hands. Her sobbing filled the dining room. Valeria sensed it was her turn to remain silent and let her friend speak. She waited. Words would come eventually; words that explained the unexplainable.

"When the internees got off the boats, the Italians immediately separated the children from their parents, the men from the women. They led the adults to Draga, where there were hundreds of tents. That was *Kampor*, the actual concentration camp behind the walls and the barbed wire. The children were assigned to a former hotel that was converted into a children's department...They called it Children's Hospital, but it had nothing to do with healing. All the little ones did was die...The first few days after being taken from their families, they were crying, 'Mama! Tata! Mama! Tata!' We tried to console them as best we could. We caressed their hair, held them in our arms, rocked them gently...but they kept crying...They were hungry and thirsty. To put it plainly, the children were starving; they were dying of hunger."

Marjana looked at the painted bowl with hot milk and crumbled bread that Valeria had put in front of her. She felt sick and turned her look away. She continued, "They were howling and wailing until their voices cracked into tenuous whispers...into almost inaudible sobs. When they fell silent, we knew death had come for them. Their eyes turned dry and blank. They lost all the sparkle of a child's curiosity. Their little mouths, dry lips with protruding teeth, couldn't even form that last question: Why?"

Finally, Valeria found her voice. "Oh my God, Marjana. I am sorry, so sorry. I didn't know..."

"Of course not, *pupa* moja...My little girl, who could imagine such a thing? Italians have large families and they are famous for their love of children. They are also supposed to be Christians, aren't they? Bastards! They crossed themselves every time a baby died of starvation...I couldn't do anything. I just held their tiny hands while their innocent souls went to Heaven..."

"I'm sorry, Marjana..." Valeria was trembling all over her body as she closed the gap between her and Marjana, who resumed her story.

"There were four to six little children in a single bed. In a couple of weeks, those who were five- to four-years-old shrank to the size of a baby, weighing no more than a couple of kilos. At first, they just pissed in their beds; later, once they caught one of the ravaging illnesses going around, they started vomiting and shitting, too. No bed linen, no covers, just plain mattresses filled with straw. The stench in the rooms was unbearable. Some were still babies, only a couple of months old. Oh, Lord! But who am I calling on? God turned his back on humanity long ago. I lost my faith in God in that slaughterhouse …"

"How many were there, Marjana?" asked Valeria in a low voice.

Marjana looked at her and shook her head. "I don't know, Valeria. We were four nurses and hundreds, maybe thousands of children … I don't know. They passed away so quickly. They contracted diarrhea within days of arrival. We gave them some water, but they became dehydrated. You see, they simply evaporated like drops of water. The rooms stank like a plague. We couldn't clean them. There were no diapers. The staff of the former hotel finally procured us some old bed linen that we tore apart and wrapped the babies in. But it was not enough. The children were peeing and defecating all the time. They had no solid food, only stale bread soaked in tepid water. There was so much filth that diseases spread like wildfire. In the end, we just laid pieces of newspaper under their skinny bottoms to catch the feces … They didn't last long … the poor ones …"

Valeria stood behind Marjana, staring blindly at the wall in front of her. She could see the suffering as her friend saw it. She put her palms on Marjana's shoulders; her green eyes filled with tears. Despite being a fighter, for once she could not utter a single coherent word.

Marjana went on: "All we could do was hold their tiny hands while they died. I will never forget the touch of those lifeless fingers and the looks of those huge blank eyes. It was a crime. No, crime is not the proper word. It was pure evil. The kind of evil only Man is capable of. Then I asked them … I mean, the Italians …"

"What did you ask them, Marjana?"

"I asked to be transferred to the adults … I couldn't cope with touching and holding those tiny hands any longer. I …"

"Marjana …"

"I begged the Italians to assign me to the general camp, where people were dying in the tents under the hot sun, but when I left the hotel for the first time in months and breathed in the harsh salty air, I fainted. I didn't feel the blow on my head when it hit the pavement. I don't know what happened. They said I was working in *Gonars* for a few weeks, yet my first memory is arriving at this apartment. I've been to Hell...I still cannot escape the prison of my memory. Every night, all I can feel is the touch of those tiny children's fingers...still and lifeless...cold and alone, like the bones of an animal that died in the desert." She was howling the last words, her gaze fixed on the ceiling as though there could be some explanation in the sky beyond the tiles on the roof.

"Oh, my God, Marjana..."

"No God, Valeria, Devil. They are so vicious and such bigots, the Fascists. They could not shoot the children in the face...oh, poor little cherubs...They just looked away as the little ones died. They simply looked the other way."

Valeria sighed. "Now I understand why food makes you sick." Taking away the bowl in front of Marjana, she placed a cup of corn coffee with milk in its place. She sat down and looked at her sick friend across the table. "Marjana, were you eating at all during those months?"

Marjana frowned and sank into her thoughts. Then she lifted her eyes toward Valeria, feeling for once understood. "I must confess that I did and didn't. All four of us nurses, we were part of the staff and our food rations were plentiful. We put aside most of the food for the children. But we could feed only a few of them; there were too many. So we had to choose. Which child to feed first? The weakest or the strongest? Should we help the youngest or the oldest? Who had more chance to survive? We discussed it over and over again." She shook her head, showing there was no real solution to the terrible dilemma.

"So you played God, well, or at least some kind of Providence. What a task!"

Tears showed in Marjana's eyes, a couple of them paving their way down her cheeks, under the stiff blouse collar around her scrawny neck, toward her heart and the limitless sorrow of human existence in the face of torture. "Right, Providence...What an indifferent institution, Providence! Every small decision pierced my heart and wounded my soul. I carried my cross and felt the thorns penetrate my forehead and my cheeks. It was more than pain. It was guilt, Valeria, the disgrace and responsibility of personal guilt that each of us hides inside. The guilt you feel when a child you did not feed or give to drink must breathe his last breath. The guilt is tearing me apart. Well, the basic ingredient of this choking guilt has been food. It started right after we understood the Fascists' death-dealing system. When they served our meals, we were unable to eat. A minute ago you were holding the tiny lifeless hand of an innocent, the next minute you had a chunk of roasted chicken before you. Whenever I ate, I had to leave the table in the middle of the meal to go to the restroom to throw up. Memories of those huge eyes haunted me, the smell of death in my nostrils, the evil I witnessed. I ate less and less. All of us did. But I drank water and coffee, real coffee, Valeria, not corn coffee. The Fascists can get everything, you know, everything for the heroes of Italy who have conquered Mare Nostrum. Now and then I convinced myself I was not really helping anybody by fasting, so I would eat a full meal…Afterward I wept while my stomach digested the pasta, meat, or potatoes. I felt the guilt in my stomach. Like having stones, bricks in my bowels. It was very painful. I had cramps as though I were digesting rocks and iron instead of food."

"When did food started to disgust you, Marjana?"

"I don't know. Maybe a year ago."

Valeria sipped at her coffee and Marjana subconsciously did the same. They were silent for a long time. Then, Valeria told Marjana the news about their home village Kozjane. In a vivid narrative, she related life under the Fascists before the occupation, the beginnings of the *Liberation Front* and the partisans' battle in Kozjane. She also told Marjana how united and brave all the villagers were, how they helped the new partisan army, and how the Italians burnt down their village to the ground to stamp out the resistance. Yet, for the life of them, the Italians could not annihilate their spirit. Valeria knew the latest news: once again, their home village Kozjane was rising like a phoenix from its ashes, proud and rebellious. She was prudent not to mention any names to Marjana, for you never know, but she took the risk and laid out her own involvement with the *Liberation Front*.

"Marjana, we must drive the Fascists out of our land even if we have to eat grass. The Americans and the British are gaining territories in North Africa. Before the year ends, they will invade Italy and kick out the Fascists from their own boot."

Marjana listened. "Valeria, my dear girl, I don't think Andrej agrees with you. So far neither the Americans nor the British have shown any wish to support the *Liberation Front*. I guess it must be because of the Communists."

Valeria sighed. "I know, and we lack for everything: ammunition, explosives, uniforms, and money. Still, we are the only ones opposing the occupation, so one day they will have to acknowledge us."

"Do you think it is possible in spite of the Communists?"

Valeria's cheeks burned with enthusiasm. "I would not take so much notice of the Communists at the moment. They're only one fraction of the *Liberation Front*. Besides, they are very efficient. They know how to lead the guerrilla war; they're the only ones among us with some real experience. Some of them were in Spain to fight against Franco. They are skilled. I say let them lead the fight. Once the war is over, they will be just another political party, maybe a stronger one than before, but just one of many. Of this I am sure."

Marjana shook her head. "If they win the war, they may take over completely, like in Russia."

Valeria shrugged. "Let them, Marjana. Nobody can be worse than the Fascists."

A pregnant silence fell between them. Would the Communists torture their opponents as they did in Russia? Andrej told them about his sister's suffering. Two sick sisters from two sick tyrannies.

Valeria looked at Marjana with purpose. "I guess we will have to leave that question for after the war. We'll cross that bridge when we come to it. First, we have to win this war. Will you join the *Liberation Front*, Marjana? We need people like you, we really do."

"Do you really need disillusioned cripples like me? I am a mad woman. Can't you see that? Either you must be joking or the *Liberation Front* is already on its knees."

Valeria slowly got up from the table and took the bowl with warm milk from the stove. She was determined, although her green eyes glistered with tears. She held the dish above the table like in a religious ceremony, like a precious offering to gods.

"My dear Marjana, if you want, you can be stronger than steel. Your will and your energy will come back. Please, have some bread and milk. I beg you, take this bowl." She put the bowl formally in front of Marjana. Her face was solemn and sincere, as though she were performing a rite, as though she were following the rules of an invisible protocol. "Please, eat my friend and get strong for the fight. Meanwhile, I will entertain you."

Marjana's face slowly relaxed into a smile. She lifted the spoon, still looking undecidedly at the steaming milk. "What will you do, Valeria? Will you sing to me?"

Valeria burst into a soft laugh. "Not exactly, but I will tell you how I managed to disarm a troop of ferocious Fascists with a song."

"What did you do, Valeria?"

While Marjana was spooning her food, Valeria recounted the *Giovinezza* story, acting out the roles of the commander and his men and their surprise. They had danced to her tune in the end – and it was a tune sung by a machine gun. Marjana laughed until tears flooded her eyes, her first tears of joy in a long time. They made a pact that morning: Marjana started to eat, and Valeria introduced her to the conspiratorial activities of the *Liberation Front*. It was a turning point.

So many months later, on a hot summer day, Valeria quickened her steps at the thought of Marjana. She approached the wired gate to Ljubljana and smiled warmly at a trembling Italian soldier on Trieste Road. It was time to concentrate on the sentinel, a soldier of the regular Italian army, a young man probably recruited in haste and by force, since the big Duce was running out of options. Good. To her surprise, she found a pair of teary blue eyes looking back at her. A question slipped from her tongue:

"What has happened, soldier?" she asked in a soft voice.

He shook his head as though he did not want to answer, yet words spilled out of his mouth. "Oh, my brother...killed by Americans. I am from Gela, Sicily, you know."

Valeria's first emotion was joy. She had to suppress a smile: finally, Italians were beginning to lose the war. "I am sorry. What about your parents? Are they all right?"

"Yes, they wrote me, you see." He focused his eyes on her papers. "What was your errand in Postojna?"

"I am training to be a nurse at the Italian Red Cross there."

"The railway at Borovnica was bombed again. Those Ščavis ...damn them all!"

"I know. I took the train to Vrhnika and had to walk all the way to Ljubljana. So, do you plan to return to Sicily and defend your land?"

"No, my orders are to stay here," he said, inspecting Valeria's papers more thoroughly. He hesitated to take them to the office and crosscheck her name which was, of course, fake. At last, he said, "Papa and Mamma are alive. So is my sister. They all mourn for our little Antonio."

Valeria could not help but sympathize with the young man. He was probably a good boy before the flood of violence brought him to Ljubljana where he had to act as the oppressor. "I'm sorry. This bloody war!" She reached out to take her pass, but the soldier kept it in his grip.

"War is war. What can we do? You're a fine girl, Ginna. Take care!"

She looked into his watery eyes and nodded. "Thank you, soldato. I hope we live to see each other at a better time."

She turned toward the center of the city deep in thought. War makes enemies of us all. Men against men, women against men, soldiers against civilians. Nobody actually wins. All losers in the end. Yet what is war? Is it a conflict of political forces unable to reach an agreement by diplomatic negotiations? Or, is it in the nature of Mankind to fight and bleed for ideals irrelevant to the majority? Are the causes of wars material like wealth and goods? Valeria knew that Hitler averted poverty in Germany by building the war industry, highways across the country, war ships, and railways. Many powerful capitalists supported the dangerous dictator with a funny moustache. For each battle lost or won, no matter how many soldiers fell, they were sure to make a profit. Was it greed then that propelled the first and now the second world slaughter? Would they ever escape this vicious cycle? She shivered at the memory of Hitler's words, which she read in one of the newspapers: "The day of individual happiness has passed." How true the tyrant's words rang. Everyone was equally miserable in this chaos, the oppressors and oppressed alike.

~~~

When Valeria opened the door to their apartment, she found Ada, Marjana, Sanja, and Andrej sitting at the table. There was a bottle of spumante and a bowl filled with almond biscuits in the middle of the table.

To Valeria's surprise, Marjana stood up to embrace her. Why …Then it dawned on her. Today was her eighteenth birthday. She had completely forgotten. She stuttered something incomprehensible while the rest of the group kissed her on the cheeks and stroked her hair.

"Thank you all. Spumante and biscotti – what a feast!"

Ada looked Valeria solemnly in the eyes. "We have another reason to celebrate, Valeria."

Andrej added casually in a husky voice, "Ada and I are getting married in September. We have asked the priest at the Church of *Saint Nicholas* to publish the banns on Saturday. We're officially engaged, Valeria."

Valeria looked at Ada with fondness. She had known for some time that Ada was in love with her sister's doctor. She raised her half-filled flute. "Cheers! Long live Ada and Andrej!"

With laughs and cheers, they quickly emptied the bottle. After a lunch of baked baby potatoes with bacon strips and fresh salad, they all went to the cinema. A famous Italian movie L'ultima carrozzella (The Last Wagon) was attracting masses of young and old to the Kodeljevo cinema. The merry party of three women and two lovers walked slowly along the Ljubljanica River. They were careful to stay in the shadow of huge wild chestnut trees, for the sun was burning hot.

"We should go swimming at City Pool Ilirija instead of sweating in a movie house," lamented Valeria.

"It'll be cooler inside the cinema. By the way, can you swim, Valeria?" asked Andrej.

"She can, but I can't. When I was a girl, women did not undress to swim and sunbathe," said Marjana.

"I learnt to swim in Russia," said Sanja. "Russians are crazy about water. When I was in Leningrad, we went swimming every day. They made a real spa on the banks of Neva River; they did not swim only in summer, but all year long. The bravest of them dive in the water even in winter when the outside temperatures are below zero, sometimes even minus forty degrees. Their friends would wait for them with warmed blankets so they don't freeze to death." Sanja gave a light shiver at the thought.

"Send a breeze of that cold air from Russia," Valeria sang mockingly to the melody of Katyusha, a melody she heard from Mario's partisans one evening back at home, "just to dry my skin and cool my head…"

"Valeria! Hush, hush!" shouted Ada.

Sanja smiled as though Valeria were a naughty child and interrupted her singing. "My dear Valeria, don't call the Russians or they will come!"

They all laughed as they reached the long queue in front of the box office. The cinema was so popular lately, no matter what was playing. The citizens of Ljubljana wanted to escape their everyday troubles, maybe escape somewhere beyond the barbed wire and the prison that the city had become. A comedy with *Aldo Fabrizi* was a wonderful way to do it. Andrej brought them cold drinks and stepped into the queue.

"He is a gentleman, Ada," commented Valeria, enjoying the pleasant Sunday with her friends after a week of living dangerously.

Her last errand was bold, yet crucial. As usual it was an adventure. She had to carry six kilos of explosives to the sabotage partisan platoon at Pivka. She had taken the train, but after the stop at Logatec she overheard a conversation between two women. They were saying that the Italian police often came aboard at Postojna to search the train with dogs. She quickly got off at Unec and walked for more than twenty kilometers in the blazing August heat. With the explosives tied around her thighs and buttocks, she looked like a very heavy girl. Her cheeks glistered with sweat and her hair stuck to her skull, sticky and hot like a woolen cap. When she finally reached the designated house at Pivka, approaching it with precaution, she was tired like a dog. At least, the house was secure. She handed over the explosives, then washed and changed. She could sleep for only a couple of hours since she had to catch the early morning train back to Ljubljana.

"Yes, he's such a noble soul," replied Ada dreamily.

"Aren't we in love?" Marjana teased her.

They all burst into laughter that became their only language for the next couple of hours. When they got out of the cinema, the sun was setting. In the light breeze, the tiny leaves of the willow trees on either banks of the river were rustling their tickling song of a summer evening. Some of the leaves were dry, flying through the air like golden coins.

Sanja sighed. "I hope it rains soon. The heat is becoming unbearable. The autumn crops will be ruined."

"Oh, I almost forgot," Andrej said. "I have to water the plants in my colleague's apartment. He left for Italy a couple of days ago."

Ada looked at him in disappointment. She was hoping they

would spend the evening together until the curfew, which was from ten in the evening to six in the morning.

"Whose apartment do you mean?" asked Sanja.

"Franci's...Do you remember Franci Zajec? His family used to live next door. When we were children, we used to play in *Tivoli* Park together. We lost touch when they moved to Prule. I met him at the hospital. He was in charge of our laboratory before he left Ljubljana in real haste. He couldn't speak to me, but he passed me a message and left the key with our hospital janitor."

"Where is his flat? Will you be home before the curfew?" Ada was worried.

"It's only six o'clock. Four hours to go. We can take a shortcut through *Castle Hill*," said Andrej.

"We?" asked the girls in unison.

"Maybe, not all of us, maybe...I thought..." Andrej stuttered uncertainly. "I thought you, Ada, you could help me water the plants. I guess they're many...I mean the plants in Franci's flat."

Ada's eyes sparkled. The rest of the party rolled their eyes, puckered their lips, and made smacking kisses in the air.

"Of course, I'll help you, Andrej," said Ada, keeping a straight face.

In a solemn voice, Sanja said, "If you two don't make it before the curfew, you should stay in the apartment. The Italians are rather nervous these days. It would be safer that way...now that you're engaged."

Andrej nodded gratefully.

Valeria added, "The Italians seem to be on the losing side, indeed. At the entry post on Trieste Road this morning, a soldier told me that the Americans and the British have invaded Sicily. He lost a brother in the battle and was whining like a puppy."

"I guess lives are lost on both sides. Bullets don't spare anybody – they slice through flesh no matter what nationality it is," said Marjana bitterly. "Come, ladies, let's get home and have a nice cup of lime tea."

"Lime tea?" said Sanja, outraged. "I'd rather have a nice cold beer or a glass of vodka with ice. At least, Russians know how to drink."

Valeria was full of black market, illegal alcohol, and conspiratorial tips. "I happen to know someone who brews a very good beer in his cellar. Let's pay him a visit on the way home. Sanja, will you be staying with us tonight?"

Sanja nodded gratefully, hinting at the lovers with her head and rolling her eyes. So, the three women headed arm in arm toward Poljane, singing Quando la radio canta by *Alberto Rabagliati* at the top of their voices, oblivious to Andrej and Ada, who were beginning to feel awkward.

Ada wondered what Andrej's invitation meant. Were they going to spend the night together? They had been alone before, but never overnight. They had kissed and explored each other's bodies, but always with their clothes on. Did this mean they were going to ...? Ada felt confused. As she fantasized about the two of them naked under cold linen sheets, kissing and touching, she got cold feet. She had never made love to a man.

"Let's turn left on Roška Street. Would you like to climb to the Castle, Ada?"

Andrej's soft voice woke her from her reverie. She followed him as she knew she would forever. He was her man, her trustworthy man. Ada looked at his face admiringly. What a magical Sunday. There was nothing but the two of them. No war, no concentration camps, no wounded or killed soldiers, only their love in this warm yellow light of August. When they started to ascend *Castle Hill*, Ada felt his hand in hers. It was a strong warm hand with long skillful fingers. She felt as if she were floating on air.

They passed the crumbled walls of *Šance*, the former fortress, and stopped to enjoy the view over Ljubljana. The numerous whitewashed Secession facades seemed to embrace *Castle Hill* like a shy bride with a long wedding veil. Andrej put his arm around Ada's waist and gently turned her toward him.

"Let's not go too close to the Castle. The Italian guards at the prison gate are nervous."

Without taking her eyes from his, Ada nodded. Would he kiss me? Andrej moved closer, so close that his lips touched her cheeks, lightly caressing her skin, soaking in her perspiration and wandering about her flushed cheeks until they found Ada's lips, opening them like rose buds with the tenderness of early morning light. They kissed for a few long minutes, and Ada put her arms under Andrej's light jacket and slowly, through the sopping sleek shirt, she followed the lines of his lean body. Despite the blazing heat, Andrej did not remove his jacket; Ada wore a simple light blue summer dress, sleeveless and fitted, that erupted into a wide skirt around her round buttocks. They heard noises of conversation approaching. A couple of dogs were barking in the heat. Before they left, their last view focused on the lovely Trnovo Church, the Church of St. John the Baptist, where famous Slovenian poet *France Prešeren* first saw Julija, his unattainable love. Andrej and Ada smiled at each other and descended the hill toward the Prule parish.

When Andrej turned the key to the door of Franci's penthouse, they had no foresight of what awaited them. The smell of grass and greenery invaded their nostrils and hit them as though they had jumped into a river. The air was humid and heavy. The swampy warmth glittered with all shades of green. Several extra windows built into the tiled roof offered more light into this private Garden of Eden. A huge glasshouse.

There were plants everywhere: invisible tendrils holding thick green leaves against the walls, plants climbing, growing, flowering, sprouting, swelling, and thriving with the vivid colors of life. The variety was overwhelming: a couple of man-sized Monstera deliciosa, in every corner bright green fronds cascaded from asparagus fern like spring water splashing over invisible rocks. A large bright purple hibiscus bush and ceiling-high ficus stood in front of the terrace door. The apartment had two large bedrooms, a dining room, a kitchen, and a terrace. Every shelf and chest was bursting with green life. It was a magical place, and the lovers melted into this primordial growth zealously kept by Andrej's friend Franci Zajec.

"Is Franci married, Andrej?"

"No, as far as I know he lives alone. If you can call it alone ...amidst all these plants..."

Ada made a few steps toward the terrace and exclaimed with joy: "Come here, Andrej! Smell all this wonder! A lemon tree in bloom, roses ...he even has a real little olive tree in the corner. Look, here's a laurel bush, a lavender in bloom, basil, and a heap of sweet-smelling red and purple petunias ...Where does he get all these plants and seeds in wartime?"

Andrej was astonished. He had known Franci since they were kids, but never imagined he had such a hobby. They would exchange pleasantries now and then, but his friend hid his passion well. Franci never said much – he just did the analyses expected of him and after work quickly went home. Andrej looked at Ada.

"It's nearly eight. We cannot finish watering them all and get home before the curfew."

Ada smiled at him charmingly and said in a husky voice, "You're right. And all these thirsty plants must be watered first."

She took off her white kitten heels and found more than a dozen zinc watering cans filled with water to the brim. Like silent sentinels, they stood next to the plant containers of various shapes and colors. Ada recited her knowledge of houseplant care:

"You have to check the soil around the plant with your fingers before watering it. If it is still moist, you should not water it, as the plant can deteriorate. Particularly during summer. My mother used to have many plants, potted roses all over the yard and lavender, laurel ..." Ada's voice broke into a hoarse whisper; their house was a ruin after the battle between the partisans and the Fascists. The last time she went home, a month ago with Marjana, they were still trying to repair the damages. They had lost all their cattle, including the horses. Even their dog had vanished. The villagers were ploughing their fields with men, striving to secure the next crop. Father and Mother had aged a decade. Marjana went to the bank in Trieste and brought her savings. Since Valeria avoided traveling home, they also went to see the Batič family. Nadja and Bruno were desperate – all their children had joined the fight, even the little Franjo was with the partisans. The village of Kozjane offered a pitiful sight, the end of humanity. There were no roses in her home courtyard anymore. War had erased the smiles from her mother's face together with the flowers.

Andrej came up behind Ada just as she was watering a huge heartleaf philodendron in the hall. It was cascading from a chest like a huge green and yellow curtain. He put his hands on her waist, as she raised the watering can in the air. He wanted her so much, but she was so young and inexperienced. She shivered. Was it fear or excitement?

Time stood still. The particles of dust stopped spinning and hung in the hot air, glittering like golden ears of ripe wheat. Andrej rarely dared to touch her breasts. Now, his hands moved upward and cupped Ada's heavy breasts. Through the thin fabric, her skin turned hot like on fire. Her heart was pounding. His touch was slow and tender. He would stop at any moment, should she give hints that she was not ready. For several weeks, Andrej had dreamed of ways to seduce Ada, to go all the way and love her with his body and soul. Yet, he knew he should not be too hasty. Ada had never been with a man and had a very spiritual knowledge of love. He feared that his eagerness would make her repel sex forever. He knew of cases when older men had been insensitive to their young brides. Blood pounded in his temples as he tried to gauge Ada's reactions. She was tense. A violin string – will he know how to play the wonderful tunes of love on it?

"My little Ada, I love you so much," he murmured in her ear and kissed her neck.

His lips traveled again, kissing the wet hair at the back of her head, sucking the sweet honeydew of her sweat like a bee from leaves in summer. He felt Ada's body relax in abandon.

Carefully, she put the watering can on the floor. She leaned against Andrej. Stretching her arms behind her, she embraced his hips, feeling his buttocks all tight with inner tension. Her hands were awkward and unsure.

Suddenly the air around them exploded into motion. She turned around to face Andrej.

'If I can only cast a glance at her breasts,' thought Andrej. Slowly, he slipped off the strap of her dress without taking his eyes from her warm brown ones. She did not blink, as though she knew what was to come. Both straps of the dress were down.

She did not resist when he unbuttoned her dress and it fell on the floor, rustling into a pile of fabric around her ankles. Without her panties and bra, she would be stark naked. She smiled softly and asked as though she should have known the answer ages ago: "Is everything all right?"

"Yes, more than all right," he replied without lifting his eyes from her full breasts.

Her heart leaped. She might be inexperienced, but she would not fall behind in love. Her fingers shivered as she began to unbutton his shirt.

"Do you think you can hypnotize my bra into coming undone by staring at it long enough?" she asked him playfully.

"Naughty little girl," was all he could whisper in her ear while he undid her bra. He kissed her neck until all the butterflies threatened to escape her belly.

Soon all their clothes lay on the floor. Ada was embarrassed by her nakedness exposed by the orange rays of the setting sun. Aware of it, Andrej wrapped her in his arms. He kissed her lips passionately. Slowly, they moved into the bedroom. They were out of their breath and would have lost their balance and fallen. Instead they collapsed on the huge bed.

The bedroom was full of green plants, too. Bronze Roman heads with vivid green baby's tears in place of hair sat on the night tables at each side of the bed. His hand slipped between her thighs.

"Watering the plants, eh?" he said softly.

Ada knew what he wanted. She looked him in the eyes and slowly spread her legs. "That's what it comes down to, darling," she said, her lips forming the words with tantalizing huskiness.

Still, Andrej was in no hurry. Mumbling, "my love, my Eve," his lips continued to tease and excite her. From her breasts to her cheeks, neck, and lips. Caresses until Ada trembled like the earth under a volcano. Passion rolled her on its mighty waves. She wanted him to take her, to feel him inside her body and soul, to be one with him.

Her wish came true, and they flew on the wings of love into the sky to become two twinkling stars. Everything was so new to her – the strong emotions that had long ago escaped her control, the feeling that she was hanging between life and death, losing her consciousness. Tears sprang to her eyes.

"Why the tears, darling?" asked Andrej, worried.

Ada's lips formed a condescending smile. Her erudite, all-knowing fiancé might be able to analyze every possible illness and state of mind, but he could not comprehend the simplest emotion – happiness. She came to this greenhouse a girl, now she was a woman in love and loved. Her tears welled up in passion.

"I'm so happy, Andrej," she said, kissing him on his lips.

He tasted her salty tears on his tongue. It was the potion of life, the potion of love. Never in his life had love tasted so sweet.

The thriving greenery, the balmy smell of flowers, the passion in this wonderful attic apartment. It was the struggle of two scared lovers against the violence and horror of the war.

They made love long into the night, long past the curfew. Too soon, the gray dawn brought them back to reality. It seemed such a fleeting moment, which ended as though it hardly happened.

Millions were dying while Andrej and Ada created a new life.

~~~

In spite of Marjana's kind invitation to a sleepover, Sanja left after a couple of beers. Stepping onto Wolfova Street, she felt a little dizzy. At the Triple Bridge, she gazed at the monument of the poet *France Prešeren* with his muse holding a myrtle branch of inspiration over his head. Sanja's spirits rose.

"Eh, France, you're the only one who understands. Art is pain and the medicine for the pain is a drink. Cheers, my poet!" She waved her hand and went home.

She looked forward to her comfortable nightgown and a good book. The one she was reading was very avant-garde and exciting in many ways. A modern French author Albert Camus. She planned to read until she fell asleep. If sleep didn't come, the sedative prescribed by Andrej would calm her nerves and bring her nocturnal peace. She still suffered from insomnia, so reading was the best therapy.

Nevertheless, the improvement in her health seemed almost a miracle. Only a couple of years ago, she thought she would never be able to close her eyes and rest, but life went on despite the war and the fact that she knew nothing about what had happened to her Sergej. Every time she thought of him, tears welled up in her eyes. She loved him so much. Their love was so pure and unique. She could never love another man.

It was autumn in Moscow when they first met, only a month after she had started playing for the Philharmonic Orchestra. The sun was shining and the sky was blue; harsh winds from Siberia had blown the rains and fog away. White tall birches shed golden ducats from their branches, and the wind carried them along the streets for anybody to pick up: a beggar, a rich man, a Red Army soldier, or a stranger like Sanja. She picked them up and released them in the strong wind, so they streamed over her head like magical rain of gold. Russia was such a wonderful place. She thought she could stay forever. At least long enough to rent a flat.

She had had enough of her boring hotel. She needed privacy and space to practice; she never had enough time to play at the Conservatory. Besides, Sanja was a perfectionist who knew that the perfect tune came from persistent practice. Someone suggested Anna Akmerova, an older woman who adored music and would not mind renting her upper floor. Akmerova was lonely since her daughter was abroad. She had a piano that Sanja could use whenever she wanted. Thus, she set out to see Akmerova. Still learning to read the Cyrillic, Sanja was trying to decipher the name of the street, looking in vain for a taxi or someone to help her.

"May I help you, madam?" a man asked in a low husky voice over her shoulder.

She turned and looked into warm brown eyes under bushy brows. He was wearing an ushanka hat with a red star in the middle. He spoke German, and Sanja wondered how he knew she wasn't Russian.

"Yes, please. Where is this street?" She handed him the piece of paper with Lady Anna's address. He looked at her, startled.

"Oh, this is my aunt! Are you visiting Anna Akmerova?"

Sanja smiled. "Yes, I am. Actually, my friends at the Conservatory suggested she might take me in as her tenant. I'm looking for an apartment, you see, and they said she has the upper floor empty."

He gave her back the note and said cordially, "Wonderful! It would be great for *Tetushka* Anna to have somebody live with her in that big house. I'm Sergej Sokurov, her nephew."

He removed the gloves from his thin artistic hands. She shook his long warm fingers, noticing his white palms and meticulously manicured nails. Sanja's grip was icy.

"I'm Sanja Strainar. I'm sorry, my hands are so cold. It's only October but it's almost freezing. I should have taken my gloves."

Sergej held her cold palms in his, saying, "Never mind, you will get used to the cold. Better the weather is cold and the people warm than the other way around."

Sanja giggled. "I agree, thank you." She allowed Sergej to lead the way, stuffing her hands in her coat pockets while they walked. Then she gave him a side glance. "But...you're the violinist, Sergej Sokurov. I've heard of you. You are to play Rimsky-Korsakov's Fantasia with the Orchestra next month. I am the pianist."

"Indeed, I am. You should take better care of your hands, Sanja Strainarova. They are your treasure."

Sanja felt daring. She stopped and looked at him."Then warm them up, please, Sergej Sokurov. Here."

She reached out, and he simply tucked her hands inside his warm sleeves. Then he nodded briefly to the right.

"Here we are. This is *Tetushka* Anna's house."

Sanja stared at a grand villa with a wonderful garden where plane and birch trees blazed the colors of yellow, orange, and red against hornbeam bushes The villa's facade was cracked, yet the huge white windows displayed the former grandeur of the place.

"This is not a house, it is a castle."

"Sanja, I must warn you, we don't have any earls and barons living in Russia. We're all one class – the proletariat."

"I know and I love it. Russia is the dream of every European Social Democrat. My father ..."

Sergej put his arm around her shoulders to guide her through the ornate wrought iron fence. "That may be so, but European Social Democrats want like a revolution with no bloodshed. That's not possible."

The huge dark brown oak door opened.

"What's not possible, Sergej? Are you preaching again, syn moy?" A petite woman with piercing hazel eyes and thick white hair bound at the back of her head smiled at the couple. She removed her dark-rimmed spectacles to kiss Sergej on both cheeks with three loud smacks. Then she turned to Sanja. "Why look, look at this beauty. Who have you brought me, Sergej?"

He smiled awkwardly at Sanja, shrugging as if to say he had no control over Lady Anna and her outbursts of love. Before the old woman could kiss and embrace Sanja, he said, "This is Sanja Strainar, a pianist. She plays with our Orchestra."

Sanja said, "Good day, Lady Anna. My colleagues thought you might rent me the upper flat of your house."

The tiny woman moved into the house, bubbling with joy. "Yes, yes, come in, both of you. They told me about you, Sanjushka. You come from Belgrade, don't you? I have many friends in Serbia. A great place, Belgrade ..."

The stream of words was incessant, and soon Sanja realized it didn't matter what she said as long as Lady Anna could shower them with her warm hospitality. In a minute, the saloon was filled with tea, biscuits, refreshments, and fruits.

"It's so cold outside. Sanjushka, how would you like something to warm you up? Here, this is something older than our Revolution, an Armagnac from 1915. They say that plum harvest was wonderful in spite of the war ravaging through France. I was saving it for special occasions. And you, my Sergej Sergejevich, what can I offer you? A vodka lemon ... You know I have my own lemons and oranges that I keep inside during winter ..." she prattled on, and on, and on, like a rattle.

Sanja forgot to ask about practical matters, such as the price of the rent and when she could move in. Anna's kindness and warmth completely overwhelmed her.

"Alas, I cannot go to concerts these days. Please play something for me ... Sergej Sergejevich and Sanja Strainarova ..."

"*Tetushka* Anna, I don't have my violin with me ..."

"You can use Olga's. Please, Sanjushka ..." Lady Anna went to rummage in the back room.

Sanja looked at Sergej. "Shall we play some of Mozart's Violin Sonatas? An easy one, maybe E minor or C major ..."

"Number 21 in E minor, K. 304 ... I'll see if I can find the sheets in Olga's room. I'll be back in a minute."

Sergej went to Lady Anna, and Sanja could hear their high voices. It was obvious that her nephew was not too keen on giving an unrehearsed performance. Sanja could understand that. She, too, hated to play when she was not perfectly prepared. Yet, who could turn down a lonely old woman?

The aunt and the nephew soon found the sheets. When the concert was about to begin, Sanja asked: "Will I be able to practice in the apartment above, Lady Anna? I mean, during the day ..."

"Any time, any time, my child. I love music. We used to go to the opera and concerts every night. Now, I cannot ..."

"Enough, *Tetushka*. Listen. Now!"

Sanja and Sergej played together as though they had been practicing for ages, both perfect musicians, both striving for the perfect pitch. With every key, they were falling in love with each other, and the aunt marveled at their love song. She became their confidant and supporter in the months to come when they had to work very hard for the new Shostakovich concert. People were saying that even Joseph Stalin along with the most important party leaders would come to listen to them.

At the thought of Stalin, Sanja's memory froze and her smile vanished. She tried to forget what happened at the New Year's party five years later. By then, she and Sergej were engaged to be married. Sergej had made a formal request to the authorities to leave the Soviet Union for a year and accompany his bride home to the Kingdom of Yugoslavia. They promised him that he would be able to leave in spring 1939, but first they had to play some duets at a party for high-ranking Communist leaders. They were also to compose the repertoire as they wished. Sergej and Sanja thoroughly prepared their concert for the chamber music. Of course, they foresaw the favorite would be Tchaikovsky's Violin Concerto in D major, from which they took the leitmotif and arranged a much shorter version for a violin and piano duet.

A ZIS-101 black limousine brought them to the Kuntsevo Dacha in the middle of deep snow. The trip took the whole morning. It was bitter cold. Sergej had brought his violin, but Sanja worried the piano in the hall wouldn't be in tune. Although they held hands under the warm fur blankets at the backseat of the huge car, they couldn't relax. Their love had been a symphony, romantic and pure, passionate and deep. Sergej and Sanja, the perfect union ...The problem was that Sanja's stunning blond looks attracted many fans and, unfortunately, one of them happened to be Stalin's bodyguard, Yaroslav Zhurov. He refused to acknowledge their engagement. A couple of weeks ago, he started sending her chocolates, caviar, sparkling wine, and even flowers despite the freezing winter – all accompanied by passionate love letters. At first, Sanja was flattered and tried to use the connection so she and Sergej could leave the Soviet Union as soon as possible. But Yaroslav, a huge violent man, wanted her to stay. He arranged for Sergej to leave first and fpr Sanja to follow him several months later. Sanja was trying to convince Sergej to leave at once for she suspected foul play. By 1936, people had begun to disappear under mysterious circumstances and it was impossible to predict who was next. Sergej, however, refused to abandon her in that nest of vipers. He loved her too much.

When they arrived at the Kuntsevo Dacha, they were assigned separate rooms. Before climbing the stairs to her room, Sanja asked to test the piano. They showed her into the big concert and party hall. She played some keys and did some scales until she was satisfied that the piano was tuned to perfection. She was playing some popular Russian folk tunes to get a better feel of the instrument when she felt two gentle hands on her shoulders. Thinking it was Sergej, she continued to play love songs without turning around.

Then, she heard Sergej's voice from the back of the room: "Let's practice to test the acoustics in the hall. The piano seems well-tuned, Sanja."

Sanja realized that Sergej could not see whoever was standing behind her from the door. But she knew who it was. She slowly stood up to break from his embrace and smiled politely. "Yaro, Yaroslav, please leave me and Sergej to practice now. We want to make the most of the evening, don't we?"

Yaroslav put down his hands and stepped aside gallantly. "Indeed, *Koba* will attend, too. Don't expect too much, however. He doesn't care much for music."

Sanja smiled politely and waved Sergej in with her right hand.

Sergej approached the piano with determined steps. "*Tovarish* Yaroslav, we have a wonderful surprise for *Tovarish* Stalin; we've arranged one of his favorite concertos for violin and piano. I am sure he will like it very much."

Yaroslav turned around and spoke to Sergej. "Don't take too long. We are having beluga caviar and champagne with buckwheat blini and butter. *Koba* loves blini, so don't keep him hungry."

Sergej nodded. "We understand."

Sanja and Sergej remained in awkward silence while Yaroslav crossed the hall. When the door finally slammed behind the huge man, Sergej said, "What did he want?"

Sanja was careful not to worsen any hostilities. "He heard me play the piano and came to welcome us."

"You mean he came to welcome you. I bet he's been thinking for a while how to get rid of me. Gulags in Siberia are not yet populated enough."

Sanja sighed and whispered almost inaudibly, "Maybe we should not speak about it in here. Let's go to our room for a rest. Besides, I have to change for the evening. Is there a shower in your room, Sergej?"

He nodded silently, smiling at their secret code; they would be discussing Yaroslav in the shower, hopefully naked. The smile on Sanja's face confirmed his thoughts. Discreetly, so as not to raise any suspicion, they sneaked into Sergej's room and removed their clothes while kissing passionately. Then, turning on the shower, they both squeezed behind the glass wall and turned on the faucet, too. It sounded and felt like a hot summer rain. Soon, they forgot all about Yaro and his eerie advances. Sergej's hands soaped Sanja's back, touching her buttocks, then slid between her thighs and continued their loving voyage past her navel to fondle her breasts. Sanja gasped with pleasure and returned his kisses and caresses. Wet with excitement and hot with pleasure, their bodies danced to the rhythm of love while their musical minds bridged the water drops. They were reaching their peak when the water turned cold. They heard someone banging on the door of the room. They kissed once more, then Sergej wrapped a towel around his loins, checked the room for Sanja's clothes, and opened the door. It was one of Yaroslav's colleagues.

"Yaro is looking for the pianist, Sanja, I think. He's looked everywhere. Is she here?" The man in uniform pretended not to notice Sergej's nakedness and spoke to him formally, as though they were at a meeting.

Sergej faked his surprise and replied in a casual voice, "Of course not. As you can see, I just came out of the shower. She said she needed to rest until evening. She spoke about wanting fresh air. What do I know? Maybe she went for a walk."

"It's snowing. Would she dare go out alone?"

"Why shouldn't she? With men like you and Yaro, this place is as safe as it can be."

The man slammed the door and went away. They were at peace for now.

A couple of hours later, Sergej and Sanja bowed amidst shouts and applause. Judging by the noise of the guests – some in uniforms, some in traditional white peasant shirts, some in splendid evening gowns – they must have been drinking all afternoon. Their red cheeks and swollen noses suggested vodka. Sergej and Sanja assumed their positions. When the hall fell silent at last, Sergej's violin quartered the atmosphere with Tchaikovsky's music.

Yaroslav stood next to the piano, grinning widely, his deep black eyes flashing with passion for Sanja under his bushy eyebrows. His cheeks were red. He must have had a drink or two. There was something Mediterranean, perhaps Greek in his strong features and wide cheekbones. His skin was pale olive in color, his hair curling in spite of the pomade. Unlike Stalin's other comrades, he did not grow a moustache. Every time Sanja cast a look around the hall, his eyes captured hers, keeping her gaze in his black pupils like a fugitive bird. She concentrated on the music. After around twenty minutes, Sergej's well-practiced solo part came in. The public was getting impatient, the whistles and murmurs alerted Sanja to stop the concert immediately, but Sergej was too immersed in his playing to notice. All of a sudden, there was a whirl around *Tovarish* Stalin, who had put his hands to his head and was now nodding in slow motion. Then the commotion began.

Yaroslav leaped toward Sanja and lifted her in his arms. His hold was firm as he carried her out of the room. The only thing Sanja could see was a heap of men around Sergej. Then she heard the crash of his violin against the floor.

"Sergej, my God!" she cried in panic. "His precious instrument!"

Yaroslav's hand covered her mouth. She kicked and punched the steel-like body against hers in shock, trying to get free and run back to the hall. She heard Sergej cry in pain and agony. The violin was a precious gift from his father. It was worth a fortune. She must get to him. Then a cloth covered her nose and she inhaled sweet-smelling vapor. Her movements became slower and weaker, the cries and bangs from the hall softer until she lost consciousness in Yaroslav's arms.

The next morning Sanja woke up in her room, dressed in her sleeping gown without recollection of having undressed the previous evening. The winter morning was bright with sun, the light from heaven cheerfully tickling the snow crystals and making them glimmer like diamonds. It was the New Year's Day of 1939. Sanja rose to her feet and stumbled to the bathroom. Her first thought through the waves of pain in her head was Sergej. What happened last night? Why had Yaroslav drugged and dragged her away?

Later, when she asked Yaroslav, his only response was: "Sergej returned to Moscow early this morning." When she asked to follow him, Yaro smiled benevolently. "This is not possible today, Sanjushka. Kobo wants you to play for him. He wants to sing along to some folk songs after lunch, so you are advised to stay."

There wasn't anything Sanja could do. She telephoned Aunt Anna asking her to send someone to Sergej's apartment and make him ring her at Kuntsevo. When she called again in a couple of hours, Anna told her that Sergej was not at home. Sanja performed the songs in terror, smiling woodenly, faking enthusiasm, disgusted by the hung-over faces of the *nomenklatura* party. She had only one thought on her mind: "What has happened to Sergej?"

She went back to Moscow that same evening. There were some low-ranking party officials who had to return to Moscow in order to prepare everything for Stalin's speech the following day in Red Square. The great leader wanted to address the citizens' rising fears of a new war. Sanja relaxed when she saw that Yaroslav was not among the passengers in the car. She sat in silence during the ride through the night, lit by moon and stars reflecting against the crystal snow. Birch branches covered in ice and snow glittered left and right of the slippery road like a silken curtain. Pines reached for the dark sky with their elegant silver points brushed with new whiteness. Apart from the machine rumbling and coughing along the bumpy road, all was silent. Sanja had a feeling she was traveling through the realm of Andersen's Snow Queen – a cruel, yet heavenly beautiful landscape.

The next morning she was outside Yaroslav's office before seven o'clock. She knew he would come back and show up early. It was still dark outside and the corridor remained unlit. Her eyes were swollen eyes from lack of sleep, revealing her darkest fears. When Yaroslav arrived, he simply nodded to her and she followed him into the room where samovar was boiling in the corner.

"Tea?" he asked politely.

"Where is Sergej? Tell me, Yaroslav, in the name of our friendship, please, tell me what happened to him."

Yaroslav poured two cups and served one to Sanja who was standing in front of his clean desk. "Do you consider me your friend then, Sanja?"

She looked him in his black eyes. What kind of question was this? She nodded eagerly with her whole body. "I do. Where is he?"

Yaroslav's lips formed a faint smile. Then, his face assumed a serious, almost gloomy expression. "It is very complicated. Sanja, I am sorry."

Sanja realized her fears were coming true. She had to be careful and focus. "But you know where he is, Yaro, don't you?"

Yaroslav nodded briefly and turned away, taking a few steps toward the window. A gray winter dawn was breaking into the room. For a long while, they stood motionless in complete silence. Finally, Yaro spoke.

"I warned you not to take too long. *Koba* hates long classical concerts, and he was in a very bad mood on Silvester Night. He received news of *Trotsky*'s comfortable life in Mexico and the publication of his writings distorting facts about the Soviet Union and disgracing the October Revolution. He was sullen and sad. He wanted to cancel the celebration and the concert, too, but Svetlana persuaded him not to. When Sergej was playing his solo, *Koba* thought his head would burst with pain. He went pale with anger. Stalin's direct words were: 'Stop the *Trotsky* bastard and his violin, or I will shoot him.' They took Sergej away immediately. In the confusion, someone smashed his violin, I'm afraid."

Sanja listened carefully. Something was missing in Yaroslav's account of the events. "I heard Sergej cry out in pain. Did they beat him?"

Yaroslav stared at Sanja for a long moment. She could not read anything in his blank look.

"I don't really know. My main concern was to get you out of there. Of course, he might have received a couple of blows after *Koba* cried out, 'Punish him! Beat him!' But as far as I know Sergej Sergejevich Sukorov is alive."

Sanja froze. She was aware of the Great Purge. Many of her friends had mysteriously disappeared – exiled, deported to Siberia, or simply murdered. No court procedures, no legal verdicts, only the troika and their speedy execution of Stalin's orders.

"Has he been sentenced yet?" Sanja asked. When Yaroslav shook his head, she sighed. "Please, Yaro, let me see him."

"I cannot right now."

"When then?"

Yaro came out from behind his desk and put his hand on her shoulder. "Will you have dinner with me, Sanjushka?"

Sanja felt the space open to negotiations. How far would she go? "I will, Yaro, I certainly will. I will cook dinner for you after I have spoken to Sergej."

Yaroslav smiled encouragingly. "Of course, I understand," he replied and waved his hand in dismissal. "Come tomorrow at the same time, and you will visit him."

The interview was over. Sanja walked out to another terrible day of anxiety and horror. The following morning she was determined to find out more about the charges against Sergej. Impatient, she confronted Yaro in the corridor.

"Yaroslav, Sergej is a not a politician. He's a musician. Music does not bear any political color. The tunes cannot betray anything or anybody. What are the accusations against him?"

He passed by her, saying harshly, "We don't discuss anything in the corridors here."

Obediently, she followed him into his room, feeling she had lost the first battle. A young party official was on their heels.

"Sanja, please listen to me. Sasha will drive you to *Lubyanka* to visit Sergej. Please, be careful with your words. Don't put Sergej in a bigger danger than he is already."

Sanja glanced at Sasha furtively. "What is his sentence, Yaro? Tell me."

"I really don't know. It is an *NKVD* case. Please, go now. Go and be sensible, Sanjushka."

Sanja smelled foul play. Still, she had no choice but to follow young blond Sasha to the Volga. At the *Lubyanka*, the first thing she underwent was a body search. Then, for hours nothing happened. She waited and waited, locked alone in the visiting room with one table, two chairs and a naked bulb on the ceiling. In the end, she lost all faith, feeling like one of the prisoners.

Finally, she heard the door click. After only a couple of days, Sergej Sukorov, one of the finest Russian violinist and intellectuals, looked like a vagrant beggar. His face was dirty, his dark eyes deeply set in their sockets, his cheeks bruised, his upper lip broken. He did not look at her and seemed completely absent.

Sanja swallowed her tears and said softly: "Hello, Sergej Sergejevich. How are you?"

His lips trembled as the guard guided him to the chair opposite hers. Sergej hid his cuffed hands under the table. He did not reply.

"Can you speak, Sergej?" Although silence met her question, she could see his shoulders shuddering with emotions. "Darling, speak to me, please! You're alive. That's all – "

"*Kurva*, I wish I were dead!" his hoarse whispered curse interrupted her.

Sanja thought she didn't hear him well. She finished her sentence: "That's all that matters. We will find a solution. I will…"

"Go, *zhenschina*, go away and leave me alone. You've brought me enough troubles."

"But Sergej, I didn't do anything. How can you blame me?"

"You're a snake, Sanja. Fucking with Yaro behind my back and denouncing me as *Trotsky*'s friend, a traitor. Why have you come here? To see what you've done? To see the misery you've caused? Look!" As his voice rose, he slammed his cuffed hands on the table. His hands – once finely sliding on violin strings to produce perfectly pitched keys, drawing the bow with velocity and skill – were bloody chunks of battered meat. All his fingers were broken, the joints twisted in every direction. Some of the knuckles were swelling with yellowish puss; his right thumb was a bloody stub.

Sanja reached out over the table. "You…Sergej, what you say is not true. This is terrible…" Her eyelids fluttered nervously. The sight of his hands hurt her. She could feel his pain in her fingers. She opened her mouth to say something, but he cut off her words.

"I don't want to see you ever again. Go away and play your filthy games with Yaroslav!" Sergej spat on the table between them and stood up.

Sanja jumped to her feet, trying to hold him back by the sleeve. "Sergej, don't believe any of these lies. Listen to me! I love you. I will help you."

"You've helped me enough, thanks. They smashed my hands with bottles of champagne. They couldn't wait to get hold of the clubs. All this, all this because of...you and Yaroslav Zhurov...You two can go to hell! You're a bitch, Sanja, a cold-hearted bitch."

The guard pulled Sergej's vest from Sanja's grip and took him away. Sanja could not move. She was too shocked to shed Gerda's warm tears of innocence and melt Sergej's heart like Gerda melted Kai's in Andersen's "The Snow Queen." Caught in a web of lies like a helpless fly. The world around her spun in a whirlwind of terror. What malice! What evil! They must have told Sergej that she had denounced him as a *Trotskyist*. For such treason, there was only one sentence: death. It must all be Yaro's doing. No matter what the cost, she was going to have a word with that rat.

Yaroslav, however, was not accessible. In vain, she waited in front of his office for the rest of the day. He did not come out and speak to her. After besieging his door for hours, Sanja felt desperate. In her mind, she started to compose a list of people she could ask for help. Once they've treated his hands and eased his mind, he would listen to her. Late in the evening she gave up and went home. She burst into Lady Anna's salon and fell into her arms. Lady Anna stiffened and slowly pushed her away.

"You have a visitor, Sanja. He's waiting in your apartment upstairs."

Sanja climbed the stairs and opened her door. Yaroslav stood up from her sofa, naked and wet from the shower, her pink towel carelessly wrapped around his loins. With a confident smile, he approached her. Sanja's terror erupted into hysterical cries and curses. She charged him with blows and scraped his cheeks with her sharp nails. She wanted to kill him. The next thing she felt was a mighty blow on her head and she lost consciousness.

When she came to, the sun was shining. Trees were flowering in front of her barred window. She found out she was in a mental hospital. Using all her resources, she managed to get out of the mental institution and out of Russia forever. She was lucky that nobody took much notice of her – neither Yaro nor anyone else from the *NKVD*. The spring of 1939 was a very busy one for the Party, and killing a pianist whom the German musical public cherished was not on their agenda. Particularly not later in the year when Molotov and Ribbentrop signed their famous treaty of non-aggression between Germany and the Soviet Union. Her friends supported her application to leave. Why not? Why bother with this wretched woman? Sanja got back her passport and had to leave the socialist heaven at a short notice.

In that golden autumn, she embarked a train that headed south, passing the fields where the farmers harvested late potatoes, beets, turnips, and pumpkins to feed the pigs and produce the nutty oil from seeds and buckwheat for thin sweet blini. Grief and despair filled her soul. Her thoughts wandered in the labyrinth of cruel tyranny where people were like spare parts for a huge killing machine, feeding the mechanism with their obedience, devoid of emotion and humanity. Where was Sergej? Would he ever realize how much she loved him? Would he know who was friend or foe? How would they ever heal his shattered hands?

The train roll on and on without offering any answers. During the stops in the big cities, all stations were full of people. Families with lots of baggage and small children looked scared and confused. Everyone was going somewhere. The whole world was going somewhere. With detachment, Sanja observed their tears and kisses of farewell – tears and kisses she could not give or receive.

What did she care about these panicking farmers? There were just ants in an ant hill. She cared even less about the rich people in fur and elegant hats. Grotesque. She felt indifferent to their concerns.

Endlessly, the train rumbled across the countries of Europe toward the black dawn of a new world war.

~~~

For Valeria and everyone who had to endure the Fascist reign of terror for over two decades, September 1943 was glorious. On September 3rd, Italian King Victor Emanuel III signed a document declaring an armistice with the Allies, who had by then occupied a good part of the Italian map. It was still a secret, so people wondered about the evacuation activities of the Italians. Were they reorganizing their forces to strike again and annihilate what remained of the Slovenian spirit for good? However, through her connections with the *Liberation Front*, Valeria found out the reason for their sudden exodus – they were running as fast as they could. They were running to their homes, mothers, wives, and children. Italy had been defeated and the whole country was disintegrating into chaos. Their beloved Duce Benito, or "Bandito" for Valeria, Mussolini and his mistress were on the run, too. Like dark shadows in the aftermath of the fleeting army, the prisoners from the concentration camps in Molat, Rab, and *Gonars* were returning home in long lines along the coastal road. Starved, exhausted, and ill, they reported on the terrible camps of death and devastation. Once they restored their forces, the majority joined the *Liberation Front*.

Ada and Andrej got married at the Church of *Saint Nicholas* on September 5th. It was a modest affair on a sunny Sunday in the hot white streets of Ljubljana. Ada and Andrej were in their everyday clothes. Only the bouquet of pink roses and the delicate flowers pinched to their buttonholes revealed that the four women and a couple of men were attending a wedding.

In the imaginary peace that had been continuing in Ljubljana in the last couple of weeks, on the day of the ceremony, the group went to the *Brkini Hills* where they were to celebrate the wedding at Kozjane with Ada's family and friends. Yet it proved almost impossible to board the train south to Italy – every carriage was full of Italian military people, officials, and their families on the run.

Thus, Andrej borrowed the hospital director's car. One of his colleagues, acting as his best man, joined them on their journey to *Brkini*. With a glass of sparkling wine in hand, they passed the empty Italian posts, singing and cheering all the way. Andrej and Ada were to stay for a week at Kozjane in the house of her parents. The honeymoon would be as sweet as the fruits they would help picking: apples, pears, and plums to dry and preserve for winter. Outside Ljubljana, many people had already heard about the coming armistice. Empty roads resounded with cries of cheer as though the war was over forever.

Friends, family, and neighbors streamed into the tavern of the village Tatre. Dozens of guests came to celebrate Ada's wedding and the fall of Fascism at the same time. The villagers gave everything. They scraped their storage reserves as though for the Last Supper. Many lips turned blue at the vast quantities of *Teran*, the region's near-black wine. Prosciuttos, hidden and stashed in secret places for years, were cut into thin slices and savored on thick bites of sweet white bread. There was music, singing, and dancing. At one point, Father Franjo, the local priest, joined the party, lifted the hem of his black robe, and joyfully danced to a polka like a young boy. Like many other churchmen in the Primorska region, Father Franjo loathed the Fascist regime in spite of the fact that the Holy See signed the Lateran Treaty in 1929. Many priests openly stood up against the Fascists in favor of their people. So many were persecuted, deported to the concentration camps, or killed. They helped the *Liberation Front* all the way, sharing Valeria's views that the Communists would win the war and bring true social justice and democracy into the country.

Despite the wedding celebration, Valeria met with her brother and their partisan leader Karlo in the back room of the tavern. She had a package for them, and they discussed the possible partisan invasion of the territories occupied by the German forces in the north. New enclaves under the authority of the *Liberation Front* could provide important safe territories for hospitals, schools, cultural events, and meetings. Although the majority of Slovenians were rejoicing, the partisans heard rumors that the Germans planned to invade all territories under the former Italian rule. The war might go on, so provisions had to be made and quickly. On a military scale, the partisans were no match for the German war machine. It was decided that Valeria should travel along the Slovenian coast to Delnice and Rijeka, territories of the *Independent State of Croatia*, and as far as Trieste and Udine so as to bring back accurate news on what's happening.

As a result, Valeria missed much of funny pranks and mock trials that the local boys had prepared for Andrej. In order to win his bride, he had to pay for drinks and saw through logs worked with iron, which were practically impossible to cut with any blade. Moreover, he had to dance with all the grandmothers in the village as well as pass the interrogation of the elders before he could hold Ada in his arms.

On that sunny afternoon, Valeria descended the road toward Vatovlje, the village where her sister Maria lived and worked in her husband's farm. The Italians had drafted her husband a couple of years ago, but she expected him to return from the front soon since many of his comrades had already returned only to join the partisans. Valeria was bringing her medical supplies and desserts from the wedding feast for the little girls. She knew the sweets would bring smiles to their faces.

She didn't like to pass by cemeteries. These days the whole country seemed like a huge open grave. And so she climbed the hill and approached the little church. The old priest, a good man and supporter of the *Liberation Front*, engaged her in conversation. He warned her of rough Italian gangs moving toward Trieste, starved and desperate, ready to kill for a piece of bread. She retorted she had a weapon. Valeria's tears blurred her vision as the old man gave her his blessing with a shaky hand. So brave and honest in spite of the Vatican's sinister silence regarding the mass extermination of the Slovene population.

She descended the slope above the village Vatovlje. The houses were perched on the hill like a flock of scared sheep. She noticed her little niece Bernardka and her friend Anna Maria sitting on tree trunks not far from the first houses. They were nibbling on fresh bread; Valeria could nearly smell the sweet aroma of milk and white flour and taste the soft texture of the dough in her mouth. Anna Maria ate the last bite while Bernardka munched at the crust as though there were no tomorrow. Then, Valeria noticed a group of Italian soldiers slowly approaching the little girls. They were five of them. Their unshaven beards revealed that they had been on the march for a while.

They marched in silence, sullenly focused on the tip of their heavy shoes, grating the pebbles under their soles. Another thousand, one hundred thousand, one million steps – and maybe they'll reach home. If they survived, for they met nothing but hatred and danger everywhere. Their army coats were heavy with mud; their helmets were beating against their empty backpacks. Although their shoulders sagged in humiliation, they were armed men. Valeria took out her Walther and hid behind the huge oak some fifty meters away.

She saw Bernardka freeze. Did the five-year-old piss in her pants again? Valeria knew how sensitive and fragile the little girl was. Her sister Maria was worried, for every time the Fascists entered their house, her niece would freeze in terror. Ever since her father was recruited by the Italian army, she often had nightmares and so slept in her mother's bed. She wasn't eating properly and was fussy about food. Nobody took into account that she was growing up under threat of imminent death. Everyone including Bernardka was privy to the secret shelter under their barn where wounded partisans recovered their health. The underground shelter was impossible to find for every time someone entered or left it, they would build a wall and hide it behind a pile of straw. Nobody could see where the entrance was, but it was always possible that someone under torture would disclose the hiding place.

The little girls stared at the ragged soldiers. In the heat of the late summer afternoon, the men were wiping the sweat from their cheeks and puffing onward. Valeria noticed their flasks were wet; they must have come directly from the creek in the valley, bypassing the village where the partisans would have captured them. Oh, bloody war! The Fascists had had enough. Great Italy, yes, but they were not in the mood to catch a bullet in these last days when the country was defeated and armistice signed by the King.

They passed the girls, only one soldier pointing with his finger at Bernardka. Valeria relaxed her lock on the trigger. She could not deal with all five men, but the partisans from the village would surely come to the rescue at the sound of shots fired from two hundred meters above them. However, the soldiers marched on. Relieved, Valeria inhaled the sweet scent of flowering buckwheat, the last crop of the season, spreading over the fields. Above the tiny pale-pink blossoms, bees hummed their song of joy; in the crowns of trees, birds chirped happily. The world, the whole world, seemed free again.

"No!" shrieked Bernardka.

Valeria saw that one of the soldiers had grabbed the crust from her hands. The girl burst into tears. Starved, he sank his teeth into the bread. Bernardka was crying her lungs out. He stopped and hesitated. Valeria watched him trembling like a willow. What's gotten into him? What will he do to the girls? She aimed the Walther at his chest.

"What is it, Giovanni? Are you afraid of the little pisser? Eat the damn bread or give it to me!" yelled one of the soldier in a strange southern Italian dialect.

Another soldier mocked him. "Giovanni, are you going to crap your brains out? I can't believe you're afraid of a child."

The soldier held the piece of bread, shivering all over. He seemed to be crying. His comrades dismissed him with obscene gestures and moved on. Then Valeria heard him weeping loudly, his laments piercing the summer song of the fields. Bernardka and Anna Maria were wailing with him, their cries ripping her soul.

"What are we doing? Where are we going, porco dio, where?" howled the soldier, staring at the white bread as though it held answers.

His comrades shook their heads. Bernardka continued crying at the top of her lungs. Her sweet white bread, the crust that Mama had sliced for her while the loaf was still warm. Her voice plowed the dust particles in the air. Valeria held her breath. Stop wailing, you silly girls! The soldiers might lose their temper and shoot them. That little girl Bernardka, tiny like an ant, yet stubborn and strong like an elephant. Her anger, her force. She would not stop. Valeria's eyes moved from Giovanni to his comrades and back.

"Where are we going? I'm not going to steal bread from a child! I will not. May I die of hunger, but this is not right."

Valeria put down her pistol.

"Here, baby, I'm sorry," said the soldier, putting the crust in Bernardka's lap.

The girl looked at him with teary eyes and fell silent. Valeria could see that she felt sorry for him. She glanced at the bread with suspicion. The fact that the stranger had bitten into it disgusted her.

"Eat, baby, eat it." He caressed her soft light hair in goodbye. Then he followed his comrades and continued to climb the path to the church. Maybe the priest would feel sorry for them. They were his flock, too, weren't they? His flock of black sheep.

Bernardka tore off the piece that was wet with the soldier's saliva. Ants should eat, too, Valeria thought. She waited until the Italians could not see her. Then, she brought the little girls back to the village, scolding her sister for letting them wander around alone.

Valeria thought of the starved Italian soldier's misery as she was descended the Čičerija Hills in the dark toward Rijeka, the first stop in her reconnoitering mission.

She stayed in Rijeka for a couple of days, long enough to follow the hectic activities of the *Independent State of Croatia* and its head, Ante Pavelić, who turned his back on the Italians, his former allies, to lick the boots of Adolf Hitler and mobilize Croatians against the partisans. His call to arms in *Ustaša*, the newspaper he started, was affixed on every wall in the city.

Worries overwhelmed Valeria as she walked around the docks and made enquiries in the shops. The people were reluctant to speak. She could feel fear and suspicion emanating from every ally the way early morning autumn fog covered the city in silence. On one such foggy morning, she took a boat to Trieste and the vessel berthed in the old port. Valeria's throat filled with anxiety when she saw red swastika flags on the facade of the Town Hall – hanging from the third floor almost to the ground – at Piazza Unita d'Italia. The Germans were in Trieste. There was no time to waste. She must get to Ljubljana quickly and see how to continue her work for the resistance. This time it would be much more difficult. She knew little about Germans and could speak very little of the language. The only song she knew was "Lili Marleen," which was broadcast by the Soldiers Radio Belgrade, but Valeria had no idea how the occupying forces would react should she start to sing in broken German.

Two days later, Valeria opened the door to Ada's apartment. The Skarpin sisters clearly feared they would never see her again. They were sitting at the kitchen table, calculating some expenses.

"Thank God, you're back, Valeria." Ada sighed, embracing her.

"We've been really worried about you since the Germans arrived," added Marjana and looked at Valeria sternly. "Don't tell us anything about your errands. We're have no interest in such things."

Cold sweat ran down Valeria's spine at the coldness of her voice.

Ada let her go and snapped at her older sister, "What are you insinuating, Marjana? You think I will betray my friend to the Germans? Is that what you think of me?"

Marjana said in a matter-of-fact voice, "Andrej has joined the Home Guard. Their mission is to fight Communism ...and the German occupation. At least, that's what they're saying for now. Valeria, I advise you to be careful. There is no need to burden Ada with what you're doing. The same goes for Sanja and Andrej. Let's all try to remain friends, shall we?"

Valeria looked Marjana in the eye. She had said enough. Still, Ada would never ...

"I see. But Marjana, Ada is my friend and I trust her. She has hidden me once and I am sure she will do it again any time. We're like sisters. What does Andrej say about my activities? He must have his suspicions."

Ada sighed, clearly moved by Valeria's speech. She gestured to the heap of boxes and suitcases in the corner. "I'm moving in with him and Sanja tomorrow. We've just been discussing the apartment expenses and how you and Marjana can stay here. Will you get the job at the printer's, Valeria?"

"I think so."

"When do you start?"

Valeria placed her bag on the floor and sat down. Marjana poured her a glass of cold rosehip tea.

"They said I can come any time. They need me mostly for the Christmas season. One of the reasons for recruiting me was my knowledge of Italian. I don't know if they still need me now, though."

Ada nodded. "Well, the *Brothers Tuma* Printing House will still have to supply their Italian customers, won't they? Andrej found Marjana a part-time job at the hospital, at Saint Joseph's. You two should be able to make ends meet. Two months have been paid in advance, so you basically have almost three months to come to terms."

Marjana's look was blank, her eyes seemed dry and without energy. "I...I'm afraid to go back to work. I wonder what I will have to cope with this time," she whispered more to herself than to them.

Valeria said, "Come on, Marjana, you can deal with it easily. You're tougher than many a man I know."

Ada nodded in agreement. "That's what I keep telling you, Marjana. It'll do you good to go back to work. You love your job."

"I don't know..."

For a few awkward moments of silence, Valeria stared at the blank wall in front of her. "Why did he do it, Ada? His father must be turning in his grave."

Ada lowered her head, shrugging. "He said he had to. I have to stand by him, Valeria."

"I understand. But it's the wrong side. You know that. They will end up in bed with the Jerries."

Ada murmured, "I'm so afraid, Valeria."

~~~

Andrej hired a team of craftsmen to renovate and redecorate the apartment. After decades, the paint was cracking and the wooden floor needed polishing. His father, old Strainar, had been more concerned with his leftist political ambitions than with their lives, and Andrej had been away for his medical studies. Now, with Ada coming, he needed to do something. Since Marjana had gotten better, she had less compunctions about moving in with him. Besides, Marjana had Valeria staying with her, and they had become very good friends in spite of the difference between their ages.

The renovation took some time. It was not easy to find materials and workmen in the middle of the war. Yet, new curtains, new paint, and some green plants made a big difference. At the last minute, he decided to renovate the bathroom, too. It needed new plumbing, stronger heating, and a bath with shower installed. He also bought a wide oak cabinet, which could serve for washing and changing a baby. Times were hard and the future dark, yet his inexplicable desire for new life was like a personal catharsis. Andrej felt that a baby's smile could dispel his sadness no matter what.

During the renovation, Sanja went to Lake Bled where she could take long walks, sunbathe, and relax in the lovely autumn weather of 1943. She had enjoyed the simple wedding celebration of her brother a week ago. The rich food, the wine, and the warm people of Kozjane enchanted her. After a couple of glasses of wine, she sat at the shabby, out-of-tune piano and played modern jazz music for the merry wedding guests. She was pleasantly surprised to see that the melodies of Glenn Miller and Count Basie were a hit. Couples swept the dance floor to the rhythm of swing, flipping their legs and arms in all directions, jumping, sweating, as though they had been born in southern America not in some remote hills above Trieste. The drummer and the musicians caught on, and they had a wonderful time jamming together. However, the top hits of the evening were famous Russian songs. Some men, particularly those in partisan shirts, even danced *kazachok* in a circle, throwing their caps in the air, accompanied by the claps of hundreds of warm hands. At last, in the small hours of the night when the wedding guests were tired and blue, Sanja played the Serbian song from the WWI, Tamo daleko (There, Far Away). There came a chorus of female and male voices immersed in melancholy, a typical closing to any Slovenian feast. When she stood up from the piano, young partisans – just boys with thin moustache pushing above their upper lips – kissed and cheered her like a heroine. She felt their warmth and sank deeper into their wide chests and military shirts smelling of wild moss and sharp pine needles. She was one with them.

In spite of the fact that Russia had caused her so much pain by taking her beloved away, during her years back in Ljubljana, Sanja had somehow buried her hatred for the Russians and their music.

She often thought of Sergej, wondering whether he was still alive. If only she could find out what had happened to him. She wrote to Anna Ahmetova many times to no avail. All she got from Russia were harsh cold winds howling over the silence like wolves singing out their prey.

Meanwhile, Andrej was building the nest for his young wife. Sanja felt awkward about staying with them. What would she do once they had a baby? Somehow, she had a feeling it would happen soon. She would have to think about getting her independence back, the autonomy she had lost after Russia and her illness. Maybe she could take a train to Rome, or even further, to the Allied territories in southern Italy. God knows if there were any ships still sailing for America. Maybe she could head north, to neutral Sweden where she knew and performed with some musicians during her European tours. But how could she get through the heavily bombed German cities? She must write some letters. She could and should return to her career, and not be in the way of the newlyweds.

When the cab brought her home, she looked up at their balcony and saw colorful chrysanthemums in pots around the railing. Lovely, the bride was here. She sighed and paid the driver to help her with the luggage.

"Hi, everybody! I'm home!" she called from the door into the darkness of the entrance hall. She turned on the light and gasped. It was like entering a new flat. Ada and Andrej led her through the light-filled redecorated rooms painted in pale green, yellow, and pink. There were huge dark green houseplants in every corner. It was wonderful. She could not help but sit down at the piano in the drawing room, where a silver candlestick shone next to a vase of bright yellow sunflowers. Needing to express her joy, she started playing a happy little sonata by Mozart. Andrej brought two glasses of chilled white Riesling and a glass of elder juice on a tray. Sanja grinned widely, slipping into a child's song, her fingers touching the keys softly like feathers. Ada came and put her arms around her sister-in-law.

"It's due in spring next year. Enough time to get ready to become an aunt, Sanja."

Sanja stopped playing and put the lid down. She was happy for them and looked forward to a baby to brighten her life, too. Yet, she felt almost sorry for it – to be born in such a violent world. Suddenly, Ada turned pale and ran to the bathroom. Andrej waited a couple of minutes. Then with an apologetic look, he went to check on his wife.

When she came back, Ada said goodnight and went to bed. Sanja and Andrej got together in the dining room for a supper of cold beef salad and thick black bread – a rare treat during such bad times.

"Dear me, Andrej, you didn't waste a minute, did you? Is this the right time to start a family?"

Andrej looked at Sanja and shifted in his chair impatiently. Only sisters knew how to annoy brothers mercilessly. "Every time is right and every time is wrong."

"Ada is still a young girl. You could have waited a bit. The war will end one day."

"Let's hope so. The hospital is jammed full. We have people sleeping in the halls. All complicated cases…all traumatized …They would wake from nightmares, crying and screaming at all hours of the night. We're all exhausted, the nurses, doctors…We're all working double shifts."

"I understand. I'm here. I'll help Ada at home, Andrej. How is she now?"

"She fell asleep. Nausea is common during the first three months of pregnancy."

"I hope she gets better. Anyway, I wanted to tell you that I won't look for engagements under the Nazis. I think it is too dangerous to step into the spotlight right now."

"I agree. Your name might pop up in connection with Russia. The Germans might lock you up as a Communist spy."

Sanja sighed. It was such a paradox, but her brother had a point. "You're right, despite the circumstances that forced me to flee that bloody country and Stalin's so-called continuous revolution, which is just an excuse for mass killings."

"Have you had any word from your landlady, Anna…?"

"Ahmetova. No, none."

"The Red Cross…did they get back to you with anything?"

"Nothing new…Sergej Sokurov simply vanished into the thin air."

Sanja fell silent as she stared at the window with empty eyes. Probably, her Sergej was still rotting in a Siberian gulag, thinking she had betrayed him. Their love and trust were maliciously ruined. If only he could endure and stay alive. Maybe one day he would know the truth. The pain rose in her chest and choked her. Her lungs felt as if they were being stubbed by a thousand pins. In spite of the lovely orange and violet glow outside, deep sadness overcame her. The last rays of sunshine were playing a symphony of colorful nuances with the flowers on the balcony. The pain was sharp and warm like fire.

"Are you aware of the new curfew hours? It's from eight in the evening till six in the morning. The Germans want us to lead a virtuous life. No drinking and partying at night." Her brother went on and on about German practicality. Sanja's mind wandered away. Every occupying force imposed its own rules. In 1929, Serbian King Alexander's hunger for absolute power announced the January 6th Dictatorship, which gave him the right to oppress everything and anyone with a whiff of liberal thought. Sanja remembered how her father used to get excited over each announcement printed in the paper. In those days, the Social Democrats were treated like the Communists. His solicitor's office would have been out of business had he not been one of the best specialists for insolvency procedures, which were frequent during the depression years. In 1934, after the assassination of the Yugoslav king in Marseille, the situation only got worse. Thousands were starving despite the cultivation of lands as rich in soil as Vojvodina and Slavonija. By then Sanja, intent on making an international career, had left first for Berlin and Paris, then continued her path to Russia. Sanja looked at her brother and told him what she knew.

"I heard they have very few troops in Ljubljana. Only some one thousand men ...A couple of high-ranking Wehrmacht officers in the dining room of the Park Hotel were discussing it in loud voices. They seemed rather anxious about the number of partisans and other Slovenian military groups that might turn up against them. Apparently, everyone was disarming the Italians and weapons were confiscated randomly by whoever was at hand."

As always, Andrej confirmed her statement with accurate data: "The Germans have 1600 men in Ljubljana. They are working closely with our government to improve the supply situation in the city. They seem to care about how we live and what we eat and drink. I hope that our life under the Germans will improve."

Sanja observed Andrej from the side. His profile was noble, displaying the features of Ancient Roman statues made of white stone and marble. He had grown a short well-trimmed beard. Since he fell in love with Ada, his lips tended to form soft curves and his thick brows rose and fell with his emotions. He had greatly changed. Sanja wondered whether it was because of Ada or something else, something he witnessed in the hospital every day. Who would not change when confronted by human misery and illness all the time? Andrej had always been a sensitive soul. However, Sanja felt it was something more.

"I sincerely hope so, but I don't feel as positive about the Germans as you are, Andrej. The Nazis hate Slavs. They think we're just a tiny bit better than Jews, and we are no more than vermin. There are creepy stories going around as to how they terrorized the Russian villages during their famous Operation Barbarossa a year ago. Shooting babies, raping women, killing the old and the weak...I can only tell you that Russians will take revenge. I know Russians; they seem a soft and melancholic folk, yet they become horrible when blind with rage. Germans will get their just deserts should the Russians continue their progress westward into the German territory. When it comes to Slovenians, I suppose the Nazis will show their real face under pressure. They have never been friends to Slavs. Even though we think we're heirs of the Austro-Hungarian Monarchy et cetera, Germans don't see us, Slovenians as any different. We're but some one million useless souls. We can all fit in one concentration camp. It's the cheapest way to cleanse the area, definitely cheaper than to set up a supply chain for food and commodities in the city."

Andrej turned to her with an attentive expression, ready to discuss the matter. "Sanja, you are wrong there. Only in a couple of weeks, Germans have improved our lives. Give them time – "

"And they will kill us all, exterminate us like vermin."

"Sanja, what are you trying to say? Are you working for the *Liberation Front*?"

"No, brother, I've learned my lesson with the Communists in Russia. But sometimes I wish...I wish Slovenians..." Sanja trailed off.

"What, Sanja?"

She looked Andrej in the eye. "I wish we Slovenians were lords of our lands for once and for all. Nobody but us: no Serbian king, no Italian Fascist, no pompous Nazi."

Andrej's eyes flashed with admiration. Sanja was such an idealist. Like their father, nothing could make her crumble and abandon her beliefs.

"Then join us, Sanja! Help the Home Guard. We're fighting for the Slovenians and their lands!"

Sanja looked at Andrej with surprise. "What are you saying? Who do you mean but we, Andrej? What have you done?"

"I have joined the Home Guard."

"What? You have joined the Home Guard, Andrej? But that's a military group. They are shooting and killing people. You're a doctor!"

Andrej stared at her and spoke in a cold voice. "They asked me to help them care for the wounded. I'm part of the *Rupnik*'s militia as a doctor. We agreed they'll only call me when they need me, when there's an offensive going on and soldiers get injured."

Sanja had heard rumors about these new groups of Slovenian patriots. However, she also knew their resources were limited and their strength weak.

"It's plain suicide, Andrej. No matter what General *Rupnik* thinks. Unless the Allies offer you real support, you're no match for the German troops. You don't have enough weapons, artillery, planes. How do you plan to boot the Nazis out of Slovenia? By shouting at them with old rifles and singing patriotic songs?"

Andrej's face turned pale. "There's no need to be offensive, Sanja. We're doing what we can. The King of Yugoslavia will persuade the Allies to back us up. The exiled government is lobbying day and night."

Curious, Sanja asked, "Why the Home Guard? Why not the *Liberation Front*?"

Andrej shivered as though a wasp had bitten him. "Are you really asking me this, Sanja?"

She nodded.

Andrej continued: "All right, let me try to explain. Like you, I am not religious, however, I believe there is a superior power, a ruling spirit – we may call him God – which steers our lives. I think religion is something positive and I've seen patients saved by the notion of God. However, zealots repel me. You will agree with me on this. You and I, we had our father, old Strainar. He raised us in the spirit of socialism, so we are not immune to justice and humanism. I can say I am a socialist and as such I probably should support the *Liberation Front*. However, there are things which repulsed me about them. For example, their brutal assaults on peasants when they need food and supplies. Each farmer who opposes their plunder in the name of the resistance gets shot, his women raped, and his house burnt. The partisans operate without any legal rules. Their political commissioners act like tyrants crushing everything and everyone in their way. In March 1943, the Communist Party, doggishly loyal to *Comintern* and *Tovarish* Stalin, signed an agreement with all non-Communist members of the *Liberation Front* that they, as the only avant-garde force, were to lead the Slovenian resistance. Since then many of their non-Communist combatants have been disappearing; some were sent to suicide missions, others face accusations of treason. Executions happen in the deep of the night. All dead. When the Germans call them bandits, they are not far from the truth. The partisans have no respect for the law and civilization."

Sanja was shocked. She knew that Valeria was an active member of the *Liberation Front*. It seemed a noble cause to her. "But, Andrej, many of them have already fought against the Italians. They are now fighting the Germans to liberate our country. They risk their lives. Just look at Va …"

Andrej nodded. "Valeria, I know. However, the situation in *Brkini* is different, Sanja. There, even the clergy oppose the Fascists. The *Liberation Front* has a wide support and its members are less Stalinist than in other parts of Slovenia. Yet, some partisan leaders, the so-called *vojvoda*, are as evil as Satan. A visiting relative came to see his mother at the hospital the other day and told us a sad story. You remember Misliče, the village in the *Brkini Hills*, close to where we had our wedding party? Not even a hundred people live there. Like everywhere in the country, its school was in the hands of the Italians. A young teacher was teaching the children reading, writing, and arithmetic. Whenever she could, she would sing Slovenian songs and read Slovenian texts to them. She was a local girl, a daughter of one of the villagers, very gifted. The nuns sponsored her to finish the Teachers' College in Trieste. Anyway, during the Italian occupation, she fell in love with one of the soldiers. They planned to get married once Italy surrendered. He had to leave and wanted her to come with him. Uncertain about what would happen, she didn't want to leave the school and the children at the beginning of the school year. Who would send another teacher at such short notice? She decided to stay behind and follow her fiancé later. When the partisans came to the village, they did not ask anybody any questions. They arrested her and without a legal procedure shot her in the orchard behind the school building. The villagers were terrorized. Many lost their trust in the *Liberation Front*.

The fate of three generations of women from Notranjska is even worse. I've been treating them. A grandmother, her daughter, and her granddaughter, a young girl of twelve, have been all raped and tortured by a group of drunken partisans a couple of months ago. They are catatonic; the young girl is suicidal. I heard that the partisan commander received some sort of formal reprimand. There was a kind of sentence. But nothing really happened to him. After a week in prison, he moved to another unit. A particularly violent fighter is too precious."

Sanja realized her brother would stick to his decision. However, she would prefer him not to meddle with politics, especially now when he was expecting a child. His job as a doctor was to help people, not to cooperate with the militia no matter on whose side they were or what role they played.

"Andrej, can I ask you a question?"

"Of course you can, Sanja."

She knitted her thin brows in concentration. "In case such a partisan, a rapist, was brought to you wounded ... would you ..."

Andrej finished her question. "You want to know whether I would treat him. Naturally, I would. But I would also see to it that he undergoes a fair trial for his criminal acts."

"And which court would you trust to be fair? A Nazi one?"

Andrej fell silent. Things were getting more and more complicated. There were no straight answers to his dilemmas. "In spite of everything you think, General *Rupnik*'s idea is not to collaborate with the Nazis. We want to fight along with the Allies to liberate Slovenia and chase the invaders out. The representatives of our former government in London are lobbying for our cause. As soon as the Allies acknowledge our military forces, we plan to take the defense of Slovenia in our hands. We all want Slovenia to be a democratic state in federal Yugoslavia. Nobody wants to see the Communists in the center of Europe. I think the civil courts should review all criminal acts after the war. I can assure you I would have not joined the Home Guard were they working for the Nazis."

Sanja took a deep breath. Her little brother was still so naïve! She saw evil everywhere. Her brother's ideas were honorable and humane in the world of darkness and crime. She abhorred the Communism following Stalin's ideology of terror. On the other hand, all former anti-communist militia ended up as collaborators. Andrej's brilliant and sophisticated mind failed to deduce this simple fact.

She tried to warn him.

"I know, Andrej. I know you hate barbarism no matter from which side . Maybe you can promise your professional support to General *Rupnik* without taking an oath to serve in uniform or take up arms. You can always justify your neutral position as a doctor. You have taken the Hippocratic Oath for life. They would understand this."

Andrej looked at Sanja sadly. "I think the historical moment demands sacrifices from all of us. I hope the Allies will come to their senses regarding the *Liberation Front*. Stalin and Hitler are two sides of the same coin; they're dictators interested only in their power. Human lives are nothing to them. We don't want either to ravage Slovenia. I'm afraid we must all take sides in the war eventually. I have made up my mind. I've been given the Home Guard uniform and a pistol."

Sanja shook her head in disbelief. "What about your job at the hospital? Doesn't it matter to you that so many patients need you? What about Ada? She's only nineteen. What if something happens to you? How will she raise the baby? She hasn't finished her studies and has no education."

Andrej said in a low voice, "We all live dangerously, Sanja. I'm not going to fight on the front. I will continue my work at the hospital. Now and then maybe I'll need to go away for a couple of days and fight for the Home Guard."

"Action you say …Are you going to harm Valeria? After all, you're fighting the Communists and she's working for the *Liberation Front*."

Andrej shook his head. "Of course not. I would do everything to bring both Slovenian armies together first and drive the Nazis out of Slovenia. I intend to talk to General *Rupnik* and suggest that the Home Guard join forces with the partisans. This way the Allies won't have to decide which group to support, and the Slovenians will be united."

Sanja sighed with sorrow. "Andrej, you're dreaming. Too much blood has run down that stream. Like your zealots in the Home Guard, the Communist partisans are possessed with their ideology. Believe me, these people see only red. Their ideas are as powerful as the Ten Commandments. Stalin is their Jesus Christ. You can never bring the two together."

"Maybe I can. Maybe we can," Andrej murmured in reply. "At

least, it is worth trying."

~~~

Since Ada moved out, Marjana and Valeria became very close friends. Their affection grew in a meadow sown with the color of blood. The fields of war poppies were endless, the sorrows numberless like seeds in a single pod. The Germans reigned with an iron fist. Slovenians, who were against the Communists and the *Liberation Front*, helped them with the saddest of ardor. Once a slave, always a slave. Like servile dogs, licking the hand of their master as long as he turns his back. Then bites. In that autumn of 1943, Marjana faced bites of various kinds.

After months of delusions and pains, Marjana started to work part time at the hospital. She was a nurse with precious experience. The situation was very difficult. The staff of the hospital kept disappearing. One day her superior did not show up for work, two days later a doctor abandoned his job, the day before yesterday a nurse went missing. The nurse vanished without a trace. Her friends were whispering that she escaped to Italy with her husband, who was Jewish on his mother's side. A young doctor, still in her training period, failed to come to work. They said she followed her husband into the woods to take care of wounded partisans. Many times nobody knew why certain people disappeared. They could only hope that their colleagues hadn't ended up in prison or a concentration camp.

Everyone was stealing sanitary and medical provisions, mostly for the *Liberation Front*. Medicines and bandages found secret ways to reach the wounded like a river flowing to the sea. Although her colleagues suspected each other of stealing, no one said anything. No matter their political convictions, they were all there to heal people. At least, it seemed to Marjana that everybody was covering for somebody, including her brother-in-law Andrej, an ardent Home Guard. She realized many times that he knew the goods were disappearing, yet did not say a word.

Her shifts became longer and longer. Often she came home in the middle of the night. By October, she was leading one of the nurses' divisions and supervising the medicine supply as well as the work of the nurses and orderlies. It was her job to provide good care for the patients in spite of the war.

After long hours at the hospital, she would return home where Valeria had usually cooked a warm meal. A stew or minestrone with corn bread as yellow as polenta. It was Valeria's turn to cheer her friend up with jokes from the print shop. Ridiculing the Germans made it more tolerable to live with the terror. The scarce supply of food in Ljubljana continued despite Germany's promises to amend the situation. Nevertheless, the two women managed to cope, and Marjana finally found her inner balance.

Yet, one day a patient turned up at the hospital, a patient who nearly pushed Marjana over the cliff, into the void of her sickness and pain, and into death.

He was not much of a man. Small, middle-aged, maybe a few years younger than her, handsome in his way. Mihael Mlakar came to the hospital on a Saturday afternoon, long past Marjana's working hours. The week over, she had made her way home tranquilly. On Monday morning she was still not aware of his presence despite the strict admission procedures for each new patient. She personally checked that everything was all right before visiting them. There were a few new admissions on Sunday, and she asked the head nurse of each department about the particularities. Finally, she entered the separate wing of the hospital where they treated patients with infectious diseases. Each had his own room to avoid spreading contamination. Lately they were treating many cases of typhus, mostly people from poor areas living in poor hygienic conditions.

The admission office was empty. The entire department was silent as a grave. The corridor floor shone in the first morning rays of the sun. While waiting for someone to appear and report, Marjana leafed through the book of admissions. No new cases. She verified the medical storage and saw that all the instruments were sterilized and everything was in order. Venturing a few steps into the corridor, she heard moaning from Room 12. When she opened the door, she found a dirty and unshaven man in filthy clothes lying in the bed.

"Water, give me water," he gasped in a hoarse voice.

Marjana paused, a chill running down her spine. Did the activists admit a wounded partisan to the hospital? They would all end up in prison.

"Certainly," she replied, closing the door behind her. She went to fill a glass with water and approached him. There was no medical chart fastened to the bed. She helped the man to prop himself on his elbow and gave him to drink. His cracked lips touched the glass and he drank in long, hasty gulps as though parched from the desert. His cheeks burned with fever. Thin, reddish strands of hair were glued to his skull. The wrinkles on his forehead were black and gray with dirt. He smelled of rotten flesh as if he were disintegrating alive. Marjana was well aware of that smell, too well. After drinking, he sank back on the pillow and closed his eyes. She put the glass on the nightstand and waited. Maybe the man would tell her who he was, but he didn't.

"Sir, my name is Marjana Skarpin. I am the head nurse of this hospital. It is my duty to care for all our patients. And I mean ALL – no matter where they come from or who they are. You can trust me completely."

"Then tell me, why doesn't anyone give a shit about me in this hospital?" he snapped in reply.

Marjana's eyebrows arched in surprise. Indeed, there was no one at the admission office this morning. "What do you mean, sir?" she asked carefully.

The man jerked up and grabbed her wrist. Pain. Marjana's blood froze in her veins.

"I've been lying here for two days, two goddamn days! Nobody came to take my temperature. Nobody brought me a meal or a glass of water. Why?" he cried in despair, gripping her tightly.

Rancid-smelling saliva sprayed Marjana's cheeks, making her stomach turn. Yet her professional ethics won. The man had every right to be furious. This was all very wrong. She gently touched the hand clenching hers. He let her go and lay down. What a disaster. They had dumped the man in the hospital bed without washing him.

"I am really sorry. I was off duty on Sunday. Let me find out what went wrong. Were you conscious when you were brought in?"

"I'm not sure. Maybe. I've had fever and hallucinations for days. Reality and nightmares follow one another, so I don't know which is which. And these headaches, these terrible headaches ..." He tried to keep his voice under control. "And the vomiting. I don't think I can keep down anything, not even water. Do you understand what I mean? I'm leaking water from my ass."

He looked at Marjana's bruised wrist. "I'm so sorry, madam."

She tried to rub off the pain and managed a polite smile. "I'll live. Don't worry," she said. "I'll have a nurse give you a bath. Afterward we'll fill up the admission form. Then you'll be ready to be examined by the physician. What is your name, sir?"

"Michael Mlakar, a proud soldier of the Home Guard," he whispered, visibly exhausted. "May I have another glass of water, please?"

"Of course, but please drink very slowly. Until we find out what is wrong with you, it's best to limit your water intake, Mr. Mlakar," said Marjana, passing him another glass.

"I'm so tired. Can I sleep for a minute?" said Mlakar in almost inaudible whisper.

"Please do. It may take a while before I gather the crew," replied Marjana.

She hurried out of the room, livid. Had everyone gone crazy? If the man really had arrived last Saturday afternoon, this was a bloody disaster. Why hadn't any of the physicians examined him?

As she stalked toward the office, she realized the reason. Since the nurses hadn't completed the admission form, none of the doctors even knew the man existed. But where were the orderlies? Why hadn't they sanitized the room much less checked it? And, for God's sake, where were all the nurses in the Department of Infectious Diseases?

From afar she noticed that the office door was ajar and she hastily entered. Maria, the youngest of the trainees, sat at the table, hiding her face in her hands, her back shaking in spasms. She was crying. Marjana had no patience with snivelers at work. This seventeen-year-old girl should learn to control her feelings. No matter, she had to start working full time before she completed her education.

"What's with the waterworks, Maria?" she asked severely.

The girl looked up with her teary gray eyes. Her blond hair had strayed to her oval face, some strands glued to her reddish cheeks.

"It's horrible, Miss Skarpin, just horrible," she said, trembling.

"Of course, it's horrible. We have a patient in Room 12 who claims to have been in the hospital for two days, and nobody has even checked in on him. Nobody has even given him a bath!" Marjana shouted, losing her temper.

"So you don't know yet, do you?" the young nurse said.

"What are you talking about?" retorted Marjana impatiently.

"Nurse Anita was found Saturday night. Hung herself at the attic of her house. The Italians took her husband away last year – to prison or one of the camps, nobody knows. He never returned. She left three small children, two girls and a boy."

Marjana collapsed in the chair at the news. "She hung herself? But why?"

Brushing her tears away, the girl tried to explain what she knew: "They brought in a man who they said was a Home Guard at *St. Urh*. When Anita heard that, she dropped everything and went home without a word. It was Saturday night; nobody paid much attention. She was supposed to come to work yesterday, but didn't show up. I was alone the whole morning. I managed to cope since the patients were undemanding and there were no emergencies. I didn't know there was a man there until I found Anita's little note. Look!" She showed Marjana a scrap of paper, the edge of an old newspaper.

I'm not coming back as long as this man, Bloody Fox, is here. I refuse to touch this man. No sense of duty or professional ethics can make me treat or help this human vermin.

Anita.

"The note was stuck next to the blank admission form. Miss Marjana, I immediately went to see the physician on duty, and he sent a janitor to Anita's house. She was nowhere in sight, only her children were there, alone and scared. The oldest girl is only nine. He brought them back with him to the hospital, where at least they had something to eat. Then her eldest told us. She was the one who found Anita. The Holy Sisters came to fetch them that afternoon. Oh, my God!"

"Stop wailing, Maria! We must put things in order immediately," ordered Marjana. The girl shut up.

"Who is this man, this Bloody Fox?" Marjana asked, almost fearing the answer. The smell of rancid blood and human debris explained it.

"He must be the one in Room 12, the new patient," stuttered little Maria.

"So why didn't you report it to the physician on duty?"

"Oh, I did. Doctor Karlovšek said he would see to it. I don't know …"

Marjana was still not satisfied. "But before the doctor can examine a patient, you must complete the admission form. Weren't you were trained to do that, Maria?"

Head lowered, Maria mumbled something, saying she forgot in the confusion caused by Anita's suicide. Yet, it dawned on Marjana. Obviously, everybody except her knew who Mlakar was – a Home Guard villain. A bad rumor seemed to herald the man. Nobody, be it a doctor bound by the Hippocratic Oath or an orderly with a broom, wanted to touch a killer. If it was true that this Mlakar was a torturer and executioner, the whole thing made sense. The hospital staff had simply put him in quarantine and pretended he didn't exist. Why did he end up in the Infectious Diseases ward? Who made this decision?

Although Marjana didn't understand much of Ljubljana politics, which got more complex every day, she knew about the Home Guard's stronghold at *St. Urh*. These anti-communist fighters, a special death squad, arrested, tortured, and killed activists of the *Liberation Front*. The incarcerations and tortures took place right in the sacred areas of the vicarage and the church. According to rumors, even the priests took part in the torture sessions and nobody came back alive from *St. Urh*. The prisoners were mutilated into a pulp, then taken to Kozler's Thicket, killed, and their bodies dumped in the Sava River. The activists had a saying: "Be careful or you'll end up at *St. Urh!*" Valeria was more afraid of the Home Guard than the Germans. She often said, "The Germans are priggish, but the Slovenian Home Guards are devils!"

"What about Andrej, Valeria? Aren't you afraid of him?" Marjana would retort. Deep down she worried that the girl would be forced to flee into the woods and leave her alone on Wolfova Street.

"Andrej is different. He honestly believes the Home Guard is against the Communists. I think he's just naïve and doesn't know he's consorting with the devil. He will never betray anybody but himself. Yes, Marjana, he will betray only himself," replied Valeria.

'And Ada and their baby,' thought Marjana.

She was, however, reluctant to share Valeria's fears when it came to the Slovenian Home Guard and the police. People must be exaggerating. Why would a Slovenian hurt another Slovenian? It was preposterous. She refused to believe that people, even the Communists, could be tortured in a sacred place like a church. People were people. Jesus Christ was the epitome of grace and mercy. Let him who has not sinned cast the first stone.

Marjana's thoughts returned to Maria and their patient in Room 12.

"Give me the admission form! Must I have to do everything around here?" she grumbled. Her knees weakened at the thought of her patient. Although working in proximity to death every day, she hated the smell of it.

She bumped into Marko, the strongest orderly in the hospital, and sent him to Room 12. Then she went to find a physician. Doctor Karlovšek was nowhere in sight, but she found his superior, Dr. Majcen. She quickly described the situation and saw him blanch at the thought of possible political troubles arising from it.

"Thank you, Marjana. To be on the safe side, please burn his clothes. Have the orderlies sterilize the room, too. What did he say was wrong with him?"

"He has terrible headaches, nausea and vomiting, fatigue, frequent loss of consciousness, nightmares, loss of reality. He's very aggressive, too. He grabbed my wrist. Look!" She showed the bruises. "He apologized later, though," she added as though her pain was not important and the violent nature of the man Anita had called Bloody Fox was only a symptom of his illness.

"As you fill up the admission form, ask him whether he was bitten by bugs or a wild animal lately. If he was, find out how long ago. Call me once you're done, so I can examine him."

Marjana heard the tremor in his voice. Still, the hospital had a schedule to follow. "What about the daily ward rounds?" she asked.

"Let's start an hour late today. We must handle this case first. If we don't make this right, we'll have the police and who knows who else in the hospital. That's the last thing we need right now. I'll speak to Doctor Karlovšek. That careless idiot! How could he do this?" he hissed. Marjana shivered.

She went to fulfill her duties and, in a quarter of an hour, she was sitting on the bed of a freshly bathed Michael Mlakar.

"Now then, Mr. Mlakar, I need to complete your admission form, so that Dr. Majcen can examine you. May I have your full name?"

"Mihael Mlakar."

"Your father's name."

"Mihael Mlakar, Senior. Deceased. Never returned from Galicia."

"Mother?"

"Angela Močnik. Like my father, she's from the village of Polje."

"Date of birth?"

"April 25th, 1905 at the Štepanja village near Ljubljana."

"Profession?"

"Farmer. I inherited around fifty acres of land from my grandmother."

"Oh, how nice, so close to the city," she said with a friendly smile.

Mlakar shook his head. "It sounds wonderful, but everything has gone to hell. The hired hands and servants have stolen everything. Nasty bastards. They would steal a penny off a dead man's eyes," he said bitterly.

Marjana read between the lines. Mlakar was obviously lazy and incompetent. She dared not imagine who this man had taken to *St. Urh* in his lust for vengeance.

"Marital status?"

"Married. My wife took the kids to America where my brother lives. There's no war there."

Marjana put everything down meticulously. "Your address, Mr. Mlakar?"

"*Štepanja Vas* 23. Although I'm with the Home Guard most of the time. First battalion, various divisions and posts."

Marjana braced herself. She needed to get more accurate data as to his movements and living conditions.

"I'm sorry, Mr. Mlakar, but I need to know precisely where you've been in the last year. Your symptoms indicate you might be suffering from an infectious disease."

Mlakar cast her a contemptuous look. What did this woman want from him? Her questions sounded more like a police interrogation. Where was the bloody doctor anyway?

"Don't push it, miss. After two days, it's high time I get examined by a doctor, not cross-examined. Even if I disclose where I've been, you wouldn't know what's wrong with me," he said peevishly.

Marjana hid her real sentiments under a polite smile. She looked him in his reddish eyes. She didn't like what she saw – undisguised hatred for the world, contempt, and malice. She breathed deeply and continued.

"Sorry, Mr. Mlakar, but you're wrong. Location and circumstances are essential in coming up with the right diagnosis. Based on your symptoms, you could have the typhoid fever, rabies, or something else. But just the first two are lethal, not only for you, but for everybody around you. Your Home Guard comrades, your family and friends. So, please be so kind as to reply to my questions."

"I was around Ljubljana and at *St. Urh* the whole year."

"How are the hygienic conditions in the army? Have there been problems with ticks or mites?"

Offended by the questions, Mlakar jerked up aggressively. But he quickly fell back on the pillow in exhaustion. Beads of sweat trickled down his forehead. He had fever.

"It was those Communist bastards that brought the vermin into our stronghold. All stinking scum. Our commander had to have all the rooms disinfected and all our clothes were changed."

"Were you bitten?"

"Yeah, we all were. When we were outside, in the woods, the vermin soon found us, too."

Marjana gave a compassionate nod, although the mention of woods made the hair on the back of her neck stand up. She scribbled his answers. "What about wild animals? Have you been bitten, for example by a rat or a fox?"

He gave a vicious smile. "Are you making fun of me, miss? Do you think the Bloody Fox has bitten my ass?" he said in a rough voice.

Marjana froze. Luckily, with her eyes focused on the papers, the man could not see into her soul. Hangmen were vile psychologists. She must cut off all the feelings and do her job, then Dr. Majcen can deal with the man.

She replied coldly, "Nobody is making fun of you, Mr. Mlakar. As I told you earlier, I'm responsible for the patients here and I mean it. Had a wild animal – a rat, a fox, or a stray dog – bitten you, you could have gotten rabies, which is a deadly disease. So it is in your best interest to tell me whether such a thing happened to you."

To Marjana's surprise, the patient laughed heartily as though they were sitting together at a party. His sudden mood changes made her suspect rabies.

"You really are a doll, miss! Has anyone told you how pretty you are? Where are you from, love?"

She gently replied: "Thank you for your nice words, Mr. Mlakar. We can't waste time on chitchat. The doctor wants to see you shortly. Tell me, did you get bitten then?"

Mlakar propped himself on his elbows and looked fiercely in her eyes. "All right, no chitchat. Let's keep to the point: Around my birthday, in April, I fell asleep in the thicket. I was so exhausted I didn't feel a fox nibbling on my leg – until it chomped on my lower right leg and ankle. I killed it. Our medic cleaned the wound and bandaged it. It healed quickly, only a scar reminds me of it now."

"Can you show it to me, please?" asked Marjana.

He pulled his leg out of the blanket. "Here, look." He pointed to an ugly, reddish scar. The animal had bitten off a whole chunk of the skin.

"Did you have stitches?"

"Yeah, the medic stitched it up. Nothing serious."

"Do you remember if you got rabies shots afterward, maybe at the doctor's?"

"Come on, I never go to the doctor's. The wound healed just fine," said the patient, his energy dwindling.

Marjana nodded with a smile; she had everything she needed. "Thank you, Mr. Mlakar. I'll fetch Dr. Majcen now. Please, rest a little."

Like a good boy, he closed his eyes and fell asleep immediately. When she returned with Doctor Majcen, they could not wake him up.

The following day the lab tests showed that Mihael Mlakar had rabies. The disease had badly damaged his nervous system and brain. Whenever he was awake, he would shriek with rage and beat around himself. They had to fasten him to the bed. He refused to eat and drink. Water, in particular, formed one of his nightmares. The orderlies took turns in changing his bed linen, which was a challenge. As Mlakar lost his mind, he got confused and sank into hallucinations, blurting out all sorts of names, probably of those he tortured and killed at Kozler's Thicket. There was no cure. Bloody Fox was doomed to die in agony and pain.

Marjana Skarpin managed the whole situation with great difficulty. The medics, nurses, and orderlies were all upset. The whole hospital was buzzing like a nest of wasps, which the war jabbed with its sharp blade. Everybody at the hospital was whispering about the crimes committed on the hill of *St. Urh*. A black fog of cruelties and crimes incomprehensible to human nature enveloped the patient. Although they were surrounded by the presence of death during wartime, this was different. The abyss of human malevolence was deeper and darker than anything the world had ever witnessed. Bloody Fox became the sign of evil.

Piece by piece, they were able to put together the nature of his crimes. Bloody Fox's nickname came not only from his zeal for torture and killing, but also from his thirst for blood. According to rumors, he didn't care when blood sprayed his uniform or splattered from his victim's face onto his cheeks. He could go on for days without changing out of his bloody clothes, at times even going to the pub in them still covered in vomit and human excrement. He was a notorious gambler and a drunk. He squandered his fortunes at the pub and lost his lands playing cards. His wife, destitute and desperate, fled with their children to America. While administering lashes with a short whip and pulling out the teeth of his victims, he took long gulps of brandy. After he finished with them, he would fall asleep in the thicket, while foxes came to nibble at the body parts of the miserable corpses around him. Although the bodies were dumped in the river, a leg or arm would go astray and lie around forgotten. Devious predators waited until the shots stopped before gorging on their human feast. One night they got their claws and teeth on the drunken Mlakar. His blood was as sweet as the blood of his victims. Afterward his comrade bandaged the wound and nicknamed him "Fox." People from nearby villages, who knew what was going on the hill, but didn't dare to speak of it, added "Bloody" to his name.

Every time Marjana entered his room, the stench of blood and death hit her nostrils. As the only nurse in the hospital that Mlakar would let near him, she forced herself to overcome her nausea. Only Marjana could calm him down. Kept under strong sedatives, he slowly slid into a coma from which he did not wake up. The whole hospital breathed a sigh of relief when the undertakers took his body away. Michael Mlakar was granted a funeral with full military honors.

Valeria was the first to notice Marjana's lethargy and loss of appetite. When she came home, she would say she had eaten at the hospital, but Valeria knew it wasn't true. Worried, she talked to Ada and Andrej about it. Times were hard and they feared Marjana would have a relapse, particularly in the face of her difficult job at the hospital. Together they decided that Andrej should try to have a word with Marjana under the pretext of discussing work.

It was on a late October afternoon when Andrej called for Marjana to see him at his office. Mlakar had died the previous day after two weeks at the hospital. Andrej, too, had heard the stories of his heinous deeds. He wanted to find out the truth and address his questions to the headquarters of the Home Guard where he had friends who respected him. General *Rupnik* in person reassured him that the rumors were nothing but enemy propaganda, all lies. The general could not speak for what happened before his time under the Italian rule, but he knew for a fact that nothing illegal or criminal was taking place at *St. Urh*. However, Andrej was aware of Marjana's fragile mental health. If she was living in the shadow of all these terrible, tragic tales, she could sink into lethargy and depression again. He also knew that Nurse Anita had been her friend.

Like a silent shadow, Marjana opened the door and sat in the chair in front of his desk.

"Hello, Marjana," Andrej said kindly. "How are you doing? Can I offer you a cup of coffee?"

The dark circles under her eyes and pale cheeks expressed more than she could. Still, she tried to smile. "Thanks, only if you have real coffee. I've been drinking corn coffee at home."

"It's your lucky day, my sister-in-law. One kilo of real Arabica, a gift from a grateful patient. The aroma is heavenly."

He went to talk to his secretary, and Marjana heard him ask for sandwiches from the cafeteria or biscuits, whatever the girl could find. Then he returned and closed the door. He started on the safe side:

"I hear you saved the hospital from a great calamity. Considering Karlovšek's negligence, we could've been all be in trouble."

"It wasn't Dr. Karlovšek, it was the system. The Department of Infectious Diseases is a debacle. There was only a young apprentice handling everything. Nurse Anita ..."

Andrej nodded knowingly. "Anita had terrible mental problems."

Marjana sat up. "How did you know?"

"Sometimes she came to see me. Just to talk."

"Did she suffer from a condition?"

"Nothing that would endanger her work. She clung to her job, you know."

"I see. Was it because of her husband then?"

"It was not only her husband. Marjana, I'm sorry, but I can't discuss it with you."

Marjana bowed her head. She understood. Still, the whole thing was so difficult. For the first time in weeks, her eyes filled with warm tears.

"The children are with the Ursulines. I visited them on my way home the other day. They look after them well, poor darlings. The little boy and the younger girl seem all right, but the eldest should be in therapy. She looks really sick. She was the one who found her mother in the attic."

Andrej nodded in understanding. "Yes, it is terrible. Just breaks one's heart. I'm seeing Metka twice a week. We're working on her trauma. It's not going to be easy, but I hope though she will make it."

Marjana brushed tears from her face. "Sorry, Andrej, I just can't stop myself."

"Come on, Marjana, you must know that tears are a blessing."

"Well, I don't allow any of the hospital staff to shed them." She tried a faint smile.

"We all curse tears, but during times of illness and war tears flow. Tell me, Marjana, how's your workload? It is too much for you? You're working full time now, aren't you? Ada says you work six days a week."

The door opened and Andrej's secretary brought in a plate tinkling with cups and saucers.

"Why, Cvetka, that's a real feast," remarked Marjana when she saw the army biscuits thickly spread with butter and marmalade.

"We keep this homemade marmalade only for special occasions, Nurse Marjana," said the young woman. She quickly left the office.

"Have some," offered Andrej.

"Thank you," replied Marjana and poured herself a cup of aromatic coffee.

For a few moments, they savored the hot drink in silence. Then Andrej spoke. "There are some nasty rumors going around the hospital about the man who died of rabies yesterday."

Marjana looked him in the eyes. "Anita's suicide is connected in some way to him. Maria showed me the note Anita scribbled on the corner of a newspaper."

Andrej was taken by surprise. "What do you mean? What kind of note?"

"In the note, Anita said she refused to touch and treat this man. She called him human vermin. It was written on Saturday before she went home."

Andrej sank into his thoughts. His talks with Anita had been quite frequent even since they took her husband away in 1942. With some hesitation, she told him how she found out that the anti-communist police had arrested him. She never mentioned *St. Urh*, only her guilt and distress due to having started a relationship with another man, hoping he would help liberate her husband. She said he was a big shot in the Home Guard, but didn't drop any names. Could it be this man?

"Where's the note now?"

"The police must have taken it. Evidence it was suicide."

Andrej's cup swayed in the air. "Marjana, what do you think about all this?"

She gave him an inquisitive look. "Do you mean Anita or Mlakar?"

"Both."

Marjana sighed. "You know full well, Andrej, that this world cannot surprise me anymore. However, Anita's death has shaken me more than I thought anything could. She was an outstanding nurse, always organized, confident. Very reliable. She must have had some strong reasons to leave that note and do what she did, leaving three orphans behind."

Andrej paled. He felt their roles reversing: Marjana could see clearly in the heart of truth while he was somehow blind. She sensed his insecurity.

"Andrej, maybe for the sake of our hospital work, it would be better if you told me what you know about Anita. It would help me understand and manage the staff accordingly. You know my lips are sealed. Our professional ethics are one and the same."

His eyes strayed around the room. He didn't know how to start. Finally, he looked at Marjana's face, wrinkled with age and painful experience. She was still a remarkable woman and her eyes reminded him of the eyes he loved deeply. In spite their age difference, it was plain to see that Ada and Marjana were sisters. She was right. It would be best to tell her everything.

"I think the reason for Anita's suicide was indeed this man, Bloody Fox. He embodies her deep feeling of guilt. Anita was obsessed with guilt. It was like poison. Let me explain. In winter 1942, they arrested her husband. Through her older sister, who went to school with Mlakar, Anita found out that the man was an important commander in the anti-communist police, so she made an appointment with him to find out more. They met at the local pub. Mlakar fell in love with Anita at first sight and they talked long into the evening. Finally, he told her that if she slept with him, he would help her with her husband. Outraged, Anita rejected him. When her husband continued to rot in jail – she didn't even know where, she looked for Mlakar again. This time he was polite and courteous; she gave in to his obscene proposal. It was only after their affair had been going on for a while that she realized Mlakar was the one in charge of her husband. In the morning, he would torture the man, a father of three; in the evening, he would get it on with his wife. She found out when he bragged about it at the pub. It was horrible. He had pulled out her husband's teeth, hung him upside down, whipped him, burnt his flesh with charcoal, cigarettes, iron, then met his wife, who did not know she was in bed with the Devil."

Marjana stared out the window where the leaves of a majestic maple tree were burning orange and red. Was it possible, such perversion in a human being?

"How did Anita find out it was Mlakar who kept her husband in prison?"

Andrej shook his head. "The waiter told her. When she confronted Mlakar, the Devil laughed in her face, revealing more than she wanted to know. She demanded that he keep his end of the deal."

"What did he say?"

A sad shadow passed over Andrej's face. "It was this summer. He told her it was too late. They had just shot her husband. Should she say a word of it to anyone, she would be next. Their children would be given up for adoption. There was a real demand for children in Italy. Although Anita was terrified, she hit him in the face and never saw him again. She wished nothing but death to that man."

Marjana wondered about Andrej. He was such an intelligent man. Why couldn't he see the kind of people to whom he gave his commitment and support? As though reading her thoughts, he continued.

"I'm going to see that what's happening at *St. Urh* comes to an end. It brings shame to all of us. I will report these heinous deeds to the Home Guard command. I despise the Communists for being outlaws and brutal, and I cannot tolerate our soldiers acting so, either. When I inquired about that damn hill, they said it was only enemy propaganda. Anita's death is no propaganda. Facts are facts."

Marjana rose from her chair and put her right arm around his shoulder. "Thank you for your trust. Do what you think is right. This man, Bloody Fox, brings shame to the human race – not only to the Home Guard, but to all of us. He died as he had lived. We were unable to stop him, and wild beasts did our job for us."

He squeezed her hand. "You're more than worthy of my trust, my dear sister-in-law. We must all stand up against the brutes who see war as an opportunity to live their sadistic fantasies. It doesn't matter on which side they are fighting."

"You're right. Use your connections and report him. He can't be alone. There may be others at *St. Urh*. Crimes against humanity should be punished. One day the war will be over, and eventually we will have to live together, winners and losers."

"I sincerely hope the Germans can settle our fighting, too."

"Oh, if we're not able to do it ourselves, then they cannot help us. Let it be. How is my little sister doing?"

Andrej's face lit with tenderness. He loved Ada so much. "Much better. No more morning sickness. Come visit us sometime. You can also bring that little red star of yours, Valeria. We can go to the movies together, like we did in summer."

Marjana nodded. "That would be lovely. Maybe next Sunday then. I don't know about Valeria. She's working long hours since it's the peak season for printers. Before Christmas, you know."

As she went out into the corridor, she heard Andrej console Cvetka who lamented that they had not touched the biscuits. He was such a good doctor and such a good husband to Ada. Hell, she couldn't understand what he saw in this Home Guard gang. Like an echo of her thoughts, Dr. Karlovšek crossed her path.

"Have the undertakers removed the patient with rabies, Nurse Marjana?"

"Yes, yesterday."

"Thank God. The fox needn't have bothered to besmirch its teeth; that son of a bitch was already born with rabies."

"True. Sadly, the world is full of such people these days, Dr. Karlovšek."

"Well, I wouldn't say so. Look at us, Marjana, we're the good ones."

She returned his smile. Well, look at that. So, he was stealing medical supplies for the *Liberation Front*, too. He had not examined Mlakar on purpose. She should tell him how irresponsible this was. The hospital could get in trouble.

"Is Majcen angry with you?"

"Angry? He was furious. He would have fired me had we not been so understaffed."

"Maybe next time you deal with such bastards, too, Dr. Karlovšek. It would be wiser."

"Well, no, dear Marjana, certainly not. He was a son of a bitch. And I am a physician, not a veterinarian."

Marjana sighed and shrugged. What could she say? He was right. She headed to her office to change and go home.

Suddenly, the memory of Rab and *Gonars* assailed her and her knees buckled as though her life force was ebbing. Emptiness was all she could feel. Her pace got slower and she dragged her feet along the corridor, reliving the cold fingers of those tiny hands begging for help. Guilt, this sleazy mud which sucked at one's feet, preventing movement. Guilt in war. She could have given herself a shot and end all this, leave this world of slaughter and sleep forever. Was she responsible for the deaths since she had worked for the Fascists? Could she have done something to stop the deaths, prevent the crimes she had in a way abetted for months at Rab? Should she have tried to shoot one of the Fascist murderers instead of trying to get one child through the camp alive? What was her role in that? What was the range of her guilt? Was there a measure for guilt? Why did she follow the rules of the criminal Fascist system like a sheep? Had she been so afraid for her own life? Had she been such a coward, shutting out all common sense although it told her to fight back?

How many times did the nurses whisper in the silence of their dormitory about their terrible duty? There were daydreams, too. What if ... what if all the prisoners were to fight the guards at the same time? Maybe they could throw down the fences and run to freedom. If the people from the other side of the fence, the people, who lived in a separate world as though the concentration camp was none of their business, although they could be put inside one day or the other, if they would tear down the walls and kill the guards. If the nurses simply went home. Who would look after the camp children then? Guilt is mud, blocking the brain cells like black pine tar that show in the wounds of a tree.

She lost her balance and almost collapsed to the floor. She leaned against the wall, upset, her temples throbbing. She stood there blinking. She was alive, she breathed. Was it fair that someone continued to live and breathe after escorting so many children to their deaths? Could one survive and not feel guilty?

Guilt was sleazy black mud. Like sticky tar, it invaded every cell in her body and every glimmer in her soul. Guilt must have devastated Anita. How could she have saved her husband by sleeping with his torturer? In the end, she lost everything. And Mlakar thought he was a war hero until his last stinky, drooling breath. The world upside down.

In the distance, as if through fog, she could see the young trainee, Maria, approaching. Soon the girl would notice her tears. Marjana swallowed hard and turned back – back to Andrej's office. To the future. We must fight for tomorrow. She would deal with the horrible memories once the war was over. She entered the antechamber.

"Cvetka, Dr. Strainar and I, we are so silly. While talking, we forgot about your wonderful marmalade biscuits."

Cvetka was all smiles. "Here, Nurse Marjana, I saved them. I was hoping you'd come back," she said, offering the tray. "Please, have a treat – you deserve it, Marjana."

Marjana sat in the chair and bit into the sweet treat.

Life must be lived. Sweet or bitter, it must be lived.

~~~

On her eighteenth year, Valeria had very little time to mature, learn, or mingle with friends. After her stressful missions at odd times and at odd places, she needed Marjana's warm embrace to cradle her to sleep. Here in the big city, far from the tranquillity of *Brkini* and Kozjane, Marjana was all the family she had. With her work at the printing shop, the flat mates got along so well that they could keep sending some money to their families. Still, Valeria had to interrupt her studies. It was for the best. She couldn't enroll under German occupation for fear that they would find fault in her papers. She decided to continue her education in literature and art history once the war is over. It should not be long, for 1943 was a disastrous year for the Axis powers: Italy had capitulated; German cities were under constant aviation fire, leaving thousands of civilians bombed and destitute; the soldiers who had returned from the Russian front were disillusioned and depressed, their fighting spirit down to zero. Only the Japanese forged on assiduously in spite of their losses at Midway.

Autumn turned to winter overnight on *All Saints' Day*. Light snow whitened the flowers and the graves and snuffed out the candles burning for the dead. The city of Ljubljana became an icy landscape, and days when the sun still tried to shine from the blue sky were rare. On such a bright chilly Monday, Valeria was headed home. She stopped by an acquaintance at the black market and bought stuff that had become rarities: white flour and butter. She approached the apartment from another side, different from her usual route. When she turned into her street, she noticed two men in trench coats leaning against the doorframe of Zvezda, a pastry shop opposite her front door. Police! Someone had betrayed her. She must flee now.

Unnoticed, she left the same way she came. She found a lobby of a house that was unlocked and slid into the hall. It was pitch-dark. Using the banister, she felt her way down the wide stairs to the cellar and sat on the last step. What now? Where could she go? If she wanted to stay alive, she had only one choice: go to the woods and join the partisans. It was too dangerous to stay in the city. She needed a warm coat, some heavy boots, woolen sweaters, and a change of clothes – which were at the apartment. It would be too risky to fetch them later. During all their trainings, the instructors kept repeating that once the police were on your trail, you couldn't risk going home to pick up clothes or food; you had to abandon your place of residence forever. Turn around and walk away if you can! Then report to your contact and wait for orders. Her contact was the printing shop. Would the police look for her there, too?

For a while, she did not move. She found a secret dark corner where she could hide in case any of the residents visited the cellar. Shivering with cold, she waited for the light of the day to fade away completely and fell asleep leaning against the wall. It was light again when she woke up, her legs stiff with pain. Once the voices in the hall had ceased, she stepped out into a new day. After she reported to the printing house, they hid her in a shipment of cellophane gift wrap scheduled to leave Ljubljana. The truck was going to Gorizia. They dropped her off at the pass above Cerkno, where the woods were so thick that even deer had to step carefully over the rocks. A courier was waiting to bring her to her unit. While walking in her light city shoes along the snowy frozen path, Valeria wondered who betrayed her. She dismissed the thought that it could have been Andrej. They were close friends, after all. He would never do such a thing. Nothing could change his good nature, not even the lousy war and his vicious collaborators. Andrej Strainar might be a Home Guard, but he was a man of honor.

~~~

Loud ringing and banging on the door roused Marjana from deep sleep. Valeria had not come home and she knew why. The two men across the street at Zvezda's were rather obvious. Who were they? What was so urgent that they had to wake her up in the middle of the night?

Wrapping a thick cardigan around herself, she ran to open the door. Before she could say anything, a man crossed the threshold and struck her in the face. She fell into a corner of the hall. Warm blood filled her mouth; her nose started bleeding profusely.

"Where is she? Where's the Communist slut?"

Marjana pulled herself together and replied in a low voice, "I don't know. She didn't come home."

One of the men took a pistol out of his pocket. "Did you warn her? Where has she gone? Tell us or I'll blow your stupid head up!"

These were not the same men waiting in front of the shop across the road the whole day. They were in black SS uniforms with menacing skulls on their caps. As the two Germans interrogated her, three local police officers searched the flat. They opened drawers and overturned the furniture, lifting and cutting pillows and mattresses. Marjana knew they would find nothing. Months ago Valeria had meticulously removed every little flyer and every book that might compromise them. She had told Marjana about stashing her things in a safe place, and Marjana trusted her. The two Germans standing over Marjana threatened to kill her anyway, their faces pale and angry. One of them cocked his pistol and aimed at her.

"Tell us and we'll let you go, woman."

Marjana felt warmth spread down her pajamas. To her alarm, she found that she had wet herself. She tried to concentrate. She must withstand this. She must be strong now. She hoped the men wouldn't notice her fear.

"I can't tell you. I don't know. This is the first time I learn that Gina is a Communist."

The man without a gun kneeled and brought his face so close to Marjana's that she smelled schnapps in his breath.

"Her name is not Gina," he lashed out. Marjana's stomach turned as he spattered her with saliva. "She is Valeria Batič from Kozjane. You know that, don't you? You also come from Kozjane."

Marjana stared at him nonplussed, but not for long. He gripped her hair and chin, forcing her jaw open, while his partner stuck the muzzle of a *Luger* into her mouth. Marjana's eyes bulged with terror.

"Are you ready to speak now, bitch?"

That was it. All of a sudden, the tension left Marjana's body. Her strong will vanished like drops of water on dry sand. She could have fallen asleep right there. If it meant dying, she was ready. There wasn't anything she could do.

"Nod your head if you want to say something!"

Marjana did not move. The men deliberately interpreted her inertia as a yes and took the warm muzzle, wet with her saliva, out of her mouth. She wiped her tears on her sleeve and regained some composure.

"Gentlemen, arrest me if you want to, but I'm telling the truth. Gina or Valeria... whoever she is was living with my sister Ada when I returned from *Gonars* almost a year ago. I was working in veteran hospitals around Italy, mostly at the *Custoza* Veteran Hospital; I hadn't been in Kozjane for decades. When I last saw Valeria Batič in the early twenties, she was still a toddler," she explained.

Then she stood up and offered her wrists. "Here, take me in," she simply said.

Both SS men exchanged a look; better one than none. They handcuffed her, and a police officer took her warm winter coat from the hook. Marjana slipped her bare feet into her shoes and followed her torturers outside into the cold autumn night.

The following morning when she did not show up for work at the hospital, all hell broke loose. The hospital director started shouting at Andrej Strainar, asking where his sister-in-law was. Had she fallen ill and failed to call in? Andrej sent the hospital janitor to her home address to find out what was wrong. The janitor, a peasant boy from Dolenjska, with a trustful smile and clear blue eyes tried to extract some coherent piece of news from the frightened neighbors. At last, he hurried back to Dr. Strainar and reported what he had learned. They quickly guessed the rest. Andrej called General *Rupnik*, who called the Chief of the Ljubljana Police. Phones were ringing all morning and by mid-afternoon, Ada and Andrej were waiting for Marjana to get out of the underground cell of the Court

House, where the Germans kept prisoners often for an indefinite time without undergoing any court procedures, denying them all contact with the outside world. Marjana, however, was special. She was the sister-in-law of an important psychiatrist.

At last, at five o'clock on that gray Tuesday afternoon, Marjana walked free. She didn't talk about her night in prison, yet her bruised face spoke of the ordeal she had suffered. Andrej complained bitterly, and the two overeager SS officers were transferred to Maribor the following day. For her part, Marjana had reached a decision: no one would ever have another chance to lock her up. She had to make her path to freedom. But where could she find freedom in an occupied and fighting world?

~~~

The snow was knee deep and kept falling from the sky in heavy wet flakes, like scraps of white tissue blinding Valeria's view of the path ahead. She was cold and tired, her clothes and shoes drenched with icy water. The platoon stumbled on up an endless, winding path fraught with slippery rocks and protruding roots. The sharp pains in her legs had ceased a few hours ago. Now and then a stinging cramp would seize one of her feet, but she could not stop and wait for it to ease. Being the only female in the group, Valeria had to grit her teeth to keep up with the relentless pace of the men.

She felt sad and bitter. For the first time since she joined the unit, they were retreating after a lost fight. Two of her fellow combatants were killed and one wounded. For fear the wounded man would slow them down and let the Germans catch up with them, they hid their bleeding comrade in a small karst cave above the main road. Alone, with some painkillers and a bottle of brandy, he had to wait for a carrier. With the help of a local nurse, it might possible to organize his transport to the *Franja* Partisan Hospital, whose location remained a carefully guarded secret. Sometimes the fighters even wondered if its existence was more fata morgana than a real hospital.

Valeria could handle the fighting. It was straightforward. When men aimed their guns at her, all she had to do was shoot them before they killed her. In such moments, her blood would fill with cold calculation as she raised her rifle with a steady and firm grip, her brain focusing on the task ahead: shooting. She was really good at it. Valeria's marksmanship was better than any other fighter in the platoon. She proudly shot Jerries like rabbits. Her commander Joc was quick to acknowledge her skills. When there was a particularly tricky shot, Joc would ask Valeria to take it. The German uniforms with stripped insignia around the collar made a perfect target. She stopped keeping count. She must have hit at least a dozen men since she joined the partisans in the woods a month ago.

One would think that such prowess would make the men respect Valeria. However, they took every opportunity when their commander was not around to make jokes and laugh at her expense. It was degrading. Valeria felt hurt, but did not report it to Joc, their commander. Joc was his partisan name; in the unit, they all used nicknames and did not reveal their real names to each other for fear of betrayal under torture. Valeria changed her fake Italian name Gina to the diminutive of her real name – Valchy. Nobody could have guessed who she was and where she came from. When she spoke of her home, she spoke of cherry trees in blossom, cockerels singing in the morning, and hot corncobs grilled over late summer fires. After occupying the former Italian territories, the Germans, alarmed by the popularity of the *Liberation Front*, became meaner than junkyard dogs. For the death of each German soldier, they rounded up a dozen hostages among civilians and shot them, regardless of gender or age. Among the victims were old women and young children. For an angry Kraut, anybody could be helping the partisans, even a tiny baby.

Upon joining the partisans, Valeria deliberately burnt all bridges behind her. On her flight from Ljubljana, she destroyed the identity papers of Gina Novella; it was better if they caught her without papers than with the wrong ones. When she made it to the woods, the platoon was not too happy to welcome a woman in their group. They tried to get rid of her at every stop. However, after their first skirmish against the enemy, they saw she could shoot like a hunter and shut up. She also earned the respect of her commander Joc. He was a peasant from the Gorenjska region, a real hulk of a man in his forties. There were rumors among the men that he used to work as a mountain guide in the Julian Alps before the war. Indeed, he could find little hidden paths across the Cerkljansko hills like a wild goat. His receding hair was turning gray, and his brown eyes lost a bit of a sparkle every time one of his combatants was killed or wounded. He joined the first partisan units in 1941, and the men whispered about his wounds in the *Dražgoše* battle. Valeria admired him for his stern justice. She turned to him like to a father. On his part, he felt sorry that an eighteen-year-old girl must confront bloodshed and killing. Instead of facing death, she should have been facing suitors and choosing a lover. She was a lovely girl, so full of life. Often Joc would slip an extra piece of soap or another pair of warm socks in Valeria's hands, saying: "Take this, you brave little lady warrior." In such moments, his smile would reveal love and recognition. When Valeria first joined the unit, she got a full dark-green winter uniform with a coat, a pair of good quality warm boots a size too big, a rifle, a couple of hand grenades, and a Titovka, a green side cap with a shiny red star in the center. Like everyone in the platoon, she always turned her cap around before battle; she did not want the shiny star to make her forehead an easy target for their enemies. She was surprised that the partisan units were so well stocked with ammunitions and gear. Joc told her that they managed to confiscate the big warehouses in the caverns along the *Rapallo* border after the capitulation of Italy. The Italians had run home as quickly as possible and abandoned everything. And so the partisans had everything a soldier's heart could wish for: weapons, clothes, food, alcohol, and radio equipment. Indeed, at every stop, they ate canned tuna or sardines with biscuits, sometimes they even made real coffee or pasta with canned tomatoes – luxuries long forgotten in occupied and starved Ljubljana.

As much as Valeria got along with Joc and held the men in attention, Ivan, their political commissary and a fervent Communist, was another story. The tiny colorless man with thin blond hair, an oversized moustache for his tiny face, and cheeky gray eyes reminded Valeria of Gabrielle D'Annunzio. The similarity was particularly strong during Ivan's political speeches, when his inflated words resounded off the black trunks of the deep winter forests. From the moment Ivan and Valeria first set eyes on each other, there was no love lost between them. Ivan kept nagging Valeria that she was too weak, a nuisance to the troop, and a distraction to the fighting men. He had her under constant surveillance. She could not even retire to a private spot to wash herself because he suspected she would run away and betray them. Valeria was livid. She had a choice: to wash in front of the whole platoon or continue smelling fouler than a dung heap. Why was he being so difficult? Where did his hostility come from? For a while, Valeria hesitated. When she looked to

Joc for guidance, he simply shrugged. Obviously, Ivan indulged in privileges unknown to Valeria.

"All right, Ivan, here's what you've been waiting for," she said in a loud, firm voice. Then for the first time in her life, she slowly undressed in front of the whole platoon. She thoroughly washed her bra, underwear, and warm undershirt in the stream while the men stared with hungry, bulging eyes at her breasts and the dark bush between her legs.

"Stop gawking like apes, men," Joc said. "It's not as if you haven't seen a woman before, have you? Valchy, hurry up and finish your washing before the troop's morale sinks in the water next to your bra. Ivan, be sensible. I suggest we let Valchy wash separately in the future. After all, we are gentlemen, aren't we?"

Ivan just nodded absentmindedly. The girl had made a monkey out of him. He flashed Valeria an evil look that said he would not forget the event so easily. Defying the political commissary in the partisan army in the late autumn of 1943 was maybe a bit over the edge.

"No, my comrades, no more hide-and-seek. You've seen everything there is to see. I am one of you," retorted Valeria with a wicked smile.

"Uhuhu, not bad."

"So young, so firm. Christmas will come early for the guy who gets some of it."

Laughter traveled from face to face and released the tension. Valeria sensed she had won this round. If she could only tell them about her missions as an activist in the *Liberation Front* and the Italians she managed to scare off after performing their national anthem. Her mind was sharper than the razor Ivan used to trim his grayish Stalinist moustache. She could see through him as if he were a cellophane bag she used to quality-check at the *Brothers Tuma* printing shop. She despised Ivan's tedious political speeches on the Russians and their perfect society. She knew from Sanja that the Soviet Union was far from perfect and Stalin an ageing monster. However, she kept her mouth shut. There would be time enough for the truth once the Germans were beaten. Now, she had to listen to Ivan grunting behind her back.

"Come on, girl, quickly! Do you want the Jerries to find us?"

On the last atoms of her energy, Valeria quickened her pace. Why was Ivan always walking behind them all? Deep down, she suspected he was a bragger and a bluff, nothing but a shitty coward. He probably always took position in the back in case they were ambushed. Valeria frequently observed that as soon as the shooting started, Ivan slipped into a hideout to watch his fellow partisans during the fight. He rarely fired his weapon, as though to avoid revealing his position to the enemy. She loathed him as a man; he was a coward, brave only in words. She made up her mind to report him to Joc tonight: while bullets hissed over their heads and everyone was sweating blood, Ivan had stayed hiding under the thick crown of a pine.

"Ah, girls are nothing but trouble."

"Silence in the back," Joc barked. Ivan shut up. Valeria held back a tiny smile. Luckily, Joc knew how to deal with political loudmouths like Ivan. She was lucky to fight under his command.

"Valchy, to the front!" Joc's order meant there was a target again. She raced through the ranks of tired men to reach the head of the line. In spite of the heavy snowfall, her eyes perceived a tiny little village with a church across the white field. A guard in peasant clothes with a funny cap was walking along its wall, shivering in the cold blizzard.

"There, can you see the man by the wall?"

"You mean the peasant boy?" Valeria guessed the fellow could not be older than her little brother Franjo. A boy of fifteen, maybe sixteen.

"Shoot him!"

"But Joc, he's only a kid!"

"He's a Home Guard. If he sees us first, he'll run for reinforcements – then we're dead. Fire! That's an order!"

Valeria aimed and, for the first time in her life, her hand shivered. She steadied her grip and pulled the trigger. The boy fell like a clay pigeon. When she put her weapon down, she looked at Joc with tears in her eyes. He tapped her on the shoulder.

"It's war, Valchy. You have taken an oath."

Valeria nodded in silence. Turning around, she let her comrades go first. How could she forget the oath of enlistment with the partisans?

"I, Valchy, a partisan of the National Liberation Army of Slovenia, will fight together with the Workers' and Peasants' Red Army of the Soviet Union and all other nations struggling for freedom, for the liberation and unity of the Slovenian nation, for brotherhood and unity among nations and peoples, for a better future for all working men. I hereby solemnly swear before my nation and my comrades that I will devote all my forces and abilities to free the Slovenian nation and every working man and woman, and to support and defend progress and freedom-loving humanity in the sacred war against Fascist occupiers and barbarians. Herewith, I also affirm that I will not abandon my partisan formation, in which I enlisted of my own free will and personal conviction, and that I will not put down arms until total victory over the Fascist and Nazi occupiers and the freedom of all Slovenian people have come to pass. And last, I state under oath that I will defend with my blood and sacrifice my own life for the honor and integrity of our partisan flag. Power to our fight! Life for freedom!"

She hurriedly wiped her cheeks. The oath didn't mention killing peasant boys protecting their church. There was a sentence about uniting all Slovenians, though. She felt a black stain in her soul, as though a single shot had branded her life forever. It hurt despite the fact that the boy was on the enemy's side. Her reason told her that the Home Guard collaborated with the Nazis as the *Milizia Volontaria Anti Comunista* did with the Italians. However, the enemy she just shot felt different. The boy was a target she hit inside her body – a target whose center was deep in her soul. When she lifted her head to catch Joc's understanding look, her eyes surprisingly met Ivan's watchful gray ones.

"At least, Ivan, I can shoot," she hissed in a low voice, "unlike others who hide their asses under the pines."

A couple of men chuckled in their beards, grasping the allusion.

Ivan stiffened and said in a low voice, "Women don't know a thing about politics."

"Silence!" Joc ordered.

Hidden behind thick hazel bushes, the partisans waited to see if anyone came running to retrieve the boy. They wanted to observe how many Home Guards were there. After a while, only a priest in a long black robe came out of the church and, seeing the body, crossed himself. The partisans heard him shout something. Women and old men came out of the houses. Valeria saw a woman kneel next to the body and heard her cry in mortal pain. Her heart missed a beat. The boy's mother! My God, what had she done? Valeria thought of her own mother and brother. Terror overwhelmed her: all the Germans, those invaders, she had killed had mothers and sisters, too. Bloody war! It was time to end it.

~~~

Two weeks after *Saint Nicholas*, the nicest feast day before Christmas, Valeria was keeping watch during a cold, cloudless night. She wondered about the children in Slovenia, whether *Saint Nicholas* would bring gifts and sweets to them as was the custom. The stars shone brightly and twinkled among the sleek pine branches cracking under the thick snow. The moon was almost full, its silver beams playing with the snow crystals on the plain. The woods, like an open stage in a theater, was illuminated by the glittery shine.

The show, however, was a tragedy. In spite of all their losses, the Germans continued the war as though there were no tomorrow. Valeria counted herself lucky for surviving the previous week, originally meant to be a winter rest.

Their platoon had climbed to Mount Blegoš so that the partisans could get some rest, wash and dry their clothes, cook a few warm meals, and sleep for a couple of days in one of the cottages. However, on the second morning, the Germans surrounded the cottage and a plane bombed it from the air. Luckily, a steep overhanging slope walled one of the corners of the hut. The woods, thick with climbing pines and bushes, offered them enough cover to get away. Not everyone, though. Three of their comrades lost their lives on Blegoš. At Leskovica, a small village, they informed the courier about the German ambush, but Joc was reluctant to disclose where they were heading. The boy told them that Cerkno was safe: the Germans were concentrating all their troops in the north where they were obviously preparing for another offensive. And so they returned to Cerkno, following the little wild trails in the woods. It was arduous to march in the knee-deep snow.

Despite the cold, Joc forbade the men to light a cigarette or a fire when they camped. Only a bottle of strong fruit brandy was passed around in the shelter that they hastily built from pine branches and held fast with wet snow.

Valeria was freezing at her post,. A branch cracked at the lower end of the slope near the stream; she stiffened to attention. Aiming her rifle in that direction, she peered through the scope and saw a man with a Titovka cap climbing the hill toward her. He seemed strongly built, although not too tall; more importantly, he was alone.

The cap meant nothing, so Valeria kept her aim steadily on his forehead until he was close enough for her to cry out.

"Halt! Give the watchword!"

Trembling, the man hid behind a thick trunk. He could not see Valeria and did not know whether she was a partisan or a Home Guard. But the voice came from a woman. He relaxed; the Home Guard did not have women in their units, so it must be Joc's platoon. The aim of his visit was to share the latest news of the developments and lead them to join the rest of the Notranjska Battalion.

"A tit has flown on a branch up high ..."

They both breathed easily again. The watchword, a verse from a popular children's folk song, was right.

Valeria added the second verse: "...and sang a song of joy and cheer ..."

She put down the rifle and waited until the man came closer.

"Hello, I'm Borko. I come from the Slovene National Liberation Committee of the *Liberation Front* with wonderful news for all of us."

Valeria looked into his blue eyes. Like all of them, he had a nom de guerre.

"You're not telling me the war is over, are you?"

Borko's smile showed a row of white teeth. His light hair curled at the edge of the cap that he took off. "And who are you, comrade? Is this a women's battalion or Joc's unit?"

"I am Valchy, a partisan like any other," retorted Valeria in a cold voice. "We're the 3rd Platoon of the Notranjska Batallion. Well, at least the ones who are left."

Knitting his brows Borko asked: "Have you lost many fighters?"

"Since I joined the troop around two months ago, seven men have either died or have been wounded. There are eighteen of us left, nineteen including you. I am the only woman."

She looked him in the eyes and he held her green gaze. What was this beautiful girl with a rifle doing on sentinel duty? Where were the men?

"Can you shoot, Valchy?"

"I could've shot you in your left eye while you were looking from behind the trunk of that pine. Yeah, Borko, I can shoot. You're lucky I also saw the Titovka on your head or you'd be food for worms."

Borko sighed. His conservative sexist views had become obsolete in the face of atrocities. Women, children, old people – all were part of this bloody circus either as victims or as fighters. He respected women who decided to act. He moved closer and reached out for a friendly embrace.

"Thank you, Valchy. Thank you for your bravery and thank you for my life."

She leaned against his hard chest, alarmed to feel her heart beating like crazy. She closed her eyes. She realized how lonely she had been. Her days revolved around obeying orders, killing, and running. There was no place for sympathy or friendship. Despite the many partisans who tried to maintain polite camaraderie with her, she could use a real friend.

Their embrace lasted too long. At last, Borko broke away.

"Will you lead me to the shelter?"

Valeria straightened up and blew a series of whistles. Shortly, Joc appeared. Recognizing Borko, he stretched out his hand in greeting.

"You're lucky she has not blown your head off, Borko. This is Valchy, our best shot."

Borko nodded. "We've met, thank you."

Joc threw his arm around Borko's shoulder and led him away, saying: "Valchy, half an hour more, then I'll send Mato to replace you. We've lighted a fire in the cave nearby. It is very warm inside."

Valeria smiled in reply. The hills were half karstic and full of natural caves, which provided excellent hiding places. Stalagmites and stalactites shining in wonderful yellow, orange, and white colors filled many of the caves. Their greatest fear was, should the enemy track them down, they would get trapped in the cave. However, the nights spent inside were comfortable. They could build a fire since the smoke went up the narrow slits between the rocks without ever emerging to the open and betraying them. In the small hours of that frosty day, Valeria curled up in the corner of the cave and soon fell asleep in spite of her grumbling stomach. In the other corner, Borko and Joc were whispering secrets about the war, yet few men in the platoon cared to eavesdrop. The long march took the better part of their strength away.

The following day Borko led them to a lonely farm on the valley of the Sora River. Wet and cold, they entered the barn. Out of nowhere, two young women brought them a huge pot of thick heavenly-smelling *jota* spiced with rosemary, pork cracklings, and smoked ribs. Loaves of fresh bread cheered them up. As the evening approached, Borko told them the news on the front line.

"The Allies have finally started sending ammunition and medical staff to our troops. Roosevelt, Churchill, and our friend Stalin have officially recognized the Slovene Partisan Army as a force against the Axis. What else could they do after the resolutions of the second meeting of the Anti-Fascist Council for the National Liberation of Yugoslavia or, in short, *AVNOJ*? On November 29th and 30th, 1943, delegates from all six counties, representing the people of the former Kingdom of Yugoslavia, met in Jajce, a little Bosnian town that lies in the free zone. The plenum reached decisions that will improve our lives for good: Slovenians, Croatians, Serbians, Montenegrins, Bosnians, and Macedonians. After the war, we will create a federal Yugoslavia, a democratic state acknowledging all human and nationality rights. We will elect a temporal government for each territory. Marshal *Tito* will lead us as head of the National Committee of the Liberation of Yugoslavia. The meeting has revoked the Yugoslavian government-in-exile and has denied King Petar II *Karadjordjevič*'s return to Yugoslavia – as least until after the war when we can hold a referendum on the monarchy's status. All German population and all collaborators of the occupiers will be evicted and their property seized by the state. It is the beginning of a new era for all of us."

Everyone stared at Borko in wonder. His words sounded encouraging, yet the men knew they had to walk many marches and fight many battles before the Germans were beaten. All these new alliances only proved how powerful the invaders were compared to the Allies.

At last, Joc said, "Thank you, Borko. We will do our duty. Let's cheer for the new Yugoslavia!"

A bottle of sweet wine from Vipava moistened the lips of the tired fighters. Only two pairs of eyes maintained their clarity in their vision of the future, maybe a future together. Borko searched for Valeria's hand under a heap of hay and gently squeezed it. She gave him an understanding look. They could not deny their love to each other, but they had to hide it from their comrades. Partisans should fight, not fall in love.

~~~

Valeria's platoon joined the Notranjska Batallion and engaged in several fierce battles to liberate the territories left of *Isonzo*. Borko had to leave and their parting was sad. Although they had no way to live their love amidst the horrors, they both floated on clouds of powerful emotions. Borko was Valeria's first love, the man she had been waiting for her whole life. Full of yearning, she started to write poetry in the little notebook that Borko gave her shortly after Christmas when he went to face new challenges and carry out new orders. He was a member of the new intelligence division within the Slovene National Liberation Committee, a kind of spy, a man of many faces, who traveled between the woods and the cities, always changing his identity like a chameleon. Valeria was the least concerned about it. It was part of wartime normality. Didn't she change names and papers almost daily in order to serve the *Liberation Front*? She had even confided in Borko some of her more successful coups against the Fascists. He knew who she truly was anyway, so there was no point in keeping secrets. On one of their lonely night watches, when they stole a kiss or two from the stars, he asked whether she was willing to return to Ljubljana and occasionally do some undercover work for him. Valeria did not have to think twice. She would go through fire if he asked her to.

The spring of 1944 brought supplies from the Allies' and new hope to the tired partisan formations. They managed to liberate a large territory south of Ljubljana where the provisional Communist government had set up schools, cultural life, and political propaganda. They wanted to reach every Slovenian and persuade them to fight against the Nazis. However, the Home Guards, *Chetniks*, and other opponents of the Communists were numerous and continued to grow like mushrooms after rain.

While the partisans liberated most of the countryside and the thick woods of Gorjanci Hills, the Germans tenaciously held out against them in the towns. The citizens of Ljubljana lived under their terror and the threat that the Allies might bomb the city, particularly after the Americans dropped bombs on Floridsdorf near Vienna in March. Everyone was extremely nervous. Intelligence and radio news reported that the Allies planned to invade the French Atlantic coast soon, which would open another battle line for the Germans after Italy and the Eastern Front.

On Hitler's fifty-fifth birthday, April 20th 1944, thousands of the Slovenian Home Guard, also called the Legion of Death, gathered at the *Bežigrad* Stadium, the biggest multi-purpose stadium in the city, and swore a solemn oath to fight against the Communists and the

Partisans.

The news was devastating. Instead of joining forces, the nation had split into various factions, their forces spent and burnt like splinters on a funeral pyre. Valeria could not stop seeing the image of the boy she had shot in front of the village church a couple of months ago. Her only consolation was that the Notranjska Batallion was moving into the territories where the Home Guard did not join the Germans, mainly the Primorska and Gorenjska regions. There only the Civic Guard remained to fight the partisans. They were protecting villages, farmers, and their property against numerous partisan raids, in which Communist freedom fighters confiscated food from the peasants, often leaving them to starve. The cleft between the two major Slovenian formations and ideologies had grown so deep that it would outlive the war.

One sunny spring morning, Joc called for Valeria.

"Valchy, are you ready?"

She flashed a brave smile. "I'm as ready as I can ever be, Commander. What is it this time?"

Joc smiled broadly. "Borko wants you to come to Ljubljana and help him in one of his operations. You'll be a city girl again."

Valeria's face lit up and her eyes shone with anticipation. She tried her best not to display too much excitement.

"Well, that will be like transforming a frog into a princess. Look how dirty and unkempt I am! I need a week to wash and clean myself."

Joc looked at her with thoughtful interest. "Is that the first thing you worry about, Valchy? You have no questions about your papers, the location, or what tasks are in store for you? I'll never understand women."

She sighed deeply. She wanted to tell Joc that he would never survive undercover work in a city. The essence of deceit revolved around one's appearance. And she looked awful. Disheveled and scruffy, she would immediately incite the unwanted attention of the first German guard who came upon her. Or maybe Joc suspected she wanted to look her best when she met Borko again. She decided to put his mind at ease.

"Dear Joc, you're the bravest partisan I know, but I have to say you know nothing about intelligence work. Appearance is everything. Unless I dress and look normal, I'll get shot at the first checkpoint."

Joc realized the girl was right. They had come to look at women fighters as one of the men. Of course, when women and men marched, fought, slept, and lived so closely together, stirrings of love occasionally emerged despite the rules of celibacy. Relationships were stifled the moment they were discovered, the couples divided and sent to different units. Joc sensed there was something at play between Borko and Valchy, but they never outwardly displayed anything but camaraderie. Valchy had a point, though: she couldn't go to Ljubljana in her muddy boots and thick overcoat. Borko had left this part of the operation to him.

"Do you know a place where you can get new clothes and have your hair done?"

Valchy shook her head. "No, my village has been burnt twice and my folks can hardly make ends meet. The only friend I have is in Ljubljana."

Joc scratched his head impatiently. "Well, you can't go to Ljubljana looking like that this."

"How much time do I have?"

"Borko needs you a week from today. Can you find your way to Idrija alone without getting caught?"

"I guess so. We've been on the town's outskirts a couple of times together."

"All right, here's what you will do: go to Idrija and see my friend, Karmen Komac. She teaches French, German, and Italian there. She gives private lessons to children who are applying to prep school. Karmen has traveled around Europe and knows the ways of the world. She lives alone and occasionally helps the resistance. However, she's not a party member and is very critical of Communists. So be careful of what you tell her."

Valchy nodded. "Joc, you don't have to worry. I've survived almost a year in Ljubljana. The undercover missions I was entrusted with were all very dangerous. No one knows anything about it, not even you. What's Karmen's address? Will you write me a letter of introduction?"

Joc liked it when Valchy stood up for herself. Strong women impressed him. Besides, she knew how to do it without offending him.

"Karmen Komac lives in the big Miner's House next to Anthony's Shaft. You know, the mercury mine. The excavation profits are now filling German pockets, I guess. The Italians have already filled theirs, the bastards."

Valeria touched Joc's elbow lightly. "Write the letter for Karmen while I get ready. Where do I leave my weapons?"

Soon they had everything arranged. Valeria's false papers joined Borko's letter. This time, her name was Andrea Maleo, born in Udine. Her picture was pinned next to her birth date and address. She breathed in deeply; whoever was in charge of her new identity was an amateur fool. In Italy, Andrea was a male name. Well, it would have to pass for a girl now. Valeria shook hands with her comrades and started off on her lonely march. She was almost glad when the heavy clouds broke into heavy rain. Because of the weather, few Germans and fewer Home Guards would leave their warm dwellings. Better to be wet than discovered.

Karmen Komac turned out to be a middle-aged woman, close to Marjana's age, and a true woman of the world. Joc was not exaggerating. Without asking a lot of questions, she helped Valeria change from a ragged freedom fighter into a stunning, modern-city woman. First, she dyed Valeria's hair to almost red using ground canna seeds and egg yolks, then she twisted the locks into a stylish chignon split at the nape into two parts: one falling down Valeria's back, the other reaching to her forehead in a soft curly mass. She dressed her in a dark green woolen dress with regular side pleats and a row of buttons in the middle. Fashionable brown high heels, a purse, and a matching brown belt that displayed Valeria's narrow waist assembled the outfit. Food scarcity and all the marching had made Valeria lose her curves. Nothing was left to chance – not even the silken underwear in champagne and elegant black stockings. Valeria had to spend hours dipping her hands and feet in milk seasoned with lemon juice before she could touch the delicate garments. She bleached her teeth with baking soda and exfoliated her cheeks with melted honey. After scraping the honey off her face, Valeria licked every drop of it, mumbling her approval at such a treat amidst the war and hunger. Karmen explained that many clients could not pay her money, so they brought her food instead.

After three days, Valeria mounted the bus for Ljubljana. The first inspection of her papers could have almost gone wrong.

"Is Andrea not a name for a boy in Italy?" asked the German SS officer who was checking her passport at the stop in Logatec.

"I am the fourth daughter, and my father wished so much for a son," replied Valeria in broken German with the most charming smile she could fake.

"You should consider yourself lucky not to be German, Andrea. In that case your name would be Fritz or Klaus," replied the man in the black uniform and gallantly gave her back her papers. A last bow and a kind smile, then he turned to another passenger.

Valeria had to go to the printing shop first. Then, in the evening, to the address Borko indicated in his letter to Joc. Reveling in her new elegant self, she walked with a light step along the Ljubljanica River, where birds chased each other with lively cries amidst the falling branches of the century-old willows. The surface of the river was smooth and mirrored the green trees along the banks. At the *Ljubljanica Sluice Gate* on Poljanska Street, she stopped to lean on the railing and observe the slow-flowing river. What did the future have in store for her? What was the reason behind Borko's request for her assistance? Did he love her the way she loved him?

As Valeria daydreamed about how their meeting again after so many months would go, she barely noticed that all the windows of the printing shop were dark, the door shut and locked with a thick chain. There was no chatter of printing machines. Only menacing silence echoed in the light spring breeze sweeping the yard. Valeria quickened her pace and hid in the shadow of the trees in a nearby park. She walked around the shop a couple of times, but nothing stirred inside. She grew more worried by the minute. The address she had memorized was on the other side of the town, twenty minutes away. What would she do the whole day? Given her lack of money, she couldn't even go to a pub. The cinemas started later. She felt like a sitting duck. As she racked her brains about how to kill time, the only person she could trust came to mind – and she decided to pay her a visit.

Ada answered the door immediately as though she were expecting her. She looked at her friend with disbelief. Then her face widened into a smile.

"Valeria, thank God, you're alive! Oh, and you look every inch a lady! Where did you come from? Milan? Paris?"

Valeria threw her arms around Ada's round body. "Hello, my dear. You look wonderful. Blooming...How are you feeling?"

Ada laughed and tapped her round belly. "I'm fine, thank you. But what happened to you, Valeria? You look like a French model. Have you found yourself a Rockefeller husband?"

"No such thing, Ada. I'm still free as a bird." Valeria wriggled her fingers to show she had no rings on them.

"That may change soon. That hair color really suits you. I guess you're here under a new identity."

"I do. My name is Andrea."

"You mean 'Andrea' like a man or 'Andreja' like a woman?"

"Who cares? They can't arrest me for my name, can they?"

"Be careful, Valeria. They arrested Marjana on *All Saints' Day* last year. They took her in the middle of the night. That one night has changed her completely. They beat her up, and it has since then fueled her rage. We cannot discuss politics now, you know, and it's breaking my heart. My dear sister. She has suffered so much. Please, go and see her, will you? She's working long hours in the hospital, so maybe in the evening. I suspect she has secretly joined the *Liberation Front*."

Valeria felt guilt-ridden. Her friend had to go to prison in her place. "How is she now, Ada?"

"Fine, I guess. She rarely comes to visit. Well, Andrej sees her almost every day at work. He says she is the engine running the hospital."

Valeria nodded; she'd always thought Marjana would join the *Liberation Front* one day. In small Partisan hospitals in the woods, they needed trained medical staff badly. Not to speak of secret volunteers to smuggle medicines, bandages, compresses, and instruments.

"How is Andrej? Is he still with the Home Guard? They've sworn an oath to the Führer, Ada!"

"I know. Andrej avoided that gathering. He was on duty at the hospital that Thursday on April 20th."

Valeria looked at her friend's face inquisitively. "But he hasn't left them. He still works for them, doesn't he?"

Ada hastily replied, "It's mostly medical work like treating the wounded and administering medicines to the sick. I'm so frightened. Sometimes he's away for many days in a row without so much as a word. I don't know what I would do if..."

Valeria had to control herself. Wounded partisans had little chance to survive since they lacked professional medical treatment and medicines. They were left alone in some cave or wood cabin until someone could come and take them to a secret hospital. The Home Guard had doctors treating them and hospital beds they could lie in.

In spite of her seemingly comfortable life, compared to Valeria's winter in the woods, she felt sorry for Ada, who was helpless and lonely. Is love in such times worth living? Her friend ended up pregnant without finishing her studies and had never had a job. However, Ada's cheeks gleamed with the aura of approaching motherhood. In a way, she looked like an angel ... like the mother of all mothers: Virgin Mary. Her love made her blind to reality. Like Andrej collaborating with the Nazis. Valeria had to take precautions. She had better leave this apartment immediately. One last question:

"Where's Sanja? I thought I would find her here with you."

"Oh, Sanja ... You don't know, of course. Before Christmas, she left for America. Since the occupation, Germans have been spying on anyone who might have Jewish ancestors or who had been to Russia before the war. Everyone knows Sanja lived and performed in the Soviet Union for many years. She had to leave in haste, really. Her Italian colleagues arranged for her to travel via Trieste to Marseille. She found a passage to Casablanca and finally to the United States. Although they say the Axis controls the Mediterranean and the Atlantic, it looks like ships still sail to America. Well, we were awfully worried for a month, then we received her letter through one of Andrej's friend. She is safe, thank God. You cannot imagine, Valeria, how it is. Germans suspect everyone and everything. We cannot listen to the radio, we – "

The doorbell cut off her words. Ada looked at the old clock in the hall. It was not yet four o'clock in the afternoon. Andrej usually came home at seven. A moment later, they heard a key turning in the lock. Valeria and Ada looked at each other.

"Quickly, into the bedroom," whispered Ada. "Andrej may not be alone. You better hide somewhere – under the bed or on the little balcony."

Valeria rushed into the room and squeezed herself under the double bed in the middle of the room. She would sneak out the moment she had the chance. Clouds of dust and dirt soiled her elegant dress and filled her lungs with the heavy smell of grime. She lay on her back, using her soft napa leather bag as a pillow and her coat as a blanket. It was important she remained calm. She could hear voices from the kitchen, yet could not say many people there were. Of course, Ada would come and get her once it was safe. She had to report to Borko's given address in the evening, just before the curfew.

What a frustrating day full of ugly surprises. After a while, tiredness overcame her. She stopped listening to the voices and noises, relaxed, and fell asleep. The squeaking and creaking of springs woke her up sometime later. She opened her eyes and couldn't see a thing. It was dark. She had overslept and missed her meeting with Borko.

"I'm sorry, Andrej. I'm really not in the mood tonight." Ada's distressed whisper reached Valeria's ears.

'Oh, no, he can't be serious,' she thought. 'Isn't she pregnant?'

She could hear nothing but the sound of kissing. The bed stirred lightly. His fingers were probably fondling Ada through her nightgown.

"I'll be very gentle. I promise you'll like it, darling," Andrej said in a sweet voice. She shuddered. Should she come out and let him know she was there?

"But we might harm the baby," Ada said almost in tears.

Then silence... They were kissing and touching each other probably. At last, Andrej's explanation came to Valeria's weary ears.

"No, our baby will like it, too. Intimacy is healthy for mothers and babies. Besides, it is not due for another couple of months. And you're so exciting, so sexy... I'm crazy about you. I love you so much, Ada."

"I love you too, darling. But..."

Again, everything went quiet. After a moment, which to Valeria seemed like an eternity, Andrej spoke.

"I need you, Ada, today more than ever."

"Why? Did something happen at the hospital?"

"Do you remember that little peasant girl – no more than twelve – who was raped together with her mother and grandmother by a troop of vicious bandits?"

"Of course, baby, you've been treating her for what... something like eight months?"

"I failed. She committed a suicide." After a pause, Andrej's voice sounded harsh and angry. "We found her body hanging in the shower today. Bloody criminals! They should be hanging, not her – every one of them!"

Valeria froze. Whatever happened now, she couldn't leave her hiding place until Andrej was out of the flat. Her presence might also put Ada in trouble. Poor Ada! She knew Valeria was hiding somewhere in the room and could hear their every breath and moan. What a disaster!

"Don't cry, Andrej! You did your best. It was simply too hard for the girl to live with such a burden. God, how I hate violent, irresponsible brutes! Wild beasts, not human beings. I hate them and I hate this war."

Valeria could hear them sobbing together. She could not stop the tears sliding down her cheeks, too.

"While we are so happy, Ada, about to have our first baby...the girl, she was so frail, as thin as a shadow, her wide eyes filled with sadness...she hung herself with an electric wire. She tore it from the wall installation. I...I was her doct–"

"Andrej, darling, it's not your fault. You were trying to help her. You were doing your best. You know the body can be healed, the members and tissues put together, while the soul is easily lost forever. Please, Andrej..."

This time the silence lasted longer than before. Valeria wondered if they had fallen asleep at last. Maybe Ada could comfort her husband with tenderness and love. Valeria started to think about how to get out of the apartment. She could slip out of the room, then silently open the front door...Or she could hide in the cellar until morning, then sneak out and run to her meeting. It was better not to walk the streets during curfew hours.

"I need you so much, darling..."

"I need you, too, baby..."

The mattress moved, the bed frame screeched. Valeria froze. Oh, my God, they were doing it. They were making love.

"Uhuhuhuh...uh...uh"

"Am I hurting you?"

"No, no, baby...it's just so..."

"I know."

The stillness meant they were kissing. Valeria's heart was beating like a drum. She could smell of the heat of their bodies, the smell she remembered from her parents' bedroom when she was a little girl. Their soft sighs and the little noises of their parting lips almost made her taste their kisses. She closed her eyes and imagined Borko's lips on hers, his sharp taste of tobacco sweet and sour like a cherry. The squeaking of the bed springs became an orchestra to the aria of joyful moans and sighs on the bed. Her eyes wide open and her senses fully alert, Valeria shivered with lust. The warmth and wetness between her legs made her feel ashamed. What was this? Was she transcending into the body of her best friend? She felt panic rise in her mind as the bed creaked and banged loudly against the wall. It was about to break into pieces just like her brain was about to explode. At last, Andrej came with a loud cry. In a second, all was quiet. The room sank in the warm darkness of the night. Valeria's eyes filled with tears of gratitude. She choked to stifle a sob.

'Thank you, Ada. What a friend you are!'

~~~

After a sleepless night on the floor under the Strainars' bed, Valeria washed and put her clothes in order before she left Ada late that morning. After Andrej left, the girlfriends ate their breakfast in silence. Neither of them wanted to bring up the events of the night. At the door, Ada, on the brink of tears, put her arms around Valeria.

"Valeria, I love you. You're my best friend. No matter what political views made Andrej join the Home Guard. I am his wife, but I use my own head and have my own opinion. You know, you're always welcome here, don't you?"

Valeria hugged her tightly. She was so close she could feel the baby kicking inside her friend. A kick in her heart, a kick in her soul. Life and love can move mountains.

"Ada, I know," she whispered in her ear.

"Be careful, Valeria. You're walking on thin ice."

"Don't worry about me. I'm a survivor. You take care, and best wished for the great event. Kiss the kicker for me, will you?"

They parted, and Valeria went to the assigned address. When she stepped into the hall of the old apartment building near the city stadium, the click-clack of her high heels brought a tall, rough man out of the cellar. His tiny prying eyes stared at her bluntly.

"What are you doing here, madam?"

"Visiting."

"Who?"

Valeria couldn't give Borko's name for she did not know what kind of cover story he had made up for them. She still tried to be polite. Just in case.

"Thank you for your interest, sir. I'll be off now."

The man nodded, not too happy with Valeria's taciturn reply. "Well, I just want to warn you. There are bandits living in this building, men who walk in and out during curfew. The Jerries have surely noticed it. The next time they come knocking, I won't be surprised if they arrest all of us."

Valeria could detect fear in his voice. Everyone feared for his life these days. She tried to sound more encouraging.

"Thank you, sir. Don't worry, I am no bandit as you can see, and I'm sure not visiting one. Have a nice day!"

Grumbling, the man replied something, but Valeria started to climb the stairs and his words were lost in the sound of her heels. She had the floor and apartment number memorized. It was a moment of utmost concentration. She had to watch her every step in order to avoid any trap laid by the counterintelligence or, even worse, betraying her lead. The man in the hall was a nuisance; unless he returned to the cellar, he would block her escape route.

She rang the bell. The door opened. Two strong arms drew her into the apartment. Her breath caught. What – ? Then she felt Borko kissing her on the lips. She nearly fainted. Her legs turned to jelly. Her mind seemed to melt in the heat of fear and passion. Still, Valeria protested halfheartedly, saying they were at war and had no time for love. Borko silenced her with more kisses.

"I love you, Valchy. Let's get married once the war is over."

Valeria's heart was beating loudly. In her head, she could still hear the banging of Ada's bed from last night. She felt ashamed as she remembered the lust she felt at the thought of him. She was in love, but her dreams of love were misplaced. It could not be.

"Borko, this is not the time …"

"Darling, we don't know whether we'll be still alive tomorrow. It's now or never." He started whispering sweet nonsense in her ears and kissing her neck tenderly. Valeria gave in and returned his kisses. Still, her mind would not follow her heart.

"I don't know, Borko."

Suddenly, he understood what she was saying. Valeria was so young. "Is this your first time, Valchy?"

Like a helpless child, she looked into his pale blue eyes. "Yes. Sorry, I – "

"Oh, my Valchy, my brave little girl. You're so mine, only mine …" His passionate hands became gentler. He murmured into her red curls: "Besides, we must do it, darling. It's our cover. We are Mr. Janez and Mrs. Marija Novak. At least, on our papers …"

Valeria's breasts were bursting with excitement, her belly arched in desire. She surrendered. They made love that morning, and all the following mornings and nights, too. Like a happily married couple. Their nights echoed with sighs of lust while days went by in hectic action.

Their job was to smuggle important resistance fighters out of Ljubljana – lawyers, doctors, and teachers who chose to work with the *Liberation Front* and the Communists and whose knowledge was necessary to build a new provisory government. It was important that their departure for the liberated territories around Kočevje took place in secrecy and provided solid alibis. Otherwise, their families would be put in great danger. The police and SS spies mingled among normal people like harmless poisonous flies on a soggy summer afternoon. The Nazis continued to ravage the towns, taking and shooting prisoners or sending them to the work camps. The Allied invasion of Normandy and the obvious fact that Germany was losing the war proved to be gasoline spilt on fire. Many soldiers in Germany had lost their homes and families during the fierce Allied bombing of German cities. Here, in a foreign country, they often witnessed their comrades being killed by Partisan bullets. It made them all murderous, deadly with their proverbially precise efficiency. Life wasn't worth a schilling.

Valeria paid Ada a visit a few more times, carefully avoiding a meeting with Andrej. When Ada gave birth to a healthy boy in July, she did not dare visit and only sent flowers and a christening gown embroidered with a dark blue lace pattern for little Martin. Ada thanked her in a letter. Reading between the lines, Valeria understood that Andrej had tightened his bonds with the Home Guard, whose members came to be regular guests in their house. It was a warning for Valeria not to visit them.

Valeria was enjoying her days of happiness that untwisted in short moments. Borko soon opened up to her, recounting his life before the war. He had finished his studies in History and Philosophy in Vienna and used to teach at the Klagenfurt grammar school. The Nazis fired him after the Anschluss, and he fled over the border to Yugoslavia. Many Slovenian families had to leave their homes because Hitler wanted every inch of Carinthia to be German. Not without some difficulties, Borko found a teaching job in Ljubljana where he joined the Communist Party. He had faith that only the Communists were powerful enough to stop the German invasion. In 1939, the pact between Stalin and Hitler shattered his as well as the trust of many of his colleagues. Only a few parrot-like officials continued to blindly repeat Stalin's foolish mantra of peace between Germans and Russians, the superiority and collaboration of their nations against corrupt Western forces. Borko experienced the Nazi terror and knew well that Hitler wanted the world for himself. Borko, whose real name was Boris Lukman from Kapla, a village on Drava River, refused to support such ideology.

"I quit the party then, but joined again later. The pact was absurd. Hitler and Stalin massacred Poland, dividing it like an apple pie. All the while, our Communist leaders praised their pact as a guarantee of peace. Crazy! All of Europe watched while people were being shot next door," said Borko angrily.

"Oh, Borko, the whole world also praised Wilson for annexing half of Slovenia, Istria, and Dalmatia to Italy. Those black shirts, the shitty cowards, they ran from Caporetto in 1917 like there would be no tomorrow, then came back with the pomp of glorious invaders. That crazy poet and warrior D'Annunzio and his drinking buddies terrorized Rijeka for years and nobody lifted a finger. Besides, what is Europe, Borko?"

"You're right, Valchy," replied Borko. "Without the Blitz and Pearl Harbor there would be no Allied forces. What do Americans care about the French, Dutch, Serbians, or Slovenians? What do they care about poor Jewish people? They knew about the Pogrom and the concentration camps. What did they do? Nothing, nothing but sit on their fat well-fed asses."

Valeria loved their political discussions. At last, she had somebody she completely trusted. There was so much weight on her soul, so much anxiety and horror. She needed to talk about it.

"Yes, the bloody Italians ... A friend of mine worked as a children's nurse on the island of Rab, where the Italians had set up concentration camps for people from the Karst, Primorska, and other regions. They settled their immigrants from southern Italy on the farms there. People said those southerners were so poor that they marched into the houses with bare feet. The horrors of the camp were such that my friend lost her mind. It took her almost a year to return to herself. Those starving children dying with questions in their eyes ..."

Valeria could not hold back her tears at the thought of Marjana. Borko tried to console her. He knew everything about Valeria's friends. When he returned under the wing of the Communist Party, the leaders sent him to Moscow to train as an intelligence officer.

His knowledge of German and his inquisitive talent soon made him an important VOS (Slovenian Communist secret service) operation commander. He felt sorry for Valeria when he saw how fragile she was in spite of her brave posturing. After all, she was only eighteen. Life had not been kind to either her or her family. He couldn't help but hold back the sad information about Kozjane that he had picked from his contacts the other day: the Germans had arrested her father and her mother. Deported, nobody knew where. He embraced her and hid his face in her hair. In between sobs, Valeria asked in a low voice:

"Will they ever be punished for what they've done?"

~~~

By the end of July, Borko and Valeria had completed their assignment. They marched with their last group to Bela Krajina, to the enclave of freedom. At their departure, the night was as bright as day. The full moon illuminated the atmosphere cleaned by the afternoon storm that had washed away the summer dust. The peaks and crowns of trees marked the line of the horizon as sharply as a pen would mark it on a sheet of paper. At the post below the village Orle, they changed from their city clothes into uniforms and heavy boots. Unfortunately, the weather changed. Heavy clouds hid the moon, turning the night dark and gloomy. Borko was leading a row of twelve men and women. With them were the two Tuma *brothers*, who owned the printing factory in Ljubljana where Valeria worked, a young physician badly needed in the villages where typhus had spread mostly among children, three nurses who were caught stealing medicines, and a few young students who decided to join the fight rather than wait for the absent lectures at the University of Ljubljana. Valeria was walking at the end of the line, her gun ready in case of an ambush.

Around midnight, they arrived at the post just below Krim, where couriers were waiting for them. After leaving the shed where they ate a copious meal, they followed a narrow uphill path lined with black bushes and high rocks on both sides. Warm summer rain drizzled from the sky. The humidity made their shirts stick to their backs. Valeria did not like the terrain; the dark shadows behind the rocks appeared like dangerous traps. Yet, the couriers assured them it was the safest way. So they were marching for a couple of hours and the night was closing in when all of a sudden Valeria heard a series of shots. Instinctively she ducked behind a nearby rock. Visibility was near zero that first morning with the fog trailing them along the way. She groped around until she felt the branches of a thick pine tree reaching to the ground. She rolled underneath. In the mist, Valeria lifted her head a couple of times to scan the situation, but to no avail.

She tried to summon into mind exactly what had happened. First, a couple of shots were fired, then some more shots followed by the sound of her comrades running, branches cracking under their feet, a couple of cries, then nothing, complete silence. Valeria desperately struggled to count the shots and footsteps in her mind. Who was hit? Could they have escaped into the thick grove to her left or to her right? Where were the enemies? Morning light was beginning to flicker through the leaves and on the moss-covered white rocks. At last, Valeria could see the narrow path meandering uphill. She focused on the gray mist ahead. Dawn was breaking. Where were enemies? Were they gone?

She cautiously stepped onto the path, moving along the rocks slowly, one step at the time, toward the spot where shots were fired an hour ago. From behind a rock, she saw Borko stretched out on the ground, his uniform pierced by bullets, warm blood oozing from his chest wounds. Approaching with caution, she kneeled beside him and felt his pulse. He was alive. She looked around to assess the position. Some fifty meters ahead, she could see the sleeve of a uniform peeking from behind a trunk and the barrel of a Gewehr 41 rifle. A bit further, behind the thick trunk of a tall beech, she spotted a dark gray lapel betraying a Wehrmacht jacket. Three soldiers of the Heer. Alas, she failed to see a fourth one sitting high up in the beech. When a crow cried in alarm and took flight, she looked up. Too late. A shot was fired; Valeria felt pain burn through her left arm. She collapsed to the ground next to Borko.

Through fuzzy haze, her ears were recording shouts and more shots. She had no idea what was going on. She felt Borko's blood wetting her trousers and smiled at the thought of his body so close to hers. A deep warm feeling of love inundated her brain.

'Now, it will be forever. My love, we'll be married in Heaven,' she thought. 'We will pick cherries and make love on the soft grass. Forever, Borko, forever …'

The unbearable pain in her arm and chest cut through her reveries. It was as if sharp knives were severing her organs and slicing deeply into her flesh. Terror and panic made her heart pound wildly. Her stomach shivered with cramps. She must keep calm. A cry flooded her ears. It could have been hers. She opened her eyes to the blue sky that raised green leaves and dark pine needles toward the sun. God of Nature. She must think of something beautiful.

> How sweet are the cherries,
> how bright is the sun,
> my love steals my kisses,
> until we are one ...

Valeria smiled, savoring the sweet taste of the ripe red fruits filling her mouth. She could not swallow the juice as her throat ached too much. A couple of white cumuli traveled lazily overhead like a flock of docile sheep. She lost the strength to follow their path. Everything became a blur; all pain vanished. Silence covered her like a soft warm blanket.

'I'm so tired.' She closed her eyes. A deep sense of peace cradled her into strange dreams. Borko was holding her in his arms. She rested her head against his chest and listened to his heartbeat. It was so nice. She let it go.

After what seemed like eternity, she felt pain again. It must have been much later. The sun that she hadn't seen rise that morning was setting, leaving the day to the shadows of the night.

"Where am I?" she asked, but could not hear her voice.

"Peter, she said something! Come here, quickly!"

A man leaned over the makeshift stretchers on the wagon. "Hello, Valchy. Hold on. We're taking you to the hospital. Are you in pain?"

Unable to speak, Valeria simply nodded. The man gave her a package of white powder and a swig of water. She swallowed with difficulty. The liquid burned in her throat like fire. After a while, she dozed off in spite of the jolting as the wagon jounced over gravel and roots.

When she came to her senses again, it was pitch-dark. She was being moved on a stretcher. Although she could not see them, she guessed that four strong men must be carrying her. All she could hear were the hushed sounds of their feet. Maybe there were others. She could hear their steps. Maybe their soles were padded with cloth. Indeed, men carrying several stretchers formed a line as they stumbled along a tiny canyon path somewhere in the woods. More distinctly, Valeria could hear a burbling brook somewhere close. She needed to empty her bladder.

"I have to go," she said.

Nobody replied. Maybe they could not hear her.

"I have to go. I have to take a leak," she said in a louder voice.

Now a man replied, "Hush, Valchy, don't talk now. We're on the secret path to Hospital *Franja*."

Only then did Valeria realize she was blindfolded with a black cloth. She shivered in fear. "Where am I? Why can't I see?"

They lowered the stretcher, and another man leaned over her. "Valchy, this is the path to *Franja*. We cover the eyes of all the wounded so they can't betray its location in case they are captured or tortured. You know that. You've heard of *Franja*, haven't you?"

Her thoughts ran confusedly. She was not sure what she could remember. Like thunder, the sharp pain in her chest returned. It shattered her body and a loud sigh escaped her mouth. Then, unable to contain herself anymore, she felt warm liquid between her legs. She began to sob like a child.

"Now I've wet myself. Why didn't you let me go?"

The man tenderly caressed her cheeks and dried the tears that inundated the black bandage. "Don't cry, Valchy, our brave little hero. Some people piss their pants in battle, in the face of enemy guns, but not you. You're a hero, Valchy. What does a bit of bodily fluid matter? We have another half an hour to go and we're there. Then you're saved."

Valeria turned her face toward the man. She was still scared to death. "How do you know my name? Who are you?" she said, perplexed.

The man wiped her forehead with some sticky gauze. "I am Tone, one of the medics. I usually accompany the wounded until Doctor *Franja* is ready to treat them. Please, let's not talk anymore. Are you in pain?"

Of course she was in pain. However, Valeria finally grasped what was going on. She was on her way to *Franja*, the partisan hospital that many fighters considered a myth, a hidden place of salvation. She felt soaked to the skin. She knew it was not only urine but also blood, her blood mixed with Borko's. She remembered the cherry taste in her mouth hours ago. She realized now it was blood, not the sweet fruit. Another thought struck her.

"How is Borko?"

The face of the man slid into shadow. Even if she were able to see him, she wouldn't have been able to read his mind.

"He's on the stretcher behind you. We must hurry. His wounds are serious."

Valeria nodded in silence. She must hold on. They lifted her stretcher and continued walking. From time to time, she could hear passwords whispered softly like late summer breeze through leaves. They were taking a lot of precautions. Good. A feeling of gratitude and security overcame her tired mind.

"Thank you," she murmured, knowing the men couldn't hear her. As the pain returned, she wanted to stifle her cries with her hand. Yet her muscles wouldn't obey the commands of her brain. She tightened her lips and gritted her teeth. Suddenly, she heard the hollow sound of boots on wooden flooring. Someone removed her bandage and light blinded her. A quick needle pierced her arm, and the tension in her body left completely.

'See you soon, my love,' she thought. She closed her eyes. In her mind, she traveled to the *Brkini Hills*, where she walked with Borko among the cherry orchards in bloom. She heard the bees buzzing and the birds singing, and she could see her lover moving his lips. He was telling her something, but she could not hear what he was saying. She focused all her attention on his words. Still, his voice couldn't reach her. Only the buzzing of bees and the chirping of birds filled the meadow, echoing in her ears.

~~~

When Valeria woke up, a beautiful, young woman in a white hospital coat was sitting on the side of her bed.

With a smile, she caressed Valeria's cheek. "Hello, Valchy. How are you feeling?"

Valeria considered the question. "I'm alive. Thank you."

The woman shook her softly curled light hair. Her blue eyes shone with warmth. "You needn't thank me. I should thank you. You risked your life for our cause."

Valeria nodded, immediately feeling an affinity with the woman. "Are you a doctor?"

The woman smiled and took Valeria's hand in hers. "Yes, I'm *Franja*. I performed the surgery. You had three bullets in your body. One in your upper right arm, in the *humerus*. The bone will heal, but you may feel weather pains later. Other two severed the muscles in the right part of your chest. You were more than lucky. No lung injuries, no major arteries damaged. However, there is something, I'm afraid..."

Valeria was barely listening to her words. The kindness in her soft voice held her senses like the song of cicadas. When *Franja* paused, Valeria tried to focus on what she was saying.

"What is it? Nothing's wrong. I can take the pain. So, you really do exist, don't you? You are Doctor *Franja*. Oh, thank you, Doctor. Thank you so much."

Franja looked her in the eyes, her face serene and full of compassion. "Valchy, you were in a relationship, weren't you?"

Valeria's eyes widened. "Yes, Borko...How is he, Doctor *Franja*? Tell me quickly, please! He was on the stretcher behind me. Did he make it?"

Franja slowly shook her head. "I am sorry, my dear. He was shot several times in the chest. His lung collapsed – he had what we call 'pneumothorax' – and there wasn't anything we could do. He died a couple of hours after they brought him in. I'm sorry. You two must've been in love."

Valeria closed her eyes. Tears welled up. A pain much deeper than her wounds filled her body. Borko, her Borko was dead. She would never be able to walk the *Brkini Hills* with him. They would never get married. There was no future for her..

After a while, she said in a small voice, "You should have let me die, too, Doctor *Franja*."

Franja did not reply. She waited for Valchy to bring her tears under control. There was more. She had heard so much about this brave young woman who, without realizing it, had become a legend. Why must all the best ones go? When would this agony pass? She took an envelope out of her pocket.

"Please, Valchy, don't say such things. Borko would want you to live and fight, not to give up like a coward. Look, here, I found a letter for you in his pocket."

Valeria took the envelope from *Franja*'s hands. There were brownish stains of blood all over it. Like a complex lace pattern. Still in shock, she stared at her name written on it: Valeria, not Valchy.

Borko, of course, knew who she was. She tore the yellowish paper open.

Dear Valeria,

If you're reading these lines, then I know I'm no longer in this world and the war is not yet over. I know you will shed bitter tears. You will miss me as much as I will miss you if there is indeed life after death in one form or the other. But don't despair, my love. Be strong like only you know how! You're young and you must live to tell future generations what it's like to live in the woods and fight for freedom. I'm counting on you, Valeria.
Please, cherish our love, but do not remain the prisoner of it. Find a new man and start a new life. Our love was so wonderful because you're so wonderful. Your kisses inspired me, your body kept me warm, and now your caresses are guiding me into a new world. I love you, Valeria. I love you more than anybody or anything in the world. Should you bear the fruit of our love, a child, please keep this letter as official proof of paternity. It would be wonderful if our child could bear my name. It would be the name of our eternal love.
Forever yours,

Boris Lukman (Borko)

Silently, Valeria folded the letter, inserted the crumpled sheet into the envelope, and planted a long kiss on the paper. Her tears were almost dry when she formed the question:

"So, Doctor *Franja*, tell me: am I with child?"

Franja caressed Valeria's sticky hair and answered with a sigh, "I'm sorry, Valchy. You were."

"What do you mean, Doctor?"

Franja took Valeria's hands in hers. "I think at some point, after you were wounded, your body triggered a spontaneous abortion to protect you. Trees do that, animals and people, too. Nature is cruel sometimes, but it is always right. You came in a very bad state. You had a high fever and one of your wounds had begun to fester with infection. It took two days to bring you to the hospital. You cannot remember, of course. Most of the time you were unconscious."

Valeria nodded and looked at *Franja* with expectation. The doctor continued.

"When I lifted your blanket, you were soaked in blood from the waist down. I saw the wounds on your upper body and knew immediately what had happened. Miscarriages are common with women fighters. The strain is simply too much. We took off your clothes and washed you. Our first priority was to extract the bullets and clean the wounds. Luckily, we had some *penicillin* in stock. Our last American supply. This medicine does miracles. It made you better in no time."

"What was it?"

Franja looked up in surprise. "The fetus was a boy, about fifteen weeks I would say."

"What did you do with him?"

"We gave him cremated him, Valeria."

"What do you mean?"

The doctor let go off Valeria's hands and stood up. "We made a pyre and set him on fire. He rose like a phoenix. Valeria, be strong. There will be another life in freedom."

Valeria shook her head as though denying the sad facts. "What a terrible time to live when everybody is telling me to be strong!"

Franja wiped the beads of sweat from her forehead. "I know. I'm sorry. Do calm down, Valeria. You have a bit of fever. I'll send a nurse with a sedative so you can sleep."

Valery turned her sobbing face to the doctor. "Can you keep my pregnancy a secret, Doctor?"

"Of course, I must keep it a secret."

"Thank you, Doctor *Franja*."

When Valeria was alone again in her corner of the room, her thoughts wandered to Borko and their unborn baby boy.

'If there is God in Heaven and you're holding his hand, tell him to unite you with our baby boy. Our angel, our angel of love …'

~~~

Another winter of war began. Big white flakes fell from a light gray sky. Andrej paused from reading a medical file and looked through the window. He took a few steps closer to admire the wonderful white curtain as it shifted, changed, and glowed with a pale new glory. Winter white, winter cold, winter of 1944.

It was the time of year when all children in Slovenia eagerly awaited *Saint Nicholas* to bring them sugary treats and toys. Although *Saint Nicholas* couldn't make them all happy, each one hoped and prayed to get a special gift. Children were children. Andrej smiled to himself. Martin was five months old. He knew the boy would not remember his first Advent or Christmas, however, he and Ada would. Tonight Andrej expected Ada would prepare a large plate with dried figs, lard-baked biscuits, and a caramel lollipop he got on the black market a month ago. They would put little Martin between the pillows in the middle of the sofa. Andrej imagined the baby's round red cheeks shining with pleasure as he licked the precious candy and dripped sticky brownish saliva on his white bib. His two tiny lower teeth would smile for the world of them.

'My God, how much I love them both,' Andrej thought.

He glanced at is his watch. Three o'clock, not yet time to go home. He reopened the medical report. He was supposed to be home for supper at six. He opened the folder of Janez Turk, an eighteen-year-old lad whose treatment for anxiety and depression continued to bear no result after almost a year. Andrej sighed. Another victim of the terrible war, another broken soul he cannot put together again.

Young Janez was among the few Home Guard survivors of the Battle of *Grahovo*. Only a year ago, the news of the partisan massacre in the village filled the front pages of the newspapers. The boy was seventeen at the time. He was alive thanks to the goodness of a local blacksmith who had saved him from the burning church. Yes, burning church...A partisan commander had ordered to burn down the church because Home Guard machine gunners were shooting at partisans from its tower. That same November night in 1943, several civilians, accused of collaborating with the Germans, were killed either by partisan bullets or by fire.

Janez came to the hospital a couple of months later. His uncle, a priest in Ljubljana, brought him to Andrej. The boy was catatonic. His uncle knew the horrible trauma Janez Turk went through in *Grahovo*. Like every Home Guard, Janez was tasked to defend their position at the church tower. As the eldest boy in the family, he fought shoulder to shoulder with his father. The partisans outnumbered the Home Guards and were better armed. They quickly won the village and herded, the women, children, and the elderly to the market square in front of the church. The partisans threatened to burn everyone alive unless the gunfire from the tower ceased. Janez and his father were told to put down their weapons and surrender. Yet, they refused to abandon their cause and continued to shoot. Their bullets killed two more partisans. The commander became furious and shouted to one of his soldiers, who grabbed a girl and used her as a living shield to get into the church. Other partisans followed. Janez and his father could hear the planks of pews being wrecked below them. Through a slit, they saw the partisans building a pyre in the middle of the church. They smelled gasoline. Several villagers were pushed inside. Then, the fire was lit. Janez and his comrades could hear piercing shrieks and fists banging desperately on the thick door. The partisans locked the people in. The Home Guards returned their attention to the machine gunners in the tower and continued to shoot. Janez saw their priest approach the partisan commander. He supposed the priest was trying to save the church and the poor villagers in it. The commander pointed to the tower, said something, and the priest stumbled away, lucky not to get a bullet to the head.

Suddenly, a cry came to Janez's ears: the familiar voice of his mother. He could not hear her words, but supposed it had to do with him and Father. Mother knew they were up in the bell tower. The commander motioned to one of his brutes, who then pushed Mother into the blazing church. Mother was nine months pregnant, the baby due any day. Father dropped his machine gun and hurried downstairs. He did not return. His parents died in the flames. Janez could do nothing but cry and wait until his lungs filled with smoke and he fainted. The bell tower did not burn down. The next morning he came to and climbed down the ladder that the village blacksmith was holding for him and another survivor. He fled to Ljubljana to his uncle.

The elderly priest tried everything. He prayed with him, talked to him, and tried to get through his wall of sadness. Yet the boy wouldn't utter a word or move his lips, not even in prayer. When someone spoke to him, he would burst into tears and clap his ears. At night he woke up shrieking from horrible nightmares. Mother and Father burnt, his siblings sent to live in other people's homes, his family broken. Death was better than life in the face of such terror. One afternoon Janez's uncle found him in the attic trying to tie a rope to the beam and decided to place him in Andrej's hands. However, no treatment had any effect on Janez. Electroshocks, sedatives, therapy – all was pointless. The boy wanted to die and was under suicide watch most of the time.

Andrej sighed. Maybe such a wrecked life wasn't worth a dime after all. Maybe the boy would be saved by death. How could he ever get the cries of his mother dying in agony out of his head?

There were no medicines to cure such pain. Better to quit a world where a man can push a pregnant woman into a burning church. What kind of man was that, anyway? Andrej thought of his sister. She was the reason why he hated the Communists. They poisoned the minds of resistance fighters with propaganda about Stalin and the Red Army. About social justice and life being better under Communism. In truth, it would be a better life only for the few leaders who planned to come into power after the war. All violent parvenus with no scruples, no morals. He was glad Sanja had made it to America.

A knock on the door made him lift his head from the sad report.

"Doctor Strainar, can I talk to you for a moment?"

He nodded to Nurse Benjamina, who hesitated on the threshold. She looked around as though she were afraid of something. Then she quickly entered the room and came very close to him, so close that he could smell her sweetish breath when she whispered in his ear.

"I have a message for you, Doctor."

He moved back to distance himself. She reeked of a poorly washed old woman. Her grayish hair was thick with oily pomade, her cheeks sullen and wrinkled. Cheap perfume did more to accentuate than to cover her unpleasant odor. Andrej's nostrils quivered; his brows knitted with impatience.

"I'm sorry, Doctor. I've been on duty since yesterday." She sat in the chair opposite his desk. "I must speak to you in private."

Andrej nodded, ashamed that she had guessed his thoughts. He was a doctor and nothing human should be alien to him.

"This is private, Nurse Benjamina. Speak up. Who sent you?"

Sister Benjamina smiled and shook her head. "Not the *Liberation Front* or anything like that. I have no interest in politics, you know. One of our old friends has sent me. He needs your help, Doctor."

Andrej noticed that packages of sedatives and narcotics went missing occasionally, but didn't say anything. He imagined Nurse Benjamina knew where the supplies had gone. He ignored it simply. Nobody deserved to suffer pain, not even a partisan.

"Who is it?"

"Franci Zajec. He's waiting for you in his apartment. He's on the run, but he fell ill. I'm not sure who's after him, Doctor."

"It doesn't matter. I'm glad he's alive. I was wondering what happened to him. How did he reach you?"

She stood up. "He phoned me from somewhere. Judging by the symptoms he described, I think he has some kind of infection."

Andrej thought of Ada and Martin. He knew that, as a result of poor hygiene, typhus was ravaging the armies and the fronts of Europe. It was a very dangerous and practically untreatable disease. He read an Italian article about the British and the Americans curing their soldiers with a new medicine called *penicillin*, but the hospital had nothing like that.

Nurse Benjamina figured out his fears and added quickly, "I'm sure he took all the necessary precautions. He's waiting for you in his apartment. You should not be in greater danger than we usually are at the hospital every day."

Andrej looked her in the eyes. "Of course, I'll go and see Franci, Nurse Benjamina."

He decidedly stood up and put on his winter coat, hat, and gloves. He took his medical bag and together they left the room.

Benjamina whispered into his ear, "One more thing: he said you should enter the apartment using the key you have. As I said, Franci is on the run. No one must know he's back."

Andrej nodded and quickened his pace. Where had his friend been for nearly two years? Andrej hated secrets that might put him and his young family at risk. Looking at the thick veil of falling white flakes, he sighed and walked into the snowstorm.

Half an hour later, he inserted his key into the lock and opened the door. There was no sound. The apartment seemed abandoned except for the masses of plants that Ada continued to care for and seemed to thrive better every day. He and Ada even took some into their own home. Just as Andrej removed his wet coat and dripping hat, he noticed it was pleasantly warm in the flat. He put his medical bag on the floor and noticed a pair of new heavy boots wetting the linoleum floor. Franci was home. Andrej stepped into the bedroom – memories of him and Ada, their first time, flashed through his mind.

"Hello, Franci. How are you?"

"Oh, Andrej, my dear friend, how happy I am to see you!"

Andrej stepped toward the bed and took Franci's wrist in his hands. Automatically he measured the heartbeat. It seemed normal although his body was feverish. He wanted to lift his sleeve to get a better feel when Franci yanked his arm away. Andrej shrugged and sat on the bed.

"Now, tell me, Franci, where have you been all this time?"

With Franci lying under thick blankets, Andrej couldn't perceive how thin he was. His round cheeks were gone and his skin was pale.

Franci's lips trembled when he finally stuttered, "Andrej, won't you give me away if I tell you? It's terrible, really terrible, you know …"

Franci raised his arm to his head. Andrej noticed the number tattooed on his lower arm. Realization struck him like lightning.

"Are you Jewish, Franci?"

Franci looked at him with pleading watery eyes. "You won't tell the Germans, will you, Andrej?"

Andrej said with compassion, "Of course not. You're my friend. Besides, I think this practice of concentration camps is horrible. I loathe all sides that employ it. Were you released?"

Franci shook his head. "Not really, I escaped."

Andrej's eyes widened. "Really? How?"

Franci's blue eyes shimmered with pride and pain. "I got lucky. I played dead and climbed out of the mass grave during the night. They don't really dig deep graves."

Andrej tried to ameliorate the horrible facts. "It seems the one they're digging for their people is deeper than any grave on earth."

Franci returned his smile reluctantly. "Yeah, that's for sure. How are you? Are you on friendly terms with them?"

Andrej sighed. "Kind of, I joined the Home Guard a year ago. I was hoping we could defeat the Communists with the help of the Germans and establish democracy after the war."

Franci froze. "On my way home I heard people say that the Home Guard denounces Jews."

"Dear me, Franci. You're safe with me. Please, don't worry!"

Franci slowly shook his head. "You're playing a dangerous game, Andrej. He who sups with the devil should have a long spoon," he said in reply.

"Well, I do hope mine is long enough. The Communists have executed thousands for no other reason than their greed for absolute power."

Franci looked at Andrej with a serene expression. "Does it mean going against your own people, too, Andrej?"

"The Home Guard only fights against the Partisans. They don't kill civilians. They're protecting us against brutality and plunder.

Oh, it's complicated, Franci. Which camp were you in?"

"*Bergen-Belsen*. It took me a month to get here. On foot, by bike, by train – I was lucky. My fever started these last few days. I wouldn't have put you in danger unless it was urgent. I have to leave as quickly as possible."

Andrej nodded. With some mockery in his voice, he ordered, "All right, my lady, take your clothes off!"

Franci laughed. He replied with a faked, woman's voice: "You won't like what you'll see, Doctor."

Pushing away his blankets, he unbuttoned the top of his pajamas and exposed his emaciated torso for inspection. Andrej had to control his face muscles not to show alarm. Franci was no more than a skeleton, his navel protruding like a newborn baby's. The telltale red rash on his stomach area made Andrej suspicious.

"Does your stomach ache?"

"Not really, but I've been eating and drinking moderately since I escaped. I know I can die unless I do so. I have to increase my food intake carefully."

"Gradually, yes. You've clearly suffered from starvation. How do you get food? I guess they have food coupons in Germany, too, don't they?"

"Of course. I've eaten well here since I came back. There was still some rice, corn flour, and beans in the pantry. You never took anything. What a shame. The mice could have gotten to them."

"That's good. You should only have light food and drink a lot of tea – chamomile would be best. Do you have any?"

"Plenty. I picked lots of it the last summer I was here. Well, I must tell you, Andrej. You have one hell of a green thumb. Who would have thought you had such a talent under your doctor's coat?"

"Well, all credit should go to my girlfriend. I mean my wife."

"She has really done an amazing job. I felt revitalized when I saw all the greenery – my plants waiting for me. It also gave me the courage to call for you. I must say Nurse Benjamina was totally against it. I understand now. Well, she's wrong, isn't she? You are a friend."

"Yes, Franci, I am."

"Not everyone in the Home Guard is a traitor."

"Of course not. How did they find you? We've been close friend for years, but I would never have guessed your family is Jewish."

Franci sighed. "They didn't arrest me in Ljubljana but in Rome. You remember my message when I left you the key?"

Andrej inclined his head in confirmation. Franci continued.

"I fell in love with an Italian. Chiara was the wife of Judge Rizzo, an Italian who chaired the court in Ljubljana. We met at the hospital when she had a light accident."

"I remember. She came in with some scrapes after falling from her bike."

"It was madness. I honed in on her like a drone on his wedding flight."

"Wasn't she older than you?"

"Yes, she was in her late thirties. But age didn't matter. It was love at first sight. She couldn't stand living with Maurizio any longer and ran back home to Rome. I followed her blindly. I was completely infatuated with that spoilt beauty. I sent her flowers, courted her, took every possible opportunity to see her. By then we had kissed and talked, but I didn't want to share her bed with the judge so we never did anything here in Ljubljana. The night I arrived in Rome, we made love in my hotel room. After that, her attitude changed. She became aloof and cool. You see, my grandfather circumcized me when I was a baby, but we've never been religious in our family. I didn't give it much thought. In the heat of love, I forgot all about it. No more than a week later, Chiara denounced me. Two Gestapo men arrested me and put me on the train to *Bergen-Belsen*. So much for love in the time of Aryan Laws ...Can you imagine? One day she's moaning in ecstasy in my arms, the next day she denounces me to the Jerries. I bitterly swallowed my disappointment and fought to survive. It's impossible to describe what they did to us. It's better to be a dog than a Jew these days," he said, his voice breaking.

Andrej looked into Franci's teary eyes and took his hand in his. "That's a very sad story, Franci. We will help you. Ada is less suspicious, so she will do the visits. Just get some strength back to travel to Italy. The Allies are in Ravenna now. You should get there and go to their infirmary. If they can give you their medicine, it will cure your typhus."

"I have typhus?"

"I'm afraid so. Did you disinfect your clothes after coming home?"

"Yes, I stole some civilian clothes, just rags actually in some village in Germany. The jacket was alive with lice and fleas. I burnt everything in the oven, but couldn't undo the bites. To think that I took so many precautions at the camp! I boiled the water whenever I could. I volunteered almost every day to do the laundry. I never ate scraps or drank anything suspicious despite the constant grumbling of my stomach. I had no time to wash the clothes I stole. Still, I should have found a creek and built a fire …"

Andrej stood up from the bed. "You'll get better, Franci. I'll visit you every few days and Ada, my wife, will come, too. The neighbors have gotten used to her."

"That's wonderful. So you got married after all, Andrej. When? Who is Ada?"

"We celebrated our first anniversary last September. Ada is the sister of one of my former patients, Marjana. We have a little son, Ada and I. His name is Martin. I'll tell Ada to be careful. And Franci, don't leave the apartment and don't turn on the lights."

Franci opened the nightstand's drawer. "Can I ask you another favor, Andrej?"

"Of course."

He handed Andrej a folder filled with papers. "Here are some shares and securities as well as the documents for the apartment. I rang a friend of mine, a lawyer, and transferred everything to your name. Sell everything and buy gold. Gold is cheap now. Keep ten percent for you and Ada. And keep what I owe you for your trouble and the apartment expenses. We'll get together once the war is over. Please, Andrej."

Andrej hesitated. He might arouse suspicion doing such business. Then he saw Franci's pleading face.

"Please, Andrej. Had the Germans known this was Jewish property, they would have confiscated it ages ago. Their competence is not all that perfect, as you can see."

"I'll see what I can do. Give me the folder. Now, get some rest."

Franci closed his eyes and fell back on the pillow. "Enjoy your *Saint Nicholas* evening. Thank you, Andrej. You're a true friend."

~~~

On the morning of *Saint Nicholas* Day in 1944, a boy was hiding behind the huge trunks of the century-old beech trees in the school courtyard. His name was Henrik Šmit. He was eight years old. Last evening, joyous for so many Slovenian children, brought Henrik no gifts, no plates laden with sweets. The image of his kind mother in the soft candlelight, her soft pale face as she arranged dried figs, apple and pear slices, juicy oranges, and tangerines on the plates that bear his name and those of his siblings – was all but a fading memory. For what seemed like eternity, Henrik had been alone. His family was gone. Instead of gifts from *Saint Nicholas*, early last evening the Panther Lady gave him a good thrashing with her horse whip and, like so many times before, for no good reason. The children in the partisan orphanage feared the black-haired woman in her black uniform and high riding boots. Her blows were frequent and painful. Henrik's behind was sore, his back stained purple as new bruises inflamed his old, unhealed ones. He knew there was no point in asking why. He was the reason. It was a just punishment for what he was.

He trembled in the cold, his chestnut hair tucked under a woolen bonnet, nose dripping from a light cold, cheeks red from frost, and gray eyes watery. Henrik tried to remain still in his oversized thick coat that used to be his brother's. In the heavy snowstorm, he was outside the school building, waiting for his teacher, Valeria Batič. He was afraid to enter the classroom alone.

Since autumn Valeria had been working in the elementary school in Metlika, a small town on the liberated territories of Bela Krajina. She came late for the beginning of the 1944-45 school year because her wounds wouldn't heal so quickly. They reopened the school in October, happy to have a teacher at last. The first problem was, the children's age differed from their level of knowledge. Many parents resented sending their girls and boys to German schools so they kept them at home. The second problem was the lack of textbooks, pencils, and paper. Resourceful as always, Valeria got in touch with her former business contacts, and a truckload of low-quality paper on its way to Vevče Paper Mills arrived at the schoolyard instead. They cut the paper rolls into sheets. A blackboard with chalks turned up, too, as well as a few copies of *Breznik's Grammar* Book and Orthography. She borrowed some literary texts from priests and local merchants, who kept ample private libraries. The last problem was, Valery had no learning plan and had to rely on common sense to organize the lessons. She felt sorry she did not study harder at the Teachers' College in Ljubljana.

In spite of the hard work, she couldn't sleep. Valeria's faithful companion through the long white nights was sorrow. War and its horrible crimes against civilians had finally crushed her bravery. In the small hours of the day she mourned her first love and her unborn son, the brave little hero on his way to freedom. She was alone with her dark thoughts. She desperately wished to see and talk to her best friend Ada. Although her little boy was growing up in comfort and safety in Ljubljana, Ada's position was precarious. The Germans and their allies were losing the war. The time would come when Andrej and Ada would face more danger in the city than Valeria on the battlefront.

In the evenings, Valeria worked hard to think of new exercises and lesson plans. She would turn off her lamp only when her vision started sliding over the characters and her mind stopped understanding their meaning. Then, her thoughts would wander to her pupils, children of terror and war.

The morning after *Saint Nicholas* Day, when she mysteriously found a sack of dried plums on her doorstep, she noticed Henrik Šmit hiding behind the trees. It was snowing heavily.

"What are you doing outside, Henrik? You'll catch a cold," she told him reproachfully.

"I've been waiting for you, *Tovarishitza* Valeria. I want to ask you about '*The Water Man*,' the poem we were reading yesterday. Did pretty Urška survive the waves of the river or not?"

"Silly boy, you shouldn't be standing in the cold. You could've asked me inside. Of course, she didn't survive. No human can stay alive underwater for more than a few of minutes."

"Why?"

"Why what, Henrik?"

"Why did the poet kill her? She was a pretty girl, wasn't she?"

"It's based on an old legend, a folktale. As you remember, she was also haughty and arrogant. It served her well."

As they entered the school building, Henrik let her pass first. "Maybe death is too much punishment. A good lesson would've been enough."

Valeria nodded and, opening the door to the classroom, had him go in first. With a smile, Henrik stepped into the room.

"It's him! Get him!" cried his classmates. Thick grenades of horse manure struck Henrik all over his body. One flew directly in Valeria's face as she stepped in behind him. The battle cries and stenchy missiles ceased the instant the children saw her. Silence fell across the room, external sounds muffled by the falling snow.

Valeria was furious. She assumed the stance of a partisan on a battlefield.

"I don't care whose idea this was. All of you will be punished. All of you. Now, go and wash your hands."

One by one they went to the sink and washed their hands with soap and chilly water. No one dared to look at either Valeria or Henrik. When Henrik stepped toward the sink to clean his face as well, she held him back.

"No, Henrik. Since they smeared us, they'll have to clean us. Now, one by one ...take the towels and start cleaning our faces."

The children obeyed. With shaking hands, they wiped the feces from Valeria's face. At first, they didn't even dare touch Henrik, but Valeria pointed at the smudge of filth drying near his mouth and they set to work. After some long minutes, they were more or less clean. Valeria wrote on the blackboard:

WHY DID I THROW HORSE MANURE AT MY FRIEND?

She looked around the class. "I want every one of you, save Henrik, to write down the reasons for your appalling behavior just now. The essay should be divided into three parts: introduction, body, and conclusion, and must be at least two pages long. While you're writing, I'm going to fetch the Chief Officer of Metlika and report your deeds. We'll consider what to do with you savages."

She turned on her heels and was about to leave the room when she heard Henrik's whisper.

"Can I come with you, *Tovarishitza* Valeria? Please?"

She immediately realized his fears. Left alone with the mob. She winked at him to follow her. As they passed her room at the rectory, she pushed Henrik inside.

"Please, wait for me here. I want to speak to *Tovarish* Marko alone. Put some logs on the fire and write a short essay about winter."

She strode angrily toward the main office, which was located in the old fire station. Marko Robič, a law student from Trieste, was in charge of managing the city of Metlika under the Partisans' jurisdiction. A member of the Communist Party for years, he had fought for the Republican cause in the *Battle of Ebro* in Spain and had traveled to Russia to absolve the rules of the New World Order – the socialism. Marko was a short, stout, and very energetic man with cunning hazel eyes that were always scrutinizing somebody. He gained authority over the locals, particularly over poor field laborers, after he managed to coerce the big landowners into sharing their food with the rest of the population. It was said that his whole family, including his mother and his little sister, perished in *Risiera*, a concentration camp in Trieste, after an Italian spy found out about him and betrayed him to the police. Almost tangible guilt shrouded him like a dark cloud. His dark eyebrows were knitted in permanent distress, and his thin lips rarely bestowed a smile on his fellow fighters. Valeria had always viewed him from afar, but the behavior of the children needed his authority. Unless he resolved it as she deemed right, she would volunteer for the battlefront. Getting a bullet to the head was better than horseshit in the face.

"Good morning, *Tovarish* Marko!"

He looked at her with a tiny sparkle in his eyes. Smoothing his chestnut hair with his left hand, he offered his right in the greeting.

"Good morning, *Tovarishitza* Valeria. Isn't it school hours now?"

Valeria shook his hand and sat on the opposite chair. "It is, but I have a problem. I need your advice and, I guess, support, too."

Briefly, she described the humiliating event. Marko's face showed disgust.

Jumping to his feet, he said, "I'll give them a good thrashing, each and every one of them! How dare they do such a thing!"

"I don't think a beating would the best strategy. We must come up with a punishment that would have a longer effect and make the children reflect on what they've done."

"Who did you say the boy was?"

"Oh, I didn't. I forgot to mention. Henrik Šmit, an orphan …"

"I see."

Valeria looked at Marko, a question in her eyes. "What do you mean?"

"His parents were part of the Home Guard. I thought you knew."

Now Valeria stood up, excited. "I do! Henrik's parents may not have been on our side, but it still doesn't justify the children's behavior. It was an attack on our *Slovene Partisan school*. It was an attack on me, personally. This is not about the boy. What do we know about how he'll see his parents when he grows up? Henrik is eight, he's very bright, but he's just a child. He did not choose to be on any side. He's a good boy, and I'm sure he'll understand our values when he's older. Students cannot behave like animals, not in my school. I will not tolerate it. I've come a long way and I won't swallow their shit, *Tovarish* Marko."

Some of her words whistled past Marko's ears as he dreamily looked at the black curls trembling with the angry moves of her head. He had liked Valeria from the moment he first saw her. He had heard about her bravery, her wounds, and Borko. However, as a woman, blinded by the childcare, Valeria missed the point. He tried to console her.

"I agree completely. But if it were up to me, I wouldn't let Henrik go to school at all. There are children in the classroom whose parents died in Dachau because Henrik's father and mother, both fervent Nemškutars, Germanophiles, denounced them to the police. The parents of little Anna Komar ..."

"I know about Anna." Valeria nodded sadly.

"She escaped into the woods when she heard the police car in their courtyard. When she came back a couple of hours later, their house was burnt down and her parents gone."

Valeria fell silent. What could she say in reply? War fought over the fragile sentiments of children ... Yet, Henrik was a child, too.

"What happened to Henrik's parents? He told me they simply left him at the parish and escaped to save their lives. He fantasizes that one day his mother would come for him."

Before she could finish with another question, Valeria caught the gleam in Marko's eyes, now almost black with anger.

"They were tried and taken away. His eldest sister escaped; the rest of the family – two older sisters and a brother of two – went to different orphanages. They will learn human values and receive an education. Maybe the little one will get adopted."

Valeria masked her horror. But at least the Partisan government allowed the children of their enemies to live while the Nazis were starving or gassing them together with their parents in concentration camps. She understood Marko's point.

"It's terrible how war divides not only us, but also future generations. We still have to think of a sensible punishment for the class. They have to know what is right and wrong."

Marko looked at his watch. He had other business this morning, yet he didn't want to disappoint her.

"*Tovarishitza* Valeria, let's get you back to the school. We'll think of something along the way. Otherwise, we can meet again afterward. It would do them good to breathe some respect into their savage minds."

Valeria was grateful to Marko. She needed him to reinstate her authority. "Yes, thank you, *Tovarish* Marko. Let's go."

They walked past the sentries and the busy citizens on their morning errands. Someone whistled behind them. Valeria flushed and threw a side glance at Marko. He was blushing, too. She smiled. Maybe she should go on with her life as Borko told her in his letter.

"Death to fascism!" he exclaimed upon entering the classroom.

The children jumped to attention.

"Freedom to the people," they responded in firm voices.

"*Tovarishitza* Valeria told me about what you did this morning. Young partisans do not throw horse manure at a hero like your schoolteacher. When she was a mere girl of seventeen, she disarmed a troop of Italian soldiers. Alone! She fought in the woods and received the highest military medals for her bravery. Do you understand?"

The children stared at Marko with huge eyes, murmuring something incomprehensible. A few looked shyly at Valeria.

"Do you understand?" Marko shouted in the silence of the classroom.

"Yes," thin voices replied in unison.

"I say, does she deserve to be sullied with horse shit?"

"No, no," they replied as one, their soft young cheeks turning scarlet with embarrassment and shame.

"You must be severely punished. I'll think of something appropriate later," Marko said, concluding his sermon.

The silence deepened. Outside, the snow fell in big flakes, transforming the landscape into a vast white desert. The classroom was cold. At Marko's angry words, many of the children trembled with foreboding and fear. Punishment could mean many things in war.

"*Tovarishitza* Valeria, please continue your work. Come see me in the afternoon."

Valeria nodded. After he left the classroom, she cleaned the blackboard and started some math exercises. It was easier to deal with numbers. In the heat of algebra, the class returned to normality. Henrik, however, continued to wait for Valeria in her room, shaking with fear because he didn't know what was going on at the school. He wrote his essay and waited. Nobody came by. He opened a couple of books and finally plunged into The Beavers, a novel about pile dwellers by Slovenian novelist Jalen. He felt safe. His teacher's room was like a sanctuary. Later, after putting a couple of big logs on the fire, he snuggled under a woolen blanket and fell asleep.

His dream of Christmas was shaken back into reality as *Tovarishitza* Valeria gently tried to wake him up.

"Come on, Henrik. You'll miss your lunch at the orphanage. Quickly, put on your coat and go. Here's a letter for your principal, *Tovarishitza* Zdenka."

It took Henrik's mind a while to come back to reality. *Tovarishitza* Zdenka was the Panther Lady. She would beat him up despite the letter. Politely he took the sealed envelope from Valeria's hand. He wished he could stay with her. Valeria seemed to read his thoughts.

"I must go see *Tovarish* Marko. You'll be all right. Just give her the letter as soon as you get back. It explains everything. You're under special protection from *Tovarish* Marko until this thing is resolved. Don't worry, Henrik, you'll be all right."

Valeria gave him a big red apple. "Eat this on the way. Nobody can steal it from your belly." She ran her fingers through his thick hair. Henrik closed his eyes and pretended it was his mother touching him. For a moment, the time stood still. Then he thanked her and left.

Valeria went to Marko's office. It smelled of fresh black coffee. She inhaled the heavenly aroma that seemed to be right out of One Thousand and One Nights. Where did they get real coffee? Marko had an explanation ready: his men had found a black market dealer who, besides selling ill-gotten goods, also spied on people and passed the information to the SS. Deep down, Valeria was beginning to doubt whether all the partisans were always so brave and noble when it came to procuring supplies. She had seen a lot in the last two years. Still, the coffee filled her mouth with bitter sweetness and transported her home, to Kozjane, to the times when her family would sit around the table, enjoying desert after the Sunday roast, sipping coffee, and chatting. What was happening back there? She tried not to think of the scattered news about the difficult situation in the *Brkini Hills*, which had become a favorite escape route for *Chetniks*, *Ustashas*, Germans, and Home Guards on their way to the Trieste port. She brought her focus back to the present.

Being a practical man, Marko came up with a punishment for the children that would also get some useful work done. Two at a time, the pupils would help the groom at the stable clean the boxes and feed the horses for one week. Both were to sleep on the hay in the barn and eat their meals there for the whole duration. They would continue to attend school and do their homework. Valeria agreed that it was a just punishment. Soon they began to chat about other things. The war started by the Germans was turning against them. The Allies continued advancing in the East and the West, German towns were bombed night after night. The SS terrorizing Russian civilians could not mirror the Red Army's ruthlessness on their march to Berlin. Italy became an important point of entry for the supplies being sent more frequently now by the Allies. They were all hoping the Germans would surrender and spare more lives and suffering. However, their fanatic leader refused to admit defeat and continued give out insane orders that sent his men into the final bloodbath.

As for the pupils' punishment, Marko and Valeria did not foresee that Henrik would be the first to volunteer for it. The stable seemed like Heaven compared to the orphanage. That night when he returned from school, the Panther Lady whipped him so hard that he lost his consciousness and thought himself dead. She took black revenge in her own vicious hands in the name of the partisan children.

In the following months, Valeria and Marko met as much as their work permitted. Their afternoons sipping black coffee turned into evenings spent together. Marko was spoiling Valeria with meat, honey, and wine. After so many years she finally got to melt a bar of chocolate in her mouth. On Marko's free evenings, their dinners lasted longer and longer and eventually turned into long winter nights spent together. Valeria's room at the rectory became the sanctuary of a new young love. In February 1945, while rough winds and bitter colds made even fighting impossible, Valeria realized she was pregnant. Marko was thrilled. They were the first couple to exchange marriage vows under the new *Liberation Front* authorities. The judge smiled with enthusiasm during the ceremony. Finally, he could preside over something else instead of trials for war crimes. Their way to freedom was paved with thoughts of a new life in a new society.

~~~

In May 1945, the train compositions at the Ljubljana station seemed endless. The sun heated the roofs of the passenger cars mercilessly. Like a swarm of killer bees, the cacophony of hushed voices spoke the language of fear and insecurity. The sorrowful wails of women and the sharp cries of children revealed there were many civilians aboard.

Valeria sharply observed the skinny, ragged boys with buckets of waters distributing drinks among the sullen passengers, who were moaning angry complaints because of the delay. Ljubljana was free. The National Liberation Army had marched into the city two days ago. The wives, parents, and children of the Home Guards, who haven't yet managed to escape to the Austrian Carinthia, were eager to leave the city as quickly as possible. The last train came from Rijeka. Families of Serbian *Chetniks* and Croatian *Ustashas* filled almost all compartments. The freshly shaved soldiers, who were shooting at each other just a few days ago, were now sharing the flight path to the north, away from the winning partisans. Absurd. Running from peace.

Valeria noticed how nervously women clutched their jewelry and fine furs. A sorry lot who lost the war, filthy collaborators, losers …She could not ban from her mind the image of what could have happened to the Partisans if the Germans and their traitorous servants had won. She bet they would not let them simply leave the country.

Well, it was better this way. There was reason to kill half of the population to prove a point, was there? Her orders that day were simple and clear: supervise the transport and shoot any troublemakers. Her superior, Major Niko, was marching up and down at the entrance to the railway platforms. A boy with two buckets went from car to car distributing water. She followed his every move carefully. He meant well, but many women refused to drink from the filthy glass he offered. The "ladies" in fur made her sick with their burning cheeks and sweaty hands clamped on their possessions. They would be gone soon, hopefully forever. She waved her hand to let major Niko know everything was all right.

However, nothing was all right. She felt sick and tired. The heavy rifle strained her shoulder. Warfare was unkind to a pregnant woman. While her belly was slowly swelling, the military shirts could still hide her pregnancy. She was married but hadn't seen her husband for more than two months. The worse was, she had little or no news at all from him. She knew through some contacts that he was busy in the final war operations concerning the politics toward the collaborators. She lived in constant fear for his life. Desperate bullets could be lethal, too.

She had followed the winning partisan battalions from Bela Krajina to Ljubljana. What an amazing welcome! The citizens of Ljubljana showered them with flowers and kisses. They, the partisans, were their army, their heroes and liberators! Like all of them, Valeria was drunk with victory, the most powerful drug of all. She was dancing and singing for the whole day and a large part of the night. She completely forgot to spare her energies, which the baby under her heart needed. However, life must go on and the victory day was over too soon. There were so many new tasks ahead of them. They were to build a new democratic society, a new socialist government that would care for justice and equal opportunities for all citizens. A cry from the rail car brought her back to the present.

"Valeria, Valchy! Look at me! Here!"

She recognized the voice of Ada and froze. Should she speak to her? What would Major Niko say if he saw her talking to the wife of a Home Guard? Valeria threw a careful look in his direction. She could see his wide back entering the railway station. Her cheeks turned red with shame. Ada was her best friend. How could she even hesitate for one second? She remembered the long, sleepless night under her friend's bed, how selflessly Ada had given herself to Andrej while hiding Valeria in the room. She smiled and looked up.

"Hello, Ada. Where are you going?"

Ada smiled and stretched her right arm outside the carriage to touch Valeria. In her other arm, she was holding a red-cheeked baby boy, who was sitting and kicking from the open window of the car. Valeria could not hold back her smile.

"Is this little Martin?" she asked, touching the chubby little foot hanging over the car window. Tickled, the boy screeched with joy. Valeria played with him for a while, then said, "He's lovely, Ada. He has your eyes, like two little chocolates."

"And you, Valeria? You look a bit round to me. Have you fallen in love?"

Valeria sighed and lifted her palms in defense. "I can't hide anything from you, can I?"

"Then it's true! Who's the father?"

"Marko Robič. He's from Trieste. We were the first couple married under the new Partisan government in Metlika."

"Where's he now?"

"He's on duty with his unit somewhere in Dolenjska. But he's alive, this much I know."

"That's good, so you will have a family. I want to kiss you and put my arms around you. Can you come aboard, Valeria?"

Valeria suddenly realized how foolish she was. If the major saw her chatting with somebody from the train, she could get in real trouble. Yet, the entrance of the station remained peaceful. She made a few steps and turned around. She did not want anybody to read her lips.

"Where are you going, Ada?"

Little Martin seemed amused by her serious voice. He reached out his tiny hands, slimy with saliva, toward Valeria. A cute a little cherub with golden curls. Ada had to hold him tight with both hands before he propelled his tiny body off the sill. His bare legs kicked so hard in the air that his right sock fell to the ground. Valeria observed him first, then Ada, who was dressed in her best silk dress and wore a lot more jewelry than usual. They were well-sheltered while the war blazed in the woods around Ljubljana. For a fraction of a moment, she felt bitter. While Ada nursed little Martin, Valeria was wounded, losing her first love and their baby in battle. But then her warm feelings for her friend quickly returned.

"So, where are you headed, Ada?"

"We're going to join Andrej in Carinthia, Bleiberg. He telephoned last night," she said, looking at the red star on Valeria's cap. "They say the Russians are coming. That they will govern Slovenia and Yugoslavia. Andrej said we should run. If we stay in Ljubljana, we could be in danger, little Martin and me. Who knows what awaits us in Austria? People say everything there is in ruins and everyone is scrounging the streets for food," she added with an inquisitive look, fishing for more information.

Valeria knew how much the Communists hated the Home Guard. While victory made them drunk with joy, revenge could make them mad with fury. Anything could happen to the collaborating soldiers and their families. They were traitors, and traitors must be disposed of, quickly and silently, like a pack of wolves killing a flock of sheep. While the question of Trieste, still in the hands of the Dalmatian and Slovenian partisan battalions, remained territorially unsolved, anything was possible. The war could go on.

"Come on, Ada. You shouldn't believe everything people say. The Russians are allies, brothers in the fight, no more no less. We have our first partisan government. There's no reason to panic."

"Everyone who didn't take the Partisans' side is scared to death." Ada's voice trembled with emotion. She saw the pride in Valeria's eyes. True, they had won and the whole country should respect them now. "So be it, Valeria. I am proud of you. I am proud to have a friend so brave and strong. You are the victor, Valchy, the victor!"

The conversation was getting out of hand. One more word and they would both be crying. Valeria must regain control over the situation. She looked toward the station. In contrast to the blazing sunshine outside, the dark entrances to the lobby seemed peaceful. However, Major Niko could be watching her from inside. She turned her back to the station and spoke to Ada.

"Ada, listen to me! This is serious. We have orders to shoot anybody who makes a wrong move. Join Andrej at Bleiberg and go away. Don't come back to Yugoslavia! Quickly, go to America or to Switzerland. Don't believe anybody, just run."

Valeria paused, watching the effect of her words on Ada. Her friend's face darkened with worry, and tears glimmered in her big brown eyes. Her lips trembled.

"Valeria, Valchy, you won't shoot me, will you?"

Valeria just stared. She came closer to the window, the baby's feet almost touching her hair. "No, Ada, no ... I love you. You're my best friend. You've lost the war, you'll lose your rights, everything. All I'm saying is, run, my darling, run, and don't look back, ever."

Little Martin turned his round face to look intently at his mother as only babies could. When he saw Ada's eyes flooding with tears and felt her body shaking with sobs, he broke into a loud cry, too. Valeria looked toward the head of the composition and saw it would be leaving soon. Indeed, the train conductor blew a whistle and slowly the cars filled with refugees began to move. Still, the major was nowhere to be seen. She cast another furtive look at her lifelong friend and followed alongside the car.

"Take care of yourself, Ada."

"Valchy, please, Valchy, help me, please ..."

Valeria looked up and thought she was dreaming. Ada lifted little Martin, his short legs kicking up in the air, away from the sill. Valeria saw her friend plant a long kiss on the baby's damp hair. Then she tossed him out the window. Valeria instinctively opened her arms. Like a package of grief, the crying baby landed in her embrace. His chubby arms wide open, trying to hold on to something, to grab anybody. She stared at Ada. 'What is this? Is she crazy?' Yet, her face was drawn further away as the train gained more speed. In a few moments, Ada's face became smaller and smaller until her head was only a dot jutting out of the window. Martin continued to cry his lungs out, his hands clutching at her hair. Valeria felt as if she had fallen into a deep black hole. What was she going to do with the baby? Her legs seemed unable to hold her. Was she going to faint?

"Oh, I didn't know you had a baby, *Tovarishitza* Valeria," a deep voice next to her said cordially.

She spun around and faced Major Niko. It took her several tries before she managed to say, "Yes, we were very much in love, Borko and I."

"Do you mean Borislav Lukman – THAT Borko, Valeria?"

"Yes, we used to work undercover together. Unfortunately, Borko died before his son was born."

The major nodded in respect and understanding. Borko was a legend. Little Martin stopped crying and looked curiously at the medals on Major Niko's chest. Then he turned to Valeria and shyly touched the red star on her cap.

"Yes, your mamma is a real partisan. When you grow up, you'll be a partisan, too, won't you, little fellow?"

"Martin, wink at Major Niko, will you?"

Martin just stared at the man. Ada's train was only a spot in the hot vapors of a May afternoon. Valeria had to finish this absurd farce and think of something quickly.

"I'm sorry, Major Niko. My friend, a nurse, was looking after Martin while I was serving the Partisan cause. She heard I was back and brought the baby here. I had to hold him, just once, after so many months. But ..."

"It's all right, Valeria. This was the last train for those nasty traitors. Your duty is over. Go home and take care of your brave little boy."

She made a military salute, which little Martin clumsily imitated.

The major chuckled, saying: "Finally, we'll have time for some laughter and joy! Have a great day, little Martin! Farewell, *Tovarishitza* Valeria!"

Valeria escaped the railway station as though hounds were chasing her. She turned around the corner of Miklošičeva Street and thought of Marjana. She hadn't seen her since she returned to Ljubljana. Now, she would. Marjana was the boy's aunt, for God's sake. She should look after him. Not Valeria, just married and pregnant. How could she explain the child to her husband? First, to the hospital.

Angry and worried in the midday heat of the warm spring day, Valeria had trouble catching her breath as she walked. Maybe, she could leave the boy in an orphanage. She heard there would be a place for the Home Guards' orphans somewhere in Štajerska. That was what she had to do. But how could she do that? His face was silent and serious. She looked into his brown eyes. How old was he anyway? Not even a year, by God. Her heart filled with pity. He could die in such a place… And somebody would hold his tiny hands …No, she must think of something else, a way to keep him with her. First, Marjana. She must help Valeria. Provide pacifiers and bottles, nappies, socks and blankets…

What was Ada thinking? Why did she do such a thing? She must have gone mad. The baby could have fallen on the rails and died.

Her heart sank. Nobody must know who little Martin is. About his father and mother. Nobody. First, she would have to forge or arrange Martin's birth certificate – father: Borko, mother: Valeria. Yet who would sign and stamp the document? And what would she tell Marko when he came back from the front? Maybe, it would be better…

She stopped and leaned against the shop window. She and the boy cuddled cheek to cheek, so that she could feel his warm tears. Poor baby. She kissed him on the forehead. He smelled so sweet – the scent of wide meadows and sweet life ahead. By God, she would never let him go. The light bounced from the glass in the window and ran over her face. Martin smiled. Valeria got an idea. She had to find Doctor *Franja*. God knows whether she was alive and where she was.

"First, we'll go find your auntie, Martin," she said, hurrying toward the hospital.

~~~

Traveling among a crowd of nervous, sweaty, feverish people, Ada closed her eyes. The air was fraught with a distinct smell – sour and sharp, the smell of despair and angst. In the aisle, particles of dust from the passengers' dirty boots and garments danced with the rays of the sun. In the cramped space, she leaned on the man's back behind her and felt his muscles through his light vest but didn't care. He could think what he wanted, she didn't give a damn. Her strength was gone. It was over, all over. This was the end. Two tears slid down her cheeks. Tears of pain or relief?

'So you won. Now you'll take everything from us. Have my little baby, too,' she thought bitterly. Her will crushed, her senses dulled.

However, in her nausea and dizziness, thinking back to that empty platform in Ljubljana, she stuck to her decision. It was the only sensible thing to do.

"Valeria will take care of Martin. It's better this way. Who knows what awaits us in Austria. We're the traitors, the losers. Nobody wants us."

She felt a hand on her shoulder and opened her eyes. An elegantly dressed man in his forties was looking at her with empathy and concern. His dark hair and beard glistered with silver threads.

"Madam, you've done the right thing. Your friend is a good woman," he said softly in Croatian. His voice almost broke, but Ada in her anguish failed to notice. She stared at him, scared that he might be an enemy spy, a threat to her baby and her friend.

"What friend?" she asked suspiciously, brushing her tears in haste.

"Don't worry, madam, your secret is safe with me. I will not tell," he whispered, feeling almost sorry for his indiscretion.

Ada closed her eyes again. If only she could die! Lose her consciousness so that she wouldn't know what was going on. Memories of little Martin seared every muscle and nerve in her body. Her nose still remembered the scent of his damp hair, her fingers longed for the velvet touch of his skin. In her palm, she could still feel the weight of his plump little bottom in the diaper. Her breasts were bursting with milk, longing for Martin's mouth to suck on the nipples. The sharp pain traveled from her areola to the life-producing gland straight into her heart. Warm jets of milk stained her silken blouse. The milk wanting to reach Martin, the honey of love only mothers can give. How much she loved her little boy. How terribly afraid she was for his life. On the run, toward unknown, perhaps hostile places and things. God knows whether Andrej was still alive, and whether she would be able to find him.

In Ljubljana, the liberation brought chaos. Everyone was cheering, singing, shooting, drinking, hugging each other and acting as though in a huge madhouse. Amidst all this joy, many among the liberators were looking to get revenge. There were no rules. The terrible tension brought about by the last months of the war seemed ready to erupt into a volcano of evil. Andrej joined the Home Guard army in their flight north in the first days of May. It seemed wiser for Ada and Martin to follow him later. Once the partisans had installed some order, the traffic would flow and life would go on. Who would think of harming a mother with a baby? Then rumors began to spread about the partisans' thirst for blood and revenge. People said they were killing all their opponents: old people, women, children, babies. Ada panicked.

For days, she searched for a way to escape and temporarily leave Martin with relatives or friends. She pleaded with Marjana to look after him until things got better. However, her older sister feared the new authorities would find Martin in her house and take him to an orphanage. She was privy to the horrible conditions in such a place, particularly for the children of the enemies. Babies were dying there. They tried to reach their family in Kozjane to no avail. All communications had broken down since the Germans left. God knows whether Mother and Father were still alive. Ada thought of her friend Valeria, but had no idea where she was since last summer. Besides, Ada had her doubts. Valeria could have become a Communist fanatic and turn little Martin in to the authorities. Days went by until this train was her last chance to flee. She packed only the necessary clothes, sewed jewels in the lining of her skirt and jacket without knowing whether they would be of any help. Marjana hid the Strainar's family silver, paintings, rare books, and antiques. Everything should be safe with her. After all, she had helped the *Liberation Front* throughout the war.

When she saw her beloved friend at the railway station, she had a premonition. Valerie looked every bit the proud victor with her red-starred partisan cap on her black curls – tired, yet glorious. Ada noticed right away her slightly swollen belly under the military shirt. A home for one child could be a home for two. Then Valeria hinted about Carinthia being dangerous, that they might find death there. There was no mercy for traitors. Wasn't Valeria indirectly offering a safer way out for Martin? Of course, she was. Ada still couldn't fathom how she gathered the strength to do what she did – an unspeakable crime. Abandoning her child. With every village and town they passed, her doubts rose like black clouds before a storm. Anxiety made it difficult for her to breathe. It was as if a mass of sticky, spongy matter were filling her lungs and invading her body and soul.

"Please, madam, do sit down," she heard the man say. He gently pushed her to the seat by the window. Ada gave in without wondering how he found an empty one in the crowded train.

"Thank you," she stuttered and carefully added, "I am Ada. You are very kind. Who are you, sir?"

In times of war, you should not reveal too much to strangers. Instead find out as much as you can about them.

"My name is Marjan Pučić. A businessman from Split," he replied.

"Why are you leaving?"

"Oh, my dear, during the war, I had to work and cooperate with everybody: Italians, Germans, *Ustashas*. However, I willingly helped the partisans. My family, wife, and children went to America before 1940. I stayed in Split to protect our estates and companies. Why? There was no reasonable way to sell them once the war started. So be it. I hope to keep my head on my shoulders." He loosened his tie and smiled at her.

Ada's suspicions lessened. "How many children do you have, Mr. Pučić?" she asked quietly, still thinking about her child.

"Five, my dear Ada, five," he said, cheering up. "My oldest daughter, Nina, is sixteen. Probably a real damsel by now. My twin boys, Marko and Luka, are twelve and, according to my wife, bloody rascals as though pirate *Kačić* were their real father. My other daughter, Manja, is a quiet and good girl. Baby boy Franjo was born in the States, so I haven't seen him yet."

'Valeria's little brother is called Franjo, too,' said Ada thoughtfully.

"Who's Valeria?" Pučić asked, showing more interest than Ada liked. She trembled. 'What a fool I am!' She was telling her life story to a stranger on a refugee train. He might contact the first guard he sees and sell her story to his advantage. 'Why is he on this train if he helped the Partisans? He must be their mole.'

"Ah, the niece of my acquaintance," she said, improvising. "She's six and speaks of her little brother all the time. I bought her a puppet to play with."

The man seemed to look right through her, reading her lies like an open book. He silently nodded and looked out the window. The train was rolling past recently plowed fields and winter wheat that spread a lush green carpet across acres of land. The farmers had sowed the wheat last autumn – during the war – and would harvest them in peace. Yet what kind of peace was this? Everyone was leaving, running, heading for a better world. This train was full of people who panicked in the face of the new guerilla power, a handful that brought life in Yugoslavia under their control. Pučić sighed. What would happen to his Mediterranean villa in Šibenik, to his vineyards in the Pelješac peninsula and his house in Split? He had helped the partisans until the very last days. He kept asking the couriers what would happen after the war to no avail. When a Serbian commander took over their communications with him, Pučić realized he had to run for his life. The man was one of those old military cadres who could not hide his contempt for rich business people. Pučić was trying to get to the passage across the Adriatic, where the Allies could help him get to America. The captains, however, didn't want to risk their ships before the fighting was really over. Minimize the damage. He had to take the sorrowful Balkan route north.

"Where are you going, Mr. Pučić?" kindly asked Ada.

Pučić smiled. The woman was chatting, as though she were taking a Sunday trip while minutes ago she had thrown her baby into the arms of her friend. Maybe she would never see her little boy again.

"To the Allies, like all of us. And you?" he said.

"Me, too. My husband has been in Austria for a couple of weeks. He's waiting for me in Klagenfurt."

"May I ask what your husband's profession is, Mrs. Ada?"

"He's a psychiatrist. Outstanding man, only ..."

"On the wrong side of the political equation," Pučić said, finishing her thought. He gently patted her hand. "Look, Mrs. Ada, I was on the right side. I worked for our cause during the whole war. Never liked the Fascists or *Ustashas*. Bunch of butchers. But in order to avoid suspicion, I had to do business with them. You see, my dear lady, I am on the run, just like you. War knows no rules."

Ada looked at him with purpose. "I've been wondering what your story was. I mean being on this train, Mr. Pučić. All traitors – real or not – hiding behind masks, ready to set a trap. What's the point? The winners take it all, don't they? There's nothing more I can give, nothing." She hid her face in her hands and started to cry.

The young man sitting next to her stood up. "Eh, women, all wails and cries!" he said, voice trembling in contempt, and stepped into the aisle.

Pučić sat in his place and offered Ada a handkerchief with his initials. She grabbed it, but could not stop the sobs. The horror of the loss, the possibility that she might never see little Martin again was piercing her heart. In the dusty railcar, her decision didn't seem as sound as in Ljubljana. Tears fell on her beige blouse already soaked with the milk from her breasts. She felt as though life were deserting every inch of her body.

"I shouldn't have done it. What kind of mother am I?" She sighed.

Pučić took her hands and shook her slightly to make her look at him. "Dear Mrs. Ada, you are a good mother and you did the right thing. I observed your friend. She seems tough on the outside, but good at heart. She loves you. She was devastated to see you and your baby on this train," he said, trying to persuade her.

Ada calmed down. "Do you think so?" she asked him shyly.

"Of course. The last thing I saw was your baby leaning his head on her shoulder. Don't worry. She will take care of him. She will find a way to deal with the situation, this partisan friend of yours. Then one day, when all this hatred and thirst for revenge is gone, you'll go back for him."

Ada wept, this time with tears of gratitude. The thought that she would soon hold her little Martin again transported her into a warm sea of expectation. The chance of tomorrow was stronger than the pain of today.

"Do you think we'll be able to come back? I mean soon?"

Pučić knew it would not be so soon, yet he wanted to comfort her. "Of course, we will. Let all this chaos calm down. When the authorities establish peace and order, we'll be able to return. You'll see, you and your husband and I and my wife, we'll all spend a holiday on the Adriatic coast. Let's say, in Šibenik. We'll go for a swim, go to restaurants, enjoy the sweet taste of scallops, and investigate the Krka waterfalls. Thank God, the war is over."

A beep finished his reverie. The train stopped in the middle of a muddy field. There wasn't a soul around. Pučić looked out the window. At the head of the composition, he could see a group of partisans quarrelling with the locomotive operator, who was eagerly explaining something to them. The men were swinging their rifles like toys. Menacing. Pučić couldn't understand what they were saying. It might be safer to get away from this, to continue the voyage on foot. He turned around and bumped into Ada, who was assessing the situation, too.

Cheeks still wet with tears, she whispered, "Let's get off the train before it's too late. I fear they'll kill us all."

The man was surprised. This devastated woman. Was it her intuition? How did she find the courage to act? No time to think about it.

"Madam needs to go to the toilet," he said in a loud voice, pushed Ada through the aisle toward the door of the railcar.

"And you're going to help her?" a rough man's voice said loudly. The passengers burst into laughter as though his quip had made their odd Sunday trip even more perfect.

Ada and Pučić jumped onto the gravel alongside the rails. Gripping their travel bags firmly, they squeezed against the side of the train. After a moment's hesitation, they ran into the alder thicket, still leafless at this time of year. The seeds cones pelted at their cheeks, the brambles scratched their skin, and insects bit and sucked through their sweaty skin. Without looking right or left, they just kept running over the roots and rocks. In spite of their city clothes, they were both wearing boots under their silks. Ada had thought of this ahead. Her bag contained warm trousers, a pullover, and a huge scarf that should have served as baby carrier. She wanted to have her hands free in case she had to march for a long time with Martin.

After a few hundred meters, her new friend whispered across the bramble bush: "Maybe we should wait for the train to leave."

"What if it doesn't? Let's run. Better to be far away," Ada replied. She didn't trust this unwarranted stop. Maybe the train was a trap. Maybe the partisans wanted to kill them all here, far away from the eyes of witnesses.

Pučić nodded, and their steps led them faster and faster onward until they reached a worn path deep in the woods. They were climbing toward the mountain pass, toward the border where the Allies occupied Nazi Austria. In the bushes, they changed out of their city clothes.

Pučić commented on her transformation: "You're a practical woman, Ada. I can hardly believe my eyes. You've shown so many faces in the short hours we've known each other. Where are you from, Mrs. Ada?"

"I'm a farmer's daughter," said Ada firmly. She was not going to tell him too much about her. "I suggest we stop using formal titles. You're Marjan and I'm Ada."

"All right, Ada," he said, staring at the baby clothes in her bag. She stashed them deeper and pulled out the scarf to turn the bag into a backpack.

"This will be easier to carry," she said.

She was determined to live and return to her little son one day. Should she not find Andrej at Klagenfurt, she must start alone from scratch. A thought passed through her mind. Maybe Andrej was dead. Alone, she could return to Ljubljana sooner. She hadn't done anything wrong. She hadn't worked against the Communists. Maybe, she could live with Valeria again. Then, remorse brought bitter bile into her mouth. Didn't she love Andrej? How fragile could be love amidst war and horror.

Marjan offered her a tepid drink of water. While she drank, he studied a military map and a compass to determine which way they should take.

"The last train station was Lesce." She pointed at the dot of the village next to Bled. "Where did you get this map and a compass?"

"Well, Ada, I took some precautions, too. However, the trains went smoothly until Rijeka. Afterward, we were stopping at each train stop. The heat and the stench were unbearable. Well, when we reached Ljubljana, it seemed to be the end of our ride. I thought of jumping off the train. The map and the compass are essential if you want to avoid people on the road. I've had them since WWI. I was an officer on the *Isonzo* Front and know how to orient a map. We'll take the less traveled paths. I am sure the roads are jammed with carts and refugees – guarded by the partisans, of course."

"With only one thought on their mind: revenge. We're nothing but trash to them."

"Ada, true peace will come one day. You'll see. Let's go!"

They walked for a week or so. During the day, they hid in the thick woods. Nighttime was travel time. When the rocks in the mountains were too steep and dangerous, they climbed them at first light. They drank water from the creeks and bought food at lonely farms. The farmers, deprived and poor after the plunder of the war, charged them a shamelessly high price for each bite. Over the border in Carinthia, many farms stood empty, abandoned. As though the farmers had left in haste. They rested, ate what they could find, washed, and slept. Where were all the people fleeing? From ruins to ruins, from barrel of one gun to another.

Every day, Ada was more convinced she did the right thing. How could she have carried a baby with her along these wild paths and climbed the rocks? How could she have silenced him when they were hiding in a ditch, waiting for the partisan patrol to pass by? She doubted she could have traveled with Pučić had she taken her baby with her. Pučić was an honorable man. Yet, saving his skin was his priority. Ada was useful. She could speak Slovenian. Croatians were shot on the spot – every one of them was considered an enemy, an *Ustasha*. Where a path came closer to the main road, they could see the endless columns of refugees, carts, trucks, and other wheeled vehicles. People were marching into exile. Sometimes the partisans would pull out men and drag them away. The echoes of shots sealed their fate in the distance.

In the first days of June, they managed to reach the suburbs of Klagenfurt. The weather was rainy and cold, their route heavy and muddy. They paid for information and found out that there was a refugee camp for Slovenians and Croatians at Viktring. Ada wanted to register at the Red Cross post, yet Pučić persuaded her not to. Until her money lasted, she was free. Once registered as a refugee, she would have to stay in the camp and could not go where she wanted. They found a cheap boardinghouse at Wörthersee. Ada was surprised to find out that Pučić had a car waiting for him at Klagenfurt. He was going to Switzerland. But first he wanted to help Ada find her husband. It was the least he could do in return.

"What was the arrangement with your husband, Ada? Where can we look for him?"

It was very agonizing. Finding Andrej among the ruins of Carinthia was like finding a needle in a haystack. He had called from Bleiburg. Where was the place? She couldn't speak German or English. She was afraid of uniformed officials. Besides, Martin was registered in her passport and people might ask where her child was. She shivered at the thought of being suspected of killing her baby.

During long walks among colorful carpets of early spring flowers in the meadows and pale green trees that were pushing out their first leaves and buds, her eyes would become blinded by tears. Milk continued to flow from of her breasts like a long-forgotten natural spring, seeking to find the streambed where there is none. Every evening she squeezed the milk out of her breasts for fear of infection. It was like letting blood. Sadness drenched her body and soul. The pain in her heart was such that every now and then she would miss a step, at times falling over a root, at times catching her balance just in time. In her mind, she would be talking to Valeria, Andrej, and Martin. Where was he, her little heart? Her little darling. Was he eating properly? Could he sleep at night? Was he crying and calling for her? They had never been separated for more than a few hours. Now they would be apart for days, months, maybe years. At least, he was in the safe hands of the victorious. The last thought comforted Ada while she was panting uphill, climbing the steep mountains that would bring her abroad. One day she would return. Andrej had told her to inquire at the Red Cross. He said he would offer his help in treating the sick the moment when he got across. Pučić's question was still hanging in the air.

"The Red Cross, a British station. He called from Bleiburg the other day. My husband speaks English among other foreign languages. He said he would try to find a job with them as soon as he comes to Carinthia."

"Right, I'll go to check there. I can speak English. Don't worry, Ada. Please, give me his full name and all the information I need."

Ada wrote down Andrej's details on a piece of paper. She held it in her hand and hesitated. Doubt invaded her thoughts. Might Pučić have an evil plan for her and Andrej? She had no reason to suspect him. No reason at all. Yet, a feeling of inexplicable distress could not leave her mind. The anxiety that had traveled with her since Ljubljana. The angst that had suffocated her weeks before the Liberation Day.

"Wouldn't it be better if I, as his wife, make the inquiries? Marjan, maybe you can come with me and help with the translation."

"I'm afraid not, Ada. If he's not at the Red Cross, they might put you in the refugee camp. My dear friend, that would not be easy, believe me. I told you about my engagement in the Great War. I spent a couple of months as a prisoner of the Italians. It was horrible. I survived only because I had money. If not for my resourcefulness, even money might not have saved me from starving. Once you lose control over your life, you must follow the orders of the occupying forces. The British have guns, too, you know."

"But Andrej left Ljubljana before I did. On the fifth of May."

Pučić looked silently at her. His face was impassive, like a rock.

"You think he's died," whispered Ada, withholding tears.

He simply nodded. "Ada, you saw for yourself what a dangerous journey it is," he said. "If he was in Home Guard uniform, it could have been fatal even though Slovenia was still occupied by the Germans."

Ada contradicted him. "No, he didn't wear his uniform. He took it with him, but was dressed as civilian."

"Clever man. May I have this piece of paper then?"

Ada was uncertain. She remembered Valeria's advice not to trust anybody and just run. Maybe Andrej had gone to Switzerland and was safe by now. She must cope on her own somehow. She said slowly, "Marjan, you've been so good to me. Thank you."

"My dear Ada, I owe you my life. Without you, the partisans would have caught and killed me. You saw how they shot Croats like rabbits. We're all *Ustashas* for them."

He was telling the truth. Ada made up her mind.

"Right. You can say you know him from Ljubljana, that he was your doctor or something. You found out at the hospital where he had gone."

Pučić nodded. "You read my exact thoughts, Ada. I'll take my car. It will help me pass for a wealthy patient of your husband."

She smiled. "Dear God, Marjan. Your car really is impressive. How did you ever get one in the middle of all this chaos? Why did you take the train and travel on foot with me? Wouldn't it be more comfortable to drive to Austria?"

He smiled and took the little note out of Ada's grip. "Sometimes I thank my lucky stars: I was in Vienna in March when my car broke down. The situation was a mess. There were Russians at the city gates and I couldn't wait for the garage to repair it. You can imagine how impossible it was to find spare parts. So I offered a deal to the mechanic, who was a Slovenian from Carinthia, from Unterloibl. He wanted to flee Vienna with his wife, who had just given birth to a little boy. Vienna was in shambles. There was a shortage of everything. He was hoping the situation would be better in the countryside, at the farm of his parents. We agreed that he was to leave the car documents and the keys with my banker, Mr. Androsch. He had difficulties getting the spare parts and sent me a couple of telegrams. In the middle of April, the car was ready. The man offered to get somebody to drive it to Split. In spite of my cooperation with the partisans, I was afraid I would end up on the run. Leaving the car in Carinthia seemed a good idea."

"You're unbelievable, Marjan. You've thought of everything," said Ada, impressed.

"Oh, it's nothing. I'm a businessman. In this lifetime, my affairs have survived different laws and a couple of states. Four to be precise. I make sure to always have plan B, C, and D ready. Now this is plan X – penniless."

Ada shook her head. "Listening to you, I'm sure you took great care of your family and your affairs. Here and in America. Your family won't lack for anything."

Her voice sounded bitter. She could almost taste it on her palate. Why did Andrej join the Home Guard, leaving her and the baby on their own? In such a terrible time, too.

"I hope to bring back Mr. Strainar with me. Cheerio!" said Pučić cheerfully, making a bow.

Then hours went by and day turned to night. Ada sat in the lobby, reading old newspapers and magazines she couldn't understand to kill time. Around her, voices in a sharp German dialect chopped through the silence. The only person she saw was a Slovenian housekeeper, who addressed her from time to time and brought her a fresh cup of tea from the kitchen.

When finally Marjan returned, he told her he had found Andrej. He was in Bleiburg, in the camp for soldiers – Home Guards, *Ustashas*, and other formations – who collaborated with the Axis during WWII. In truth, he was working as a doctor. They went to a restaurant for dinner and agreed to fetch him in the morning.

They had to drive for several hours. The roads were jammed with refugees traveling aimlessly. Some were headed east, others west, most of them from south to north. They spoke different languages. It was as though the Lord wanted to scatter them all over Carinthia. God was the war, which was sowing sorrows all over the face of the earth. The only common thing among these people was the pain engraved in their stony faces. Pale, dusty, and hungry, they were moving toward the new peace that was a thousand times worse than the war.

As soon as they reached the camp, Pučić sent a boy with a note for Dr. Strainar saying his wife was in the office. Even though Andrej and Ada had been apart only a few weeks, it felt like years had passed. When he finally came in, he was in uniform and looked very serious. Yet, when he saw Ada, he cried with joy and opened his arms. She rushed into his embrace and for a moment hoped that tomorrow held a bright future for them. They would be one body and soul. Only love mattered. She gave him a summary of their voyage, how she and Mr. Pučić abandoned the train and went on foot, climbing the mountain passes to get to Carinthia.

"Where's Martin?"

The question sliced the air like the blade of a guillotine. Uneasy silence hung over their heads.

"Mrs. Ada left the boy with a friend of hers," said Pučić as though her child were merely staying with a babysitter for the afternoon.

Andrej's face turned purple. "Ada, what friend? Who, Ada, who has our little Martin?" he said, voice rising in panic.

She looked into his eyes and saw flashes of anger, horror, shock, and disappointment. An abyss of hate came between them and widened. A big, black hole. How could she explain that it had been for the best? Mountains, soldier camps, and fields of war were no places for a baby.

"Valeria," she whispered.

Without another word, Andrej pushed her away roughly, turned around, and started walking back to the soldiers behind the barbed wire. Fierce flies buzzed in the hot air like a ferocious diatribe. Ada leaned against the wall. She must be strong now. She observed the room through the thick fog of her fears. She must not lose him.

"Andrej, we'll get Martin back when things calm down! Please, Andrej," she pleaded, crying.

Yet, he did not look back. He marched on. She couldn't comprehend the world around her. Pučić gently led her back to the car and started the engine. It blared to life like an angry wild animal. She burst into hysterical weeping.

"Why can't he understand?" she repeated again and again between her sobs.

"I'll go see him tomorrow, Ada. Again. It must've been the shock. I promise I'll bring him back. Let's not drive back to Klagenfurt, but stay at that little inn near Bleiburg. Ada, I will use all my skills to persuade your husband. I will not fail, my dear," he said in a firm voice.

They drove along the blooming orchards of apple trees along sweet-smelling elder bushes and tall acacia trees. Everything seemed to be bursting with new life, only her life was over. This was the end.

She had abandoned her child – her body and soul. She would blame herself to the end of her days. Her husband would never forgive her. God would never forgive her. Not for this mortal sin.

All night long she sweated and panted in bed. Guilt tortured her mind, which burned with self-recrimination and sorrow. When she finally managed to close her eyes, gray light had begun to invade the room. Soon she heard Pučić's car roaring out of the yard. Ada had little hope. She knew Andrej. Once hurt, he had a hard time seeing things from a different perspective. His heart bitterly froze in outrage. While he was an empathetic doctor, open to the sorrows of his patients, he couldn't open himself to his wife or family. Why was he wearing the Home Guard uniform now? He used to avoid military activities before. Why couldn't he put her and their baby first? Who would leave a young mother and a baby in the chaos of war?

Ada felt let down. Her marriage, which she had imagined as the marriage of two souls forever inseparable, was a failure. Her husband didn't seem to love her enough. He kept his distance, as though their union were merely a social convention that an aging bachelor had to fulfill. As though he were pressured into finding a wife and a mother of his children. Ada cried most of the morning. In between, when her tears dried in her burning eyes, she sank into black thoughts. She couldn't see a way out.

At one o'clock, there was a knock on her door. Andrej entered the room, wearing civilian clothes. Ada stared at him in confusion and pain, as though he were an apparition. Finally, she realized it was her husband in person. She stood up.

"Andrej," she whispered, surprised.

"Ada, my darling. I'm so sorry about yesterday. I was so shocked, I didn't know what to do. Please, hold me, my darling, hold me tight."

She couldn't believe her ears. "What did Mr. Pučić tell you, Andrej?"

Andrej sighed and took her hands in his. He looked into her eyes, swollen and red from tears. "We talked for a long time, Ada. What a lucky coincidence that you two met and he accompanied you to the camp. Pučić spoke to the Croatians there. They told him that people are disappearing back home. Soldiers who board the trains to Yugoslavia under Allied supervision have been disappearing without a word. I'm not going to play the sacrificial lamb. Our time will come,

Ada. We'll be happy anywhere we are. One day the red bandits will be gone and we will return."

She sighed heavily as though able to purge evil from her lungs forever. She embraced Andrej and hid her face in his shoulder. Tears of gratitude and love welled in her eyes. They could be happy again. She wished he would kiss her as fervently as he did that summer night at the Ljubljana Castle. Her beloved, her good man.

"Thank you. You understand. Thank you," she said serenely.

He held her in silence. No kiss, his body stiff. After a while, he slowly let her go. "I shouldn't have left you alone with Martin. Please, forgive me. Do you think Valeria will take care of him?"

Ada said in a firm voice, "Certainly, I'm sure she will. Marjana is also there. They're friends. It was better this way. I'm not sure, Andrej, whether our little boy would be alive today had I not acted as I did."

His eyes sank to the floor. "I know. Pučić told me he wouldn't have traveled with you had Martin been there. It would have been too dangerous. The train that you left – all its passengers are now in the concentration camp at *Teharje*. Not only men, also old people, women, and children were made to walk for fifty kilometers without food or water. Anybody who couldn't go on was shot on the spot. My God, it's far worse than the Nazi occupation!"

Ada nodded. Finally, Andrej was seeing reason. "What will happen to the Home Guards then?"

"There are rumors that the British will take them to *Palmanova* by train. They say the conditions are better there. Some will leave tomorrow. I'm not sure, you see."

She felt relieved. "But you'll stay with me, won't you, my dear?"

"Yes, Ada, I will stay with you. You know how much I love you, darling."

Her dark thoughts and bitterness in the last weeks evaporated. She lifted her head and kissed him on the lips tenderly. "I love you, too, Andrej."

They held each other for a long while. When they heard the tinkling of cutlery from the dining room below, they wondered where their savior Pučić was.

They found him in the dining room, where he was devouring potato salad with fried elder flowers – a wartime dish. People ate what they could get. His spirits were high. Raising a tall glass of beer, he toasted to them.

"Good, you've come to an agreement. You're both coming to Switzerland with me. It would be easier to travel together. Then we'll see. No matter what, I have to find a way to reach my family in America."

"I'm sorry, Ada. I forgot to mention that Mr. Pučić offered to have us travel in his car. This is very kind of you, Mr. Pučić. I just have a small errand at the camp's infirmary tomorrow, then we can start off. I have a friend in Engadin, in the wonderful town of St. Moritz. We studied in Italy together. Maybe I can find work in Switzerland. This way we're close to Yugoslavia and Martin."

Ada smiled at him gratefully. She still felt the anxiety and pressure in her breasts, however, the steel coldness around her heart was melting. Ada and Andrej were together again – everything else was unimportant.

"Thank you, Mr. Pučić, you've been so good to us," said Ada in a bright voice.

Pučić acknowledged her thanks, wondering to himself what the future would bring. He had a long talk with Andrej Strainar and couldn't understand how rigid and backward his convictions were. The doctor seemed to crave a martyr's death. What did those priests preach to Slovenians? The appeal of mass suicide? Pučić had serious trouble in persuading Andrej not to join the soldiers on the train to *Palmanova*. As a tough and experienced mediator, he knew about the fragile moral ethics of the British, how they could go back on their promises in a flash. All they were after was profit; they could not resist temptations and cheated their clients for tiny percentages here and there whenever they could. Their empire was based on lies and violence. God knows what would happen to thousands of anti-communist soldiers on their return. What would happen to the Croatians? The way he saw it, the *Ustashas* should account for the war crimes they had committed, but not the innocent people who were fleeing with them. What would be their fate?

Marjan Pučić watched the Strainars with only one wish in his mind: to embrace his wife Miljutina and every one of his lovely children. However, in 1945, the journey to America was as long and as difficult as the journey to peacetime life.

~~~

The world on that golden September day was nothing less than perfect. The sun was shining brightly as if at the peak of summer, while fresh autumn breezes thick with the scent of ripe fruits and harvested fields played with the gray curtains of a private hospital room – a rare privilege in 1945, even for victors and heroes such as Valeria. Her eyes bright like diamonds, she waited for Marko and Martin to come and welcome a new member to their family: baby girl Anna. After a night of birth pains and exhaustion, Valeria felt dizzy and drunk with tenderness and love. She could have embraced the whole world. Every couple of minutes she softly kissed the forehead of her daughter, who was wrapped in white linen. Valeria had never imagined being so happy.

Last night when the contractions started, soon followed by her water breaking, Valeria was overcome with panic. Although she had gone through tough times and long winter marches in the woods, the new swelling sensation and sharp pangs inside her body seemed to squeeze the breath out of her. The tension in her belly grew unbearable. Her labor pains were sudden and sharp. She had to concentrate on her breathing. However, nature soon took over and, like a wise goddess, guided her in focusing and gathering her physical forces. For a couple of hours, she was straining her muscles and pushing without uttering a cry. Grinding her teeth, she bravely defied the pain. After all, Valeria was a warrior. In the distance, she could hear the doctors' whispered conversation in the room. They were saying that the hardships faced by women partisans on the battlefront had taken their toll on their bodies and drained their strength. Pregnancy and labor were risky for every one of them. Luckily, Valeria had spent some time teaching in Bela Krajina. In those months, her young body recovered and regained its natural rhythm, like her menstrual cycle.

In spite of her thirst for life and longing for a new love with Marko, Valeria was not overjoyed when she found out she was pregnant. The war seemed to last forever. How could they take care of the child? Marko, however, was thrilled. His joy soon infected Valeria, although they saw each other rarely during the victorious spring of 1945.

One would think the new freedom in the new country would give their life stability and impose social justice. Unfortunately, it wasn't so easy. In autumn, the food supply broke down. In spite of the help sent by the *UNRRA* to the devastated lands and destitute citizens of Europe, people were starving. In the spring of 1945, with fighting still going on, the farmers couldn't plough and sow the fields. And there weren't enough men for the task. Despite it being peacetime, millions of people wandered the wasted lands, many living in refugee camps. In ragged clothes and torn shoes, they simply sought a bite to eat and a place to sleep – homeless, humiliated, scattered into billions of tiny particles like their blown-up homes and towns. Shame and despair replaced dignity. The situation was particularly hard on the children. Weak and lost orphans in rags begging for scraps of food were crying from every corner of the towns that used to gleam with culture and splendor before the war. International humanitarian organizations like the Red Cross lacked resources and could not look after them. Moreover, in Slovenia, a rumor that twenty thousand Home Guard soldiers had disappeared after being deported from Carinthia caused widespread horror among those who had no knowledge of what had happened.

Because of her job at the OZNA headquarters, Valeria was well-off. Everything was ready for the new family member. And now that day came. Just before dawn, Anna – a tiny baby of less than three kilos, her lovely head matted with soft wet hair – was born. Her loud cry resounded in Valeria's ears like a concert of a thousand violins, the music announcing the biggest miracle of all: life. After a bath, little Anna was cradled happily in the arms of her mommy whose breasts were bursting with milk.

"Hello, darling." Marko bent down to kiss Valeria on the lips. He was in the uniform of *Tito*'s partisan army. His shirt smelled fresh, yet the trousers were filthy, smeared with cracked mud of dubious origins. He couldn't stop staring at their baby.

"What do we have here?"

Valeria smiled to her husband and lifted the wrapped baby to him. "Here, take her. I need to rest for a while. She's been at my bosom the whole morning."

Clumsily, Marko held his little daughter in his arms. She made a grimace as though about to start crying, yet stopped and opened her tiny lips into a wide yawn exposing reddish, toothless gums.

"God, Anna, your daddy is boring, isn't he?"

Valeria and Marko broke into a laugh. Anna opened her blurry eyes. She wanted to see who was laughing at her. She observed Marko's face attentively.

"She can't see you properly, Marko. Her vision will clear up in a month. But she knows you're an important person in her life. Maybe she can memorize your features if you move your face closer to hers."

Marko did so, kissing Anna's rosy cheeks and tiny nose tenderly. "I should have shaved before I came. I don't want to scratch her skin."

"Babies are tougher than you think. So the nurses keep saying. Maybe we're the ones, the mothers, who need more rest."

Valeria relaxed on the pillow with a sigh. She closed her eyes and breathed deeply. Anna's eyelids were closing, too, and she fell asleep in Marko's arms as though meeting her father for the first time had tired her.

"Marko, you can put Anna in her cot and sit on my bed. Tell me, where is Martin?"

A cry from the hall answered her question. The day nurse came into the room with the screaming toddler in her arms. His cheeks were purple and gleamed with tears. He was pushing his body away from the nurse who was trying to hold him in her arms.

"We were playing airplanes. I was lifting him up and down, throwing him in the air. At first, he shrieked with joy. Then suddenly his joy turned to panic, and he started to cry like there's no tomorrow. I was trying to comfort him so you could have more time alone. I'm sorry."

Valeria thanked her. She stretched her arms, and Martin cuddled close to her with his huge brown eyes filled with tears, his tiny body still shaking with deep sobs. Valeria kissed him on his slimy cheeks. "Why's my darling Martin shedding crocodile tears? Come on, my boy, give me a kiss!"

She wiped his eyes and tickled his neck. Through the fog of tears, Martin's lips opened into a smile adorned with tiny white teeth. He looked around with wonder in his eyes. He had never been to a hospital before, nor he had ever seen Mother lying in bed. He couldn't understand what was happening in this gray room.

"Come, Marty Smarty, meet your little sister," Marko said, taking him to the cot.

Martin first looked at his father, then curiously at the little worm wrapped in linen. Was this it? Was this the sister he had been waiting for? He exchanged a surprised look with his dad.

"Yes, Martin, I know. She doesn't look like much, doesn't she? It's not easy to come into this valley of tears, you see. Don't worry, your sister will grow up before you know it, and you will be able to play together."

Martin stretched his arms, and Marko held him close so that he could caress his sister's head. She did not move apart from the barely visible spasms on her face, her mind probably wandering through her baby dreams.

"They say I'll be able to go home tomorrow."

Marko, holding Martin in his lap, sat down on the bed and gave Valeria a kiss. "I'm on leave and will be able to spend a week with you. Marjana has been coming over every day. She makes lunch for us and helps with the cleaning. She said it would be best if she moves in with you for the first couple of weeks while I'm away. She said you should take it easy and rest, Valchy."

"We'll see. You know how my boss needs me. Is Marjana working full time now at the hospital?"

Marko shook his head. "I don't really know. But she's not looking very healthy. I think she even works double shifts. I don't know what's wrong with you girls from the *Brkini Hills*. Why are you all so pig-headed?"

"Come on, you need somebody to fight with. Are you a man or a mouse?"

"A tiger, grrrhhh ..." Marko snarled into Martin's belly as though to bite him. The boy shrieked with joy.

Valeria laughed only to grimace with pain, her stomach cramping. She held her breath for a moment, then asked: "Where are they sending you, Marko?"

"I've been placed in Kočevski Rog for now."

Valeria nodded. She'd heard the rumors about the trials there of collaborators – the Home Guards, the police, and civilians who fought against the *Liberation Front* during the war. She did not really like what she managed to gather from the reports. People shot without trials just because they were wearing the wrong uniform. She thought she knew the real reason behind the vengeance. It was fear mixed with political calculation. The Communists were preparing the terrain for the first democratic elections after WWII. The date hadn't been determined yet, however, the new provisional government, founded by the *Liberation Front* and *Tito*'s partisans, was eager to convince the majority of Slovenians to vote for them. Their methods of persuasion were brutal. Valeria was well-informed. She worked in the *Slavija* building, the seat of *OZNA*, as the general secretary of Josip Traven – Joc, her former partisan commander. The path to him and this job was not easy.

"By the way, I met Ivan, your former political commissary, the other day. We exchanged a couple of words, nothing personal. He promised me a big job in one of the new police forces."

Valeria's face darkened at the thought of that awful man. "You mustn't tell him about us. He loathes me. I happen to know a few secrets about him. For example, I remember how fast he hid in the bushes at the whistle of the first bullets. He's nothing but a rotten coward!"

Marko kissed her on the lips. "Don't worry. I told him we're married; he sends his regards. He's as docile as a lamb. In fact, we may get along quite well. He's not such a bad chap. And you're safe now, darling. You're working for Joc at *OZNA*. He cannot touch you."

"I wish you were right, Marko. I don't know what will happen in the next few weeks. I have to get up and start working as soon as I can."

Marko nodded and donned his Titovka cap. The red star in the middle shone like a drop of blood on his forehead. "Give Mommy a kiss, Martin. You better to rest, darling. Take care of our girl."

He carried Martin out and closed the door, the merry shrieks of the little boy echoing from the corridor. Again, she was alone with her baby. She dozed off. The nurse woke her up with dinner. She forced herself to eat a few bites and drank two glasses of milk. "Milk makes milk," the old women's voices from her village echoed in her head. After the nurses changed Anna's nappies and the baby had a drink, too, Valeria was finally left in peace. She picked up a book. Such a rare luxury, a poetry collection by Ivan Cankar. Yet, she could not focus on the verses. Her thoughts wandered to Martin, and to Joc, and to the dramatic changes in her life during those early days of May, the days that remained in people's minds as the most beautiful days of liberation. If Marko only knew, she would be doomed.

She closed her eyes. The memories of baby Martin in her arms as she hurried along the streets on that hot day in Ljubljana haunted her. The boy was crying like mad and people were looking at them as though they were aliens. They must have seemed strange. Valeria in her uniform and rifle; the boy with a missing sock, his cheeks turning purple as he shrieked...His tears and mucus dotted her uniform. With his right hand, he was fiercely pushing his body away from her. She had to tighten her grip to keep him from falling on the ground. She was running away from the railway station, trying to ignore the sad reflection of them in the dirty, empty shop windows.

Valeria's first thought was to get to the hospital and speak to Marjana. After all, Marjana was Martin's aunt. The boy was her responsibility, too. She found her in the staff kitchen, smoking, resting on a sofa, completely exhausted. When she saw Valeria with Martin, her eyes nearly popped out of their sockets.

"Oh, my God! Ada, she really did it."

"Did what, Marjana? What do you mean?"

Marjana stood up and rummaged in the kitchen cabinet. She turned around with a piece of chocolate in her hand. "Here Martin, stop crying, my boy. Everything will be fine."

Nothing was going to be fine. What was her friend thinking? Valeria tried to compose her thoughts. She placed her rifle in the corner of the small room. The tiny window was open. She could smell lime trees in sweet bloom and hear birds singing their spring song. Yet now, the world was crashing on Valeria's shoulders. She looked at Marjana.

"You don't mean Ada was planning to dump her little son on me all along, do you? It was pure coincidence. She couldn't have known I'd be on duty at the station today."

Marjana shrugged and lit another cigarette. "Of course not. She came over a week ago begging me to take Martin to Kozjane. I told her they would find the boy and put him in one of their orphanages. You know, they came to see Father Skarpin and asked him about Andrej. Ada was desperate. She wasn't sure they would leave Yugoslavia alive and had big doubts about the situation in Carinthia. They do have some money and jewelry, but you know the risks. You should know she was desperate. She asked me about you many times and lamented that you simply disappeared. She nourished the thought that Martin would be better off with you, on the side of the victors."

Valeria sank on the sofa. Ada was saying that Andrej had called her only yesterday. Who knew if that was true? Were the telephone lines working? Apparently her friend took advantage of her. Like bitter bile, anger surged inside Valeria.

"Ada and her bloody Home Guard husband can go to hell! I'll bet they're scared. They should be, too. We've sent them packing ...That's what we do to the Führer's friends. Their own fault, completely ...I wonder what they would have done to us had we lost the war. They wouldn't have let us leave ..." Valeria covered her face with her hands. She was trembling all over. "That madwoman, completely mad. I don't think she could have planned it though. My dear God, what am I going to do with the kid, Marjana? I just got married. I'm expecting a baby of my own."

The toddler followed them with his huge brown eyes, straining to comprehend Valeria's angry words. The chocolate kept him quiet for now, but he was not consoled. Where was his mommy? He wanted his mommy. Salty tears melted with the sweet chocolate in his black-smeared mouth. One look at his aunt and his short high-pitched sobs made it clear he wasn't done crying yet.

Marjana lifted Martin in her arms and cradled him softly. Then she put him on the sofa and gave him some rags to play with. His attention shifted to the new game. Occasionally his brown eyes would scrutinize the scene and try to catch his aunt's gaze. Marjana caressed his hair and found another piece of chocolate in the cabinet.

"Here," she said, giving to Valeria with a nod toward her belly, "it'll restore your strength. Where's the father of your child?"

Marjana sat down on the other end of the sofa.

"I don't know, somewhere in Dolenjska. They haven't discharged him yet. Me neither ...I'll soon be able to place the rifle on my belly if this goes on much longer. The baby will be able to shoot the enemies from my belly! Bang, bang ...beware of a red baby sniper!"

Marjana broke into a laugh at the rather macabre joke. One hell of a woman, this Valeria. "That's my Valchy. Come on, talk to me. Tell me everything you've been up to since you spied on Andrej and Ada that spring night a year ago."

Valeria threw a furtive look at Martin, her cheeks flushing. "Did she have to tell you that?"

Marjana lifted her hands in defense, pointing at the weapon in the corner. "I didn't ask her to. Anyway, if you must know, Ada has been alone most of the time since then. Andrej was either at the hospital or on the battlefront. He was patching up the people you partisans hit with your new American rifles. Some of them might have been the victims of that rifle, too, Valeria."

Valeria trembled. She wasn't proud of shooting Slovenian farmers and civilians who were known collaborators. She wasn't proud of the fact that they had to shoot any Slovenians at all. It was absurd, but she had to obey orders. They had to end the war that at some point had turned into a social revolution.

"Give me a smoke, Marjana!"

"No way, you're pregnant. No smoking for you."

Valeria sank into her thoughts for a while. She chewed on the chocolate. Then she took Marjana's hand in hers and started to talk. About the night when she had to flee into the woods, her return to Ljubljana and the undercover, often illegal, activities she carried out. She didn't approach either Ada or Marjana for fear of putting them in danger. She knew about Marjana's terrible ordeal in the hands of the SS men. She recounted her first love with partisan Borko, then losing him and their unborn son in an ambush, then the time she spent at the *Franja* Partisan Hospital where she met the wonderful young doctor everyone thought was a fairy tale invented to sustain the Partisan morale. Then the winter months in Bela Krajina, which led to Marko and their marriage, the first under the new authorities. Marjana listened attentively, brushing tears from her eyes every now and then. Valeria was her little hero, so young, so brave. She had suffered so much.

"My dear Valchy," Marjana said, embracing her, "you brought me back to life once. Now it's my turn to help you."

"Thank you. You already have. You went to jail in my place."

"Think nothing of it. It wasn't a party, but it's over. I still owe you, *pupa*, I do."

"Then take Martin. You're his aunt, Marjana."

Marjana's face fell. She stood up and went to the window. She inhaled the sweet scent of flowering trees outside as though gathering the strength to explain things to her friend.

"If I take him home, everyone will know he's the child of my sister and her Home Guard husband. They would take him away and put him in one of those orphanages the partisans have set up for the orphaned or abandoned children of collaborators. I hear terrible things happen there. He's so little, Valchy, for God's sake, not even a year old. Babies are dying in large numbers there. Diarrhea, malnutrition ..." Her voice cracked. "According to the reports, those places aren't much better than Rab."

Valeria jumped to her feet and put her hands around her. "I'm sorry, Marjana. What was I thinking? Of course, I'll take him. Ada saved my life twice, she trusts me. I'll figure out what to do with his papers."

Marjana trembled in her friend's arms. She felt very grateful. The bonds forged among the *Brkini Hills* were stronger than any politics. After a while, she asked, "Didn't you say Doctor *Franja* treated you when you were wounded? She was the one who told you about your miscarriage. She works in this hospital now. Maybe she can turn the miscarriage into childbirth and issue a fake document ... You can say that the boy was living with a farmer's family, but they all died in the war. If you carefully hide the traces of the story and dispose of all proofs, it can work out. Martin can pass for yours and Borko's."

Valeria looked at little Martin. Tired after the commotion at the station and bored with the women's chat, he fell asleep on the sofa. His face was peaceful, his chubby cheeks flushed with the purple dreams of an angel. His light hair stuck to his forehead in sweaty curls. He stretched his arms across the sofa in the complete abandon and trust that only children had. The little boy was so vulnerable, so alone.

"When is Doctor *Franja* on duty? Another woman who had saved my life, and I don't even know her real name."

"*Franja* Bojc Bidovec. I think she may be on duty now. I'll try to find her in the ward. Wait here, Valeria."

Valeria relaxed on the sofa. She must have dozed off for she came to at the sound of the door opening. Doctor *Franja* stepped in, thin as a straw. Her lovely oval face with blue eyes looked exhausted, but smiling.

"Valchy, how good to see you! I'm so happy for you."

The fact that they both survived the war abolished the distance between them. They embraced, and Doctor *Franja* instinctively touched Valeria's round belly. "Is everything all right?"

Valeria nodded. "I've seen a midwife in Metlika a couple of times. She always suggests I rest. After leaving the hospital, I worked as a teacher in Bela Krajina, where I recovered from the rigors of living in the woods. I donned my uniform and joined the liberators on their victory march to Ljubljana. Days of joy, I tell you. Today I got posted at the railway station to guard the train compositions."

"Yes, it's crazy. It seems as though the whole world is going somewhere. Sometimes you can't tell the difference between who's running away and who's pursuing them." *Franja* noticed little Martin asleep on the sofa. "Is this your baby, Nurse Marjana? He's so cute. How do you do it? I mean, balancing your work schedule and motherhood ..."

Marjana and Valeria exchanged glances. Neither said anything in reply. How do you do it, indeed.

Looking at the clock on the wall, Marjana said, "I'm sorry. You two have to talk, and I have to look after a patient."

Once they were alone, Doctor *Franja* politely said, "I can see something is bothering you, Valchy. What is it? How can I help?"

Valeria pointed to the sleeping toddler. "He could have been mine. A few months, no more than seven apart ..."

Franja sat down on the wooden chair opposite the sofa. She smelled trouble in the air. Valeria sank to her former place on the sofa. For a few moments, the room was silent. Valeria's face darkened. She didn't know how to start.

"What is it, Valchy? Whose baby is this?"

Valeria looked at the doctor and the need to cry on her shoulder became almost a physical pain in her chest. She slowly caressed Martin's shoulders and checked his fingers whether he was cold. He was soft and warm like a kitten. His warmth unbound her silence. She told *Franja* about Ada and their childhood in the *Brkini Hills*, their friendship throughout their school years, always helping and loving each other. She recounted Andrej and Ada's wedding, her pregnancy, his hatred for Russia because of his artistic sister and her unfortunate fate there, the reprehensible actions of the Communists that caused Andrej to join the Home Guard. Finally, Ada's flight by train. She gave a deep breath.

"*Franja*, I met Ada this morning. She was on that train to Carinthia when she saw me. I was on duty. Luckily, my superior went inside the railway station so we were able to talk for a while. Otherwise, I could've gotten into trouble. These days everybody suspects everybody of treason, you know. The train was packed. Home Guards, *Ustashas*, collaborators of all sorts, and their families. Anyway, when the train started moving, Ada literally threw little Martin into my arms. There wasn't anything I could do. I caught him, and my superior found me still in shock with a crying baby in my arms."

"What did you say?"

"I told him Martin is Borko's son. You remember the letter Borko left for me? It must have come to my mind subconsciously..."

Franja said almost to herself, "But the father of your child doesn't know anything about you and Borko, I guess."

"Well, some bits and pieces, but not much, really ...Marko and I don't talk about the past. You know how it is in war. You live for the moment. Every day could be your last. I don't know what Marko will do." Valeria's voice broke into sobs. Her life seemed to fly out of her veins. "I'll go home to Kozjane and leave everything behind. I'm sick of Ljubljana."

Franja took her hand in hers. "Don't lose faith, Valeria. We all know and respect you. Is there a way I can be of help?"

Valeria looked *Franja* in the eye. "Would you be able to change my medical record? Write 'childbirth' instead of 'miscarriage'? I can make up some story from that point, but I need a birth certificate for Martin."

Franja shook her head. "You're asking me to tamper with a medical report from one year ago. It's impossible. They transferred the archives of the *Franja* Partisan Hospital to Ljubljana. I don't even know where they are. I can try to find out, of course. I can try to find your file and remove it. You know this is a criminal offense. I can go to jail if I get caught."

"I'm sorry for asking this of you, but I'm desperate. What will happen to Martin if our people find out he's the son of a traitor? It was stupid, so stupid of Ada to do what she did... A baby belongs to his mother. Yet, I owe her my life, not once, but twice. There must be a way to get a birth certificate in this chaos. I still have Borko's letter – the words of a hero."

Franja lowered her head. "I understand you, Valchy, really, I do. But these are difficult times. I was under investigation myself after you left the hospital. Suspended for a few months. The allegations were of all kinds, from sloppy care of my patients to manipulating medical protocols. You can imagine how I felt. Honestly, I cannot get involved in something like this now. It may put you and your baby in danger."

Valeria sank into gloom. How could she legitimize Martin's existence? She felt as if she were living under the Italians and the Nazis again – trying to come up with ways to trick the new authorities, the people she had fought side by side with. Her faith in the new just society dwindled in Bela Krajina. Their treatment of the enemy's children was terrible. They let them live only to abuse them. Children shouldn't be held responsible for the deeds of their parents. Children were innocent. Henrik's image appeared before her eyes, his scared face bathed in filth...

"I cannot, I'm sorry. But I may know somebody who can."

Valeria's face tensed up with anticipation. "Who?"

"Wasn't *Tovarish* Josip – Joc your commander?"

"Yes, Joc ... What about him?"

"He's the chief of OZNA now. While you were with us, he wrote me and asked about you. He's a good man. He helped me when I was in trouble and managed to put things in order. I know he works in the *Slavija* building. I'll give you his phone number. Go to him. He will help you."

Valeria thought of Joc and the last time they saw each other in spring 1944. He was the one who sent her to Idrija where teaching had transformed her from a ruffian into a city girl. With a bit of imagination she could thread a credible tale about Borko's son. She must involve her family back home. They were the only people she could trust. Should she lie to her partisan friend and commander?

"If necessary, would you confirm my pregnancy, Doctor *Franja*?"

"Yes, but the best thing to do is to remove your medical file. The abortion has been noted, I'm afraid."

Valeria's thoughts rushed from fact to fact. So many possibilities of getting caught in a lie and then into trouble. "What do I say to Joc regarding Martin? If I had asked people to look after him while I was away, I would have given them his birth certificate, too, wouldn't I?"

"Oh, Valchy, choose a house or a family whose members all died in the war. You shouldn't trust anybody. Only Marjana. Say she brought your baby to the railway station today."

In the peaceful sound of Martin's breathing, Valeria's words sounded like a funeral sermon: "So I'm to abuse the memory of victims for the life of a baby, smear their death with lies. This is like defecating on their tombs."

Franja sighed. "My dear girl, life comes before death. It is the nature of things."

Like many times before, Valeria banned morality from her decisions. Doctor *Franja* was right. Inventing a story about the baby, finding the right details, yet not too many. The whole series of events should be watertight. This was how she would get the paper from Joc.

"Thank you, Doctor *Franja*, thank you so much. Has anybody told you what a great woman you are?"

Franja stood up and embraced her. No words were needed between the two lonely shipwrecked women in this war. Valeria felt *Franja*'s body tremble with emotion. Hot tears drenched their cheeks. Affinity and boundless love overwhelmed them. Valeria realized that this was what she had been fighting for all those years she faced danger and death. Life and love, the essence of existence. Everything else was pointless.

~~~

The Carnegie Hall lay illuminated; the concert was sold out. The American high society continued to celebrate the end of the WWII in every possible way. Many American soldiers hadn't yet returned from overseas, though. At their various posts around devastated Europe, they tried to set up basic administration structures and put order in the lives of millions of homeless and starving savages. Europe, the cradle of humanity, was in ruins, lawless, rotting, her people hungry and her spirit crushed. It was worse than a desert. In the aftermath of the slaughter and revenge among various ethnicities and religions, the taste of blood was bitter. The victors were losing their human face and hiding behind the death masks of history. They forged the truth for the future generations.

At forty-six, Sanja Strainar was on her way up in her second or third musical career. A shining star, a brilliant pianist playing under the baton of famous conductors. After years of giving concerts on the West Coast, tonight she was about to perform in the East Coast, in New York, for the first time. The public knew of her: thanks to the recordings she had done, they were broadcasting her concerts and selling her records all over America. The suspense before the concert played in the faces of the orchestra members, who were tuning their instruments.

Through the entrance on the left came Maestro Arturo *Toscanini*, who had conducted Tchaikovsky's famous Piano Concerto No. 1 with Vladimir Horowitz as solo pianist. The public burst into applause. The Maestro bowed and shook hands with the major soloists. Then, looking toward the entrance and with a dramatic gesture, he summoned Sanja to the stage. She came in like a fairy, long black dress opened at the back, silken light hair fastened in a bun. Her pearl necklace – her mother's gift for her first solo success in Ljubljana – shone like her cheeks. She offered her right hand to the Maestro, trembling for fear she might fail. *Toscanini*, almost a head shorter than her, held it firmly and looked in Sanja's eyes with confidence. She would not let him down. His lips brushed her elegant fingers before he let her sit down. Focusing on her music, she nodded to the Maestro. He lifted his magic baton, commanding silence filled with suspense and anticipation. Wind instruments softly started the concert.

Eyes wide open, never blinking or hesitant, Sanja waited to play her first notes. Tchaikovsky's concerto was full of ups and downs, grace and love, pain and tragedy. If music could describe her life, it would have written it with these very notes. This concerto was her soul mate not only on the stage, but also behind it. The moment before she struck the first keys had always been an enigma. Would she play well or fail? Like that winter night during the war in Ljubljana.

Yet, Sanja could remember other times she performed it. The first time in November 1921 at the Ljubljana Philharmonic Hall in celebration of the armistice. The new state of Slovenians, Croatians, and Serbians rose from the ruins of the Austro-Hungarian Monarchy. Sanja was only fifteen – and the soloist's understudy. Her piano teacher and the conductor did not yet trust her with such an important part. They thought her performance was still insecure and the soloist role too demanding. Yet, Sanja Strainar had been working very hard. When the day came, the soloist fell ill and could not perform. With all the nobility of Ljubljana and even a few members of the *Karadjordjević* royal family present, it was Sanja or nobody. At her first performance, she captured the public with her clear and accurate play. After a standing ovation, she had to return to the stage and repeat the finale. A star had been born.

A look from *Toscanini*. Her fingers touched the black and white keys, at first with force, then gently as though merging with the piano. It was the touch of two lovers transforming into one being, resounding in one melody. Like a lovely summer song of cicadas, the strings played their tune. Music was love and love was music. In thousands of melodies and keys, with different faces and facets, music had resounded in Sanja's heart since she could remember. The music of love had always been the strings, the perfect sounds of violins.

On that long forgotten evening in November 1921, her whole family was there. Her elegantly dressed mother in her thirties and her middle-aged father, a politician, a member of the Parliament and a lawyer, who was writing laws for Yugoslavia, the first democratic state of the Southern Slavs. His compassion for poor workers and farmers brought him closer to the Social Democrats. He became one of their leaders. Little Andrej sat on Mother's knees, carefully watching Sanja's hands, as though he feared she would slip on ice.

He was only five at the time. The Strainars conceived him at the dawn of WWI when they lost all hope of having another child. The little boy was their joy. At the end, when she bowed to the public, Andrej climbed the stairs to the stage and gave her a bouquet of red carnations.

While her fingers artfully played the keys, Sanja's memory led her to that Sunday lunch long ago when they almost lost Andrej. Guns started to blasting in the middle of the meal. Their house in Gorizia was at a safe distance from the *Isonzo* Front. However, in spring 1916, the Italians had occupied new strategic points from which they were bombing the city. The images surfaced in her mind as though from yesterday.

Their housekeeper Mari was serving strong chicken broth with noodles. It had been only a month since Andrej's birth, and Mother needed to recover her strength. Steam rose from their plates. Her father nodded, and Mother wished everyone "Bon appétit!" They never said grace before meals for Father hated the Catholics and their conservatism. Sanja recalled a white tablecloth with blue cornflowers and lace, fine Blue Onion china dinnerware, and silver cutlery so shiny you could tease your daddy by flashing his eyes with it. Of course, Sanja could tease Father. She was his darling. The crystal glasses scented with red wine and elder syrup from last spring. The housekeeper brought in dish after dish as usual. Fried asparagus, bitter and sweet. In spite of the war and scarce supplies, they had meat on Sundays. Fried chicken, the pieces from the soup, and roast beef, then steamed potatoes and spinach with pine nuts as side dish. First salad leaves served in little bowls. Sanja ate with appetite. They were discussing the situation and their plans should the front line reach them. The detonations were coming closer.

"Maybe we should go to the cellar," Father said.

"I'll check whether Andrej has woken up," Mother replied, hurrying to the back of the house.

Sanja waited for dessert – a fluffy egg dough with sweet nuts and honey. She was bored. Father kept asking the same questions about school and her piano lessons. She excelled in everything, after all. Mother soon returned with little Andrej in his baby stroller. He was asleep.

"Mommy, look, isn't he a little angel?" said Sanja merrily.

Mother and Father exchanged glances and smiled at each other. Only years later did she find out how much they wanted more children, yet all of Mother's pregnancies had ended sadly. Now, at wartime, a baby was born. It was a miracle.

A loud blast sounded nearby, but the baby boy merely shuddered and slept on.

"Let's have dessert, then go to the cellar," said Mother. "Mari went in search of the ingredients all morning. We shouldn't disappoint her."

Father nodded. The Sunday meal was a family celebration, a weekly ritual. In spite of the devastating news in the papers about thousands of dead soldiers in Belgium, in Galicia, and now here, in the wonderful mountain slopes of the Alps near the emerald-green river of *Isonzo*, war seemed very far from their Sunday lunch ceremony.

Masterfully, Sanja finished the playful part of her solo and smiled. Her now wrinkled cheeks had been so smooth back then. Little Andrej spent hours behind her piano, while she went through exercises and endless scales. Her little brother was her first and most devoted fan.

And they almost lost him that Sunday in Gorizia. Sanja had just taken a bite of her savory dessert when a bomb crashed into the house. It wrecked the back part where her parents and little Andrej slept in a vast room.

"Under the table, all down!" cried Father, taking the baby out of the stroller. Another bomb hit the house. From under the thick oak table where they hid, they could see splinters of wood and pieces of the wall crushing the crystals in the elegant showcase in the corner. Then nothing. Only ominous silence.

"Maria and Sanja, take Andrej and go to the cellar. I'll look for Mari," ordered Father. He rushed to the kitchen, while Mother took the baby in her arms. Sanja, pale with horror, could not say anything. Little Andrej was crying his lungs out. Bits of milk spilled out of his tiny mouth as he choked and spit in terror. They went to the dark cellar. Mother passed the crying baby to Sanja and lit the candles. Another explosion. Father! They remained speechless save for Andrej, who was shrieking like hell.

A few moments later, there was a knock on the door. It was Father carrying their unconscious housekeeper. She was alive. Father and Mother bandaged her wounds, while Sanja tried in vain to calm down her little brother, whose agony was prophetic as though he foresaw that the world and humanity would drown in hate forever.

Marica came to her senses for brief moments. She suffered pains and lost her hearing. The gunfire went on until evening. Then, Gorizia sank into menacing silence.

"Where's our army? Where are the guns and defense we had approved huge sums for in the Parliament? The Italians are shooting without restraint at civilians. Damn those Austrian military agitators and war profiteers!" Father was angry. Slowly the residents of the border town came out of hiding. Their house was in rambles. Father decided to move to Ljubljana. Little Andrej had been a sleepless and nervous baby ever since.

The song of violins brought Sanja back to the black and white keys. The harmony of sounds was like an invisible palm stroking her cheeks. While her fingers touched the piano, she felt like talking to her lover, kissing and caressing the hidden spots that only her loving lips could reach. Violins were love. Violins reminded Sanja of her infinite love.

Andrej grew up in haste. For decades, they went their separate ways. In order to succeed in her career, Sanja had to study abroad and train under some great world teachers in Vienna, Paris, and Berlin. She followed her calling without hesitation and dedicated all her love to music. She kept in touch with her family through long letters. In spite of the distance, she loved Andrej, who in turn respected his older sister and appreciated her support. When he made up his mind to study medicine, Father did everything to impose his will on his son and successor. Sanja stood up for her brother and persuaded old Strainar to let him pursue a medical degree. Andrej was so grateful. His admiration for her artistic genius knew no limits. In the weekly long letters that they exchanged from one part of the world to the other, they discussed everything. Words overcame distances and continents, communicated thoughts and expressed feelings with the lightness of a flute airing its bright clear tunes over the piano. The music was playful, sincere and clear like the emerald stream of *Isonzo*, rushing over white rocks and meandering past green meadows.

Sergej. He came into her life, her man, her lover, her violin player. Their love was so tender and absolute. The lyrical tunes were so gentle and strong that Sanja's heart galloped in thunder and pain at the memory of its beauty. The years they spent together in the Neverland of socialist idealism were too short. Old Auntie Anna Akmerova was the witness and the fairy of their love. They were thinking of marriage. Then evil struck them. The Devil himself feasted on the music of their instruments, breaking the chords until they fell silent forever. Stalin's bloodsucking killers had taken their toll.

Sergej, my darling, my one and only, I will never stop loving you, Sanja thought, barely able to hold back her tears. She must not cry. A pianist might share her sentiments with the public, yet the Maestro must see that she kept them under control at all times.

She struck the black and white keys rhythmically until she reached the lowest tones of the concert. The oboe raised her hymn to the goddess of Beauty followed by Sanja's dearest violins. Oh, only the Beauty of music, which mirrored the depth and richness of the Slavic soul with its shades of genius, could make her forget the sorrows of this world. Beauty was higher than grief. Beauty was more powerful than any sorrow out of Pandora's box.

Toscanini held his baton while Sanja played her part. His face shone with trust and intensity. She played so well. Her performance was like her life: beautiful, precise, and sad. It was the body of the concerto, which the American public cherished and accepted years before the Russians. Americans fell in love with the concerto's childish spirit and novelty. Tchaikovsky had composed a piece of perfection that spoke magic to open hearts.

The first part was over. Sanja bowed to the Carnegie Hall public, which burst into roaring applause. The flute led the lyrical theme introducing the second part. Sanja's piano solo took over, her thoughts wandering to Andrej, Ada, and the little nephew she had yet to see. He must be as cute as baby Andrej was. She smiled.

She was grateful to the fortunate series of events between 1943 and 1944 that had brought her to America. The Nazi secret police was at her heels all the time. They systematically executed anybody who had anything to do with the Soviet Union. Here, in the land of the free, she'd had to start from the scratch. She was playing in bars and halls along the West Coast to a public who couldn't distinguish between the wailing of a cat and classical music. However, she was alive and she got by. After the war, she attended a concert of the famous London Royal Orchestra and met many of her old friends and colleagues again, now refugees like herself. They introduced her to the director and her star started to shine again.

Tours, recordings, radio performances, fame and glory. She was rich and successful, but also lonely. Each passing year she missed her family more. She had nobody but Andrej, Ada, and the baby. All her efforts to find Sergej had been in vain. The evil machinery of Stalin's apparatus had totally devoured him. Andrej and Ada were lucky to find passage to Argentina after the Communists had won. They lived in Buenos Aires, however, without her little nephew Martin, who grew up in Valeria's family. In her letters, Sanja tried to console Ada that it was only sensible to leave the boy in Yugoslavia given the circumstances. That she had saved his life. When she confronted Andrej about it in her letters, she got a very cold reply. Her brother hated being separated from his son. His heart and soul breathed poison. He abhorred the fact that his boy lived in a Communist state, raised by an enemy in the so-called new Yugoslavia. Sanja could see that Andrej had donned the trappings of a wronged man, an exile of absolute injustice. His world was getting smaller and narrower. There was almost no room for his wife and his sister left. Sanja was worried. Ada's last letter was a cry for help.

It was high time she went to visit them in Argentina. After this concert at the Carnegie Hall, Sanja planned to take a couple of months off. She would fly to Buenos Aires to embrace her brother Andrej and comfort her sister-in-law Ada. Then, she would find a way to give a concert in the new Yugoslavia, in the white city of Ljubljana, and personally check on how her nephew was doing. Little Martin must be something like five years old now.

The merry sounds of violins launched into the finale, accompanied by her dramatic solo part and the crescendo of all instruments. Sanja sighed with regret. The concert was nearing the end. The beginning remained the most beautiful part, when all the keys still lay ahead and you embarked on an adventure of sounds and harmony that were both familiar and puzzling. The Maestro was a light that never faded. When he lifted his baton, the sun rose over the horizon and every creature in the planet woke to a new day, new growth, and new life. How complicated and enigmatic, how accurate and perfect, how sad and merry, how harmonized yet chaotic, but always short – our lives were always much too short. Simple solutions did not exist. Like a concert, life resonated through a thousand notes and facets, always the same, yet different every time. Music and life were ambiguous and enigmatic. Only death and silence were plain and simple.

Sanja concentrated on the majestic finale. Afterward she smiled with happiness before the standing ovations and the cheering of the audience. In two weeks' time, she hoped to bring the same joy to

Andrej and Ada.

She did not know that Andrej and Ada were no more, never foresaw Ada being gone or Andrej turning into a grumpy old man, aged and bitter before his time.

~~~

A couple of years went by. Despite the challenges and difficulties that life brought, Valeria prospered in the new Yugoslavia. She was also able to keep her secret. She had approached Joc, her former partisan commander, on that sunny day in May 1945, requesting a birth certificate for Martin. Joc studied Borko's last love letter to Valeria. His fingers smoothed the surface of the paper, still smeared with blood, as though caressing the hand of his fallen friend. After a while, he looked at Valeria.

"Valchy, I never told you Borko was a distant cousin on my father's side. We loved each other. I'll take you and the boy to meet his family one day. They will be happy that Borko has a son."

Valeria was relieved. Tears of gratitude blurred her vision. "What about the birth certificate, Comrade Joc?"

In a few days, the papers for Martin Lukman arrived, giving the baby identity and protection. Joc never asked Valeria where she had left the boy while she worked as a teacher in Metlika. After some long weeks, her husband Marko joined her in Ljubljana. By then, she had woven a web of carefully reasoned lies.

A family from Kozjane, by the name of Likin, had been looking after him. Their house was outside the village, so nobody noticed the boy. Only their yard could be observed from village Tatre, which was on higher ground. One early spring day in 1945, a German artillery officer saw through binoculars that a group of partisans were strolling around the Likin yard. They bombed the house and took the family members to Dachau. Nobody knew what happened to them. They never returned. Little Martin, by miracle, was at her sister's place in Vitovlje at the time. Valeria and Marjana meticulously discussed every detail. Valeria's sister Marija backed the story. Thus, she managed to pass off Martin as Boris Lukman's son. When Marko returned home from his assignment, he was a disturbed and broken man. Valeria wondered what had happened to him. Like a child, he was quick to tears and laughter. Without asking a lot of questions about Martin, Marko sagged into Valeria's arms, demanding only her warm love – hers, little Martin's, and the love of the baby that was on the way. The little boy touched Marko's heart so deeply that he soon asked Valeria to adopt him. She refused, wanting Borko to live on through the name of his son. Marko wasn't very pleased, but accepted her decision. Or so it seemed.

Nevertheless, May 1945 was important to Valeria. She started working as Joc's personal secretary in OZNA, the Department of National Security. She found that she could manage the documents well enough thanks to her knowledge of Italian. She started learning English and French, too. Her job gave her family some protection and also kept nosy questions about Martin at bay. Fortunately, the war was not a conversation topic among comrades. As though their silence could banish the terrible memories that often invaded their nightmares.

That May she also joined the Communist Party, which advanced her career even more. Life went by peacefully, but not for long. Whenever Valeria tried to analyze what happened in the summer of 1948, her brain erupted into flashes of pain and flames of horror.

First came the Informbiro Resolution, then the cursed letter.

For former *Liberation Front* activists and Communists, the Informbiro period was a nightmare. Valeria had never truly trusted the Russians. She considered them wild and violent folk. Indeed, the first condemnations of the Yugoslav Party leaders began in Russia. The Information Bureau of *Comintern* reproached the leaders of the Yugoslav Communist Party for abandoning the path of Marxism-Leninism and living in luxury after acquiring the riches of their former opponents,. Valeria knew what the *Comintern* leaders meant. She herself had observed that in nationalizing factories, houses, and cars, Party officials ended up with the bulk of the wealth. She was sure that the Russian apparatchiks were no better, though. They had everything while Russian citizens were starving. One thing led to another until good friends and old comrades of Stalin, such as *Tito*, *Djilas*, *Kardelj*, *Pijade*, and *Ranković*, were expelled by the *Comintern*. Behind the ploy was the Soviet Union ambition to place a new Communist leadership in Yugoslavia, a leadership blindly subordinate to Stalin. Valeria and Joc agreed they couldn't let this happen. The horrible Informbiro Resolution was the last act in a drama of bad relations between the two Red Tsars: Stalin and *Tito*. The times were chaotic and dangerous. Since the summer of 1948, Valeria had seen many of *Tito*'s loyal fighters rotting in prisons all over the country.

No trials, no legal defense.

They were all very nervous. One day you were a respectable party official, next day you disappeared in one of the prisons or concentration camps that were mushrooming around Yugoslavia to intern thousands of Stalin's followers and *Tito*'s opponents.

Tito was in a difficult position. The country was poor, the people traumatized, the scarce infrastructure in post-war ruins. Since the breach with Stalin, Yugoslavia appeared to be in a political vacuum. It turned into a kind of no-man's-land between two blocs: the USA and the Western European countries under the Treaty of Brussels, an alliance that would later be called NATO, on one side; and the Soviet Union with the Warsaw Pact countries on the other. The peoples of Yugoslavia, from the Vardar River in Macedonia to the highest peaks of Mount Triglav in Slovenia, feared that the Red Army would invade and occupy the country. In a state of shock the lawlessness of the Informbiro Resolution seemed the least of all evils. Yugoslavia was getting ready for another war.

If Yugoslavian party leaders wanted to survive and keep their positions at the top, they had to act quickly and efficiently. Overnight *Tito*, being a true disciple of Stalin, proceeded to suppress anyone who praised Stalin and the Soviet Union. Only a day ago Stalin was the country's big brother, his portraits hung next to *Tito*'s on every wall; now he became its biggest enemy. After having fought the war side by side with the Russians, the officers and soldiers in the National Liberation Army were particularly confused. A special law, so-called the IB directive, enabled the authorities to disappear people overnight without any legal procedures as long as two Party officials signed off on the action. Valeria knew everything about it. She was the one who typed the warrants and stamped them, while her boss Joc signed them every day. Once Joc and another one of his colleagues have signed the order, the field agents took over and brought the person charged with pro-Soviet views to prison. By 1949, all the prisons in Yugoslavia were full. The word was about hundreds of thousands became Informbiro prisoners.

Tito and his clique needed a better solution to deal with the huge number of their enemies. In spring 1949, a barren island in Northern Dalmatia called *Goli otok* (Naked Island) proved the perfect location for their gulag. It was a huge rock with practically no vegetation; the couple of bays it had were poorly protected from rough winds. With little effort, it became a high-security prison for *Tito*'s political opponents. Separated from the mainland by the powerful winds and currents of the Velebit channel, it was less than half a mile from the island of Rab, and even less distant from its twin island *Grgur* where the women's prison was put into operation a couple of years later. The prisoners worked in the stone quarry, pottery, and joinery under any weather condition, lashed by the icy *burja* or literally frying under the hot summer sun. Their daily menu consisted of violence and thirst.

Years later, in the fifties, Valeria had to visit both islands – *Goli otok* and *Grgur* – to inspect their activities and organize the sales of their products to Slovenia. She was horrified. The barracks where the prisoners lived were in appalling state, not to speak of the sanitary conditions. The stench was terrible. Food and water were scarce; the prisoners starved and lethargic, with everyone just waiting for death. A subtle hierarchy of violence hung in the air. She remembered Sanja's stories about Stalin's gulags as well as pictures of horrible Nazi camps with their motto: ARBEIT MACHT FREI! She was shocked. She never expected the society she was helping to build would turn into such a horrible institution.

Freedom under *Tito* and the Yugoslavian Communists had many facets. The enthusiastic shouts of "*Tito, partija!*" during the big public gatherings in the post-war years echoed in her brain as she sailed back to the mainland.

Valeria ceased dwelling in the Neverland of justice under *Tito*'s Communist sun. She was part of the system and had seen too much. She was ashamed of herself whenever she thought of the tumultuous years when the *nomenklatura* replaced the former capitalists in their homes and positions of power in the new, socialist society. Her family was one of them, for better or worse. Still, Valeria worked hard and kept her mouth shut. In the darkest nights when she berated herself for being a cog in the state's evil machine, she always found justification in the fact that she was doing it for her fragile young family. If she spoke up and show resistance, it would mean trouble for all four of them. She started to censor what she said in the company of friends and family, including Marko, Marjana, and Joc. Her own mind slowly burned away until only cold gray ashes remained where once emotional fire and political engagement enflamed her actions. Valeria was beginning to see the world and the people around her through the red goggles of the Communist Party. Their mind was her mind. Right and wrong merged into only one notion: survival.

Yet, her merry and positive nature also brought her joys and a good life. Her marriage to Marko Robič was a good and stable one. He was a supportive husband and a loving father. Valeria had to admit she loved him more every day. Their home was a sanctuary of love. She learned to leave her office work, the terrible orders she had to follow, and the suffering of prisoners outside her home. She was happy for Marko when he was promoted to Chief of the Ljubljana Police in the last days of 1945. His position brought about new responsibilities and privileges. Because of their tight schedules, their family life soon became stressful. They went to work in the morning, then to the party meetings in the evening when important gatherings still took place, as though the Communists still had to operate under cover. With Marjana living with them, she was the one who looked after the children. However, Marjana soon grew tired and wanted to go home. Retiring in spring 1946, she went home to Kozjane. They found a housekeeper from a tiny village near Postojna, Zdenka to care for the children, prepare meals, and keep the household in order.

In March 1946, Valeria helped Marjana move to their home village. The OZNA driver put all of Marjana's belongings in his big Opel Olympia and drove the friends to the ruins in the *Brkini Hills*. During the war, the village of Kozjane was burnt down three times. The first time was on March 13th 1943 during a fight between the Italians and the partisans; the second time, in October 1943 between the Germans and the 3rd and 4th battalion of the Šercer Brigade; and the third time, on September 14th 1944 when the Germans avenged the attack of the Istrian partisan regiment on their stronghold in Tatre. The villagers soon returned and started to rebuild their homes with optimism and zeal. However, after a year of *kolkhoz* – collective farming imposed by the Soviet Union – their fields became barren, their livestock grew ill, and the inhabitants were starving. Young people abandoned their homes and migrated to towns where they could find jobs and build lives. The old remained on their lands, hopeless but stubborn, waiting for the Grim Reaper to decimate them as the scythe would cut ripe meadows in summer. The flow of goods and natural produce to Trieste became difficult with the territory divided into two zones.

Marjana found the Skarpin house locked, although part of the roof was missing and the kitchen lay open to the weather. Her parents had survived the war, but were destitute. Unable to find the energy to rebuild their home again, they had rented a tiny room at the Planina Retirement Home. After two wars, Marjana's father was distraught and broken. He passed away shortly after the liberation, and her mother, disillusioned herself, followed him soon after. There was no news of Ada and Andrej, which was a relief in a way. Thus, Marjana was the only person left in her ruined home. She still had her savings, wisely transformed into gold before the war and deposited at a bank in Trieste. With the help of the village men, she restored the house and planted orchards and fields. The surplus produce went to numerous orphanages around the country. Marjana personally brought the red sweet apples and honey pears to the children. Their grateful eyes were like the golden sunset of her days, warming Marjana's tired body and soul, giving her the will to go on and be brave.

The Batič family had been decimated, too. Only Father and Mother remained in the house. Marjo never returned from the woods and nobody knew where his remains lay. Maria's family survived, her husband and all their children. The twin brothers had gotten married and moved away – one to the heart of Istria, the other to Čičarija, a region between Croatia and Slovenia. There was no news of their sister Justine. After searching, Valeria at last found out about her fate. During the war, she was working at a hotel in Rijeka, where she smuggled food and information to the partisans. A young *Ustasha* kitchen maid gave her away one day and she was imprisoned at the Jasenovac death camp, where she perished. Old Bruno and Nadja Batič continued farming despite the stupid *kolkhoz* policy since it was the only way to enable Franjo to study at the high school in Koper. Franjo wanted to continue studying law and chose Trieste as his home for it was closer to Kozjane.

Marjana and Valeria were very careful about the story regarding little Martin. At first, Valeria's parents were shocked that their daughter had a baby out of wedlock. However, when they met Marko and saw the young family together, their fears vanished. Valeria was afraid to tell them the truth and felt ashamed when her mother cuddled the boy tenderly.

After the liberation, Marjana had moved in to the two-bedroom apartment on Wolfova Street with Valeria and her family. Living conditions were cramped, with no privacy and space for the children. However, early in the summer of 1946, Marko arranged for them to move into one of the lavish villas surrounded by a vast green park with ancient trees in the center of Ljubljana. The place had remained abandoned after being confiscated from collaborators, probably some rich merchants or noblemen, they didn't know. The representatives of the *National Heritage Committee*, who inspected such properties and collected precious antiques, famous paintings, and other riches for museums, or so they claimed, had yet to empty the villa.

Valeria moved in with the children while Marko was at one of his professional trainings in Belgrade. She was awestruck as she entered the house. She wandered about the rooms with dusty linen over beds, obviously abandoned in haste. The house was thick with dirt. After taking the curtains and bed linens to the cleaners, Valeria and Zdenka got down to cleaning. Water simmered on the big stove in the kitchen. When they reached the bathroom, a curious rat came out of its hole to check on what was happening in its so far abandoned realm. Valeria shrieked in terror. And so rat poison was distributed around the corners, and builders called in to fill the cracks with fresh mortar. Valeria decided on the spot to have a couple of rooms repainted. Thus, the decorators dragged the old clocks, heavy beds, trunks, and chests to the attic.

The house had three floors. Each floor had a separate bathroom and a balcony. There were eight comfortable bedrooms, a huge dining room that could easily accommodate twenty people, and an elegant saloon with a door to the terrace and the park beyond. Huge trees provided ample shade as well as the scent of flowers and wild grass. The estate was far too big for them. Before approving all the repairs, Valeria consulted her boss Joc, who was very knowledgeable about everything, whether the authorities eventually planned to place other families in the house with them. He reassured her that she and Marko deserved to live in decent conditions after what they went through in the woods. When she wondered out loud why the villa had remained uninhabited for so long, he reluctantly explained that it had been originally given to Ivan, but he didn't like it, preferring a remote estate in the outskirts of Ljubljana, which had a bigger garden where guards were easier to place. Ivan's indecision regarding the villa also prevented the *National Heritage Committee* from inspecting it and turning over the valuables to the socialist state.

Valeria felt almost relieved that Marko was away while she assessed their new home. During the hot July days following the move, she discovered famous Impressionist paintings hidden in the attic, including a small study of *Rihard Jakopič's The Sower*, one of the most famous Slovenian paintings. She carefully put it away in a trunk. There were also numerous antique pieces of furniture, centuries old, inlaid with mother-of-pearl, ivory, and precious stones, and wall tapestries woven with golden threads that depict scenes from the Bible. While heavy oak and walnut wood furnished the huge rooms, the real treasures, including artistically carved trunks and chests inlaid with jade, ivory and amber, were stashed in the attic. Valeria felt awkward in the face of the luxury. As a precaution, she decided to hide them from prying eyes under some huge war blankets and old paper. She always suspected the *National Heritage Committee* to be nothing but a bunch of thieves. Apparently the residents had left in haste. Maybe they had thought one day, they would come back and retrieve their valuables. She didn't say a word, not even to Marko, about hiding the paintings and precious antiques in the darkest corner of the attic.

She felt a strange, mellow kind of melancholy. Although it seemed right that the partisans get rewarded after their victory, she felt like an intruder in other people's lives, almost like a thief. Every object in the house had a history that she could only guess. The porcelain, the delicate linens, the clothes left behind in the wardrobes.

After a week of cleaning and decorating, a new visitor came by: a robust black-and-white tomcat. His fur was in tatters, his ears bitten off in parts; he must have gotten into a hell of a fight over this summer's love. Valeria decided to keep him. Cats were much better protection against rats and mice than arsenic powder in every corner. He was very shy at first, but after a couple of bowls of milk, he moved about the house as though it were his home. After a long day, while she was sitting on the bench in the park and smoking a cigarette, he even came over for a cuddle. It was like Christmas for the children.

"Kitty, kitty, kitty!" Martin kept shouting at the top of his voice.

"It, ity, it," little Anna echoed, following her brother on all fours for she couldn't move as fast or keep her balance on two legs yet.

The children's voices meant clumsy cuddles, which rang an alarm bell for the graceful animal. He escaped to safety up the regal walnut trees in the park. Disappointed, Martin and Anna gazed up at him. Yet, nothing could lure the handsome cat from his place. Valeria and Zdenka laughed at the scene: two hasty puppies chasing a cat. At the time, Martin was two years old and Anna ten months.

They owned a car – a Fiat – and both Marko and Valeria had a driving license. On Sundays, they would take the kids to the sea, visit Marjana at Kozjane, or go on excursions around Slovenia. Valeria enrolled at the university to pursue Comparative Literature and French as a foreign language, however, she never had enough time to study properly. Often her professors turned a blind eye and let her pass the exams anyway. She always vowed to study later, but failed to do so.

Now, three years later, Martin was attending school for the first time, and Anna was the leader of her kindergarten's group. In spite of the hardships and uncertain times, Valeria and Marko led a nice life, filled with parties, friends, and seasons by the sea. They felt secure and protected under the wings of the Party. However, silence and mistrust grew like weed in the post-war socialist society, taking its toll on them, too. Marko started to drink a glass too many after work. On many evenings his drinking buddies brought him home almost unconscious. He had no control over his drinking, as though he wanted to drown out memories. It was not until late 1949, when Joc promoted Valeria to Head of the Archives of the OZNA, did she find out the real reason. She loathed his drinking. Marko got sloppy with his words, and it put the family in danger. In such dark times, alcohol was a dangerous vice.

"Valchy, I may drink, but I never get drunk," he often said to ease her worries.

"Darling, I see men like you sent to *Goli otok* every day. You really should be careful. Everyone is your enemy, everyone, remember that!" she would reply severely.

"Don't worry, my love. When I'm drunk, I only talk about my childhood, my youth, and memories from before the war. I trained myself like a dog. Sometimes I have to think whether I still exist. My mind wanders to the *Risiera* concentration camp or to Kočevski Rog, and I think I am dead," Marko replied in a sad voice.

Valeria nodded in understanding, but worried nonetheless. His drinking sprees soon got worse, and Marko became quarrelsome with his friends and violent toward Valeria and the children. People started to avoid him. Frequently, bartenders rang her in the middle of the night to come and fetch her drunken husband. She would take their car and drive to wherever he was, trembling with fear that their little children would wake up alone in the big house. The situation was getting out of control. They started avoiding society, which only worsened the situation for Marko drank himself to oblivion on weekends. Once, he fell into a coma and almost died. Valeria managed to save his life in time.

After a couple of days, he came to his senses and decided to stop drinking. Valeria banned all liquor from the house to remove temptation. He stayed clean for a couple of months. Their love revived; hope twittered in the air. It animated their evenings, lively and eager like a swarm of moths around the fire. Every night when they returned from the meetings, they brought out thick blankets and sat together in the garden. They smoked, drank coffee, and talked. Soon hope infused their bedroom and life continued in merrier tones. Only a pink pill hinted at the demons in Marko's mind. He had to take the pill in order to sleep. Marko admired his Valchy, who could separate her job from the family, war from peace, friends from foes.

Not long after they moved to the big house, her boss Joc called for Valeria.

"Valchy, you're being promoted. Please, follow me!"

They descended the stairs until they came to the cellar of the *Slavija* building. Joc took a bunch of keys from his pocket and searched for the ones to unlock one of the rooms with heavy metal doors. There was a loud click and he pushed it open. Valeria could see nothing but a black hole. Joc reached for the switch and a dusty yellow bulb illuminated the room. Hundreds of boxes filled with papers, documents, and some carefully sealed boxes were scattered around.

"What is this, Joc?"

"These are the documents of various people, mostly collaborators, exiles, and criminals. Your job is to put them in order and guard them from curious eyes."

She looked at him, astonished. "That's impossible. I'll be locked away with these papers for ages. Have I done something wrong, Joc?"

Joc put his right arm around Valeria's shoulder. "You don't understand, Valchy This job is proof of our deep trust in you." He gestured toward the dusty piles. "Most of these people were eliminated in 1945. Their relatives may be alive somewhere and present a threat to our communist society. Some are out there, and they want their property back – the factories, the houses, the lands that underwent nationalization. We cannot let this happen. You know how reactionaries are always plotting against *Tito* and Yugoslavia. We must have an overview of who they are and what they're doing. You won't work alone. You'll be in charge of a small group of people – maybe something like ten employees, who will be helping you. You must keep them under thumb and guarantee the secrecy of the archives."

Valery remained unhappy about her new job. The windowless room in the cellar seemed like a tomb filled with evil spirits. The souls of the victims and the dark forces of the assassins were lurking in the dark corners. She continued her protest.

"But I thought the officials from the ARS have long since dealt with the collaborators who deserted Yugoslavia and are now living abroad. What have they been doing all these years? Were they sitting on their fat asses or what?"

Joc smiled – his Valchy and her work ethics. He said, "You're right. Those in the ARS are indeed a bunch of lazy, worthless bureaucrats. Their boss is barely literate. However, they are doing something. They keep track of emigrants, but these records are too sensitive. Our party leaders preferred to stow the papers until they could find someone trustworthy to handle them. I think you'll be able to put this mess into order."

"And you said this is my promotion … In what way?"

"It is a promotion, Valchy, and a huge one, too. First, you'll travel to Belgrade for special training at the Central Committee. Upon your return, you're to hire ten people and instruct them about the work. You must be very careful in your selection. A special building, probably on Beethoven Street, will be allocated for the purpose of organizing and storing all these papers. You'll be personally responsible for security procedures and the safety of these archives. Not a fly must leave that building."

"Who will be my boss?"

"That'll be me. The archives are ours, *OZNA*'s archives."

"Oh, good." She sighed with relief. Always practical, she added. "Is there a raise in it for me as well?"

"Cash is difficult, but you will get a nice little house by the sea in Ankaran. Marko can visit his relatives in Trieste there. Maybe he'll drink less. How is he?"

"Visiting Marko's relatives isn't possible."

"Why? Doesn't he have a special passport for Zones A and B?"

"Yes, but his folks died in the *Risiera* during the war. He hasn't got anybody."

"Oh, all of them? I'm sorry, I forgot."

"Well, losing his whole family has been tough on Marko. The summer house sounds nice, though. Will we be sharing it?"

"No, it'll be yours only. But how is Marko? You don't say much about him."

Her face darkened. Although Marko had been clean for some weeks now, she could sense his unrest. He was trying so hard – she could see that. However, he had a short fuse. One wrong word out of her and he went to sleep in the guestroom while Valeria cried in her pillow until dawn. Joc watched her, waiting for an answer.

"You knew how it was. He was drinking a glass too many here and there."

"And now?"

"At the moment, he's managed to keep sober. But he's grown edgy. I have a feeling he's about to explode in front of my eyes any day now. Anything I say or do can set him off."

"I'm sorry to hear this. I hope he gets better. You'll see, the sea will lift his spirits. Ankaran is a good idea. Well, let's go back to the office."

Valeria nodded. She took the keys of the accursed room from Joc and locked the door behind them. "When does my train for Belgrade leave?"

"Tomorrow at six in the morning."

"Oh, tomorrow already?"

"Yes, we want you to start as soon as possible. I'll tell you more on the train. We'll be traveling in our own compartment."

"We?"

"I have to come along and vouch for you, Valchy. It'll be like old times in the woods," Joc said, his eyes bright with cunning.

It wasn't until two months later that Valeria understood the corruption and the atrocity of the new system. She found out why Marko was a ruined man and why he drowned his pain in vodka and brandy. In those months after the liberation, while she was pregnant with Anna and striving to save Martin, Marko was in Kočevski Rog. His job was to kill. Every day hundreds of Home Guards, young and old, were felled by his bullets. The evil saturated his mind forever. He came back to Ljubljana half-deranged. Then, overwhelmed by the birth of their daughter, he was too confused to ask any more questions about Martin.

As Valeria considered her job to organize the documents of the traitors, she thought about her role in the war. She had killed many men. Some were guilty, others were innocent. Why didn't she, a woman, break down, too? The only answer she could think of was motherhood. Her fight was the one of a lioness protecting her cubs. Maybe women really were the stronger sex. They had to be in order to keep the bloodline going.

While the train was rambling toward east on that gray autumn morning, Valeria remembered the readings from her philosophy course. A saying by Abdu'l-Bahá: "Yes, a scorpion is evil in relation to man; a serpent is evil in relation to man; but in relation to themselves they are not evil, for their poison is their weapon, and by their sting they defend themselves. Thus, evil does not exist, and is relative to man." Have the people of the new Yugoslavia turned into poisonous serpents and scorpions? Was it because of communism?

~~~

A week later, Valeria was walking across the Congress Square in Ljubljana. The sweet smell of roasted chestnuts filled her nostrils like the promise of her warm home. She had embarked the train from Belgrade the day before, and it arrived in Ljubljana early this morning. She found the *OZNA* driver waiting for her. He immediately took her to the *Slavija* building for a meeting with her boss and dropped off her baggage at her home address. Her desk was full of papers, both new and old cases. Joc had yet to find her replacement so she had to work almost double shifts. The hours until she could go home to Marko and the kids stretched on and on, they seemed like years. When at last, she could leave for the day, she couldn't wait to open her suitcase and distribute the gifts that she had bought in a special shop in Belgrade. Chocolate for the kids, Cuban cigars for Marko. She also had a pair of warm green gloves for Zdenka.

The sun was setting behind Rožnik Hill. An evening fog embraced the city, shyly rising from the Ljubljanica River, hesitant like a bride lifting her veil. The surface of frozen puddles glistered in the last rays of the November sun.

It was so nice to be back home. Belgrade was a challenge. Everyone kept reading her lips, trying to understand what she was saying in her broken Slovenian-Serbian. She should learn Serbo-Croatian better or she would be handicapped at her career. She had bought a few books to that purpose. She was particularly looking forward to Ivo Andrić's *The Bridge on the Drina*. Everybody praised it as the symbol of brotherhood and fraternity among the nations of Yugoslavia. She must read it.

Valeria smiled at the memory of how nicely Joc had presented her to his superiors. They all laughed their heads off at the story of *Giovinezza* and sympathized with her for losing Borko. Valeria was particularly moved by their sincere and deep compassion. Complete strangers comforted and embraced her, saying praises and talking to her as though they were all part of a big family.

'Slavs have big souls,' thought Valeria, 'willing to open their hearts to you without any shame or restraint. Like children, happiness and sadness, smiles and tears, laughter and fears move their minds simultaneously and passionately. Why hide your emotions after all this suffering?'

She felt uneasy when strange men smacked wet kisses on her cheeks – three times, with the third one landing directly on her lips. At first, she flushed in shame. Only two men had kissed her lips in her lifetime. Soon she accepted their warm outbursts of brotherhood and learned to welcome them with an open heart. Joc's dramatic and picturesque interpretation of her activist and partisan career embarrassed her. She was tired of the same stories. However, judging by the warm acceptance of *tovarishi*, she realized how cleverly her boss had introduced her. Anecdotes and tales of brave fights were like invisible threads, distinct milestones that make a person worth remembering and promoting. A lovely young woman who scared Italian soldiers and made them run was sensational.

Her steps were light as feathers along Rimska Street. When she rang the bell of their home, Zdenka opened and the children rushed into Valeria's arms.

"Mommy, Mommy!"

Kisses flew from cheek to cheek, little hands grabbed for the lap where they could always find comfort. Valeria barely managed to remove her coat. The table was set for one in the kitchen.

"Where's Marko?"

Zdenka gave her a strange look, as though she to warn her. "He phoned a while ago. He has a meeting of some kind. It may last long into the evening."

"Well, when he comes home, he'll be able to have a cigar. From Havana, a Cuban," Valeria said in a light voice, ignoring Zdenka's sharp words. "What has Mommy brought you from Belgrade, my little darlings, what?"

"What? What?" Martin and Anna shrieked in unison.

Valeria unlocked her leather suitcase. First, she gave Zdenka a pair of wonderfully embellished gloves. The children waited politely for what would come out of the heap of clothes and papers. She pulled out two square packages.

"Chocolate!" they cried out with joy.

"Only after meal," Valeria added firmly.

Zdenka grinned from ear to ear. "They've already eaten. An hour ago."

"May we try it now, Mommy?" asked Martin excitedly.

"You may, but save some for tomorrow," she said in a soft voice.

The children twittered to the drawing room, counting how many bars they would eat today and how many tomorrow. Zdenka placed a heavy pot on the table.

"Here. My *jota* doesn't taste like yours, but there's a dry sausage inside. Enjoy your meal!"

Valeria inhaled the pungent smell of sauerkraut and her mind wandered to her childhood memories of Kozjane in wintertime when the dish was often on the table.

"Lovely, Zdenka, thank you. After one week of *čevapčiči, kajmak*, and grilled meat, *jota* is perfect. You know how men are. They eat meat and drink alcohol. Besides, they do not drink beer or wine like Slovenians. They drink schnapps, plum brandy, my God! I could feel it burning my brain after a tiny glass. I had to learn fast to pretend to drink without really drinking. I would take a gulp, keep it in my mouth without swallowing it, then spit it back in the glass. Every now and then, I'd let a plant have my šljivovica. The Serbian men couldn't believe how much this tiny Slovenian woman could drink."

Zdenka smiled and sat opposite Valeria with a mug of tea. Her employer was fun, in spite of all challenges and difficulties in the household. "Is the *jota* good, Valeria?"

Valeria nodded and ate two servings in no time. Although food was not scarce any more, her habit to gulp down food persisted. After changing from her uniform into a comfortable skirt and sweater, she joined the children in front of the lit stove in the drawing room. The smell of burning logs and chocolate filled the space and her mind. This was the sweet scent of happiness. Zdenka tended to the dishes and went home early. A bit later than usual, she put Martin and Anna to bed. After a story, she sat by the fire with a book in her hand. It seemed like hours before she heard the click of the key in the front door. She stood up to meet her husband. As soon as Marko entered, she could smell brandy on him despite his attempt to camouflage it with a mint.

"Hello, darling. How was Beeeeooooooograd?" he said, dragging the vowels to imitate the Serbian pronunciation of the Yugoslav capital.

She decided not to smell the brandy or notice his drunkenness tonight. "Fine, thank you. Are you hungry? I can warm some *jota* soup for you. It's really delicious."

Marko shook his head and put his slippers on. "Thank you. It was Ivan's birthday, and he invited us all to dinner."

No kiss, no embrace. Side by side, they went into the drawing room. Marko put some logs on the fire. Valeria reached for the box of the expensive cigars.

"Here, Marko. I don't know where they get these, but they say they're the best. Even *Tito* smokes the same brand."

Marko took the parcel and put it on the dresser. He headed for the liquor cabinet and poured himself a good dose of cognac. "Something's wrong with my stomach," he said by way of excuse and emptied the glass in one go.

Valeria came closer and gently took the glass from his hands. She kissed him on the cheek and looked deeply into his eyes. Without saying a word, her sincere face betrayed her dark thoughts. He could read it like an open book. The reproach and the shame. She was so successful at anything she did. She even got promoted. Marko found out from Ivan how much the party officials respected Valeria and how eagerly they supported her ambitions. She was hardworking and reliable. She had been to Belgrade where she met the generals and associated with top party bosses, while he played the nanny to their kids. He could imagine her trip vividly. He used to spend time with the bosses in bars. Surely, men went after Valeria, trying to grab her breasts or bottom. Ivan said that every ambitious woman had to spread her legs first. If she refused, that was the end of her career; if she was willing, then the ladder was free for her to climb.

Marko's eyes shone with fury. He grabbed her harshly and held her in his arms. His tongue violated her lips, demanding a kiss. She tried to resist his force. This was not how she pictured their reunion.

When he backed off at last to catch his breath, she shrieked indignantly, "Marko, what's wrong with you?"

"What's wrong with me? You're my wife, aren't you? I have every right. I have more right than all those Belgrade pigs with whom you've been whoring for the week, haven't I?"

He crushed her back into his arms and closed her mouth with another kiss. Valeria's eyes filled with tears as she tried to free herself from his brutal embrace. The smell of his foul breath, cognac, and cigarettes sickened her. Nausea almost made her vomit. Marko ripped the sweater from her body, tore the bra apart, and grabbed at her breasts.

"No, no, please, Marko, don't ..." she pleaded, hoping he would listen to the distress in her voice. She wished he would stop and the whole thing would remain nothing but an unpleasant memory.

Yet, rage made Marko stronger. He pushed her to the sofa and grabbed her long hair in his fist so that she could not turn away from his smell. He stared down at her. Bitch! Thunder inflamed his actions and he unzipped his pants. With the other hand, he lifted her skirt and tried to penetrate her with his swollen penis.

Valeria burst into tears like a helpless child. Nothing she did in war had prepared her for this. Marko halted. His battle-ready manhood shrank to impotence.

'Tears, my God, tears.' He saw her hurt and humiliated, writhing in pain. 'What have I done?'

Valeria felt his grip loosen. He fell against her and hid his face in her hair. They were both crying now, crying like helpless infants, crying out their sorrows and pain. They could not escape the spider's web of violence. No matter how much they tried, war was all around them.

"Forgive me, Valchy. I don't know what's wrong with me, darling," he said, sobbing against her throat.

She could not forgive, at least not tonight. Nevertheless, she whispered gently: "Oh, Marko, it's all right. We'll get past this somehow."

They lay together on the sofa, half-naked, worlds apart despite their entangled limbs, each one thinking about his own hell, each one trapped in his own abyss. The logs in the fireplace turned to ashes, and the room sank into dark coldness. Valeria felt Marko's breathing slow down. Soon, his drunken snoring filled her ears. She slipped away, relieved not to feel his body against hers anymore, the body of a man she once loved. Alcohol had taken him away. What had happened to Marko? Why was he becoming such an animal? And how could they live together tomorrow and the day after tomorrow after what happened tonight? Valeria breathed in deeply. Her stomach turned at the smell of him and she had to swallow hard to keep from vomiting.

'Marko, my Marko! Keep drinking and you will rot in your own piss,' she thought as she threw a blanket over him. She knew he would not move until morning.

She threw a couple of logs on the dying embers. Then she went to the bathroom where she stood under the shower until there was no more warm water left. She wrapped her hair in a towel and climbed into their double bed where she fell in a deep sleep. She dreamt she was a partisan hiding in the woods with her comrades. They were tired after a long march and a fight with the Germans. However, she was trying very hard to understand something – an idea, maybe an event or a word. Something about the war, something she could not fathom, although she thought she had known everything there was to know about war.

~~~

In July 1949, the weather was pleasantly warm in Buenos Aires with cool evenings and warm days. It was very different from distant Slovenia where the summer sun was frying everything it touched, firing up every concrete surface in Ljubljana to unbearable heat. The shade of the huge trees in *Tivoli* Park offered some solace. Ada remembered that soon after giving birth, she would take baby Martin for a walk there. In the green cathedral under the huge maples, they would find peace in spite of the war ravaging around them. 'Oh, how long ago was that July!' Ada thought of it as though from a previous life when she was both mother and wife.

Here in the new world, Ada was neither. She was alone and she was lonely. She got in the way of everything and everybody, especially Andrej's. Her husband had less and less patience with her. She hated herself and she hated her life. Their marriage, the unison of two souls and bodies, was over. A broken mirror with pieces reflecting light that went in every direction. The man she used to love so passionately became a stranger. The warmth sometimes resurged in old memories.

Through the open window, the wind brought sounds from the streets below – the merry cries of youths who were gathering to go dancing. Not waltz or polka like in Slovenia, they went to one of the dim, smoky bars to dance tango.

It had been ages since Ada went dancing. Ages since she last sang. She didn't care to listen to music either. Everything reminded her of the life she had lost forever. She longed for white flowers and red fruits, the sweet fruits of the cherry trees in the *Brkini Hills*. She dreamed of the scent of lime and acacia trees, the golden fields of ripe wheat, the tall corn patches with their green and gold light in August. God knows what became of her home village, Kozjane.

Her older sister Marjana was a clever and intelligent woman. A survivor with a broken heart. She had almost starved herself to death, wanting to die of compassion after the atrocities she witnessed in the Italian concentration camps. But they somehow managed to save her. Andrej healed her. A miracle. After the war, she found new meaning in life in spite of her age. She celebrated her fiftieth anniversary not long ago. Marjana used all her contacts at the Red Cross and the Catholic Church to find her address in Buenos Aires. She sent her a letter from the Trieste post office. Ada had read it so many times that she knew this greeting from the other side of the globe almost by heart.

Dear Ada!

Kozjane, 12th March 1948

At last, our Father Josef gave me your address. Do you remember him? He used to scold you when you were giggling instead of praying in church. I'm so glad I can write to you, although you may find some things unclear. The new regime is severe. We don't know whether the Allies report to our authorities about the letters that are sent from Trieste to our immigrants around the world. Thus, my little Ada, this will be the only letter I will send you.
You cannot imagine how happy I was to find out that you were able to save yourselves and settle down in Argentina before the major wave of immigrants took place. That was a very smart move. It is good to know that you are doing well in your new home so far away.
First, let me tell you about our parents and our house. Two years ago, I came to Kozjane and found our main door locked, though the house had no

roof. A ruin. During the war, our village was burned three times. Slowly, some life is coming back, yet the people are poor and cannot rebuild their homes. This Kolkhoz or collective farming based on some Soviet model does not prove profitable at all. We all hope that this way of exploiting the soil will stop, now that Tito's relations with Stalin have deteriorated. To hell with politics. Let it be.
Father and Mother survived the war, but they're weak and sick. All the horror was too much on them. Father died of pneumonia two years ago. In a few months, Mother followed him to the grave. I was the only one in the family present at both funerals. Otherwise, there was a huge crowd. The whole Batič family, save for Marjo and Justina, who both died in the war, came and all our neighbors and friends, too. There was also Valeria with her husband and her two children: a boy, Martin, the fruit of a relationship with a partisan during the war and a girl, Anna born in wedlock with her husband Marko.
Our Kozjane villagers have once more shown how close-knit we are. Father Josef laid Father and Mother in their graves. I thought I would follow them shortly. My depression returned and there was not a doctor who could help me fight the devious disease. I despaired and lived in the ruins of our house alone, lonely and sad. Like a gypsy. The foul wind kept howling through the empty walls and snow entered the only room with windows where the little stove gave no warmth at all. I had a feeling I was living in a graveyard – and only decades ago, Kozjane was a lively, modern village.
Spring came early the following year. Knowing I have some savings, the village boys came to see me. They needed a job, while I needed to fix the house, plant the fields, and tend to the fruit trees. Work started and the sun shone back into my life. The boys did not only save our land and rebuilt our house, but they also brought me back to life. In spite of my age and the pains in my bones, I work in the fields and look after the orchards, so the harvests are plenty.
Since the years after the war, I have become close to Valeria. We were friends before, you know, but the difficult times after the liberation brought us together for good. I will never forget how tired and nervous Valeria was when she came to the hospital in May 1945. She had little Martin in her arms and another child on the way. We found a solution to her problems and for a couple of years lived all together in that tiny apartment on Wolfova Street. When I returned to Kozjane, Valeria and her husband Marko moved to a comfortable villa in the center of Ljubljana.
I can imagine how curious you are about Valeria and her young family. They have gone through hell, all of them, most of all Valeria. You remember

she ran into the woods the evening they arrested me in her place. There she met the father of Martin, who was an important Communist fighter of the resistance. They were not married, however, very much in love. They were both shot while leaving Ljubljana to reach the liberated territories in Bela Krajina. He died; Valeria lived and had his child. Our neighbors, the Likin family, looked after Martin until she could take him. It is only by lucky coincidence that the boy is alive. When the Germans took the whole Likin family to Dachau, the boy was staying with Valeria's sister Maria for a couple of days. Truly, a miracle. I was so glad Valeria came to find me at the hospital. Her husband, Marko Robič, is from Trieste. A very nice man and a devoted father. He dotes on Martin even though he is not really his child. He plays with him and looks after him. However, there is one problem. Marko tends to drink too much, but who wouldn't when faced with the misery of war? Like all of us, Marko tries to forget the unforgettable. But he never hits the children or Valeria. She was lucky in choosing him, our little Valchy. Her children grow in a happy family. Every end of June when the school is finished, she brings them to our house for a holiday. They are such a blessing. Ada, I cannot tell you how much I love them. We pick cherries, wild strawberries, and blackberries, search for mushrooms, and catch crawfish in the stream. I have bought a couple of goats that graze around the house. You should see the love between the kids and the children – little wild fools, I tell you.

Valeria is not aware of my letter to you, and it is better this way. She has started a new high-responsibility job with the Information Agency OZNA. A very high position. Below I've written her address, just in case, I may be gone one day, but please, Ada, do not use it. You know how we are doing. Some better, some worse, but life goes on.

You have to take care of yourself and Andrej now, build your future. You have a new life in Argentina and you should think of increasing your family. I look forward to nephews and nieces. I believe we will be reunited one day. Not in the near future, though for the peace we live in is not real peace. Thank God, we survived.

So, my darling Ada, let us embrace in our thoughts if we cannot live together.

Have a nice time, and send my love to your man. Don't forget to love each other.

With kisses,

Your Marjana

Ada's eyes filled with tears. She had to hold back her sobs. Andrej would be home soon. She should not cry or he would have enough of her tears and sadness one day. Somewhere in the distance, the waves played an evening song at the shores of the golden land, full of opportunities. Ada stood up and lit the lights.

They had furnished a small apartment in the center of the city and somehow kept on going. Yet, their life was a pale shadow of the happiness they shared during their first two years in Ljubljana. There was war, there was danger, but they had loved each other deeply. Their hearts beat as one, their souls were fused together, and their bodies thrived on sensual pleasures amidst poverty and food rations. And they had their little boy, their Martin.

Although Marjana was trying to say in her letter that Ada did the right thing at that bloody train station in Ljubljana, Andrej never forgave her. He blamed her for abandoning their child, leaving him in the hands of Communist murderers. His resentment was silent at first, but as their relationship crumbled, his accusations became vocal, louder and more pronounced every time. His only son was living with a bunch of criminals, for Andrej considered anyone who decided to live in the new Communist Yugoslavia a criminal. As a psychiatrist, Andrej was rational and coolheaded. He weighed every case and symptom before starting a treatment. However, when he assessed anything political, he reacted with passion. His views were strongly anti-communist, and the longer he lived abroad, the greater his hatred for *Tito*'s Yugoslavia grew. Drifting apart from his beloved Ada only added fuel to the flame. His once kind heart was freezing in icy bitterness. Thus, Ada hid Marjana's letter for fear he would extract some kind of revenge and get everyone, including their Martin, into trouble. She often wondered how he could forget those two difficult years after the liberation. They were hungry and cold so many times. Little Martin could have died in the ruins of war and they would have been helpless to do anything. Nobody cared for the collaborators. The only medicine for the losers was the revenge of the victors.

She remembered their time in Carinthia. Andrej took so long to make up his mind about leaving the Home Guard troops that Pučić gave up on him and drove off to Switzerland alone in his fancy car. Supplied with fuel and food from the Allies' black market, Andrej and Ada waited and waited. It was terrible, a complete meltdown of all human values and principles. Total chaos and lawlessness. People were whispering that, besides black market goods, everything else was on sale – love, sex, sentiments, had they ever existed in any war. The only rule was to survive. It was abhorrent to see men and women acting worse than wild beasts.

In the last days of May, Bleiburg, where they were stuck, underwent a cold front. Icy rain fell as though summer would never come. Andrej took care of his comrades, who were coughing and trembling with fever. Ada waited in their rented room while Andrej worked night and day. The laden sky had no answer to the main question of what the future had in stall for them. Money was running out, its worth already declining with the general shortage. Every evening Ada begged Andrej to leave the Home Guard and move to Switzerland, to the land without any war for centuries, where they could have a fresh start. Deaf to her pleas, Andrej went back to treat the soldiers in the camp day after day. He felt it a betrayal of his homeland if he did not share their destiny and help them out.

Then some of the men who were sent to *Palmanova* by the British transport came back to Carinthia. They told the truth about the British's deceit. Right after the border, the sentinels of the Yugoslav partisans took over the trains and directed everyone into the woods where they were killed like livestock in a slaughterhouse. Only a few escaped alive, mostly by pretending to be dead under their bleeding comrades. Andrej sobered up. There was no public transport. All communications were destroyed. They had to walk. On the brink of winter, they started their monthlong march and entered the Swiss territory through the Engadin Valley. The Swiss refused to let them in the country until Andrej's friend vouched for them. In St. Moritz, they took a rest before selling all of Ada's jewelry.

In spite of his friend's connections, Andrej couldn't get a job. The Swiss had so many European immigrants with good medical education and training. They did not need another psychiatrist. He managed to freelance at health resorts here and there and acquire some private patients who paid him shamefully low fees, but not enough to earn a living. Ada enrolled at the Italian Teachers' Institute and continued her studies. In place of tuition, the management let her clean the premises. They lived from day to day without any real prospects for the future. They had no idea what was happening in Yugoslavia, how their loved ones were doing – Ada's parents, Marjana, and most of all, little Martin. Twice Ada sent a letter to Kozjane, a generic one about health and harvest, but both remained unanswered. Maybe the postal service was still suspended or the letters were being seized by the authorities. Be as it may, she stopped writing for fear of getting their loved ones into trouble. The only person she could share her thoughts with regularly was Sanja, who had reestablished her musical career in America. Sanja invited them to come to America. The passage was possible, and she would send the money. Yet, Andrej, stubborn as always, wanted to go his own way. Indeed they both wanted to stay in Europe, both hoping things would change and they could return to Ljubljana.

The following spring a glimmer of hope came to their sad existence. Ada got pregnant. For a couple of months, they floated on a cloud, delighting in the flowers and the bird songs on spring mornings. Their happiness though was short-lived. The child in Ada died, perished, the same way as the promise of joy died and disappeared from their dreams. Every day was grimmer and darker than an autumn tempest on the horizon. Ada finished her studies and waited.

Andrej wasn't happy either. Switzerland was not what he thought it would be. On every occasion, the Swiss made him feel inferior as a professional and as a man. They started looking for an opportunity to go to Sweden. However, things went differently. Through his Catholic acquaintances, he found out about a possibility to migrate to Argentina. It was the end of 1946. *Janez Hladnik*, a missionary priest, helped them. In Argentina, a community of Slovenians, who escaped the Fascism before WWII, was looking for a doctor who spoke their language. Naturally they had to hide the fact that Andrej had collaborated with the Fascists and the Nazis. Ada and Andrej celebrated their first Christmas in a modest one-room apartment in the center of Buenos Aires. The four Advent candles on the table awakened new dreams in the desperate couple. The warm flames signified a new life. Indeed, Ada was pregnant again. At last, passion and love revisited their bed. They were happy, singing Slovenian Christmas carols and making love long into the night. The candles burnt down and life died again beneath Ada's heart. She lost all hope and buried her dreams in bitterness.

The following summer she started the ritual of celebrating Martin's birthday. She baked a cake and put three candles on it. When Andrej observed her zeal in arranging the celebration, he deeply worried about Ada. Tranquilizers might have helped her condition, but therapy or at least an honest conversation would have been much better. Yet, the wall of silence and resentment that had grown between them grew higher and wider. Andrej's diagnosis – trauma from abandoning her own child – was irrelevant for Ada was living in a world of her own. For a while, Andrej tried to be compassionate and understanding, but he grew more and more weary of her pointless ritual to memorialize their lost son.

This year there were five candles on the cake that Ada lit while humming a nursery rhyme.

'Little Martin would be five today. Maybe he doesn't remember me. Why can't I let go and continue with my life?' she thought with bitterness as she stood up to close the window.

Before she could reach it, a draft swept through the dining room and put out the candles. Andrej was home.

"Oh, this macabre cake ritual again," he grumbled.

Ada played deaf and went on as though she hadn't heard him. "Will you have dinner, darling? I made some wonderful roast beef."

Without a word, Andrej went to the bathroom and came back refreshed, wearing a dressing gown. Exhausted, he sat at the lavishly set table. His day at the hospital was long and the patients difficult. He was also tired of speaking Spanish, a foreign language he'd acquired only recently. Moreover, he had to sit through a meeting of Slovenian associations and listen to groundless, futile conflicts among the members – only to come home to a stage of this absurd farce, a birthday party for the son, who vanished from their lives years ago. Enough. Enough of this.

Ada brought him dish after dish. After a glass of wine, his spirits lifted. Maybe things would improve. Maybe he could talk to her, talk her out of it. Maybe tonight they could make love.

Yet Ada lit the candles and the ritual went on.

"Blow the candles, baby, blow!" She was talking to the teddy bear that had replaced Martin on the third chair at the table. Every year it was Andrej's job to blow out the candles. He did it hoping she would overcome her fixation by playing out her fantasy. Tonight, he could not. He was fed up. Fed up for good.

"Ada darling, maybe it's time we stop with this charade. Our little boy may not even be among the living any more. Maybe he's an angel looking down on us while we carry on with this farce," he said in a soothing voice, a plea in his eyes.

Ada gave him a look as though he were insane. "Andrej, I beg you, please. You know Martin is alive. He can feel our love, and we should always bear him in mind. How could he return our love unless we show him ours? It will all be right once we are reunited."

Andrej sighed with annoyance. "Should he be alive as you say, Ada, maybe it's better for him that we're not together. You do know the repression people are suffering under the new Yugoslav state unless they side with the Communists, don't you, Ada? I hear the Communists have turned against their own people recently. Darling, why don't we get dressed and go for a walk and have some drinks at a bar?" he begged her.

Ada firmly sliced through the chocolate icing. "First, we'll eat the cake. Let's sing 'Happy Birthday'!"

"Please, darling. This isn't healthy. I miss him, too. I feel the same pain you do," he said, tears in his eyes.

"Happy birthday, dear Martin, happy birthday to you!" Ada finished the song and blew out the candles. Then she put the first slice of the cake on the plate in front of the teddy bear.

"I can't put up with this any more. Darling, I've asked you so many times to let it go, to end this terrible drama. You're torturing yourself and tormenting me. You cannot bring another child of ours to the world because your body rejects what your soul doesn't want. Accept the fact that you made a mistake. I know you feel guilty about it. Repent and confess, go to church, and get absolution for what did. It was wartime. I understand. It wasn't your fault. Please, let it go."

She put the plate with his piece of cake in front of him. Her words were cold as the blade of knife. "I did not made a mistake, and stop condemning me once and for all. Martin lives because I made the right decision. A DECISION. Something alien to you, Andrej. Here, eat your cake."

Patiently, he dug the fork into the soft cream of the cake. He knew how the conversation would go. They would blame each other for as long as they could. Distribute guilt for what had happened. She blamed him for leaving her and Martin alone in Ljubljana during those critical weeks. He had failed to look after his family, dedicating his efforts to save his Home Guard cronies instead. He was guilty of abandoning his family. He had run for his life.

"You know, Andrej, the year we stop celebrating his birthday, Martin may really die." Her voice trembled with agony.

"Where do you get these stupid superstitions, Ada? As to us, he might as well have been dead all these years."

"Speak for yourself. You don't care about him. Your only thought is to fill my body with your semen so we can have another child. You don't give a damn about Martin."

He stabbed his fork into the chocolate. "I think less and less about our child-making. You've become a stranger, Ada." His voice was cynical. He couldn't hide his feelings any longer.

Ada continued as though she didn't hear his words. "He'll be starting school now."

Sarcastically, he replied: "You really think they have schools in Communist Yugoslavia, don't you? Maybe Martin will become an illiterate lumberjack or a butcher. Primitive authorities have no need for intellectuals. Instead of doctors they breed executors and thugs."

Ada's face flushed with rage. It was precisely this stupid zeal and stupid disparagement of everyone who thought differently during the war that had brought them to these foreign shores. Far away from home, dumped with other excommunicated European intellectuals, friends of the criminal Nazi regime. What right did he have to look down on Valeria?

"What has your illustrious medical profession brought us, Andrej, tell me, what?" She raised her voice. "We live like outcasts far away from home. We have no friends and family. Alone, stranded for all time. You're right, I cannot bring babies to this world. Because I do not conceive babies out of love. I conceive the fruits of despair and sadness."

A morsel of cake fell from his fork. He stood up. "Ada, I can't go on like this anymore. I'm sorry, terribly sorry," he said in a low voice.

He turned and went to the bedroom. After a while, he came out, holding the suitcase in which they had stuffed their meager possessions years ago. Ada's eyes bulged in anger. Was this his solution? Men were such fools!

"You can't go on? You? What about me? Sure, run, rabbit, run! Coward, always running from your responsibilities. And you have the nerve to reproach me! Go, go away, I don't want to see your face ever!" she cried hysterically, spitting saliva and shedding tears as though tidal waves of rage were at work in her soul.

"I'll send money every month. You'll want for nothing, Ada," he said, trying to control his voice. "When you're ready to talk, come see me at the hospital. I'll always be there for you."

In reply, Ada lifted the plate with the cake and threw it at his feet. Chocolate, cream, candles, and shards of porcelain flew in all corners of the dining room.

"Here, you have it!"

She continued crying and swearing long after the door had closed behind Andrej.

Rage turned into sobs and tears dried up in pain and gloom. She looked in the abyss of her heart and found blackness, a tunnel without end, a road to hell. In the middle of the night, she calmed down, washed her face, and cleaned the mess. She came to a decision. Not without hesitation. Maybe Andrej would come back before morning. Lastly, she put the teddy bear away in the dresser. From the back of the dresser where she had hidden it, she took out her only thread to life: Marjana's letter with Valeria's address.

No more tiptoeing in the dark, no more guessing. It was time for the truth.

~~~

Snow fell early in the season and whitened the hilly landscape of Slovenia some weeks before the Christmas of 1949. Pure whiteness erased and thickly covered the traces of blood – remnants of numerous families torn apart by the Informbiro Resolution, the wounds of another social cleft – from which the new Titoist society was rising like a phoenix from its ashes. The magic of the Advent and *Saint Nicholas* Day, eagerly awaited by children in bygone times, were now full of sober Communist slogans and speeches depicting Stalin's hateful policy while praising *Tito*'s love for his people.

Valeria's new job was a source of constant stress. Her idealism and faith in the future wavered. She rarely smiled these days and counted her very few merry moments with the children as special blessings. Without them, she would see no light at the end of the tunnel. Basically, her job was to dig the graves, expose the facts, and document the horror. Valeria Batič Robič preferred never find out what happened to the thousands of men and women, who were on the wrong side during the war, the collaborators. She couldn't believe in the prevailing opinion that they were all war criminals. The names and dates revealed women and children, old men and youths, not only soldiers. Yet, the partisans murdered them all in cold blood, without investigation or trial. She persuaded herself that the same destiny, if not worse, would have been in stall for her and her family had the Nazis won the war. Apart from organizing *OZNA*'s archives, she started noting the criminal deeds of some collaborators – deeds she knew for sure had happened. Thus, she managed to bear in mind that the Home Guards had not all been innocent. It sort of made amends for her dance with Death among those wretched papers. For the war hadn't ended yet amidst the archives of *OZNA*, and Valeria had a feeling it never would.

Naturally, her lips were sealed. When she spoke to Joc or her superiors, she was prudent with words and careful in expressing her thoughts. She enjoyed certain privileges and became an important person. They invited her to several meetings where she gave public speeches. Valeria tried to avoid most of them, not because she had ceased to believe in the liberation and communism for she still held on to the values she had fought for, but because she couldn't stand the hypocrisy. Thus, she refused to speak at the orphanage for the children of collaborators near Celje on the anniversary of *AVNOJ* on November 29th. Snow was falling, so the travel would take ages. Besides, she wasn't sure how to approach the orphans of the people whose dossiers and deaths passed through her hands every day. Anxiety plagued her, and she knew why.

The headmaster of orphanage *Petriček* rang her up, saying he wanted to show her the positive results of their socialist education. He insisted in coming to see her the following day. They came indeed. A thin, shallow man in his mid-forties. With him a tiny boy of five, thin and scared. He could have been Martin's age. Her opulent office, arrayed with carpets and polished furniture, intimidated him. He was shaking with fear. It was her uniform. Valeria still wore one to work, complete with Titovka cap from which a red star shone. In his little hands, he was clutching a bouquet of red carnations with green sprigs of fragrant rosemary. Hesitantly, he made a few steps toward her and recited in a loud, clear voice:

> My dear Tito, can you see,
> how brave I am, a busy bee?
> My dear Tito, can you see?
> I love my country
> and I love thee.

He made a bow, staggered, and she could see he had tears in his eyes. Valeria took the bouquet from his trembling hands and put it on the table. Then she lifted the frail body, embraced and held him close, kissing him warmly on his thin blond hair. They remained silent for a while, like mother and child, both shaken by powerful emotions. The headmaster stared with surprise as though he could not comprehend her tenderness for the child of a traitor. In Valeria's eyes, children were children and in that moment she was simply holding little Martin in her embrace, not a boy from the orphanage.

"Children are innocent. I hope you've been treating them decently, Mr. ...?"

"Kovač, Kovač is my name, *Tovarishitza* Robič. Don't worry, we give them everything we can. The boy, Bine" – he motioned to the child in her arms – "will be going to school next year. He's a bright little fellow."

"Indeed, he is."

In her arms, Bine began to sob silently. His arms clung to her neck as he pressed against her throat, making it hard for her to breathe. Valeria didn't know what to do but hold him in her arms. His warm tears drenched the starched collar of her shirt, but she didn't mind. Poor little fellow! What were they doing to him? She didn't believe a word the headmaster was saying and decided to send an inspection to this orphanage estate near Celje. From the corner of her eye, she could see that Kovač did not approve of her compassion as he stared cynically at her plant in the corner. Finally, the boy calmed down and stopped sobbing. He looked at her, curiosity overcoming his fear.

"Are you a partisan, *Tovarishitza*?"

Valeria smiled kindly. "I used to be. Now we live in peace, and Yugoslavia has its own army. As you can see I just work in the office now."

"Did you fire your rifle during the war?"

Valeria wiped his wet cheeks. "I had to and I did. But I got wounded, so after that I worked as a teacher."

"Will you be my teacher when I go to school, *Tovarishitza*? I like you better than *Tito*."

Valeria gaped in surprise. "Have you met *Tovarish Tito*, Bine?"

Valeria looked at the headmaster, the question in her eyes. What nonsense were they teaching the children? The headmaster's tiny moustache shivered with annoyance. The corners of his mouth turned down, and he spoke in a cynical voice.

"Not every child in our institution is a bright, lovely boy like Bine. Most of them are a nuisance, parasites, hostile to what we're trying to teach them. Marshal *Tito* came to visit us, and Bine recited the verses to him. *Tito* was so moved that he held him just like you are doing now."

'The only difference is I didn't sign the order to eliminate boy's parents as the marshal probably did. What a perversion of justice.' Without voicing her thoughts, Valeria just nodded to the headmaster, gently placing the boy on the ground. Reluctantly, he let go off her.

"I cannot be your teacher, Bine, but I promise to come see you at your school. So be sure you learn well and be a brave boy, will you?"

The boy nodded. She reached out for a special treat in the dresser behind her. Christmas seemed to shine in his eyes as he took the bar of chocolate she gave him. She couldn't miss the avid gleam in the headmaster's eyes. Clearly, he wanted one, too,

"You know what, Bine, why don't we sit down and talk for a while? You can tell me something about your friends while you're eating the chocolate. Take a sit." Valeria motioned them over to the sofa in the corner of the room. "Would you like some coffee, *Tovarish* Kovač?"

"Yes, thank you," the man replied politely, masking his disappointment. What a waste of chocolate! One punch and little Bine would throw it up on the way back to the children's camp in *Petriček*.

Her secretary brought the best of everything. After a few shots of brandy and a tray of biscuits, not to mention being bribed with a sack of coffee and a bottle of French Cognac, the headmaster finally relaxed. She couldn't stand the sight of him. Her fingers itched to fill up one of those horrible IB forms and send him to where he belonged. Bowing and thanking her for the gifts, the man was worse than a lizard.

Long after they had gone, Valeria thought about children and the terrible consequences of war. She couldn't help but think of Martin and his falsified birth certificate. He would be living a different life had she left him in such an institution. Probably longing for the bliss of tenderness just like little Bine.

Valeria often wondered whether Joc believed her. Could it be possible that her boss was aware of her darkest secret? Like all her colleagues at OZNA, he was very knowledgeable. They managed to dig up everyone's deepest secrets whether in Yugoslavia or abroad. Although she had invented a likely story, she could never be sure. She had always felt guilty for her greatest fear during most of 1945

– that someone in the Likin family would return from the concentration camp and disprove her story. What kind of woman would wish death of her neighbors? She was turning into a snake.

What did Doctor *Franja* say? Life comes before death.

Soon Valeria's own life was at stake. She was losing her mind while floating in the purgatory of communism.

~~~

On Christmas Eve of 1949, the spider's web of lies entrapped Valeria and her family in a dangerous cocoon of forged facts and fabricated events. The drama revolved from a single paper. It was not Valeria's fault, nor Marko's despite his drinking; it was the letter, a bloody letter with a treacherous stamp on the envelope: BUENOS AIRES, ARGENTINA.

Like every Christmas under the new regime, the couple attended the party meetings long into the night. Valeria was sure Marko would go to the pub afterward as was his norm ever since her trip to Belgrade. Hurt predominated in her feelings for her husband and she could not forgive him for what he had done. She could not help herself. She moved him and his belongings in the guestroom where he slept like a stranger in his own home. For weeks in a row, he would try hard to show how sorry he was. He would stay sober, bring her flowers, and take the family on a trip. He came home early and played with the kids. Yet, Valeria's heart had frozen over. They loved their children and knew that separation or divorce would wreck their young lives. It was out of question – no matter how difficult it was for both of them. They lived from day to day, waiting for a miracle to find each other again and turn their path upward.

The moon was full, and the sky shone with millions of stars. The thought of going to the pub, hearing the same old jokes, and whining about the days in the woods turned Marko off. They were drinking nearly the whole day – beer, wine, brandy. Tonight Marko just wanted to go home, embrace the children, put some logs on the fire, and tell them a story. But the party meeting seemed endless. The speakers kept losing their train of thought, repeating the same bombastic slogans again and again. Like Marko, they were all thinking of past Christmases, of sweet *potica*, and of singing carols around the tree. Midnight Mass in church was a chance to court girls and have a drink with the village elders. Yet, ever since the Church had collaborated with the Home Guard and the Nazis in Slovenia, celebrating Christmas was strictly forbidden. No trees, no songs, no sweets, and no Mass. Lord Jesus suffered once more on the cross due to the wickedness of men. Smoking cigarettes and drinking brandy, Marko longed to go home and talk to Valeria. Once more he would tell her that he was sorry and that he loved her. He would beg her to help him once more to stop drinking. She must know in her heart that she was the woman of his life. She must take him in her arms and forgive him. Maybe she would. It was Christmas, after all.

When he finally got back to his office, he put on his coat and rushed home. Just before leaving, he downed a last shot of brandy for the road.

As he reached their door, he could feel the liquor taking hold of his blood. He fumbled with the keys, but before he could insert the right one into the lock, Zdenka opened the door. He stared at her as though she were a ghost. The smell of brandy and cigarettes made her back off.

"Good evening, Marko. I'm in hurry as I'm meeting a friend tonight. The children are asleep. If you're hungry, there's some stew left on the stove."

Marko staggered on his feet. His eyes were blurry. "I'm not hungry, thank you. Don't even think of going to church, Zdenka. No Midnight Mass, no ... You know who you're working for."

"Of course not, I wouldn't dare," the girl lied to his face. She was meeting with friends precisely for that reason: to attend the midnight service in secret. She was not religious and did not believe in God, who had allowed the war to destroy Europe and its peoples. Yet, with her days fraught with work and worries under the employment of people who were more communist than Stalin and *Tito* together, she longed for the lights, the psalms, and the miracle of the Christmas child and His magical birth. She needed to feel alive and loved, although this love was imaginary.

In his wet boots, Marko tottered to the kitchen and sat at the table. A letter lay on the immaculate white linen, embroidered with traditional poppies and bluets of a summer wheat field. The blue envelope was addressed to Valeria Batič Robič. Who would use his wife's maiden name? His eyes spotted the stamp in the corner. He swore and tore it open.

My dear friend Valeria,

Buenos Aires, 14th July, 1949

I hope my letter finds you well. You may be wondering how I found your address. Marjana wrote to say that you have a good job and are doing well. Also that your husband is a kind father to your children. I am happy for you, my dear Valchy. You deserve all the happiness in the world.

The world at peace is full of evil, not what we had expected. People bring all kinds of news about our country, mostly that it is a communist dictatorship similar to Stalin's Russia. Sanja is lucky to be in America where she has rebuilt her musical career and is doing great. Write to me, how is life in Yugoslavia under Tito?

However, I am not writing to you to talk about politics. It has been a long time since we last saw each other. I would so much like to embrace you, hold you in my arms, and chat with you until morning. We have so much to tell each other. How did the labor go? Marjana told me you have a girl, Anna. I worried about you. You seemed so tired that day on the train station.

Oh, I can't go on like this. You know why I am writing. How is my Martin doing? Is he a brave boy? When will he start school? He's five years old now. Did you celebrate? Did he blow the candles, my little darling? All these questions without answers, these tortuous thoughts and past memories, which destroy every minute of my life here in Argentina. Not a day goes by without thoughts of you, my dearest friend, and Martin. For years I haven't slept for more than a couple of hours at night. I walk about our tiny flat thinking that while darkness is falling in the mountains behind the city, it is daytime in Ljubljana and you're taking Martin for a walk in Tivoli, or you're reading him a story and singing him a song.

In 1945, when Andrej found out about what I did, he was furious. Still, I'm convinced I saved Martin's life. In you, he found his homeland. The road to Bleiberg was tough. Somewhere near the Radovljica station, the train stopped. The partisans surrounded it., I managed to escape into the bushes with a Croatian businessman. We had to walk for a week, bypassing the partisan sentinels, hiding in the ditches, trembling for our lives. The route would have been impossible with a baby. It was a miracle we survived. I know I put you in big trouble. Please, forgive me if you can. Yet, I knew you would find a way and do the right thing. You're such a good woman and a dear friend, Valeria. I hope there will come a day when I can repay you for your kindness. I live for that day, although my force is fading.

A while ago, my world fell apart; Andrej walked out on me. He has never forgiven me for giving up our son. We tried to conceive another child, but my womb went barren after that terrible escape and this eternal night of self-reproach. Ever since we came to this new, wild land of fascinating beauty and fantastic opportunities, all we did was quarrel. I let him go. I've had enough of his reproaches. Our love was a flower that grew only on Slovenian soil.

Now, I am alone in a foreign country. I have nobody and I have to make a living. I will get by, only if I can have a piece of news from my little boy, from my Martin. I am so homesick. If I only had a piece of news about him, if I only knew...I can go on. I can continue on the road to hell that the war and the Grim Reaper have set for me.

I miss our village Kozjane. If only I can embrace a cherry tree in flower. If only I can take you in my arms, my dear Valchy. If only I can kiss my little Martin. Only once. One kiss. You must think me crazy reading these lines, but please, answer my letter if you can. My address is: Ada Strainar, Avenida San Martin 89, 1420 Buenos Aires, Argentina.
Forever yours,

Ada

Marko reread the letter a couple of times without grasping the meaning. Finally, the facts hit his intoxicated brain: Martin was not the boy he thought he was.

The click of the front door announced Valeria's arrival. "Hello, I'm home. Oh, gosh, Marko, you could have taken off your muddy boots."

With a rag under one foot, Valeria tried to wipe away the mud from the polished wooden floor. The dirty tracks ran from the entrance to the kitchen.

"Damn bitch! What have you done to me?"

Valeria stopped. She could see the rage in Marko's eyes. What had gotten into him tonight?

"Nothing, nothing," she whispered, trying to console him. She wondered if it was delirium caused by his drinking and remembered the tiny pistol she kept in her purse at all times. Because of her job, Joc insisted she remained armed.

"Borko's son...Bloody whore, you planted a Home Guard's bastard in my family!"

Valeria halted in the middle of her doing. This was serious. "What – what are you saying?"

Marko stood up and lifted his hand. He made a fist and swayed toward her. For a moment, Valeria thought he would hit her in the face. Maybe he wanted to, but changed his mind. "Damn you, Valeria, damn you!"

He turned his back on her and reached for the liquor in the kitchen cabinet. He took a gulp from the bottle. The silence after his angry shouts was deafening. Only then did the letter on the table catch Valeria's eye. Another glance and she recognized Ada's tidy handwriting. She quickly scanned the words. When she reached for it, Marko turned around and seized it before she could.

"I'm going to see your boss Joc tomorrow. I'm showing him this, you vixen!"

"Don't ... Wait!"

"What, what shall I wait for?" He banged his fists on the table so hard that the flowerpot and the ashtray almost fell to the floor. "You're a snake, Valeria, a real serpent. You hid the son of a traitor in an honest communist family. How did you get his birth certificate? Who forged it for you? A Nazi spy?"

"Marko, please, it's not what you think. Calm down, let me explain everything..."

"How long did you think you could fool me? How long? I'm such an idiot! I should have suspected something. This son of yours and Borko's came out of the blue. It's a traitor's bastard, a little shitter eating my bread and butter. I will kill him. I swear I will strangle him with my own hands." He stretched his arms to show he meant what he said.

"Daddy, what is it? Why are you so angry?"

Martin's tiny voice came from the threshold of the door. Marko took another gulp from the bottle and made a menacing step toward the child. Valeria quickly stepped between them.

"Please, Martin, go to bed! Mommy and Daddy need to talk. Please, go!"

"But I want Daddy to kiss me goodnight. Daddy?" said Martin, holding his plush teddy bear in his arms. "And he must kiss teddy Jaka good night, too."

Marko's eyes filled with tears of helplessness. How could he hurt a child? He loved him like his own. No letter could change this. He turned away from Martin and said in a shaky voice, "Mommy will kiss you both good night. Daddy doesn't feel well tonight, Martin."

Valeria understood and ushered the child out of the kitchen.

Still complaining, Martin tried to get his father. Finally, she put him back to bed and returned to the kitchen. She knew they were not done yet, she and Marko. She should have told him everything the moment it happened. Maybe then, in the whirlwind of violence, he could have understood her compassion for the child.

"Please, can I see the letter, Marko?" she begged in a whisper.

He came behind her and pushed her on the chair at the table. "No, you can't. I will read it to you aloud."

Marko started to recite the words from the letter in a pathetic voice, dragging each syllable like a rope around Valeria's neck. Halfway, Valeria stood up and put some logs on the fire in the stove. For the first time in her life, she felt powerless, ambushed. How could she get out of this mess? Marko finished and reached for the bottle.

"I'm sorry, Marko, I really am," she said in a tiny voice. "Ada left me no option. When the train started moving, she threw her child out of the window. He would have died had I not caught him. You know those were difficult times. Everyone was looking for revenge. I took pity on him. He was only a baby, not even a year old. And I was pregnant. In spite of what you think of me, I am a woman."

"You're a Home Guard whore, that's what you are. Like this friend of yours, Ada. Home Guard sluts, both of you. Valchy, my heroic little Valchy, lovely and brave, always at the service of OZNA, always ready to serve her bosses ...I wonder what Joc will think when he sees this."

Marko flushed each of his excited statements with a gulp of brandy. "You stabbed me in the back. You made me raise ...damn you, and love ...a traitor's son ..." His hoarse words echoed from the walls like the sad song of a raven. It was obvious he was losing his mind. She did hurt him. It was her fault.

Taking pity on him, Valeria tried to make peace: "Marko, listen. Joc doesn't have to see this. We can burn the letter in the stove and forget about it. Martin is our son and we will teach him to be a good communist. He doesn't even remember his parents any more. No one will ever know ...Marko, together we – "

"Lies! Lies! More lies!" Marko burst out with rage, upsetting the table. A pot of evergreen thistle, water, ashtray, butts, linen, Valeria's purse, and the letter toppled to the floor. She managed to make a quick step aside to avoid the falling objects. "Is that what you want, traitor's cunt? Are you spying for the Fascists? Is it for the dirty Italians? No, no, no ...You will never sing the *Giovinezza* again, never! Do you hear me? Do you hear me, you bloody Fascist bitch!"

Valeria stood back and, from the corner of her eye, could see the letter slip onto the kitchen floor. She reached for her purse. She'd had enough. There was no point quarreling with a drunk. Still, she wanted to shut Marko up.

"Marko Robič, you have no right to insult me! We'll talk in the morning when you're sober. You will understand that I've done the right thing. You – "

"I know you're a spy!" Marko completely lost all reason. From the depth of his soul, alcohol and resentment roused the worst fears of his mind. Evil mud infused the bile with all the horrors he wanted to drown in booze. He couldn't let it go. "You're working for the Fascists and the Home Guard. You probably volunteered for the job at the ARS so you can establish contact with the traitors. That's why this woman has your address, too. Whore, traitor, cunt!"

Valeria's sharp intelligence focused on the crucial thing: getting rid of the letter. She snatched it off the floor, swiftly opened the lid of the stove, and fed the paper to the fire. In seconds, the tiny sheet disappeared with a hiss among the orange flames. It was gone. Valeria realized she would never be able to reply to Ada, never tell her that her baby was growing into a healthy boy. The grip on her shoulder brought her back to her other problem: Marko. Gathering all her strength, she pushed him away. He fell over the legs of the overturned table in the middle of the kitchen and lay motionless for a while. Then his voice reached her ears:

"You won't get away with this, Valeria. I'm going to report you. You may have burnt the letter, but other people have seen it. The postman and Zdenka ...the envelope is still in my pocket. You won't get away!"

Valeria took the pistol out of her purse. She came close and pressed the muzzle against his temple. "I'm done with your babbling. Give me the envelope or I'll shoot you!"

"Oh, go ahead and shoot me! Shoot me in the back, too, you coward! Some hero you are, shooting your own brothers in the back! I know how you got your decorations, Ivan said ..."

Valeria's coldness turned her heart to stone. She held her breath and her index finger on the trigger. "I've never shot anybody in the back. Ivan is a goddamn liar. I won't shoot you in the back either.

You're not worth the bullet, you drunken loser. Just so you know, I've seen your dossier. I know what you did at Kočevski Rog. I know about your bloody job there. You and Ivan, and the likes of you shitty bastards, you were shooting thousands in the back. Killing people after they'd laid down their arms, men who couldn't fight back. You slaughtered them like sheep. You are cowards – YOU, not me! Now give me the envelope!"

Marko stared at her as though she were a ghost. "You...Valchy, you've seen the records...You mean there are records of Kočevski Rog?"

"What do you think my job's about, you idiot? I work for *OZNA*. The envelope – now!" Valeria pressed the gun's muzzle harder against his temple.

With shaky hands, Marko took the envelope out of his pocket. Valeria grabbed it and stepped aside. There was no return address, only the postal stamp indicating "Buenos Aires, Argentina." She threw it in the fire, too. Carefully, she put the weapon back in its holster and returned it into her purse. Behind her, she could hear Marko retching on the kitchen floor.

"Go to hell, you filthy drunk. I don't need a man like you."

The following morning Valeria came down early for a cup of coffee. Marko had vanished like a ghost into the thin air. The kitchen was clean and everything in order, as though nothing had happened. She thought she heard some clatter and noise during the night. The doorbell rang: it was Zdenka.

"Is everything all right, Valeria?"

"Everything's perfect."

Nobody ever saw Marko again. That same morning Joc called Valeria to his office and presented her with divorce papers ready to be signed. From now on, she and her little daughter Anna were to use her maiden name, Batič. Martin's last name remained Lukman, the name of the hero. Earlier, Marko was arrested and would probably be sent under the IB's directive to *Goli otok*. The only way for Valeria to keep her job was to file for a speedy divorce and distance herself from her husband completely. No contacts ever with either Valeria or the kids. When Valeria asked Joc about the charges, he replied in a vague tone that he didn't know the details. Marko might have insulted some high-ranking party officials, or could be suspected of secretly supporting Stalin. Once again Valeria had no choice. Her pen glided over the paper and her fate was sealed. She had lost her man forever. The only bright stars in the cloudy darkness were the children.

Years later, Valeria found out what had happened to her unfortunate husband. Marko Robič was not a man without strong convictions. He had a mind of his own. Indeed, he loathed the dispute between *Tito* and Stalin, which was not about the truth of communism, but a struggle for power. Men who fought side by side did not matter. Marko had a sharp tongue. He criticized the so-called high-ranking partisan fighters who had spent most of the war heating their furnaces at home, yet were now promoting themselves and obtaining various privileges. Just before Christmas 1949, he aired his views to the wrong person, who reported him. Nobody came to Marko's aid. Nobody asked Valeria, for she was his wife. When he turned up for work on Christmas Day, agents were already waiting for him.

Her colleagues had no scruples in placing Marko's file in her hands. Thus, Valeria read the horrible details of Marko's death on his first day in *Goli otok*. As was the custom, the prisoners welcomed the newcomers in a special way: they formed two rows, which by the end of 1949 were a couple of kilometers long each, and the newcomers had to walk through them while being spat at, cursed, and beaten by the other prisoners. Should anyone refuse to hit the newcomers, he was made to walk through the rows himself. When they saw Marko Robič, the Chief of the Ljubljana Police, who had put many of them there, their anger and fury went out of control. They wreaked their vengeance on him – kicking and pummeling him with their fists, stoning and hitting him with sticks. After two hundred meters, Marko collapsed to the ground and was beaten to death. He died from the blows of people like him, accused wrongly based on groundless allegations. Maybe his guilt was documented in other directives and yellowed papers buried in OZNA's archives until fifty years later. Maybe Marko's guilt breathed the foul air of decay in the woods of Kočevski Rog, where the Slovenian revolution had bathed in the blood of the collaborators until, like every ravenous beast, it finally devoured its own children.

Valeria Batič was careful with the secrets of the Slovenian Civil War and the Communist Revolution. She managed the archives office of OZNA until she retired in the eighties. Nightmares of that terrible Christmas Eve of 1949 visited her from time to time. Yet, she learned to live with it, dedicating all her efforts to the future of her children. The loving siblings – Martin, the son of a traitor, and Anna, the daughter of a murderer.

Anna and Martin, 1991-2014

My exposed heart now waits quietly
for flower and grass seeds to sprout in it –
far too strange good powers sleep within me.

– *France Balantič*, Wreath, Sonnet VI, translated by
Tom M. Priestly

Anna

How can I go on living with all the power of eternal love in a world full of hate?

I think I will not. I cannot go on. The seven decades have been a lot. Despite Mother's tender arms and sweet kisses. And a childhood filled with playing and fun times with my brother, who even then was building a silent wall of grudges. And evenings around campfires with girlfriends, analyzing every word or gesture of boys. And that warm summer moonlight when my darling and I first made love. Then our wedding – the union of two young lovers with bright prospects for the future, a feast that joined two very different, maybe even out of sync, families. And last, my children – don't forget the children. Lively babies, funny toddlers, active boys, and cunning teenagers.

I have been a daughter, a sister, a wife, and a mother. As much I'm able to give and receive love, I can never get enough. Since I can remember, I yearned for more tenderness. I still do. Embraces, kisses, touches, more of everything, more, more, more...Memories of erotic sensations – according to Mother, illegal and sinful in the eyes of the Church – and passions that dwell in the secret corner of my mind still make me, an old woman today, shiver with lust.

At times, I encountered losses and failures, sad days when the world seemed more intent on stoning me than comforting me. Yet, love remained my Red Thread, the leitmotif of my life's symphony, the river running and jumping over the rapids of my passionate body and soul, both looking more like deserts these days.

Despair was my frequent visitor. The pain of love pain could cut my soul like a sharp razor. At a young age, I lost my husband. The world, including Martin, cried with me that day. He helped me financially and watched over the education of my sons. He was like a father to them until they grew up and became independent.

However, be life as bitter as it can be with "the slings and arrows of outrageous fortune" (Hamlet, Act III, scene 1), I've never run out of love. It surges from my soul and body like an eternal spring. When sorrow takes over and sadness suffocates you, you know there will another sunny day with light and hope. I bathe in love when my grandchildren come to visit. The twittering sparrows that used to sing their songs from bushes ready to burst in buds have long ago outgrown me My heart rejoices when my son in his fifties puts his arms around my shoulders and calls me Mommy, or when my daughter-in-law caresses my cheek saying how smooth my skin is. True or not, I melt in their love.

Therefore, I long only for one thing: to sow the seeds of love among people, to plant the fields so that one day a harvest of golden wheat would warm their hearts, the harvest of tender emotions when you love and get love in return. Well, if I cannot infect everyone with love – for some people have the greed and hatred of vermin – maybe I can at least help my brother Martin. I would like to see him change, make him open his chambers of solitude and resent. Indeed, my brother was dealt a bad set of cards as a child. It was tough for him to face facts and harder still to absolve them. I think he has never stopped blaming Mother for everything that happened. He begrudged her for not having told him the truth sooner.

I hope he will come to this roundtable session today. The talk will neither be about the partisan village of Kozjane nor about the betrayals, the burnings, or the deportations of our folks. There won't be any disclosures on the unjust treatment of the Home Guards' children in *Petriček* or new locations of WWII mass graves with the buried bones crying murder. Nothing about the scandalous revenge of the victors. Instead, the discussion will focus on national reconciliation. In my language, reconciliation means love. Love among Slovenians. Love that struggles to triumph over hatred and the evil resentments that cause us to continue dwelling in war crimes as though WWII did not end seventy years ago.

Why does the weight of this love sit on my shoulders like a heavy rock? Why do I have to carry it around? The weight grows heavier every year as my body grows older and wearier. The weight and this secret everybody shares. It has transformed our genes, and all the Slovenians are sharing it. In fact, many years ago, I took this weight from Mother's shoulders. It was a long time ago, so long ago, I can hardly remember.

Martin

What kind of symbol is this? It looks like a horizontal curly bracket advertising a tourist menu outside a café. Obviously it's not. This logo in the shape of a stylized book means I should be at the right address. For what? The *Trubar Literature House*? Will this plain door open the pantheon of Ljubljana's literature fans? Well, who cares?

I'm here now, and for once, I will honor Anna's strange request.

Despite her age, Anna still falls for every stupid hoax. I cannot help but wonder at her eagerness. Can't she understand that our lives are almost gone and the threads of our tangles almost spent? The only destination we can be excited about is the grave.

The whole issue about my mother and father has preyed on my nerves for far too long now. I don't care for the facts that have changed so many times. Facts are facts only in science. Even in science, facts are only true in the natural or so-called "hard" sciences. Only figures, mathematical proofs, and the laws of physics can endure the test of reality. The rest is mumbo jumbo. I feel sorry for all these philosophers and researchers in human sciences who think they can save the world. Mercy on all sociologists, anthropologists, psychologists, and physiologists who call their tiptoeing in the dark science.

The funniest of them all is my little sister, who thinks her librarianship can withstand the test of any science. She rarely says anything when I am around, though. Maybe, the librarianship might become a kind of real science should librarians ever discover some formula or procedure that would allow books to exert a force against dust particles and prevent them from settling on the covers. Thus, the librarians would have no more need to dust their books. For example, they could invent a special coating for book covers to be applied during the printing process. No such invention exists, of course, only mumbo jumbo. Well, my little sister is modest compared to the loudmouths who spew their prophecies before the media like little volcanoes of knowledge. We, the real scientists, would never aggrandize our work and perform on television like clowns. Nevertheless, our researches and discoveries are fundamental in making human life comfortable – food production, heating, energy, transportation. We generate the progress of society. Our basic researches form, as consequence, the essence of modern life.

Passing through a dark corridor, I run into a staircase. A sign points upward through the glass door. Judging by the buzzing from the hall, the discussion obviously hasn't started yet. As I take off my coat, a bald greenhorn with rockabilly-style glasses from the previous century smiles at me politely. Dear God, he's wearing an earring and a scarlet scarf, too.

"Please, sir, come in. We'll start in a minute."

Instead of saying anything improper, I just nod. In the hall, all the seats are taken. The sun blinds me for a moment and I stagger. Calm down now, old man, the least you need is to slip and fall down. I could break my arm or my leg, or God forbid my hip, as so many of my friends have recently. The pain in my chest reminds me of the lethal Grim Reaper, who is on his way to collect me. Yet I am not easy to get. He should know that.

When I regain my sight, I see Anna. She's waving her hand as though it were a propeller. I can see you, sis, all right. I'm coming. I make a sign with my hand to make her stop. People are watching. My sister and me. I feel uncomfortable. Is this circus necessary?

At last, I reach the chair on which my sister has placed her huge handbag. She picks it up and I shiver with fear, thinking of what this colorful woman's purse might spill on the floor. The "shit" would really hit the fan. I politely greet the person next to me and sit down. My sister is glowing with happiness, as though she were high on something.

"Hi, bro, how are you?" she says with a wide smile that flickers the whiteness of her false teeth in the bright light of the hall.

"Fine, thank you. How are you?"

She doesn't say a word. Her hand firmly squeezes mine. Hell, I can't help it. Her warmth slides through my veins and her emotions spill into my system. I breathe it in, the air mixed with the sweet-scented lime of her perfume.

"Martin, everything will be just fine. You'll see. Just fine."

What I will live to see, I'm not sure. To my dismay, I realize once more that Anna's viscous feelings never fail to overpower my healthy distrust and reason. The woman is terrible. She can make minestrone out of scientific facts. Since our childhood, Anna has always been like that. Like Mother. That's why we're here tonight. While I control my stony face, tears flow inside my brain and inundate my thoughts with salty bitterness. Nobody can see my tears and nobody should. The only person in the hall who can guess my pain without looking at my face is my little sister Anna.

Anna

Since I can remember, Mother meant the world to me. When I was a little girl, I could not see enough of her. She was always away at meetings and business trips. My love for Mother is so deep that my heart still aches today at the thought of her. When I was a little girl, they had to put me to bed at night with her sweater so that I could go to sleep with the scent of her in my nostrils, the scent of my mommy. I could sit in her lap for hours while we were visiting friends and family. Mother's arms were like soft feathers; I floated on clouds of Heaven.

As to Father, I barely remember him. I associate my memories of him with what Mother and Auntie Marjana told us about him. Places, events, anecdotes. I was only four when he disappeared forever one winter night. Many years later, in the late eighties, Mother told us how he died. She didn't know why, though. In *Tito*'s gulag, *Goli otok*, in spite of the fact he had been the chief of Ljubljana's police. Somebody had indicted him, and he was lost. Martin says he doesn't remember much of him either, although I heard they had a lot of father-and-son time in the Gulf of Trieste where they went fishing. Maybe we were both under the spell of the old photographs that we pored over with Mother. It was a ritual: tea, cookies, table lamp, and hard leather-bound folders filled with black-and-white photographs that portrayed people who were no longer alive.

We were living in a huge villa in the center of the city. Oh, I adored our house. It was so spacy and the rooms furnished with valuable antiques. Imposing oak bookcases filled with old books, some dating from the nineteenth century and earlier. There were works of Hugo, Balzac, Zola, Shakespeare, and Dickens as well as German pre-romantics in Gothic script that nobody could read. Books cast a magical spell over me. I would leaf and flip through them for hours years before I could read them. When Martin and I grew up, each one starting to lead our own lives, Mother divided the house into three spacious apartments. The ground floor was for her; in the middle, I lived with my family; and above us was Martin. His apartment was bright and had a huge terrace overlooking the Castle and the Congress Square.

Our house was a real *Villa Villekulla*, although I was too shy to be a strong brave girl like Pippi Longstocking. Martin and I would spend long hours in the park that surrounded our house. It was vast and full of secret places, castles and prairies of our imagination. A high wall insulated the property against the noise and bustle of the city. There was a wooden pavilion where we would play on rainy days. The orchard made part of the farthest patch of land. There were cherry, plum, apple, and pear trees. Next to the orchard was a vegetable garden maintained by our housekeeper. Sweet strawberries, black and red currents, and raspberries – we were two naughty little birds preying over the tasty berries, eating them before they could ripen and be picked. When our Zdenka retired in the seventies, Mother continued to cultivate the garden and found a lot of joy in working the land. After all, Mother was a farmer's daughter.

A few years after our mother died, we had to leave the house. It was returned to the original owners and their descendants as part of the denationalization process. Mother would have been very sad had she lived to see it, although she herself had said many times that we were not the proper owners of the house and were lucky to live in it. After Mother's funeral, Martin moved out. He broke away from us, burnt his bridges. Whatever. The precious antiques that I found in the attic helped ease my family's tight budget. I was able to sell them at international auctions for large sums. A librarian's salary was very low back then. Alone with two sons in a huge house with enormous maintenance costs was a nightmare. To make ends meet, I found tenants and slowly sold the antiques one piece at a time. *Rihard Jakopič*'s study for his famous painting, The Sower, centuries-old chests inlaid with mother-of-pearl, mirrors with golden frames, paintings – they all saved us from poverty.

Rajko, my dear Rajko! God knows if he could ever forgive me my foolishness and daydreaming. We met after graduating from the university, both on our first jobs. Rajko was working in the Criminal Court, I was in the international loan division of the National and University Library. We made a wonderful couple, although we were still trying to forget our first disappointments in love. Rajko's girlfriend had abandoned him while he was doing his military service. My first love had decided to work in Germany and wanted me to join him. It was out of question at the time. My family meant too much for me. My marriage with Rajko was a marriage of reason. However, we made a good team and endured hard times. Our children – our golden boys – were the source of joy that brought us together more than any passion ever could. Marko came first, then Luka. Each one named after his grandfather. I will never forget how much I loved and was in love with Rajko when our boys were born. The golden threads of parenting were holding us together forever.

During the week, Mother would look after us and the children. She worked in the garden, fetched the boys from school, cooked lunch – in short, she spoiled us. She adored Rajko, and they got along very well. Rajko's parents were distant and cool. They never got over the thought of our union. I should have been a Catholic daughter-in-law from Prekmurje, and their son should have been at the Court of Justice in Murska Sobota. They also never forgave me for not saying our vows in church.

Years went by. We were all working, studying, growing. Mother was so proud of us all. Martin was the first to complete his doctorate as the youngest in the institute. Mother attended his graduation and shed tears of happiness. She bought him an expensive golden watch with the long, incomprehensible title of his thesis engraved on the back. Soon after, it was my turn: International Coordination of Bibliographical Data. Mother's present was a wonderful set of crystal glasses that once belonged to no less than the Krupp family. It included a lovely decanter and twenty-four pieces each for different kinds of liquor: white wine, red wine, champagne, cognac, and schnapps. They were so beautiful we scarcely ever used them.

The whole mumbo jumbo over doctorate celebrations left me unmoved. There were no emotions in our work and achievements, only laborious study. No passion, no feelings, no sensations. Nothing for me. My home revolved around rationality and timetables. I longed for more. Handsome Henk from the National Dutch Library in Amsterdam found every opportunity to see and comfort my soul and body. It was the first of my several passionate love affairs. I needed love more than peace.

Then came the moment when Rajko told us that the doctors found out he was seriously ill. And the day when I crawled to my mother like a battered stray dog. I had to tell her the facts, although I could already foresee her reaction.

Martin

They have started the discussion. Against all my expectations, what they're saying is logical. I can see their point. For once, these men are not recounting old stories and echoed myths of the split forces of the Slovenian nation since WWII. As though one war could be the source of all evil and its axis, spreading horrors in all directions like a centrifugal force. They are denying this perspective in search of their case to defend the reconciliation elsewhere. I agree. As a man and as a physicist. The Slovenians really don't prosper by bringing up all the possible reasons for their divisions and quarrel. The demagogues of communism, of liberalism, and of Catholicism and the conservative side tend to use a language full of particular malice. The gravitation toward Evil. While ordinary folks remain trapped and powerless in their words. Stupid fish caught in the fishing nets. What about me? Am I free of the partisans versus Home Guard rhetoric? Yes, indeed, I am. The man with two family names – one of a partisan, the other of a Home Guard.

If I only had a family of my own. But I'm alone with all the riches and the fabulous names in the world. A dead branch on the tree of life. After Iris, there was not one woman in the world I could love. A few dates, and I got weary with each one. I couldn't stand that glimmer of hope in a woman's eye, hinting that I was the one, the hope of a future together when she would do anything for me: cook, wash, clean, submit to my whims, anything just to be with me. Good gracious, no! If I really wanted to have some creature submit to my whims, I would buy a dog. A wife and a life companion should be so much more. Iris knew how to be both.

Oh, my dear lovely Iris. We understood each other since the moment we met. There were no ambiguities or open issues between us. We knew to respect accuracy and discipline. She was a musician, while I followed the path of natural science. A force is a force and a key is a key. No deviations, maybe only variations. These clear and transparent systems support the most precious achievements of Mankind, the supreme goal of everything that defines a human being – Reason.

We met at grammar school where from being classmates we became best friends, and from best friends we grew into lovers. Iris came from a very respectable middle-class family who happened to be on the right side during WWII. That was what Mother claimed, and she surely had known those things. Iris was a charming girl in her own unspectacular way. Her brown hair was smooth and her eyes deep blue like a peaceful bay of the ocean. We were different from other lovers of our generation. We did not waste time counting the stars above or watching grass grow while sitting on the banks in the parks. There was no time. For long hours, Iris had to practice her violin each day, while I had to study technical books. However, the short time we managed to spend together was magic. We made love and adored each other without the use of big words and pathetic vows. We planned to spend our life together.

We both graduated with flying colors and enrolled in the University of Ljubljana – Iris chose the Academy of Music, while I chose the Faculty for Mathematics and Physics. The summer of 1963 was very hot. Iris went to Macedonia where she was to perform with her orchestra. I was bored, tired of waiting for her. The plan was to go to the seaside where we could spend time alone in our summer house in Ankaran. I was looking forward to swimming, boating, walking by the sea in the moonlight, and candlelight dinners with classical music in the background. This trivial music festival was Iris's last duty before she was free for the summer. The Ohrid Summer Festival of July 1963. Why did she have to go to Macedonia for that bloody performance after which many musicians and instruments remained silent forever? When the festival was over, the orchestra spent the last evening in *Skopje*. Iris rang me from her hotel. She was thrilled with the beautiful landscape around Lake Ohrid. The public awarded their play with wonderful ovations, and the whole atmosphere was magic. We spoke for some time. She said she missed me and could hardly wait to see me. I should get everything ready so we could go on holiday the same day she returned.

"I love you, Martin," she said in the end.

"I love you, too, Iris," I said.

Those were the last words we exchanged.

The following morning the train should have left *Skopje* at six o'clock. Two days later, I should have been holding my love in my arms. Yet, two hours before departure, on July 26th, 1963 at 4:17 in the morning, the countryside around *Skopje* shook terribly. The earthquake took thousand lives. My Iris, my love perished in the ruins of the city, and her violin was silenced forever. Although international organizations sent rescue troops to free victims from the deadly concrete rubble, Iris's body was never found. In the earth's tremor, she vibrated her last song. Her parents, devastated, organized a funeral with an empty coffin with white silk inside. Ever since then, my heart and soul were like that coffin – white and empty. My first and only love crumbled in the ruins of *Skopje* and turned to dust. Iris was to play her beloved *Kreutzer Sonata* to the crickets forever.

I was young, not yet twenty, but my luck with women was sealed: there was not to be another. I dedicated myself to my studies and my scientific career. Well, now and then, I had an affair with this or that lovely woman, and those nights were long and full of passion. However, nobody came close to being my life companion. My family was my sister and her boys. Anna was bursting with pure and toxic estrogen, so her woman's aura was more than enough for the life of me.

On the other hand, my sister Anna hasn't learned a thing about life. She is still at everybody's disposal for anything. What used to be her lovers – though she thinks I don't know about them – are now sons, grandsons, volunteers, friends, and even stray cats. When her eldest son decided to get a divorce, she sold her nice apartment and moved into some dark cell in order to help him start anew. Crazy woman. I was so mad at her. She could have come to live with me in my 200-square-meter house with five rooms. She could have gone to Kozjane and enjoyed the sunshine of *Brkini* or to Ankaran. Half of the house is hers anyway. No. Obstinate in her flood of love, she gave more than she had to Marko. Anna is as pig-headed as Mother. The only difference between them was their philosophy of life: Mother was a stern realist; Anna is a loving idealist.

My dear sister Anna has always been a victim of her emotions. Yet, in my will, I have named as the beneficiary of everything I own. Which is a lot. The heritage of the Strainar family, the Skarpin family, and my savings from all the years I worked in the field of science. Anna Banana, the girl of many without a penny, has no idea she will be a millionaire when I kick the bucket.

We'll see how my chest surgery goes. Lung cancer means more or less death. We saw what happened to Rajko decades ago. In spite of more advanced treatments now, only 8.4% of men of my age survive the next five years after diagnosis. Thus, the probability that I will die this year is high.

Say what you may, I am at peace with myself. My time has come. I can close my eyes forever and find eternal rest.

Should I live and survive, well, then I will. Maybe this diagnosis based on the roentgenogram is not true. It may only be one of the many horrible coincidences that have been steering my life since the moment I was conceived and born. Long, long ago I was destined to be Fortune's toy.

Coincidence, the roll of the dice. That's what the whole world is about. In the words of good old Einstein: "Coincidence is God's way of remaining anonymous."

Anna

My husband Rajko didn't suspect anything about my love life or maybe he just pretended not to. After my doctorate, I started to work as the City Library director. Travels to distant seminars and trainings were part of my job. Slovenians were no good as lovers. They were cold and average. Besides, the major drawback was that they were too close to my home. Who wants to sully his own backyard? Still, my major concern and focus remained my husband and my family. A warm home, a satisfied husband, and two happy sons always came before my torrid nighttime trysts. But the thrill of exploring a new body, the pleasure of an erotic adventure, and thirst for more passion often found me in other men's embraces.

Where did I meet all these willing and lustful heroes of the night? They were everywhere and they chased after me all the time. I inherited the best from my parents and turned out a beauty. The wavy chestnut hair of Mother and the striking blue eyes of Father. After both births, my breasts and hips stayed roundly shaped without being fat. I've always enjoyed teasing men and loved to have fun. Well, be they young or old, educated or dumb, tall or small – all men were crazy about me. Particularly when we had taken our clothes off. Sometimes, one would fall in love with me, really in love, and could not face the fact he was a one-night stand and nothing more. My family was sacred. My secretary soon learned how to get rid of fervent pursuers. On the phone, she simply never put them through. Being from afar, they could not travel easily to see me. Eventually, they cooled down. Men are tomcats. Once the mating season is over, their ardor abates, and their love yowls calm down. Yet, at times, things, my affairs got complicated. As a friend of mine would say: "Life is not Disneyland."

Early one spring the doctors found out that Rajko, my husband in the prime of his life, had lung cancer. He had to stop smoking immediately. It was something unheard of. Rajko was doing sports, playing tennis, mountaineering, skiing, and biking. As to smoking, in those days, everyone – from teenagers to old men – smoked. I only quit during my two pregnancies and while my boys were little. Today I still enjoy a cigarette with my coffee. At first, nobody took the diagnosis seriously, least of all Rajko. He grumbled about doctors trying to scare people with their overreaching alarms. That was their job. They earn their living by terrifying people. It was what they did.

"Of course, I cough when I catch a cold. It just so happens that I catch it more often lately, that's all," he would tell our friends, waving his arms in excitement.

Surgery was out of the question, and Rajko grimly rejected chemotherapy. He said he would get better after some rest and took a sick holiday. We all hoped he was right, but his health deteriorated dramatically. He lost his appetite and was losing weight. His afternoon naps often stretched into a whole night's sleep. Thus, he couldn't return to work. The Court managed without him and found a temporary replacement. Rajko would wander around our apartment aimlessly for days in a row. I tried to persuade him to go to Ankaran. The salty breeze of the sea would certainly improve his condition. Maybe he could plant a vegetable garden, for early greens thrived in the mild Mediterranean climate. He could take the boat and go fishing or simply lie on the veranda and enjoy the sweet scents of spring. He was not in the mood, so we spent all those sunny days in March indoors in our flat in Ljubljana.

Mother finally put her foot down. They went to Ankaran together. During the week, she would look after him, cook him his favorite foods, bring books from the library, and watch TV with him. On weekends, she went back to Ljubljana and I came with our boys. Sometimes Martin joined us, too, and took Rajko on short sailing trips. His health seemed to improved, for he was all smiles and laughter. Usually he would grill fresh fish, cook vegetables, and pour wine when we came. Indeed, he planted a patch of tomatoes and other Mediterranean vegetables. Every week, he looked forward to the news and gossip of our friends from Ljubljana. Of course, I could not imagine how difficult all this was for Rajko. He would gather his strength during the week so that he could show a merry face during the weekends. Mother, however, warned me that his condition was not what it seemed and that he should be seeing a doctor. I did not believe her. Mother was always exaggerated when it came to our health. Rajko was bursting with happiness. We loved each other and made love every night in spite of the whistling sound from his lungs and my fear that he would die in my arms after sex.

When the heat of June announced a warm summer, Rajko's health got worse. One evening he suddenly turned blue, unable to breathe, and we had to call for an ambulance. They admitted him to the hospital in Izola. When they installed an oxygen tent over his face, I anticipated the worse. I couldn't fool myself any longer. My Rajko was dying.

That summer I sent the boys to the scout camp on Bohinj Lake. It was a long, hot summer with my family scattered around Slovenia. I was alone. Only Martin came to see me for an occasional drink. His brotherly love was touching although he masked it behind a set of reasonable explanations detailing what he had to discuss with me and why. He is my rock and anchor. I can always rely on him.

However, Martin, too, went away to go sailing around the Dalmatian islands for two weeks. It was his pilgrimage every year. That year he took the boys with him to keep their minds off their dying father. They moved Rajko to Ljubljana, his condition practically unchanged and bad. I visited him every day at the hospital. Afterward I returned to our Villa Villecula, sad and in despair. The worm of loneliness bored a hole in my brain. I often drank a glass of wine too many in the evenings. In my nightmares, I negotiated with God and Satan for Rajko's life, and many mornings I woke up in tears.

At the library, I cleaned my desk and finished the work I had put on hold for months. A new project to increase our readership filled my days until a colleague of mine from Split came to visit. I knew him from our work on the interlibrary loans within the Yugoslavian library system. He was leading the working group and wanted to find out what each member expects from the system. My yearning was easy to read. Dalibor was a dark handsome hulk with desire and tenderness in his big brown eyes. We met for many weeks at his rented apartment in the old town of Ljubljana.

What a metamorphosis. A tedious, gloomy summer showed its bright colors and merry tunes at last. I could breathe again. When the leaves on the trees started to change into the yellow, orange, and red glow of the season's last rays and the first autumn rains poured from the sky, Dalibor was still in Ljubljana. Like a schizophrenic, I lived in two worlds. On one side, I was visiting Rajko every day, sharing with him my high spirits and jokes, caring for my family and my boys, and living the masquerade as a good wife facing the bitter fate of her husband. On the other side, I slipped away into the strong arms of a lover who was always ready to give me what I needed.

With the boys, we arranged their visits at the hospital in a way that only one came at a time; Rajko tired easily and his attention span was short. Marko had started his second year at grammar school, so his first duty after school was his father. He would talk about his classes, subjects, teachers and tell him funny stories about his classmates. After Marko, I came and Rajko would tell me proudly that our eldest was a great student. Before Mother and Luka came, Rajko needed to rest. They arrived during the last visiting hours. Mother was still trying to persuade Rajko to start chemotherapy and give the doctors and himself a chance. It was no good waiting for the end like this. Rajko would smile and reply that with so much love and attention, the malignant cells of the evil tumor would evaporate and he would continue his life as though nothing had happened. Yet, the cancer pursued its murderous agenda without mercy.

One morning something I'd suspected came true. As always when I was distressed, I turned to Mother. I had to confess all my sins. Shocked and furious, she called me a slut and a bad wife for betraying my husband in the worst days of his life. She shouted at me angrily as she never had before. What was I to do? Love was like a drug, and I was a junkie. Addicted to feelings, to human touch, to kisses and sex. I suspected I inherited it from her, but Mother was roaring like a beast at me.

In the end, I bowed my head and whispered the real reason for my visit and confession: "Mother, please, let it be. What's done is done. I'm pregnant."

She slapped me hard. Without a warning, without a thought. The mark of her palm burned my cheek.

"Mother! You're out of your mind!" I jerked back from her.

I had expected her help and understanding, not a slap, not at the age of forty. What was Mother thinking? Was she acting like a partisan in the woods with a rifle on her shoulder? My brain could not digest what had happened. I stared at her, whom I loved more than anybody in the world. Then I grabbed my purse and my car keys. When I reached the door, her voice, now kinder and seeking reconciliation reached me:

"Please, Anna, Annie, forgive me. I'm sorry. Come back. We'll talk and find a solution. Please, I didn't mean to …"

With tears in my eyes, I closed the door and returned to the sofa in front of the fireplace where Mother used to cradle and cuddle me for hours. Once again I was her little girl, unable to face the realities of life.

Martin

Since my first memories, I have always loved the sea. Wherever you look, there are only deep waters and an endless blue skyline around. The gray mist of the morning still hanging over the azure mirror of water. The only connection between the sea and the sky my elegant yacht *Iris*, white and swift like a swallow. I can well remember that sailing weekend with my two nephews.

We came aboard at the stern. The weather report was promising. A moderate but steady north-west wind that would fill our sails so that the engine could stop rumbling. Only the song of *Poseidon* would hiss around the mast and fill our lungs with faith and joy. My nephews were jumping around the deck like two little goats. Marko was almost sixteen, Luka was fourteen. They were good little fellows, doing well at school and helping at home. The sailing trip to Grado would present an occasion to teach them something about the forces and the physics of winds and sails. And also to explain the weather. Two days for the three of us, three real men alone.

First, the sailors, particularly those at that age, needed to eat. I opened the cooler that Mother filled to the brim for fear that her grandsons would suffer famine. There were delicacies of all kinds, nothing but the best. In spite of my vigorous complaints, she had added another sack of fresh fruits and vegetables. She didn't want to understand that men didn't eat vegetables, and that sailors in the past times did not get scurvy in two days. Vitamins are important, so here we were, with supplies for a cruiser.

"Come on, boys. Sailor's breakfast," I called from the saloon inside the hull.

They dug into the cooler and stuffed their mouths with pâté, salami, cheese, and fresh white bread. No forks, no napkins, no plates. Only a hunting knife – the universal tool for everything at sea. Under the food, we put a kitchen cloth; the crumbles would feed the fish after we finished.

"Where are we going today, Uncle Martin?" Marko managed to ask between the two bites.

I poured some black coffee from the thermos and took out a bundle of naval maps from the casing. Carefully and away from the fatty pâté and salami, I unfolded the one we were going to need for navigation.

"Our course is past Ankaran bypassing the Gulf of Trieste and heading for the border checkpoint at Trieste. There we'll register with the Italian Port Authorities. Have you got your passports with you?"

"Yeah," they replied in unison.

"All right. If we find a spot sheltered from the wind, we'll throw the anchor in front of the *Isonzo* river delta where the water is very clear. *Nona* has made some fried chicken for lunch. Then we'll slowly glide to Grado and tie the *Iris* in the old port where I will take you to dinner."

"Oh, that's the prize for having good grades at school, isn't it?" asked Luka.

Luka was eager to discuss school as he had finished his year with top grades in all subjects. Marko, who had passed his first year in grammar school, did not do as well. The change from elementary school to prep school and the illness of Father threw him out of kilter, so his results were mediocre. He didn't comment on his brother's bragging and fiddled with some ropes.

"Certainly not. We're going to celebrate our holiday. Your grades at school are your own responsibility. Your grades will influence your life, not mine," I said grumpily.

Marko nodded in appreciation. Luka nodded, too, as more interesting activities had taken over his attention already. School and its concerns were in Ljubljana, now they only had to breathe the salty air of the Mediterranean morning, which was filled with the shrieks of many birds, seagulls being the loudest among them. They circled above our boat, waiting for scraps from our table. Maybe if they had cried a bit louder, one of us would have taken pity and started to feed them. Some were already swimming around the stern, casting their little black eyes everywhere so as not to miss a morsel. Indeed, Luka tore off a piece of bread.

"Don't even think about it, Luka," I said sternly. "We're certainly not feeding the seagulls with white bread. They should catch fish if they're hungry."

Luka swallowed the bread, while Marko put away our leftovers in the cooler. I never installed a refrigerator on the boat, only a tiny gas cooker to warm up an instant soup or cook some eggs. When I sailed around Dalmatia, I liked to stop at local inns, talk with the locals, and eat and drink what they had. I had some very interesting discussions with them that stretched long into the warm night. Sea is not only wind and water. Sea is also the people who live along its shores. They usually have a hard time making a living.

"Uncle Martin, will we turn on the engine now?"

"Soon, my boy, soon. We're waiting for the north-west to pick up. I guess around noon. It'll fill our sails finely. Then maybe we'll be able to deploy the spinnaker."

The Port Authority's weather forecast that I had studied in Izola was quite accurate, though weather fronts could change very quickly in June. When I finally turned on the engine, it gave a sharp whistle and started to rattle regularly. Warming up was good for the system.

"Come on, boys, order on the boat! Clean up!"

They jumped at my command without hesitation. They knew I was very strict on the boat. As skipper and captain, I was responsible for them and they had to obey me. They never complained about anything as they often did with Anna or Mother. The women did nothing but spoil the boys. Yet, all they needed was to know the limits, to come up against a brick wall, so to speak. They needed order and structure in their lives, not kisses and hugs. Rajko understood that and kept them on a short leash. However, with his strength dwindling, he could not control them anymore. When Marko and Luka started fighting lately, all he did was watch helplessly with tears in his eyes. I wondered how long he had left. These days, he was in and out of the hospital.

"Untie the ropes!"

Marko hurried to the bow to throw the mooring rope into the sea, while Luka jumped to shore to loosen the stern ropes. Slowly, we glided away from the pier and into the blue waters of the lagoon. It was like all those times when I leave the shore: a fluttering feeling tickled in my belly, the feeling of freedom and vast horizons ahead. I liked to think that the Little Mermaid was kissing my cheeks and seducing me to sail.

In less than a mile from the shore, the north-west began to wheeze around our ears. I lifted my hand to signal that soon we would switch off the engine, but not before the mainsail fully caught the wind. The boys understood and worked laboriously with pulleys and ropes. When all was ready, I turned the key. Silence. Only the sound of ropes and sails playing their wheezy song with the breeze. Fully deployed, the mainsail filled with wind, white and elegant like a giant seagull. I steered the yacht into the right angle to optimize our course.

"Yeah, *Poseidon*'s rock'n'roll, Uncle Martin!" cried Luka excitedly. They joined me at the stern and brought me a cold beer. Another of our little sailing rituals.

"Well, boys, you can share a can, too," said I seriously. I was, after all, among real men.

Marko smiled and rushed to get one from the cooler before I changed my mind.

I started the day's lesson. "Tell me, which forces act upon the boat? Physics, my boys, everything is physics, come on."

"Buoyancy," said Marko.

"Yes, and what else?" I insisted.

"The force of the wind against the sail," added Luka.

"Yes, the force of motion. Which unit do we use?"

"A newton," replied Marko. "And there's another force – the force of gravity, otherwise the keel wouldn't be able to hold our course," he added, enthusiastic about remembering it.

I smiled and explained some extra details. They listened as though I were reading them a story. Good. The knowledge should sink in and stay in their brain for later when they start their engineering studies. Then we listened to the silence and the wind. Without a word, we handled the turns. The north-west had reared up some waves that the *Iris* rode elegantly and easily. We enjoyed the concert of splashes around the bow, the string sounds of the ropes and the distant cries of seagulls.

"Uncle, look, dolphins!"

Although the wind carried us smoothly, I switched on the engine. Curiosity is a dolphin's middle name. I wanted the boys to enjoy their trip as much as they could. There were some hard times ahead of them. Anna would not be able to bring them up on her own. Sometimes I thought my sister was still a baby, a spoilt little brat like all younger sisters were. How would she cope without Rajko? The boys could lose more than a father, they could lose their future.

My father had disappeared from my life when I was just half their age, yet I cannot forget the pain in my heart when I realized after a couple of weeks that I had lost him forever. I would never see him again, never. At first, Mother told us all kinds of lies about where he was, then she said he was on a military mission and would return in time. But he never did. Anna and I often inquired about him, but Mother would get annoyed and furious as though we were asking her for something forbidden. We only wanted to know when our father would come back. Never. Recently, Mother told us where and how our father had perished. *Goli otok*. We were shocked, Anna and I. On one of my sailing trips, I tried to approach the barren rock islet with my boat. It was so close to the island of Rab, invaded by tourists each summer. I steered into the passage with the intention of checking out how the prisoners lived there in *Tito*'s ungodly gulag. Before I could adjust my binoculars, a police motorboat accosted me, and the guards wanted to know whether I was spying. They were rude and aggressive, showing off their revolvers and rifles, threatening me with a fine. Patiently, I concocted some excuse and turned the boat toward the mainland. They let me go in the end. All I could glimpse were gray shapes of rocks and machine gun stations turned toward the sea to monitor every fish swimming in it. It was horrible. Marko and Luka, on the other hand, would see what would happen to their father. They would watch him die and attend his funeral. They would know and understand. Yet, would that make it any easier for them?

"Look, Uncle Martin, there's a school, a whole school is swimming around us!" shrieked my little sailors.

The dolphins performed a show when they reached the boat. Their light gray bodies, blocks of muscles springing into the air, raised high jets of water that splashed the bow. Their black eyes were inquisitively scanning us, winking and sending messages of companionship. The vast sea was a playground for fish and men. They whistled their messages as they swam – at times ahead of the boat, at times behind us. After a few nautical miles, they must have satisfied their curiosity for they vanished into the deep waters as swiftly as they had appeared. I switched off the engine, and we were alone again with the wind and the sea.

The day went on as planned. The Italian officers at the Port of Treviso were telling me jokes as though we were old friends. In the evening glow, we sailed into the lovely old port of Grado. I ordered rest for my sailor boys and stepped ashore. I called my sister to let her know we had anchored and were safe. She picked up after the first ring.

"Are you all right?" she asked in a shrill voice when I said my name.

I tried to calm her down. "All is fine, Anna Banana. We're about to dine with the gods."

Suddenly, I heard her burst into tears. She was sobbing and could not talk, gasping for air between confused words. In the background, the line crackled with funny noises. The frustration was more than I could handle. But instead of telling her to stop crying and pull herself together, I waited, already dreading the news.

"Martin, they took him away, to the hospital. He was hardly breathing. It's over, Martin, all is over. The end," she finally managed to say.

"Is he alive?" I said, trying to discern a solid piece of information from the mess of her words.

"Yes, Rajko's alive. But they say he has to stay in the hospital until the end. Do you understand? Until the end!" she wailed into the receiver.

Through the crackling and echoes, I shared her pain. I could feel her angst, but had no words of comfort. In the face of death, I've been a coward like everybody else. Men, women, old and young people. Terrified by the thought of the void.

"Annie, dear, please, do calm down. There isn't anything you can do. I won't tell the boys yet. Let them have another day without a worry. We'll be home late tomorrow as planned. Are you okay with that?"

There was silence on the other end of the line. For a moment, I was afraid she had put down the phone. Then, she said solemnly, "Thank you, Martin. You're a wonderful brother and a good uncle. Enjoy tomorrow and have a calm sea, my sailors."

Words that were not mine escaped my mouth: "Anna, I love you, I love all of you. You are my family, you know. I'll take care of your boys, I will – not only tomorrow on board the *Iris*, but also later."

She whispered a thank you and put down the receiver. I sighed with emotion, and a treacherous tear blurred my vision. From now on, the education and personal growth of my nephews would also be my responsibility. Prep school, university, career. I would have to keep watch, make sure that their course in life is on track and the sea calm.

Anna

Even if Mother hadn't slapped me, I knew I had gone too far. How could I have lost my head like this? With Rajko at the hospital, I had stopped taking the pill for it seemed unnecessary to keep dosing myself with hormones. After a couple of nights with Dalibor, I restarted taking them, though obviously too late. My periods have always been irregular, so I thought nothing of it at first. The pregnancy test was the only way I could be sure. Positive. My first thought was to talk with Mother.

"When was the last time you and Rajko slept together?"

"In June."

Mama gave me a look of disgust and shook her head angrily. "Anna, you have no choice. You must get rid of the child at once."

Her words slowly sank in.

"What if..." I trailed off, unsure of how to continue.

Mother guessed my thoughts. "You cannot risk it. Rajko may live long enough to see you lover's child grow in you. Think of how it would hit him. Poor man. Think of your sons, Anna! What would they think of you? Slut, that's what they'd say. Slut!"

My eyes filled with tears. "But Mommy, you know it's not true. I love Rajko. He's my husband and the father of my boys."

Mother collapsed onto a sofa. She looked old and tired. "Maybe you should think of your love for him and your family before yourself. You're spoilt. You have no control over your impulses. I know about your secret affairs with men. It's been going on for years. This Dalmatian was not the first to get between your legs."

The bitter taste of resentment rose in me. Her sermon was too much.

"It's not like I'm the only one, Mother. That's life. Carpe diem. We must live for today, not tomorrow. Only you partisans used to fight and live for tomorrow. We're now living in your tomorrow. Are we to be blamed?"

Mother flushed with anger; I shrank back, expecting another slap in the face. She raised her voice. "Yesterday, today, tomorrow, my God, folly and insolence! Call your doctor now and get an abortion! Otherwise, otherwise...I'll disown you! I will, indeed. You will not give birth to this misbegotten child."

My head dropped and my courage failed me. Indeed, there was too much at stake. Rajko, my sons, my family, my job and position. The City Library director who got pregnant by her colleague while her husband was dying of cancer. I didn't care about Mother's inheritance or money, the rest was much worse. Unable to hold back my tears any longer, I cried like an abandoned infant. A childish woman who was about to abort her own child.

Mother moved closer and took my hand in hers. "Darling," she said, her voice trembling with emotion, "you know you cannot have it. We're lucky that abortion is legal in Yugoslavia. You need not justify anything to anybody, and it will be over in a couple of hours. Besides, Rajko's condition is a good enough reason."

She paused for a moment. "I know what you're thinking. Your Dalmatian lover won't ever know about it. It's good he won't. You must not tell him any of this."

"Mommy," I wailed, thinking of the little human being inside me that I was about to kill, "I feel like a murderess already."

"Sometimes we don't have a choice. We must proceed with the realities of our lives. But, Anna dear, this is not a murder. Believe me, I know what a murder is. I'm an expert, so to speak. When I was a partisan, killing was my business. Shooting at a target. I rarely missed the enemy. In the eyes of the law, a fetus – until it's twelve weeks old – is not yet a human being. When was your last period?"

Sobbing swallowed my words, so I could not reply. Slowly, the strain of the whole year culminated to a suffocating pain in my chest. Mother was the one who put the pieces together and arranged my first and only murder. Of course, it was legal. Yet, I torment myself to this very day with the images of a little baby that was denied its right to live. Tears blinded my vision while Mother rang up her gynecologist and made an appointment for the following day. Without a will of my own, I let myself be taken to the brightly lit theatre where thousands of aborted children met their end in a dish. There was no other way. The fruit of love had become the victim of love.

Not much later, on a rainy day in October, we laid Rajko to rest. The pregnancy was over by then. I was crying for my husband, for my baby, and for me. Certainly, I didn't let my conscience be my guide. I felt so sorry. Sorry for all, sorry to be alive. I wanted to lie down in the coffin with my husband and die with him.

Martin

The year Mother's heart started losing strength will forever plague my memories. The doctors had been advising her for some time to undergo a heart valve replacement surgery or face the fact that her heart would completely stop one day. Yet, Mother had always known better and had a strong will of her own.

"Well, I will live until I die," she calmly repeated. "I cannot let them mess with my heart where I keep everybody and everything sacred to me."

She would add one or two things about bad doctors and the conversation would be over. She condemned herself to death in spite of all the progress in medicine. Nobody could help her against herself. One thing I must admit: Mother was not a coward.

In 1991, a change of seasons brought about a change of state. Slovenia was reborn. Like a bride clad in white, the country faced the international community to be admitted and welcomed among independent and democratic states. The desire for transformation was in the air ever since 1988, spurred on by the "Trial Against the Four" – more popularly known as the *JBTZ* affair – when the public rebelled against the *Yugoslav People's Army*, which imprisoned three civilians and one military officer for betraying military secrets. Spring was in the air, Slovenian spring. The communists were eager to change their colors and act as democrats. They were promising the voters to lead them into the bright future without the annoying hegemony of Belgrade. After the first free elections, the first Slovenian democratic government was elected. Yet in 1991, Slovenia was still a republic of Yugoslavia.

I volunteered at the local headquarters of the *Slovenian Territorial Defense*, which was not part of the *Yugoslav People's Army* and existed only to protect civilians against eventual foreign occupation or natural disasters. We could see that these local troops were in fact becoming the Slovenian Army. My duties were to prepare for anti-aircraft warfare and to maintain the artillery and surveillance systems involving airspace control in Slovenia. In my youth, I spent a year and a half of compulsory military service in the Yugoslav army, where they had trained me well. Only now, it was different. I was protecting my own country. As Slovenia's D-Day approached, I spent most of my days in uniform at the headquarters, changing only when I went to visit Mother at the hospital. Anna had persuaded me not to tell Mother how serious the movement for Slovenia's independence was. She was right that time, I must confess.

The fact that *AVNOJ*'s Yugoslavia, the federation of nationalities living in brotherhood and unity, was falling apart was something unthinkable to Mother. She did not and could not face the reality.

Of course, she followed every bit of news. She knew about the new political parties, then called "associations," and she went to vote in the December 1990 *independence referendum*. Still, her views were the views of her political party – the Communists – and her generation of WWII partisan fighters. Back in 1988, she even wondered why the crowds in front of the military court during the *JBTZ* affair were protesting.

"Have they lost their mind? Don't they understand that Borštner as a military man is a traitor and the other three are his accomplices? Had *Tito* still been our leader, those people wouldn't even be alive now. And those crowds of protestors would get some good beating to clear their stupid heads, too. What do they want, the fools? The nations of the Southern Slavs have never lived in such prosperity and comfort in history. Yugoslavia unites and feeds them. There's no better social order than communism. Don't you agree, Martin?"

Although I had other ideas regarding democratization and freedom, I nodded politely. In truth, I was impatiently waiting for Slovenia to become an independent state. I didn't tell Mother about my role in the process of splitting from Yugoslavia. I knew it would hurt her.

I have always loved my mother. Still today, my eyes fill with tears at the memory of her. She was a partisan, a young girl of seventeen, who according to legend disarmed a troop of drunken Italians. She was a hero, a sniper, the first to fight the Fascists and the Nazis. She received several medals among which the prestigious laurel of the National Freedom Fighters for her courage. A Slovenian poet wrote a poem in her honor. *OZNA*'s archives were in a flawless state under her administration. However, deep down Mother was a woman, a tender and kind woman. She had that feminine mercy that our poet *Alojz Gradnik* expressed in his verse: "like mother's milk, you give, give, and give." Had my mother lived in the times of the first Christians, she would have become a saint. As she lived in the times of the Nazis, she became a Communist. Or so I thought. I could always run into her embrace, always. On that cursed day when Iris did not return from *Skopje*, Mother was the only person who saw my tears. She held me in her arms and patted my back to calm my sobs.

"Martin, dear, the ways of the world are unpredictable. One day you are born, one day you die. What can we mortals understand about all this? Maybe it is better we don't or else we'd spend every day of our life thinking about dying. How could we live with a burden like that, my boy, how?"

She tried to comfort me, saying a new love would heal my wounds, as was the case with her. She reassured me I could love and feel loved again. Well, it was not to be so. In emotional matters, I am very different from Mother and the very opposite of my sister. When I turn away from something, that door is closed forever. The subject of women and love, potential children and family died with Iris in the ruins of *Skopje*. In spite of all the efforts of my mother and sister to find me a wife, I've remained single to the present day.

In May 1991, Mother's heart got weaker with every beat. She was gradually dying together with the federal state of Yugoslavia, which Slovenians had voted against in the *independence referendum* in December 1990. Almost 95% of the voting body had participated, and 88.5% voted for an independent Slovenia. "Should the Republic of Slovenia become an independent and sovereign state?" The historical question produced a clear answer. The preparations for big celebrations were ambitious. However, at the Territorial Slovenian Defense, we were preparing for the attack of the *Yugoslav People's Army*, led by conservative Serbian generals. Ironically, any aggression on their part would be funded by Slovenian money. Bitterness over that, however, was futile. The fact was that JLA was one of the strongest armies in Europe at the time. In those turbulent days, I continued visiting my mother, trying to conceal what was happening outside her sickroom.

On a warm sunny afternoon, Mother summoned us Anna and me. Her spirits were high as though she were getting ready for a party. We raised her bed and sat on each side.

"Well, my little toads, how are you doing? What a wonderful day it is. The perfect day for a trip. My destination has been set. Down to hell, I will go. Soon, very soon. I hope the weather lasts."

"Mommy, come on, don't be so pessimistic. The new medicine will work and you'll get better. You'll see, you will. There's the garden to be planted at home," said Anna kindly.

Mother exchanged a look with me. We coped with the truth and the wavelength of reality. We knew that her bloated legs, ankles like ripe watermelons, would never walk in the garden again. We knew Mother was going to die. The heart is the only muscle that cannot regenerate its cells. When it fails, it fails forever. Its beats get slower until they stop altogether. Surprised, I could see fear and confusion in my mother's blurred green eyes. Was she terrified in the face of death?

No, it was not that. The reason for her moment of panic were the facts that have brought me here today in this tiny hidden hall in the center of the capital city.

Mother took our hands and united them firmly on her chest. Through the linen of her nightgown, I could feel the withered form of her sagging breasts. I felt embarrassed, particularly after I met Anna's tearful eyes. Mother had her eyes close, her lids sealed tight as thought to keep from seeing the world as it was, as though her gaze were fleeing from invisible demons. Gray locks of hair stuck to her forehead, making the line between her skin and her scalp almost impalpable. Her lips trembled with pain as she started to tell us her life story. She wouldn't let go of our hands. She held them in her skinny fingers, united on her chest, without any intention of letting go – the grip of love, stronger than steel and harder than diamond.

It was then when my mother told me that she was not my mother. That my real father, whose name I had been so proud of – Boris Lukman Borko – was in fact not my father. It was then that the sorrow that still clutches my heart today forever invaded my soul.

Anna

The long spring afternoon at Dr. Peter Deržaj Hospital when Mother recounted her life story turned into an evening that stretched its shadows across Martin's face. He stared at Mother as though she were an alien. He could not believe what she was saying. I must say that the facts were distressing, not only to my brother, but also to me. My poor Daddy! From executioner at Kočevski Rog to Police Chief in Ljubljana, only to die in Tito's gulag in *Goli otok*. With trembling voice and tears in her eyes, Mother explained the series of events that led to his doom. Her terrible past rose in front of her eyes like a vicious monster. Often, she had to pause to gather her wits and suppress her emotions before she could continue to divide our lives, to estrange a brother from a sister.

We were both powerless. I could hardly control the anger and rage that I felt for Mother at that moment. Avoiding her gaze, I felt the fury inside me boil. Why had she hidden these facts about our fathers? Who gave her the right to be silent for years and then confess for hours whatever she wanted? Damn her. Did she expect indulgence from God in the other world?

When I finally looked up and saw her teary eyes, it was like looking into a mirror. Pure love shone from her. Love. Her ideals of justice. The honesty to reveal the truth for as long as she could. The truth that would recreate a brother and a sister from real facts, not from lies. Mother was searching for a sparkle of understanding in my eyes, like a voice waiting for an echo from the mountains. Where were her kisses on my cheeks? Would I understand?

Eventually, I smiled at her, embarrassed. The little girl, her biggest fan and admirer, was back. Whatever she confessed, no matter how terrible the facts she spelled out or concealed, she was my mother and I loved her dearly. She was a good woman. No occupying force could tear compassion out of her heart. Maybe today people would condemn her for war crimes. Certainly, they would say she had profiteered from the war. In my eyes, she was nothing but a human being, an infant crying in the darkest night of Mankind, a human being facing the most horrible historical backgrounds of all times. A human being both good and bad.

With her strength fading, I was afraid she would die without our absolution, without our forgiveness. Nobody should die without having received absolution, nobody. She focused on Martin, on the son who was not her son. Martin's face trembled with disquiet. What was he to do with all this information? Would he try to track down his lost family? He was almost fifty years old. Should he start looking for his father and mother on the other side of the globe? Now I understood why Auntie Marjana made him the sole heir of the Skarpin house in Kozjane.

The question that we anticipated with concern resounded in our ears:

"Can you forgive me, Martin?"

There was no Anna in this equation of history. I was simply not important. Her darling, always on her mommy's side. Who cared if I found out that day that my mother and father had blood on their hands? The check would be in the mail. The check to Anna Batič Horvat, a naïve and trusting librarian.

Back in the hall of the *Trubar Literature House*, we were still sitting when people burst into applause. Why? I heard the philosopher say:

"A partisan and a Home Guard, they both got caught in a big ideological machinery. One chose this side, the other that side. They were scared like sheep before a butcher. Should they meet and confess their pain to each other, admit how wrong they had been in following their chosen path, then Slovenians would find reconciliation."

My God, at home, Mother lived with reconciliation every day of her life – whether she wanted to or not. Her path was motherhood. She was able to love the children of two mortal enemies with the same passion. Like a river that inundates both left and right banks. With no possibility to leave either side untouched. Would her maternal love bring her absolution for the deaths of all the Slovenians she had killed with her bullets during the war?

My thoughts wander to that hospital room, to my mother's deathbed. Martin did not answer her question. Naturally, he hesitated. In order to camouflage his indecision, I moved forward and embraced her. Yet my brother was in her arms before me. Of course, he should forgive her. For his life, Mother had risked everything, even me in her belly, her daughter on the way to life. We held each other and, in my memory, we were crying, all three of us. Our love had conquered the war. It was stronger than the evils of the world.

The discussion on the stage agrees with what I think. These clever young men understand that each human being can only exist as individual. That each of us lives only one life of his own. However, it has not always been so easy. Martin dramatically changed after Mother's death. I realized that at her funeral.

We buried Mother in the family grave in Kozjane where she joined her father, mother, and brothers in her last rest. The little graveyard, surrounded by low walls to protect candles and flowers from *burja*, was crowded. According to her wishes, we buried her without a priest or a service. Yet, members of partisan associations, high officials of the Communist Party of Slovenia, various ensign-bearers, the local choir, and musicians came – all speaking, playing, and singing in Mother's honor. Many of them we saw for the first and last time in our lives. It took hours before we could throw a handful of earth on her coffin. Everyone was expressing condolences, hugging us and kissing us on the cheeks as though we were privy to some secret code among the chosen who had known Mother. A skinny little man called Henrik approached me and held my hand in his for a long time. He said that Mother had shown him mercy and compassion during the most difficult moments when he was a child. Yes, Martin and I, we found out about him. Later, we learned that he owned a very successful factory that made windows and doors.

That day I watched Martin closely. His face was stony and expressionless. Only when we were alone with the gravediggers, watching the soil that Mother so eagerly planted and sowed falling upon her, did he point to the Skarpin family gravestone.

"Look, Anna, my mother's not there. She's not good enough even to have her name on the plaque. Only Marjana. As though she, Ada had never been born. God knows whether I exist at all. Maybe I don't."

Sorrow and fear overwhelmed me. I was wondering whether I would also lose my beloved brother along with Mother. The harshness in his voice cut me like a knife. Suddenly, he was as cold as steel, his heart frozen into ice.

My assumptions were soon confirmed. After my mother, we also buried the state she had fought for – the new Yugoslavia. It fell apart like a badly assembled puzzle. Martin thrust his energies into the new independent Slovenia. He didn't have any time for me or his nephews. He forgot our childhood games and our past friendship. For many years, he scarcely exchanged a word with me. The boys, who adored him like a father and used to spend time with him on his yacht, were irrelevant now. They soon started their own families, yet Martin never came to my grandchildren's birthdays or other family celebrations. In his mind, we became strangers.

Based on hearsay, I know he went to Argentina and found his real father. Also, he had his mother's name engraved on the tombstone in Kozjane. Under the Denationalization Act, he managed to retrieve most of the property and inherited the wealth of the two families. He became fabulously rich and moved in to a five-room, 200-square-meter apartment on Miklošičeva Street. When my children and I got evicted from our Villa Villekula, I could have sworn I saw an expression of malicious joy on his face, though he gallantly offered a loan to help us get through the worst. The loss of our once so-called national property hit me hard. Martin got involved in right-wing politics. He was aiming for national recognition of the Home Guard as the official Slovenian army during WWII. As patriots, not collaborators, they should be cleared of blame for all they did was fight against communism.

Since his retirement a couple of years ago, he returned, seeking contact with me. At first, we spoke on the phone, but then we came into the habit of visiting. Why not? We were lonely old people. Martin had nobody besides me, and I had my children and grandchildren only in theory. In practice, they were far too busy to spend time with me. We didn't care about what the other was thinking. Like two dry trunks on a clearing, we were there, waiting for the last rays of sun to warm the bark before we decomposed and kicked the bucket. By then, the elements could not hurt us. Be it sun, rain, wind, or snow. Nothing could bring us from this world, and nothing could keep us in it for long. Sadly yet realistically, the annual growth rings showed that our time was almost up.

It is so nice of Martin to have come today to listen to these wonderful young men talking about love and understanding among Slovenians.

Shyly, I put my hand over his.

Surprisingly, he does not withdraw his.

Martin

That evening Mother breathed her last. We were with her, Anna and me, each holding her by the hand, shaken by her confession and wishing for her strength to hold us together forever. Facing the demons from the past was not easy for either of us. My father was a psychiatrist and a doctor, yet a Home Guard and a traitor, while Anna's father and my foster daddy was a murderer and executioner in Kočevski Rog. Neither of them were who we thought they were. Only Mother was Mother.

When she finished her confession, she handed me an envelope with Ada Strainar's last address in Argentina with a note: "Deceased" and information about my father, Andrej Strainar, a pensioner. There was also a copy of the note about their divorce from the *UDBA*'s archives as well as a picture of five young people in front of the Kodeljevo cinema. Written in pencil on the back: *1943, Marjana Skarpin, Ada Skarpin, Valeria Batič, Andrej Strainar, Sanja Strainar.* There was also a tiny folded paper with my father's latest address: *Andrej Strainar, Av. Corrientes 123, Buenos Aires, June 1987.* I wondered if he was still there, at that address. I wondered if he was still even alive.

Mother was observing me carefully while I looked over the papers. At last, she asked, "Can you forgive me, Martin?"

At that moment, I wasn't sure what I should forgive her for. Did she mean her care and love for me? The sacrifice that made her save another woman's baby? My tender gaze should have been enough reply, still I said, "Mother, you'll always be the only mother I ever had."

I bent over the sickbed and inhaled her sweetish scent that hinted of tenderness. As a child, I'd always felt safe in her arms.

Since the first years of my life, I could remember Mother being the backbone of the family. We all knew it was her high-ranking job at the secret service that granted us a good life in the communist cocoon, woven from thousands of lies, threats, and extortions. The threads were tiny, yet numerous and evil, so the society of terror remained a solid, seemingly unbreakable formation. Yet Mother, so kind and loving between the four walls of our home, knew how to weave these threads around her little finger, how to pull or loosen at the right time and with the right force, like a puppeteer manipulating the show. Now, she put her arms around my neck.

"I love you, Martin. I love you like my own son. My poor foundling, my darling."

I could hardly reply with the lump in my throat. "I love you, too, Mother."

Anna joined our embrace, and I could feel my sister's warm tears sliding down my neck. As always, my sister was exaggerated in her display of affection.

"Mommy, Marty Smarty, I love you, too. My dear family."

Mother and I had almost forgotten about Anna. Her dear father, Marko Robič, was a different man, not a courageous partisan hero, but *Tito*'s obedient soldier killing other soldiers, prisoners of war who had put down their arms. My daddy, as I had remembered him in the stillness of the morning, on the sea outside Ankaran where we took our boat fishing. Whenever he cast a look at the waking city of Trieste, he would swear at the fact that it was not a part of Yugoslavia. He said the day would come. He told me about his childhood in the port, sea fishing, mushroom picking in the Karst plain where Ceasar's mushrooms were as big and orange as little suns in the green grass and their taste as tender as veal. Also, he would talk about his love for Mother. Many times, he told me the life story of Boris Lukman, whose name I carried, and how Mother hid me with a farmer's family in Kozjane to keep me from danger during the last years of the war. One of his favorite stories – and mine, too – was the moment he first met me. Mother, very much pregnant, was waiting for him at the railway station in Ljubljana with me in her lap. With tears in her eyes, she started telling him about Boris Lukman. Father said I looked at him and smiled. It was love at first sight. Mother's fears as to the circumstances of my origins and birth were lost on Father. Father loved me and was proud to be able to raise the child of partisan hero Borko. Until then, I knew of only two fathers; I could not foresee that the ordeal over my parents was not over yet.

Alcohol was the blight of our house. Eventually, our good times with Father became less and less frequent. His kind nature deteriorated. As one rotten apple spoils the whole barrel, one glass of brandy would infect his brain with hurtful heat. He became stubborn in his silence. He did not beat us or scream at us. Mother was the one who did the shouting, trying to wake him up from his stupor and bring him back to soberness, back to reality. At first, we noticed her hiding the liquor in such impossible places. But once Father found her last stash in the attic, he would go to the pub and not return before dawn. It might have been there, during one of his drinking sprees that he said a wrong word that doomed his fate. Poor Daddy. History played foul with him, turning him into a murderer. He couldn't take the guilt and so drank himself to oblivion.

On my mother's deathbed, I found out I had three fathers and two mothers: Mother and Ada, Father, Borko, and Andrej. The image of war hero Borko shaped my youthful memories, Home Guard Andrej sired and lost me during my first year of existence, Father loved me and I loved and missed him my whole life. My mothers could do no better. My biological mother threw me from the train to save me. Mother caught me as a baby and loved me for life.

Yet, whom would a baby flying through the air choose to love? Maybe nobody. Therefore, at a young age, I acknowledged only one truth: the truth of facts I could see with my own eyes and verify by means of mathematical proofs. Mathematics, physics, hard sciences; the rest is smoke and darkness. The only thing that has any importance is the analysis and synthesis of forces and elements.

Psychiatrists would say I was suffering from an identity crisis. They would start digging in the most secret parts of my conscience and thoughts. Yet, the only thing they could find would be formulas, figures, hypotheses, and theories derived from quantum physics. They would find my sharp reason – the survivor's spirit of a child of the cruel war.

Anna

With my hand over Martin's, I must think of our relationship. When we were small, we were very close. One could say our love was outstanding for siblings only a year apart. Yet after Mother died, the ties between us broke. It was worse than the wildest teenage fights. We didn't manifest our hate with fists. We did it with words, poisonous words.

In honesty, it was not only Martin who changed. Mother's confession made me think about her life, too. At the time, the archives were still there, and as her daughter, I was able to access and research the facts. I found interesting evidence about her partisan commander Joc, about her first love Borko, and about Father. Yet, she was the focus of my interest. In my reading, I confirmed my assumptions that Mother was ready to do anything for the regime. Was fear her only reason for covering up the facts about my brother? Was she really so afraid they could dig up something about the events in 1945 and incriminate her, or was she ready to sell her soul for a comfortable life?

I catch the words of the debater from the panel: "Sincerity, only sincerity has the power to overcome all the differences, be it ideology, religion or nationality. It is not so important whether a *German Chancellor* knelt in front of the monument to the Nazi-era Warsaw Ghetto Uprising or not. What's important is whether he meant it sincerely. Europe is reading *Boris Pahor* because he is sincere. He returned from the concentration camp and did not feel like a victim. He felt guilty for having eaten the bread of those who died. Not a victim. A man, a human being."

Has my mother ever gone to the Kočevski Rog to shed a tear for all those men and women whose documents she had to put in order and keep secret? Who knows? She never mentioned anything to either of us. Yet, her confession planted a seed of hate between us brother and sister. The cleft was so deep that we didn't speak for years. Martin felt cheated about the truth regarding his parents, while I felt deprived of Mother's love. I had always known Mother preferred Martin to me, in spite of the fact that I loved her unconditionally and cherished her like I would a saint.

When I was small, I did everything to attract her attention. Sometimes I would let a cup fall to the floor so that it broke in a thousand pieces. I would cry, scream, and stamp my feet. Mother had a very efficient way of disciplining me. No physical punishment, just tedious domestic chores. After Father was gone, we dared not contradict her. She remained kind and loving, but only after we obeyed her wishes. Army rules, fair yet strict. Martin was born for the regime. Most of the time he ignored my outbursts. Thus, he was considered well-behaved and placid, while I was naughty and passionate. I fought bitterly for Mother's love. Martin, however, took her love for granted. Oh, I cannot forget the nights I stayed awake, planning horrible ways to make him look bad so that Mother would be angry with him and love me more, her darling. Sometimes I succeeded, and Martin received the blows that were meant for my behind. Yet he remained dispassionate and calm; he never told on me. He merely cast me a cynical look – a warning that he would settle the score accordingly as soon as we found ourselves alone.

It got worse during our teenage years. I was popular with boys, a true diva when it came to flirting. Martin noticed and updated Mother daily on my every move like a local radio news station. Mother even engaged him to follow me to parties where he would snatch glasses of liquor and lit cigarettes from my hands. I hated him, this nasty loser who was destroying my life. Mother's spy – the excellent student and the perfect son. I would daydream about him dying of an incurable illness so that I could have Mommy all to myself. I looked for opportunities to pay him back, cursing the day he was born. All he did was make fun of me. Luckily, he never found out about my extramarital affairs; my infidelity would have been endless fodder for his sarcastic comments. Cynicism is the worst form of disappointment, and my brother has been its avatar in every sense. Marty Smarty and his love for physics. Indeed, gravitation works downward exactly as he has spiraled downward ever since his only love, Iris, died. Some people experience worse things than that, yet they do not bury themselves in formulas or freeze their hearts forever. Of course, Mother had pitied him beyond reason. He was a martyr for having lost a girlfriend while I, who have lost the father of my sons, was merely a widow.

I'd never had Mother to myself. She loved both of us and tried to be fair. Yet, whatever good I might have done at the altar of maternal love, where feelings were weighed on God's scales of justice, there was also Martin, the son who couldn't care less. The son who wasn't her son. At least now, we all understand.

A year after Mother died, during one of our frequent disputes,

Martin had the nerve to shout at me: "Anna Banana, I've always known you cannot be my bloody sister. You're too stupid!"

That was it. We stopped seeing each other. Even the weekends and holidays we used to spend together at our summer house in Ankaran were planned scrupulously to keep us from bumping into each other. Thanks to e-mails, we were also spared from talking on the phone. Martin, now going under the name Strainar, supported the right-wing political view to expose Mother's communist comrades as criminals of war whose only focus after the liberation was power and theft. Oh, had Mother lived to see it! And if she did?

Nothing would be different. Hadn't she loved him dearly all those years knowing full well who he was? Martin's political delusions and his rich man's arrogance wouldn't have changed anything. She had tenderly loved the baby that war had thrown into her arms. Maybe more than if she had given birth to him.

Oh, I must be crazy. An old woman at seventy still holding childish, jealous grudges against her brother. Maybe I have really lost my mind. Perhaps if we had a father, things would have been different. However, there were only the three of us, caught in the eternal triangle: Mother, Martin, and me.

Now, we are alone. Only Martin and I are left. My sons are part of their families and belong to their children. Like shoots of the elder bush, they don't need the mother trunk any longer. Marko and Luka will pass down their genetic code to their children as I had once bestowed Mother's genes to them. No matter how angry I am with my brother, he was there for me when Rajko died. Not like all my lovers, who promised me the moon and stars for the rest of their lives.

I sigh. The moderator notices and looks at me in surprise. Do I want to speak up? No, baby, not yet. Martin casts me a furtive glance and flashes a compassionate smile. He couldn't have guessed my childish thoughts, could he? My anger fades as quickly as it came. My eyes are mellow and moist while my heart begins to warm.

Oh, it is my Marty Smarty, my dear brother! We used to climb cherry trees together and get into mischief whenever we could. Now we have climbed to be seventy. This is good. With a nod, I try to tell him that it's all right.

Maybe, at the end of this session, we'll try to speak out and declare our love to the mother of all mothers. We will sing her praise, our high song of love. Maybe we will. Unless we go home and have a glass of wine.

Anyway, we will chat.
About all those bygone years.
For the years we have left are few, perhaps even none.

Martin

The night outside is as black as coal. The windows behind the panel seem like the two square mouths of a giant monster. I cast a glance at Anna. She is mesmerized by the speaker. Indeed, like the voice of a magnificent opera singer, his velvety timbre caresses the auditory nerves in everyone's ears, the way dew brushes dry, withered plants after a long sunny day. Considering the discussion and the response of the public, Mother's fight and her role during the war and in the new Yugoslavia where we enjoyed all possible privileges of the communist *nomenklatura*, would be subject to criticism and condemnation. Indeed. Should we abstract the killings of thousands of prisoners of war and examine the suffering of thousands of civilians, who were dying in concentration camps in *Teharje* or Viktring. Disowned and banished, strangers begging for mercy, all they met was hatred. Where would all those Slovenians have gone if Canada had not accepted them or if Perón had not invited them to Argentina?

Never will I forget my bitterness whenever I thought of Mother in the weeks after her death. I blamed her for not speaking sooner, thus denying me the basic right of every human being – the right to the truth. Oh, how much I love the truth. In my mind, I blamed her for everything that was wrong with my life. Everything. Analyzing her every word, gesture, and tenderness pained me, but it was necessary. I had to understand what was true or false.

My life changed. I lost faith in people. My doubt extended to my sanity and to the sanity of the world. It poisoned my mind and covered my brain cells with black tar. I was suffocating, losing my mind. It took me a long, long time before I could comprehend Mother. Not her individual deeds, which were done on the spur of the moment. More reaction than action. I needed to understand her integrity, that strange morality she kept under a coat of grizzly conformism. I wanted to grasp her emotional nature under the mask of brutal reality. Could she have acted in a different way? She did not choose the stage; history set it up for her. A stage on which the tragedy of a nation took place and a thousand horrible scenes were played. Each individual fate mattered little, yet the protagonist was a culprit and a victim. No more, no less than a human being.

After Mother's death, years went by as I searched for my identity. Soon after the funeral in 1991, the *Slovenian Territorial Defense* command allowed me a few days off to take care of a cold that I had caught during the Ice Saints in May. I quickly got better and eagerly pursued my scientific research at the institute. I was weary of uniforms, armies, and artillery and did not want to take part in any new war.

Before, my goals were different. Slovenian independence seemed the right way to go. Yet Mother's confession dispelled my belief that a single individual could change anything in the course of history while politicians were squabbling like little children in a sandbox. Sadly, it is their decisions that have a strong influence in our lives. I found escape in science where facts are facts and never lie. No articulate argument could erase the force of gravitation; it is there for everything with a body mass, period.

And so during those foggy days in May, with winter still threatening the newly sprung buds of trees with a spring frost, I gave myself over to measurements, experiments, and scientific contemplation. The nights were short and spent with little sleep. I noticed how my colleagues felt sorry for me. Probably due to Mother's death. They tried to cheer me up with coffee and sweets and made sure I did not eat my lunch alone at the canteen. Finally, on a Friday afternoon, I was left alone in my laboratory. Fog trailed long white veils along the narrow streets of the town. The rain had stopped for a while.

Sitting behind my desk, I stared at the twilight outside and contemplated the mystery of my conception, the mystery of my whole life. Who was I? Had my existence been set by the Lukman surname as written on my passport ever since I could remember? Or was I the son of Andrej and Ada Strainar, people I never even met? In my mind, Marko Robič was the only father I ever had, though we were not related by blood. Impatiently, I banished thoughts of my mother from my head.

Of course, the question "What connects people?" kept tormenting me. Was it blood? Or emotions, like love – something my sister eagerly threw herself into as though diving into a hot herbal bath?

"The major reason for the situation and the gap between the two sides resides in the ignorance of what had happened and the consequences of the war," says the philosopher on the panel.

I strongly agree, particularly regarding the ignorance in half-knowledge. Lack of education is the major setback of humanity. However, things are more complicated than that.

When I found out about my parents, I started the long research into their motives and plans that had brought me into this world. As always, I applied scientific methodology. First, I analyzed the composition of a human body. I realized that I contained the following chemical elements: 65% oxygen, 18.5% carbon, 9.5% hydrogen, 3.2% nitrogen, 1.5% calcium, 1% phosphorus, less than half percent of potassium, sulfur, and chlorine, and very little magnesium and other so-called trace elements. I paid strict attention to the function of each one and their interaction, particularly their interaction during the process of cell division that enables the creation of a new human being. I took time to comprehensively study the human anatomy and even read scientific books on psychoanalysis.

My questions remained unsolved. By posing them, an abyss of unknown, an inexplicable void opened before my eyes. Wherever I turned, I ran into the limits of my existence. On the physical aspect, my body was vulnerable and could easily succumb to any virus or bacteria. In terms of time, my life span was too short to leave any trace on the Earth's clock. Judging by the way progress moves faster than light, even my excellent contribution to science will be superseded and soon forgotten. Besides, I'm not in the league of Isaac Newton and Albert Einstein. I did not believe in God and seriously doubted I was a part of his Divine Plan. The fact that I experienced certain feelings and observed people expressing their feelings for me didn't prove that I existed or mattered, either. Anna surely viewed her life as a network of millions of emotional bonds, silver and golden threads of joy and pain that formed her cocoon of family and friends. Her pathetic puddle of feelings was disgusting. I needed to wall off my sister and her spoilt brood. Silence made a perfect dam around muddy waters. Anyway, emotions, tears, and such were not my cup of tea. I have always pretended to show my feelings. Well, there were times when I had to do it.

Soon after Mother's funeral, I wrote to my biological father in Argentina. There was no answer. Thus, my life remained open to every possibility and direction, like an equation with too many unknowns, its solution impossible to determine.

The Ten-Day War for independent Slovenia was over. The Territorial Defense people requested my service and I did my duty. Yet,

I was relieved when the ships, laden with the same weapons and heavy artillery that caused so much loss and suffering in Bosnia a year later, sailed off from the Port of Koper with their nationalistic and aggressive commanders aboard. I used every congress and foreign visit to promote the young state of Slovenia as David winning the battle against Goliath, good against evil. The international political community remained unconvinced. However, Croatia and the Baltic countries, including former members of the Soviet Union, as well as Iceland, Sweden, and Germany soon recognized Slovenia's sovereignty and independence. Within a year, the international community added us to the map of the free world that respected democracy, the government of law, and human rights.

Like Slovenia, I was waiting for recognition, my father's recognition from Argentina. At last, after some detours, a letter came. Father invited me to spend the Christmas holiday with him in Buenos Aires. On the last week of 1992, I boarded a plane.

Not long after we took off from Frankfurt Airport and were served dinner, I fell asleep. My dream took me to a high rock on a deserted island. I was staring at the rough sea a dozen meters below. The waves were huge and tall, the kind of waves that a storm with rainy *jugo* from the southwest brings. They clashed against the rock like thunder, their foams nearly reaching my feet. I was scared. It seemed that at any moment the waves could grab and flush me into the deep sea.

Suddenly, I woke up. For a while, I had no idea what was happening. I saw that the oxygen mask from the compartment above my head had popped out and was dangling before me. The plane roared through the winds as it hit one turbulence after another, which was like being swept into those stormy waves in my dream. The passengers were moaning and crying in fear. I took a deep breath, but another turbulence squeezed the air out of my lungs. I reached for the oxygen mask and struggled to put on the life jacket under my seat.

'What's the point?' I thought. Yet I strapped the jacket on as instructed.

Panic crept into the minds of the passengers. Some unclasped their seat belts with the intention of leaving their seats. Where did they want to go, the fools? A pretty, young flight attendant came down the aisle. She took off her high-heeled shoes and tried to calm the people down. She had her life jacket on, too. With a swift thrust of her hand, she pushed the man who had released his belt back down into his seat.

"Don't panic, sir. Everyone, please stay in your seat with your seat belt fastened. We're not losing altitude. Only the turbulences are making our flight uncomfortable. It'll be over soon. Don't worry," she said with a trained smile, then put her mask back over her mouth.

It was sickening how those arrogant business people were babbling in mortal fear. I felt even more sickened by the fact that I, too, was trembling in alarm. It was too soon to say goodbye and crash into the Atlantic, far too soon.

The captain's voice came over the loudspeaker asking us to keep calm as the bad turbulence would soon be over. The stewardess went on consoling one passenger after another, always smiling, putting her hand on a shoulder here and there. I could neither read her lips when she spoke nor hear her voice. Yet, her will to do her job as it should be done impressed me. She was so beautiful. Her thick brown hair in a bun, her face composed of harmonious features and perfectly made up, her green eyes the same color as my mother's eyes.

It dawned on me like a thunder strikes a tree: this petite young girl embodies her mission, her reason to exist. Every one of us embodies his mission by what he does. We are what we do. Not chemical elements, but our deeds define our being. We are neither the faith we trust in God, nor the love we give or take. The least of what we are is the genetic code we get from our parents, which in turn lives on in our descendants. No. We are what we do at this moment in this bloody world. Our deeds can defy eternity. They can mirror our will and freedom forever. I nodded to the girl as she staggered along the narrow aisle; and when she came to my seat, I took her hand in mine and squeezed it gently. I needed to thank her. She had no idea she had just opened my eyes. I knew what to do next. I would meet my biological father with a reason and a plan. The reason I'd been seeking since the moment I was tossed off that train. For fifty years I remained suspended in mid-air; now it was over.

My father had long ago abandoned the city apartment, choosing to live in a little house outside Buenos Aires near the Costanera Sur Ecological Reserve. His life was comfortable but lonely. His housekeeper kindly settled me in a small guest room. After a long bath and an afternoon nap, I was ready to face my creator. He was waiting for me in the library. Heavy velvet curtains blinded the last rays of the setting sun. An elegant floor lamp lit the low table, the leather sofa, and matching armchairs with an orange glow. Aperitifs stood at hand, waiting to cheer us up. At the other end of the room, a huge oak desk spoke of many working hours. The walls around the room were lined with bookshelves.

"Good evening, Mr. Lukman," said a tiny gray man, who blended in with the leather of his armchair.

I came closer and shook his bony hand. "Good evening, Mr. Strainar. Thank you for your invitation," I replied and sat on the sofa opposite him.

He nodded and said nothing. He was scrutinizing my face so thoroughly that it seemed to take all his energy. Patiently, I waited for our conversation to start. Mentally, I compared him with the man I saw in the photograph – in his thirties, wearing glasses, a bit too serious, yet handsome. Next to him was my mother Ada, smiling broadly. It's been almost fifty years. His hair was gone and his murky eyes were almost invisible behind his thick horn-rimmed glasses and wrinkled eyelids. His dark eyebrows were gone, too. His face was clean-shaven and he wore a starched shirt and a tie under a smoking jacket that was fashionable in the fifties. He pressed his lips together. What kind of thoughts were running through his brain? Was he embarrassed to see me? Was he thrilled to find his long lost son at last? Clearly, he was looking to break the ice.

"Well, you have a degree in physics, haven't you, Mr. Lukman? Very interesting. Did you take your doctorate in Ljubljana?"

In short, well-formulated sentences, I summarized my career. I could see that he was listening to me with a lot of curiosity, even enthusiasm.

"Yes, life certainly continued on in this new Yugoslavia without us. Obviously, you had some good work opportunities in this socialist country, Mr. Lukman."

"Quite so. You know my mother, I mean, Valeria. She was politically very well-connected."

For the first time, he smiled. "I bet she was. One hell of a girl from the *Brkini Hills*, Valeria. A *Liberation Front* activist and your mother's best friend."

I looked him in the eye. Enough beating around the bush. "Precisely why I ended up in her arms. Isn't that so, Father?"

His body shivered and he looked away. Hastily, he took the bottle of whiskey and poured himself a glass. He nodded a question in my direction, but I shook my head and covered my glass with my hand. I wanted to talk, not drink. His bony fingers trembled, spilling half of the brandy on the table. His eyes searched for a tissue to wipe the liquid. Unable to find any, he lost his patience.

"Valentina, por favor!" he cried out in the direction of the kitchen.

The door opened and his savior came in with a mop. "The dinner is almost ready, sir. In five minutes," she said with a warm smile and rushed out.

We remained silent. I wasn't going to put words in his mouth. It would be unmanly. Let him choose the way to talk to me. The scientist in me required that things be put in their proper place.

"Father, if you doubt me, we can look into genetic testing options, you know, a DNA test. It is rather expensive, but the results are reliable. Then you will know whether I really am Martin."

"Oh, Martin, we don't need anything like that. You're the spitting image of me. Look at this!"

He opened an old photo album. The first pages showed their marriage photos. Ada and Andrej, young and beautiful. Father wasn't wearing glasses, and I recognized myself in his face and eyes, his mouth, his nose, and his smile. Only his eyes were lighter. Next to him was my mother Ada, dressed in a simple white dress, holding a bouquet of roses in her arms. I could see her eyes shining like two little suns. She was glowing with love and happiness.

My quest was out in the open and, like water released from a dam, I started to ask questions about their life. Father seemed happy to tell me everything. Little anecdotes, stories from the WWII, the black market, and the shows at the cinema. He told me about Auntie Marjana's severe depression and how he managed to cure it. I reported that according to her last will and testament I was the sole heir of the Skarpin estate. He seemed satisfied. Justice had been done for once, he probably thought. He told me I had another aunt, his older sister, Sanja Strainar, a famous pianist, who had lived and performed in Russia a decade before WWII. During the war, she had to escape to America where she rebuilt her career without ever finding out what had happened to her fiancé Sergej Sukorov, the famous violin virtuoso, in the dark years of Stalin's terror. His voice cracked as he recalled Sergej's fate – *NKVD* agents broke all his fingers and cut off his thumbs, then made him believe it was Sanja who had betrayed him. It was a tragedy. The end of a great love. When Sanja retired, she came to Buenos Aires and they lived together for a few years, sharing their love for music and culture. She adored tango and went to listen to its rhythm and watch the dancers in the numerous bars around town almost every evening. One evening, she simply fell asleep for good. Father showed me photographs of my aunt as she played the piano or bowed to the public, always looking like a movie star. In the end, he held one photo between his trembling fingers. Father embracing Mother, who is holding me, a baby, in her lap. We all smile merrily. The world in this picture is nothing less than perfect.

"This is our last photograph together, Martin. Soon after this day, I lost you, my son," he whispered weakly.

I took his hand and squeezed it gently. "Father, I can only imagine how angry you must have been with Mother for what she did. Around 1949, she wrote to Valeria. Mother was very unhappy, devastated. Father, did you ever look at the matter from another perspective? Maybe Mother was right. You know, I had a happy childhood in the new Yugoslavia. Valeria's husband loved me as his own."

When his housekeeper Valentina opened the door a crack, he waved her away obstinately. She disappeared back into the kitchen. We were alone again. Father hid his face in his palms. His body was shivering. I was afraid he was crying.

After a while, he breathed in deeply and said, "I was so unjust to my darling, Ada. Yet, I loved her dearly, my God, how I loved her. When we came to Argentina, everything was so difficult. I had to work several jobs and still we couldn't make ends meet. For many months we survived only because Sanja was sending us dollars. It was so humiliating, but there was no other option. Your mother, Ada, was such a kind woman. However, she was not a woman of strong will and action. She couldn't conceive another child, perhaps because she couldn't stop mourning for you. My love turned into hatred and bitterness. After a while, I started to blame her for everything that had gone wrong in my life. She was guilty. Guilty of abandoning you. It was her fault we were expelled us from our fatherland like a pack of wild dogs with rabies. In my eyes, she was guilty. I was not a good husband, and I might have been a far worse father than Lukman, whose name you bear and speak of, son."

For an instant, his words about guilt touched me. I had blamed Valeria for all sorts of things, too. The thought, however, soon evaporated, and I focused on the old man in front of me, the man who was my father. Although I had already given him a detailed account of the events that enabled Valeria to present me as her child, Father obviously couldn't remember half of it. Remembering who's who in my life is not easy. It didn't matter, though. I just wanted to get to the point of this meeting.

"Father, things have changed in Slovenia. People are talking about the crimes committed by the Partisans against the Home Guard after WWII. About the killings and deportations, the stolen property and wrongdoings. Two years ago, President *Milan Kučan* of Slovenia held a speech together with Archbishop *Alojzij Šuštar* in Kočevski Rog. It is time you come back and tell your side of the story."

Father sighed and took a sip of his whiskey. His gaze looked out the window, into the distance, into bygone times. "Who will listen to me, Martin? Who? Everyone's dead. Partisans and Home Guards alike. There's no point in going back. This is my home now."

How could I convince him? I stood up and took a stroll around the room. Surprisingly, there were many Slovenian series on the bookshelves. The best one hundred novels, the Nobel Prize winners, selected writings of Slovenian poets and writers. He followed me with his gaze.

"We have a bookseller who can get Devil's psalms in Arabic if you want. I had to buy all my books again. God knows my apartment was handed over to some political secretary who lit his fireplace with my collection of great literary works. As far as I heard, they were all a bunch of primitives, hardly literate."

I had to laugh at that. "Oh, Father, that's not true. We've had many highly educated friends who came to visit. Particularly, when Valeria had to raise the two of us on her own. They were of course different kinds of people, but some were great artists and sharp intellectuals."

Father gave me a surprised look. "What do you mean by the two of you? There was another child in the family? And what happened to Valeria's husband?"

A complicated series of unfortunate events. I had no choice but to restart from the beginning. When I finished, the door opened again. This time Father nodded and started to lift his aging body from the armchair.

"Let's have dinner now, Martin. Valentina has prepared all kinds of special dishes to welcome you, and we should not disappoint her. All Argentinian specialties. We'll drink a bottle of Malbec. You do drink wine, Martin, don't you?"

Nodding, I followed him into the dining room. The table was lavishly set. Among crystal wine glasses and porcelain, flowers competed with the dishes in terms of colors. Empanadas with various sauces, soups rich in flavors and vegetables, grilled beef and potatoes prepared with chickpeas or roasted. The dessert, dulce de leche, was a sort of crème brûlée with milk cooked to caramel. Not without pride, Father explained how he rebuilt his life from a poor refugee to a wealthy doctor. A couple of years ago, he retired and bought this lovely hacienda next to the natural park. Heaven. Every day he took a long stroll, enjoying the incomparable vistas. Lovely, but I needed to get back to the reason for my visit.

"Father, it would be really nice if you came to Slovenia. In summer, during my vacation, we could go around the country and visit places. You could stay in Marjana's house in Kozjane. It's very comfortable and well-renovated. You know, the village was burnt down three times during WWII. The *kolkhozes* after the war caused widespread hunger and poverty, so people abandoned the *Brkini Hills* and moved into towns. Kozjane is deserted. Only two families are still living there. Other farms were rebuilt and now serve as summer houses."

He was tempted; I could feel it. But his fear of the country where he had lost everything was huge. "There's something else I have to confess, my son. I may have caused the early death of your mother. Not long after I left her, your mother committed suicide. It was strange. She had a good life in a way. She finished her teaching degree, had a well-paid job, and was very popular with everybody in the Slovenian community. Then, one day she did not show up to work."

"Why?" I asked in a low voice.

"She overdosed on sleeping pills. I myself had given her the prescription because of her insomnia. She'd been suffering for years. Well, not only that. There were other things, too. I'm guilty, Martin, guilty of her death. I had been cruel and ..." His voice quivered, and he paused. "I was very cruel to the wife and mother, to the woman, who gave life to you, son. I'm sorry."

Words died in my throat. I knew that anything I said would have been but a drop in the sea. His wrinkled face spoke of the hours and days he spent tormenting himself. The reproaches and faults in his features have long ago drawn a map of sorrows and pains. It was an inaccessible country to me. Still, I somehow understood how he felt. He had to clean the slate. Start from scratch, so that there would not be any unsolved questions between us.

"Another thing, Martin," he added in a trembling voice.

"Yes?"

"The Home Guard was a terrible mistake. It is wrong when Slovenians kill Slovenians," he said dryly.

"The same goes for the Communists, Father. They went after fellow Slovenians, too," I said, lowering my head. "Executioners and killers."

"The Communists were a mistake, too, my son. Had they not lost, they would have remained a mistake."

"History is full of ideological blunders," I replied.

"Yes, history and ideology are abstract notions. Yet, it is men who make mistakes and men who pay for them. See how long it has taken for the two of us to be rejoined."

"I'm so glad we have, Father," I said in a low voice, adding, "Slovenia is a different country now. You'll see. Please, come visit me."

For days, we debated the issue. I had to use all my cunning not to push him too much, just persuade him gently to come home with me. During our long walks, meals, visits to the cafés and bars, I explained about politics and life in independent Slovenia. I started from the beginning. The "Trial Against the Four," the first associations that could not be called political parties yet, the presidential elections, the first Slovenian democratic government and Prime Minister Lojze Peterle, the Ten-Day War against the *Yugoslav People's Army*. Slovenians – all for one, one for all. I told him about *Jože Pučnik*, a respected politician, whom people trusted and followed. Although my decision to support the policy that demanded lustration and truth regarding the crimes of the Communists had entered my mind only recently, I related these wishes to him, too. It was time we let some light into the Slovenian past, do away with doubts and half-truths and start anew with honesty and respect. I would do anything for the cause and was ready to offer all my savings to the right people.

Finally, he agreed to visit Slovenia. As we were saying goodbye at the airport, he embraced me warmly as a father would embrace his son. At last.

For many years until his death, Father came to Slovenia for the summer holidays. Soon after my trip to Argentina, we filed a well-documented request with the Slovenian authorities for Father's estate to be denationalized and returned to us. The following year I left the big city house where I had lived with Valeria, Anna, and her family, and moved in to Father's comfortable apartment on Miklošičeva Street.

At last, the lump in my throat had relaxed and I could breathe. I got in touch with my younger nephew Luka, who was a very gifted engineer, and arranged for him to start his doctorate program at the University of Ljubljana. My sister was drowning in melancholy, unable to deal with his ambitions. Luka was like son to me. The first time my father returned to Slovenia, the three of us took a sailing trip around Istria. It was fabulous. Luka and Father rejoiced over the winds and sails like two little children. We had a great time. Our time was short, though. Father was old and soon fell ill. He died before I could buy a plane ticket and rush over to see him in faraway Argentina. Once again, I was an orphan.

My estates and properties were immense. I inherited Father's money, which included Aunt Sanja's fortune. I could have retired and gotten some peace in my life. However, it hurt me to see what was happening in Slovenia. The silence, the base denial of criminal actions, the shameless denunciation of others. I dedicated all my efforts to politics for over a decade – until *Jože Pučnik* died. Then, I'd had enough of all the demagogues and loudmouthed moonlighters. To hell with all of them. I made many enemies because when I had something to say I told it to their face without mincing my words. I was that lonely child screaming about the emperor being naked. Nobody liked me. Nobody. Still, something else gnawed at my brain. Deep down, at the core of my being, I still couldn't find peace. My nervousness, impatience, insolence, irritability, and coldness made people steer clear of me. Nobody, not even my sister, could put up with me.

Lately, my illness has made rethink the basics of my life. During my nocturnal struggles with the Grim Reaper, I realized that the quest for the Graal of my being should begin at the beginning – within myself.

After my speedy retirement, I spent most of the spring in Kozjane. When the doctors eventually agreed on my diagnosis and before they set the date for the surgery, I took a long sailing trip around the Adriatic coast and islands. In the bays from Dubrovnik to Grado, I found peace and beauty at last.

"What can we do to let the soul rest in peace? This soul, this collective conscience, it is all of us," pleads a woman from the audience.

"A decent burial conveys peace. It means that Evil cannot have the last word," says the psychologist on the panel, aiming to focus on the essence of national reconciliation.

Their words echo in my ears. 'What about me? Have I decently buried Mother? I mean Mother Valeria. Have I forgiven her? Or am I torn apart by evil like a malicious and ungrateful child?'

As always, my sister interrupts the stream of my thoughts. She wants us to go to the panel. Together. Dear God, Anna Banana has really lost her mind! This time for sure!

Anna

Although my brother's health and life were in jeopardy only a month ago, his condition has improved dramatically after the surgery. The doctors managed to remove the malignant tumor on his outer lung, so it seems that my brother has beaten the cancer. Almost daily I come to his apartment and supervise his housekeeper to do everything properly. The rooms shine with polish, and the meals she cooks are healthy and rich. I usually stay until he wakes up from the afternoon nap that I make him take. It is fun. For the first time in years, we are talking, playing chess, watching television, and reading the newspapers. Of course, not without commentaries.

"Oh, my God! They're really overdoing it! National reconciliation here, reconciliation there," says Martin one day, his nose in the paper. "We'll have our reconciliation soon enough when we all die. All of us who carry this burden on our shoulders. Soon enough, Anna. Look, like us, they were born at the end of WWII, so we're all hitting seventy now. A few more years and we will all kick the bucket. Why would anyone want to air dirty linen that will soon disappear along with the people involved in it? It's the law of nature."

Dropping the magazine on my knees, I reply, "Speak for yourself, bro! You'll be seventy this year, not me."

"Right, still quite a young girl, aren't you? Here comes the bride all dressed in white...You will travel around the world a few more times, won't you? Dear me, Anna, don't you see that the national reconciliation is like catching water with your fingers? Pure waste of time."

"Sorry, Martin, but I cannot agree with you," I answer. "I think there are still people who intentionally don't want the animosities to stop. They need fighting and while people fight, they profit. They're abusing human emotions to inflate their ill-gotten gains."

Martin takes off his glasses and looks at me with new interest. "Well, look at you! You're developing logical thinking with age, sis. I agree, all this instigation serves a purpose: greed. All you need to do is follow the words and the money. It's obvious who says what at a certain time and in a certain place. Still, I don't understand something. What's wrong with the mass media? Why can't they influence such important discussions more? They can scribble about the tits of a starlet any day, yet they don't write about the younger generation needing unity, transparency, globalization, and in Slovenia, social security, jobs, and lodgings."

I smile. "Well, they do write about all these issues. Many are critical, especially women journalists. Maybe the first thing you notice in the papers are the tits."

Bursting into laughter, Martin swats at my head with the newspaper. "Anna Banana, be serious. Know what? I've been thinking of that evening at the *Trubar Literature House*. Somehow I'm grateful you made me listen and speak up."

I wait, thirsty to know more. What kind of a lesson does my brother have in store for me this time?

"I've never been part of such a pathetic scene, and I probably never will be again. Dear me, complete strangers were crying like babies while we recounted Mother's life and her fate."

"Don't you ever feel a little bit sorry for her, Martin?"

"No."

Anger possesses me. "How can you be so heartless, so cold? You! When she saved your life. Actually, she gave you two lives. More than she ever had."

"Now you've got me wrong, Anna. I loved Mother. Not a day goes by when I don't think of her. I don't whine and wail, though. She had her life under control to some extent. Not even the war or the Communist Party had deterred her course. Her heart remained clear and honest. She had always gone her own way. Like a tanker. She couldn't change the course once it was set. Even if she was to sail into a reef."

"Yeah, Mother was a woman of strong will. A rock of the *Brkini Hills*."

"Well, you see. That's what I meant. There on that evening fifty people were crying like sissies when you said you were the daughter of a murderer and I was the son of a traitor. The old spinsters were crying their hearts out."

More than two months have gone by and this is the first time Martin mentions that evening. I know that I have challenged him with my attitude: my desire to hold all of humanity and love in my arms forever. We have always been tough adversaries. Reason against emotion. Ratio adversum emotio. That long early spring evening. I remember the audience, who have been all moved to tears, flooding the hall like April snow melting in the sun. Martin, however, did not show any feelings. Rigid as a stone, he simply stared in front of him without saying much. I knew I had profoundly shaken his foundations. It was earthquake and tsunami time in his soul. I had to. I have my own good reasons. I was afraid we would die unreconciled like any average Slovenian with his silent grudges, bitter with resentment. We are not responsible for these grudges. It was the dirty, lousy war. And dirty, lousy wars go on because dirty, lousy people-breeders profit from them. I have made up my mind that I would not leave this world before making peace with my only brother. We shall die loving each other as we used to. Unconditional friends, the brother and sister we used to be before he found out about his family, the Strainers, and before he started to dabble in politics and study the unjust treatment of the Home Guards. Had I not taken him to that debate, God knows whether I could have ever brought him out of his fortress, the path to which was paved with lessons and soliloquies.

"Oh, Marty Smarty, those people were not crying for us. They were bewailing their own fate," I retort.

"Right on the money again, Anna. Catharsis means cleansing one's soul from the inside." He has to have the last word, of course.

Although I can feel there is something else bothering him, I pause. The housekeeper brings in the afternoon coffee and biscuits, which means it is time for me to go home to my small, sad apartment. At last, my brother speaks up.

"The weather report for tomorrow is nice. I feel I'm strong enough to drive the car. Why don't we go to Kozjane? We could visit Mother's grave and have lunch on our way back. Maybe at Matavun."

I look up at him. He evades my eyes and stares at the coffee cup as though to hypnotize it. It doesn't move. Oh, I'm not going to let him off the hook so easily. No, he is going to look me in the eye and tell me why he wants to go to the *Brkini Hills*. Which mother and which grave does he have in mind? Valeria or Ada? Since Andrej Strainar's death years ago, I know Martin rarely visits the Skarpin house and the farm that Auntie Marjana renovated and left him in her will. It was an odd thing to have done at the time, and we were all surprised. Later, the reason behind it became obvious. Now, the cup still hasn't changed its position. Is he going to look me in the eye or not?

"Why don't we go to the Skarpin house, clean and air it properly after the long winter? We can cook something there," I insist.

Finally, Martin lifts his dark brown eyes, which have become grayish and blurred with old age. I realize he means our dear mother, the only mother he has known. She was the one who cuddled him, looked after him, and loved him. What's that shine in his eyes? Old age or old tears?

"No, Anna. I don't want to visit the Skarpin house tomorrow. I want the three of us to be alone: you, Mother, and me."

I nod in understanding. "All right," I say and get up from the armchair, not without ache and moaning.

Early next morning the twittering and chirping of birds from the wild chestnut tree in front of my window wake me up. It is a clear sunny morning. A perfect day for a trip to the *Brkini Hills*. I am looking forward to it. It is the place of our childhood, the place where we spent magical moments together. Every year, during the school break, we would visit Auntie Marjana. We would run about the flowering pastures and climb to the tops of the cherry trees. Many times we ate so much of the tasty red fruits that we got sick. We were two little naughty starlings who refused to climb down from the trees even for lunch. Oh, those happy childhood days without a worry in the world.

At eight sharp, the silver Mercedes stops in front of my entrance. We drive for a good hour in the comfortable car. Soon we halt in front of the graveyard in Kozjane, the village where our two mothers were born. Martin opens the trunk and takes out three big candles: white, red, and blue.

Haltingly, he explains, "I stopped by the flower shop. I thought we might want to light some candles."

What can I say? I step toward the metal gates and push hard. The rows of abandoned graves tell the story of the village. The people have long ago left their homes and gone to the cities. Apart from a couple of summer houses, where city folks turn up for the weekends to grill *čevapčiči* and drink *Teran*, the village is in ruins. Year after year, ivy and bushes creep over the cold bricks and walls – some still bearing the traces of war fires – and slowly claim their natural space back. What a waste. This land is so rich, ready to bear crops and nourish generations. My gaze embraces the soft green hills where some cherry trees still carry flowers among planted fields and blooming pastures. They are late this year, the white tree fairies of spring. My God, how beautiful this land is. These hills stretching from Mount Snežnik to the Mediterranean Sea are round and full like a mother's breasts, swollen with milk for her babies. The land is ripe with love and honey.

Surprisingly, Martin takes my hand in his. "Isn't this beautiful, Anna? So beautiful..."

"Yes. When I die, I want to be laid here beside Mother. I miss her so much, Martin." I begin to sob, though I don't want to shed tears today.

My brother takes me in his arms and holds me tightly for a long time. At last, he says, "All this aimless wandering around, all these mothers and fathers that war brought up. I've had enough, Anna, enough. I want to rest in peace here in this tomb, too. With our mother and with you. You're the only family I've ever had."

"Oh, Marty." I put my arms around him and press my body so close to his that I can feel his heartbeat. My brother. Our lives blend into one mighty cherry tree. Our feet have grown deep roots, and our arms have become tall branches that touch the sky.

"Now, let's light our candles. Mine is white and yours is red, Anna."

"Please, stop it, Martin." I get upset. "Always these divisions, white and red, Home Guards and Communists."

"You don't understand, Anna. We're doing this together. Not for war and division, but for love and peace."

"Yes, the son of a traitor and the daughter of a murderer," I add in a whisper.

"Anna and Martin, sister and brother," says Martin firmly.

We put the candles on the grave and dwell in our memories. Suddenly, a light spring breeze lifts the petals from a cherry tree next to the graveyard, and the flowers are falling on us like confetti at a wedding party. Tiny and soft as Mother's kisses and caresses. Our souls are clear and full of love, pure like the white petals falling through the air and on the ground.

"Look, Anna, the cherries are white in bloom and carry very, very red fruits," says Martin with a roguish smile.

"Oh, Marty Smarty, above all you should always remember one thing: cherries are sweet. Sweet, sweet cherries!"

We laugh at the comparison with our split lives. Martin takes another candle out of his bag, a blue one.

"Who is the blue candle for, Martin?"

He recites jokingly: "Oh, Anna Banana. White, blue, and red..."

"Slovenian banner, go ahead!" I finish the line and ignite the match between my fingers.

The blue candle kindles the brightest flame of the three.

It is the candle of truth, burning with the golden flame of wisdom.

For all enlightened men and women who refuse to argue and quarrel forever.

For all friends who are to build a new world.

For all future generations that will grow together into one mighty tree.

For all the people in the world who love white and red alike and enjoy the taste of sweet, sweet cherries.

THE END

Glossary of less known terms

Alberto Rabagliati a famous Italian singer of the time, (1906-1974).
Aldo Fabrizi Italian actor, director, screenwriter and comedian (1905 -1990); not only his films, but cinema in general was very popular in Ljubljana during WWII.
All Saints' Day Catholic celebration of the dead on November 1st.
Alojz Gradnik a Slovene lyrical and decadent poet between the two wars, born in Medana in 1882, died in Ljubljana in 1967; one of the most important poets of his time.
Alojzij Šuštar born in 1920, died in 2007; Archbishop of Ljubljana from 1980 until 1997; on December 7th 1990 he offered the mass for the Home Guard victims at Kočevski Rog, together with the president of Slovenia Milan Kučan, for the first time after 1945 in a gesture of reconciliation.
Arbeit macht frei! German: work sets you free; the slogan which appeared above the entrance of Nazi concentration camps.
AVNOJ Serbo-Croatian: Antifašističko Vječe Narodnog Oslobodjenja Jugoslavije, in English Anti-Fascist Council for the National Liberation of Yugoslavia; the second meeting of the representatives of all later federal republics, i.e. Slovenia, Croatia, Serbia, Monte Negro, Bosnia and Herzegovina, and Macedonia met in a Bosnian town Jajce (Tito's headquarters at the time) on November 29th and 30th 1943 to work out the fate of Yugoslavia after WWII. The dates were national holidays during the Communist era and were celebrated as the foundation of the new Yugoslavia.
Battle of Ebro The longest battle during the Spanish Civil War took place between July and November 1938. The Republicans fought against the Nationalists along the river Ebro and after Germany came to Franco's aid lost.
Bežigrad Slovenian, northeren part of the city of Ljubljana, close to the central railway station.

Bergen-Belsen Nazi concentration camp in Lower Saxon, near the town of Bergen.
Boris Pahor Slovene writer, born in 1913 in Trieste, notable for his Holocaust experience that he described in his novel Necropolis, translated in several languages. Until present days, Pahor remains the critical voice of the Slovenes in Trieste.
Breznik's Grammar written by Anton Breznik (1881-1944), teacher, headmaster and priest, published in 1921; one of the few books used to teach Slovenian.
Brkini Hills Slovenian area in the hinterland of Trieste (Italy) between the River Reka on the north, the Karst Plateau (town Sežana) on the northwest, and the border to Croatia in the south; 700 to 800m above the sealevel; main towns Ilirska Bistrica, Divača, Podgrad, Hrpelje, Kozina, and Pivka; Kozjane, Vatovlje, Tatre, Suhorje, Ribnica, Misliče are little villages of some 20-30 houses in the Brkini Hills; famous sight the Caves of Škocjan.
Brothers Tuma a family company by the ancestors of the author's husband; Liberation Front members; descendants of Henrik Tuma (1858-1935), a famous politician, MP, Social Democrat, solicitor, mountaineer, and researcher.
Burja Slovenian; a strong, dry and cold northeast wind, coming in wild shocks from the mountains and from the mainland; very strong at Karst, in the Brkini Hills and at the seaside.
Castle Hill Ljubljana Castle on the hill above the city makes the skyline of Ljubljana. It was originally a Medieval fortress built in the 11th century, many times rebuilt and expanded until the present state. During WWII the building was used as penitentiary. Today it is one of the major cultural venues and sights of Slovenia.
Čevapčiči minced meat grill dish similar to the Kebab.
Chetnik Serbian: a member of paramilitary guerilla defending nationalist and monarchist ideals and the Orthodox faith; the royalists. The army was established in the first half of the last century to fight against the Ottoman Empire. The Chetniks took part in both Balkan wars of the 19th century, in WWI and in WWII when their role changed from defending Serbia against the German occupation to cooperating with the Germans in the fight against Tito's partisans. Already during WWII their aim was the Great Serbia and their strategy ethnic

cleansing of Muslims and Croatians. Expulsions, torture, and rape were their ways of operating then and in the last Balkan war in the 1990s. Their foes were the Catholic Ustashas.

Close linked ... France Prešeren: Zdravljica (Toast); today Slovenian national anthem.

Comintern Russian: abbreviation for the association of all Communist parties, existed from 1919 to 1943.

Commissariato civile Italian authorities for the control of the civilians during their occupation of Ljubljana, WWII.

Custoza a field and a veteran hospital in Italy after WWI.

Djilas Milovan Djilas (1911-1995), a contemporary and a comrade of Tito's, Communist politician, WWII partisan leader, theorist and author. In 1954, he criticized the new, aspiring class of the Yugoslav Communists living in wealth and was expelled from the CPY and jailed. In prison, he wrote several international bestsellers (The biography of the Montenegrin poet Njegoš, Conversations with Stalin, 1962) and translated Milton's Paradise Lost. His biography of Tito, the inside story, is also very famous. He was released in 1966 and lived in Belgrade as a dissident until his death.

Dražgoše one of the first battles between the Germans and the partisans in Slovenia during WWII, from January 9th to 11th 1942; the partisans retreated, and the Germans took horrible reprisals against the civilians; the villagers were all either killed or taken to the concentration camps, the village burnt down and demolished. Controversy as to the true denouement of the events.

France Balantič a young Slovene poet (1921-1943), a Home Guard, who died during the partisan raid of Grahovo in 1943. Although he had written only some ninety poems in his lifetime, he has been considered as one of the most gifted lyrical voices of Slovenia. See France Balantič, Path without End, published by Mohorjeva/Hermagoras, Klagenfurt, 2005.

France Prešeren December 3rd 1800 - February 8th 1849, up to the present day Slovenian best known poet; a Romantic writer in Slovene and in German; master of the sonnet and other poetic forms, he elevated Slovene poetry to international trends and level. He wrote A Toast, the Slovene national anthem. His profound works inspired all later poets and were the source of national pride from the Spring of nations in 1848 until the

1991 Slovene Independence. Works: The Baptism on the Savica, Sonnets of Misfortune, A wreath of Sonnets, Zdravljica - A Toast. The major national award for the achievements in culture is named after him. His birthday is celebrated as the Merry Day of Culture, his death day is the Slovenian Culture Day, work-free.

Franja Slovenia: a clandestine hospital for wounded resistance fighters named after the main woman physician, who worked there Franja Bojc Bidovec. It has never been discovered by the enemies and operated until the end of WWII. Today it is a museum.

German Chancellor Kniefall von Warschau is German for Warsaw Genuflection, which refers to Willy Brandt's gesture of humility and penance before the monument of the Warsaw Ghetto Uprising on December 7th 1970.

Giovinezza Fascist anthem; Italian for youth; march song; Youth, youth // spring of beauty, // in the hardship of life // your song rings and goes! Ending in ... that doesn't unfurl the flags // of redeeming Fascism. Valeria could sing the song, as every day school started with it.

Gnocchi Italian: potato dumplings.

Goli otok Croatian: barren, naked island, uninhabited; situated in the Northern Dalmatia, north of the island Rab; POW camp during WWI set up by the Austro-Hungarian Monarchy for Russian prisoners; after WWII, cruel political prison operating from 1949 to 1989; also named Tito's Gulag.

Gonars near Palmanova; Italian concentration camp for the Slavic population from the lands the Italians gained after WWI; at Gonars some 500 victims.

Grahovo On November 24th 1943, the partisans entered the village of Grahovo where the Home Guards had a military station. The partisans burnt it down. All the Home Guards died in the flames, among them was a young Slovene lyrical poet France Balantič (1921-1943). The church from which the Home Guards were trying to defend the village was burnt, too. The civilians were tortured and killed for collaboration. The facts about the cruelty of the partisan operation were hidden from the official records until 1991.

Grgur the twin island of Goli otok; the islands both uninhabited are half a mile apart; Grgur for female political prisoners operating from 1949 to 1989.

Humerus Latin: a long bone in the arm running from the shoulder to the elbow.

Independence referendum in 1990 with its historical outcome of 88.5% in favor of Slovenia as independent state was held on December 26th and was the basis for the secession of Slovenia from Yugoslavia.

Independent State of Croatia Croatian: Nezavisna država Hrvatska, was a Nazi puppet state of Croatians during WWII existing from 1941 to 1945. Until 1943 it was under the Italian protectorate and its official ruler was the Duke of Aosta. In fact, the state was led by Croatians Ante Pavelić and Nikola Mandić, who continued after the capitulation of Italy and under Nazi occupation. The state was spread over the territories of today's Croatia, Bosnia and Herzegovina as well as parts of Serbia. The soldiers were the Ustashas. The state was persecuting other nationalities and races, particularly Serbs, Gypsies, Muslims, and Jews. They operated several concentration camps, most notorious at Jasenovac and at Sisak (children).

Isonzo the Isonzo River, in Slovene: Soča, and the Julian Mountains were one of the most cruel theaters of WWI, opening in spring 1915 when Italy attacked the Austro-Hungarian Empire. The Italian forces were led by Field Marshal Luigi Cadorna. Between June 1915 and November 1917, twelve battles were fought the last huge loss for Italians was the Battle of Caporetto (See the Kobarid Museum of WWI); Ernest Hemingway's A Farewell to Arms is partly set in this battle. Italian poet Giuseppe Ungaretti was also stationed at this Front - I Fiumi. The Front is estimated to have taken 1.2 million lives; 30000 casualties were ethnic Slovenes; many thousands of Slovene civilians perished in the Italian refugee camps where they were treated as enemies.

Ivo Andrić (1892-1975) was the only Nobel Prize for Literature laureate (won in 1961) from the Yugoslavian territory. In his novels, he described the life in Bosnia under Ottoman rule. The Bridge over Drina is his most famous novel.

Janez Hladnik was a Catholic priest and missionary, born in 1902 in Slovenia, died in 1965 in Argentina. In 1936, he was sent to support the Slovenian community of 20000 Slovenes, who had run away from Fascism. After WWII his role in obtaining permission from the Argentinian president Peron to let 10000 Slovenian refugees come to Argentina was a major one. He helped selflessly with practical matters and organized cultural life of Slovenes far away from their country.

JBTZ the JBTZ affair, the JBTZ trial or Trial against the Four was a political trial held against Janez Janša, Ivan Borštner, David Tasić and Franci Zavrl, who were jailed by the military Yugoslav Peoples' Army's authorities and sentenced to between six months to four years imprisonment for publishing in the magazine Mladina military secrets. Slovenians went to the streets and protested. All but for Borštner, who was employed in the army, were set free. It marked the beginning of the Slovene Spring.

Jože Pučnik born in 1932, died in 2003; a Slovenian public intellectual, sociologist, dissident, politician, and the leader of the Democratic Opposition of Slovenia (DEMOS); father of the Slovenian independence.

Jota thick soup with potatoes, sauerkraut, beans and smoked pork meat and bones.

Jugo Croatian; a southeast wind. It usually occurs with rainy and cloudy weather, generating high waves, but it can also blow hardly when the sky is clear. A cyclonic jugo can cause heavy storms, even hurricanes.

Kajmak fresh cheese produced from cream.

Kampor at the island of Rab; Italian concentration camp for the Slavic population from the lands the Italians gained after WWI; at Kampor some 4000 people and 150 children died of hunger and starvation.

Karadjordjević The Serbian Royal Dynasty of the pre-WWII Yugoslavia; kings Aleksander 1st (assassinated in Marseille in 1934) and his son Petar 2nd, who fled to London after the bombing of Belgrade on April 6th 1941 and remained the king in exile until his death in 1970. Today, the descendants of the dynasty live in Belgrade and are active members of the Serbian society.

Kardelj Edvard Kardelj (1910-1979) was a Slovene journalist, Communist and partisan leader during WWII; an economist, considered to be the creator of the self-management doctrine.

Kazachok Russian lively dance, often to the melody of Katyusha's song.

Kačić a famous Croatian pirate in the 13th century, operating around Omiš; was knighted in 1258 by the King of Hungary, Bela IV.

Koba nick name of Joseph Stalin (1878-1953), leader of the Soviet Union from mid 1920s to his death in 1953. He rose to power with brutality and cunning, consolidating his absolute power by the Great Purge in the 1930s when Sanja is living in the country. Stalin's purges were carried out by the NKVD troika, who imprisoned, sentenced, and executed the punishments within 24 hours.

Kolkhoz After WWII all landowners, who had more than 35 hectares of arable land and 45 hectares of all land were expropriated without compensation, the same all other institutions owing land like the Church. A number of small poorly equipped farms (5-10 hectares) could not produce enough, so after 1949, Yugoslavian agriculture was organized in Kolkhozes, collective farms following the Soviet model. The results were devastating, and in the countryside, famines made people leave and settle in the cities. The situation was better in those areas where instead of collective farms the cooperatives were established.

Kurva Russian: whore, bitch.

Liberation Front Osvobodilna fronta slovenskega naroda, shortly OF; after Yugoslavia capitulated and the Axis occupied Slovenia in April 1941, the Communist Party of Slovenia (CPS) called all Slovenes to armed resistance against the occupiers. Many political groups got involved like Christian Socialists, members of the liberal Sokol, and progressive intelligentsia; famous leaders Edvard Kardelj, Boris Kidrič, poet Edvard Kocbek, a Christian Socialist. Already by September 1941 it was clear that CPS had taken control of the Liberation Front and used the patriotic spirit for socialist revolution. The fighters of the Security and Intelligence Service (VOS) were removing all who were in the way, which caused a strong opposition among the conservative circles and the Catholic Church. The CPS finally consolidated its leading role with Dolomite Declaration in March 1943. It proclaimed itself the only representative of the Slovene people, controlling the National Liberation Struggle (Narodno-osvobodilni boj, NOB) and joined the Antifascist Council of National Liberation Struggle of Yugoslavia (AVNOJ); recognition by the Allies. Liberation Front was the base for the new Slovene government, proclaimed a number of resolutions and decrees regarding the establishment of postwar Slovenia. After the war, it was transformed to Socialist Alliance of Working People (SZDL).

Ljubljanica Sluice Gate Slovene, also called the Partition was designed by the Slovene architect Jože Plečnik and only built in 1943. It symbolizes a monumental farewell of the Ljubljanica River leaving the city.

Lubyanka Russia: popular name for the 19th century building in Moscow, where NKVD and later KGB had its headquarters and prisons.

Lucio Bini Italian psychiatrist and professor (1908-1964); researching electroconvulsive therapy for mental diseases together with Ugo Cerletti.

Luger a pistol very commonly used by the Germans during WWI and WWII; also by the Stasi in East Germany.

Milan Kučan born in 1941 in Križevci, the Prekmurje region, first president of Slovenia from 1991 to 2002; a member of the Communist Party and a high official in the former regime; in his presidency, he commemorated the Home Guard victims of the Kočevski Rog (December 7th 1990), with a plea to all Slovenes to reconcile and let the dead of both sides rest in peace.

Milizia Volontaria Anti Comunista Italian: Anti-Communist Police, shortly MVAC; the formations of the MVAC, the Legions of Death, and the Village Guards (in Notranjska and Dolenjska some 6000) between early 1942 and 1943 were the reaction to the Partisans' mistreatment of the people in the countryside (requisition of food, forced mobilization, murders of opponents); they were poorly armed and sought help from Italians. After Italy's capitulation, most of them joined the Home Guards. Valeria is confused, as there were also the Blue Guards (Chetniks), adherents to the Yugoslav King Petar in exile (London), some 300-600 military men who had mostly acted as secret agents for the Allies and were not supported by the Axis.

National Heritage Committee Slovene: Komisija za upravo narodne imovine; There were special committees that searched the confiscated houses and premises for precious antiquaries, paintings and art objects. As a rule, the art objects would be put into museums and galleries, however, many wandered into private collections of Party officials.

Natlačen Marko Natlačen (1886-1942); was the pre-WWII governer of Drava Banovina (all Slovenia northern of the Rapallo Border) who after April 1941 established a National Council of Slovenia in Ljubljana and maintained a dialogue with the Axis, trying to gain political concessions for Slovenes under the Italian rule; e.g. he ordered to destroy official lists of members of the Communist Party and its supporters, as he feared Italians would persecute them. As a leader of conservative Slovene People's Party, he was branded a traitor by the Communist Party and executed by the Security and Intelligence Service of the Liberation Front. In order to revenge, Italians took randomly people from the street and shot them as hostages.

NKVD Russia: People's Commissiariat for Internal Affairs was a law enforcement agency of the Soviet Union, also carried out the jobs as a secret police, directly responding to the Communist Party and its leader, at the time of the novel Joseph Stalin.

Nomenklatura Slovene: the expression for the privileged bureaucracy members and party officials in the Soviet Union and in other Communist states.

Nona Slovenian dialect for Italian nonna, grandmother.

OZNA Serbo-Croatian: Odjeljenje za zaštitu naroda, Department of National Security was a security agency existing between the spring of 1944 and 1946, operating under Tito's comrade Aleksandar Ranković as the counter-intelligence to Gestapo and other Axis police forces.

Palmanova The Palmanova lie: the Slovene Home Guards were told by the British that they would be moved to Italy, as the conditions would be better there than in the camps at Bleiburg and Viktring. Yet, the British knew what the Allies had agreed: all collaborationist soldiers are handed over to the troops that they had fought against, in the case of Home Guards, to the Tito's partisans. In the aftermath, most of the returned soldiers were killed in various places, most notorious the Kočevski Rog forest.

Penicillin Antibiotics; The Allies supplied the parties they supported with medicines and ammunition. Germans did neither know nor used Penicillin at the time. See Lindsay Rogers:

Guerilla Surgeon, Collins, London 1957.

Petriček The existence of the orphanage and the difficult conditions, in which had lived the Home Guard orphans after the partisans have executed their parents for collaborating with the Nazis, has been revealed only recently in a book by Ivan Ott (Otroci s Petrička) and the documentary by Miran Zupanič with the same title. A moving account of the post WWII revenge and atrocities against the enemy's children.

Pijade Moša Pijade (1890-1957) was a painter, art critic and publicist; translated Marx' Capital into Serbo-Croatian; had a Sephardic Jewish parentage and in 1948 persuaded Tito to allow some 3000 Sephardic Jews to immigrate to Israel; Communist, fierce partisan leader in Monte Negro and a close collaborator of Tito; founder of the Yugoslav Press Agency Tanjug.

Poseidon God of the Sea in the Greek Mythology.

Potica a traditional raised cake with walnut filling baked for Christmas and Easter in Slovenia.

Pupa Slovene Brkini dialect: girl, baby

Ranković Aleksandar Ranković (1909-1983), a Serbian Communist, partisan leader and comrade of Tito's, considered the most powerful man in Yugoslavia; founder of the Yugoslav secret police OZNA and UDBA. He fell from power in 1966 for allegedly having bugged Tito's bedroom; lived in Dubrovnik in political exile.

Rapallo Treaty, November 12th 1920; at the Paris Peace Conference after WWI, the border between Italy and the Kingdom of Serbs, Croats, and Slovenes could not be resolved in spite of long negotiations. The two states should determine it themselves, which was done by the Treaty of Rapallo. Italy recognized the new kingdom, which had to accept the border annexing one-fourth of the Slovene ethnic territory to Italy. More than 300000 Slovenes as well as the cities Trieste and Gorizia became part of Italy. The border remained in effect until 1947.

Rihard Jakopič Leading Slovene Impressionist painter (1869-1943); his works are exhibited in the National Gallery of Slovenia.

Risiera di San Sabba, near Trieste, Italy; was a Nazi concentration camp for the transition of the Jews, who were deported to Auschwitz or other camps. The building was erected in 1913 as a rice husking plant. Famous Slovene writer Boris Pahor was held in Risiera before being transported to Dachau.

Rupnik Leon Rupnik (1880-1946); Slovenian military man, a major from WWI, mayor of Ljubljana under the Italian rule from 1941 to 1943; founder of Slovenian Home Guards; a staunch anti-communist; set up the controversial public Home Guard oath-taking ceremony at the Ljubljana Stadium on April 20th 1944, which has been interpreted as the Home Guard allegiance to the Germans. He fled Ljubljana just before the end of the war and spent time in the Italian refugee camps with his family until the Allies handed him over to Yugoslavia in 1946. He was tried and executed as a national traitor.

Saint Nicholas In Slovenia, children used to receive sweets as presents on the evening of December 6th by Saint Nicholas. During the Communist era (1945-1990) on the New Year's Eve December 31st, Father Frost was bringing the gifts. Today, it is mainly on Christmas, brought by Santa Claus.

Šance Slovenian; the remains of the fortifications on Ljubljana Castle that in 1930s were rebuilt into a promenade, designed by the famous Slovenian architect Jože Plečnik.

Ščavi an abusive name for a Slovene, a Yugoslav or generally any other Slav living under the Italian rule; Neo-Fascists would still use it today.

Skopje the capital of Macedonia, which used to be one of the six republics of Yugoslavia. Independent since 1991. The earthquake on July 26th 1963 turned its medieval and Ottoman character into a modern city.

Slavija The Slavija Building has been the seat of the Slovene secret police since 1945, address Štefanova ulica 1, Ljubljana. Before the Communist era it was the seat of the bank, today the address of the Ministry for Internal Affairs.

Slovene Partisan School The Liberation Front organized schooling for children in Slovenian language. This was very important, as it evoked patriotic feelings and promoted the resistance. Also culture was very important for the Liberation Front and Communist Party propaganda.

Slovenec The Slovenian - a famous newspaper of the Slovene People's Party that was partly published also in Slovene during WWII.

Slovenian Philharmonic Orchestra Slovenska filharmonija; the Philharmonic Society was founded in 1701, the orchestra many years later; the building in which the Philharmonic still resides today was built around the turn of the 20th century and hosted many famous orchestras.

Slovenian Territorial Defense Slovene: Teritorialna obramba; the partly voluntary troops organized for the protection of civilians in natural catastrophes and war. In 1991, the Yugoslave People's Army (conscripts from all Yugoslavian republics) was still holding the territory of Slovenia, protecting the interests of the state of Yugoslavia. Slovenian Territorial Defense were all locals, Slovenes, who opposed the Yugoslav Peoples' Army during the Ten Days' War from June 26th 1991.

St. Urh Sveti Urh; a low hill close to Ljubljana in the community of Moste-Polje, Bizovik; during WWII the church and the parish were transformed into prison operated by the Village Guards, MVAC and later Home Guards for Liberation Front activists and their sympathizers; there is a lot of controversy as to the fact whether the Catholic priest was taking part in the torturing sessions or not. When the prisoners were at the brink of death, they took them into the Kozler's Thicket (Kozlerjeva gošča), where they killed them and threw the bodies into the river Sava. Mihael Mlakar is a fictitious character.

Štepanja Vas Slovene for Stephen's village, a small village near Ljubljana on the road to St. Urh

Teharje is a settlement near Celje; during WWII a German concentration camp that was used for Home Guard prisoners by the partisans after 1945. There are some 25 mass graves of the victims in the area. Today a memorial park.

Teran dark red Slovenian wine, authentic to the region of Karst.

Tetushka Russian: diminutive of teta, which means aunt.

The Water Man France Prešeren's famous ballad of a pretty young girl Urška seduced by the Water Man with whom she drowns in the Ljubljanica river.

Tito, partija! Slovenian: Tito, the Party! The hail to the Communist Party of Yugoslavia and its leader Tito.

Tito Josip Broz - Tito (1892-1980) was a Communist, a Marxist, a resistance leader of the Yugoslav partisans during WWII, the president of Federal Yugoslavia and the leader of the Non-Aligned movement. Born and lived in great poverty on the border between today Slovenia (mother) and Croatia (father), he soon embraced the Communist ideology and in WWI joined the Russian revolutionaries during the October Revolution. They were friends with Stalin, until they separated in 1948 - Informbiro. After his death, Yugoslavia fell apart.

Tivoli Park; Ljubljana's famous promenade and the biggest green area of the city.

Toscanini Arturo Toscanini (1867-1957) was a famous Italian conductor who in the 1930s went to America. On several occasions, Toscanini refused to play the Fascist anthem Giovinezza before the beginning of the concerts.

Tovarish Russian, Slovenian: comrade.

Tovarishitza Russian, Slovenian: female comrade.

Trotsky Leon Trotsky (1879-1940), real name Lev Bronstein, was a Marxist revolutionary, theorist, a Communist leader, and one of the seven first members of Politbiro after the revolution. He criticized Stalin and the new Communist bureaucracy after the Revolution. After having been expelled from the Party, in 1929, he was also exiled for life from the Soviet Union. He lived in Mexico and continued publishing his writings. He was murdered by Stalin's NKVD agents in 1940.

Trubar Literature House opened since 2010 in Ljubljana, UNESCO Creative City of Literature. The round table discussion regarding the Slovene reconciliation did take place in autumn of 2013 and was the source of inspiration for the author.

UDBA Serbo-Croatian: Uprava državne bezbednosti was the secret police of the Communist Yugoslavia in the same sense as the NKVD in the Soviet Union. Founded in 1946, it operated until the break-up of Yugoslavia in the 1990s.

Ugo Cerletti Italian neurologist (1877-1963) who discovered the method of electroconvulsive therapy for treatment of certain mental disorders.

UNRRA United Nations Relief and Rehabilitation Administration was an agency founded in 1943, operating until 1947; it supplied food, medicine and other basic necessities to the devastated countries of Europe.

Ustasha Croatian: a soldier of the Independent State of Croatia during WWII.

Ustaša Croatian spelling of Ustasha, the daily newspaper in the Independent State of Croatia during WWII.

Villa Villekulla the house of Pippi Longstocking, written by Astrid Lindgren.

Vojvoda Old Slavic war-leader or warlord, Slovenian vojvoda; principal commander of a military force.

VOS Slovenian: Varnostno-obveščevalna služba; Security and Intelligence Service during WWII. Its task was to fight the enemies of the Liberation Front and Communist Party; executions of collaborators, anticommunist Slovenes, and many times the people, who opposed the Communist Party took place. It created the opposition within the various fractions of the Liberation Front.

Yugoslav People's Army or Yugoslav National Army were armed forces of the Communist Yugoslavia. The origin was the partisan fight during WWII that became a strong federally organized military force. After Yugoslavia dissolved, the remnants of the army fought in Krajina (Croatian War of Independence), Bosnia and Herzegovina, and Kosovo.

Zhenschina Russian: woman

Bibliography

Printed sources

1. Lindsay Rogers: Guerilla Surgeon, Collins, St. James's Place, London, 1957.
2. Kozjane, partizanska vas v Brkinih, uredil uredniški odbor: odg. ured. Stane Koman in drugi, založila Občinska konferenca SZDL v Sežani, Ljubljana 1979.
3. Barbara Holešek: Razvoj in formacija prostovoljne protikomunistične malice 1942-1943 v Ljubljanski pokrajini, diplomsko delo, Univerza v Ljubljani, Fakulteta za družbene vede, Ljubljana 2004.
4. John Corsellis in Marcus Ferrar: Slovenija 1945, Smrt in preživetje po drugi svetovni vojni, Mladinska knjiga založba, Ljubljana 2006.
5. Mojca Šorn: Življenje Ljubljančanov med drugo svetovno vojno, Inštitut za novejšo zgodovino, zbirka Razpoznavanja, Ljubljana 2007.
6. Dokumentarni film Otroci s Petrička, produkcija Arsmedia in Uredništvo dokumentarnih filmov TV Slovenija, režiral Miran Zupanič, 2007.
7. Tomaž Štaut: Elitne enote na območju današnje Slovenije med drugo svetovno vojno, diplomsko delo, Univerza v Ljubljani, Fakulteta za družbene vede, Ljubljana 2008.
8. Anja Vovk: Brkini v postindustrijski dobi, diplomska naloga, Univerza v Ljubljani, Filozofska fakulteta Oddelek za geografijo, Ljubljana 2011.
9. Anja Kodermac: Osnovno šolstvo na Slovenskem Primorskem med NOB: šolanje kot otrokova pravica, diplomsko delo, Univerza v Ljubljani, Pedagoška fakulteta, Ljubljana 2012.
10. Božidar Jezernik: Titov gulag, Modrijan, Znanstvena založba Filozofske fakultete, Ljubljana 2013.

11. Keith Lowe: Savage Continent, Europe in the aftermath of World War II, Picador, St. Martin's Press New York 2013.
12. Kristjan Kovačič: Diverzantsko bojevanje na Slovenskem med 2. svetovno vojno, diplomsko delo, Prometna šola Maribor, 2013.
13. Brina Svit: Slovenski obraz, Cankarjeva založba, Ljubljana 2014.
14. Grahovo 1943-2014, Nova slovenska zaveza, Ljubljana 2014.
15. Jasna Fakin Bajec, Oto Luthar: Kras in Brkini za radovedneže in ljubitelje, Založba ZRC, Nova Gorica 2014.

Internet sources

1. Sigmund Freud: War Neuroses, Wien 1920, www.freud.org.uk, accessed in June 2014.
2. Objava posnetka: Veliko protikomunistično narodno zborovanje na Kongresnem trgu v Ljubljani 29.06.1944, www.youtube.com, accessed in June 2014.
3. Intervju Bernard Nežmah z dr. Borisom Mlakarjem: Domobranci med Kočevskim Rogom in rusko fronto, Mladina, 01.12.2003, www.mladina.si, accessed in June 2014.
4. Miha Štamcar, Aleksandar Mićić: Intervju z Mitjem Ribičičem v Mladini, 30.05.2005, www.mladina.si, accessed in June 2015.
5. Mladina, 06.10.2006: Zgodovino retušira tudi cerkev, www.mladina.si, accessed in June 2015.
6. Damijan Guštin: Za zapahi, Prebivalstvo Slovenije v okupatorjevih zaporih 1941-1945, članek sistory.si, Inštitut za novejšo zgodovino, Ljubljana 2006, sistory.si, accessed in June 2014.
7. Fašistična zapuščina, 1. del, pričevanje preživelih internirancev in osebja italijanskih fašističnih taborišč, www.youtube.com, objavljeno 7. marca 2007, accessed in December 2013.
8. Katja Skubic: Koncentracijsko taborišče Teharje, Dokumenti in pričevanja o povojnih koncentracijski taboriščih v Sloveniji, II. del, vir Ministrstvo za pravosodje, 2008, www.mp.gov.si, accessed in June 2014.
9. Revija Zaveza, številka 41, Nova slovenska zaveza, Ljubljana 2009: www.zaveza.si, accessed in June 2015.
10. Blog Emonec: Sv. Urh do leta 1943, objavljeno 2010, www.

11. Okrogla miza štirinajstdnevnika o umetnosti, kulturi in družbi Pogledi z naslovom Onkraj sprave: nujnost odpuščanja, vodil Boštjan Tadel, objavila Socialna demokracija 24.10.2013 na www.youtube.com, accessed in January 2014.
12. Quando La Radio Canta by Alberto Rabagliati (Swingitaliano by Trio Lescano), www.lifeinitaly.com, accessed in June 2014.

Made in the USA
Middletown, DE
05 May 2022